THE BEAUTIFUL ONE

THE BEAUTIFUL ONE

Alexandra Hamilton

FREDERICK MULLER LIMITED
LONDON

First published in Great Britain in 1979
by Frederick Muller Limited, London, NW2 6LE

ISBN 0 584 31058 7

British Library Cataloguing in Publication Data

Hamilton, Alexandra
The beautiful one.
I. Title
823'.9'1F PR6058.A552/

ISBN 0–584–31058–7

Typeset by Texet, Leighton Buzzard, Beds., and
Printed in Great Britain by offset lithography by
Billing & Sons Ltd., Guildford, London and Worcester

Author's Note

The theory as to the origin of Akhnaten's religious "reformation" is, of course, that first advanced by Dr. Velikovsky, as is also the account of the subsequent fate of certain members of his family.

The Families of Akhnaten and Nefertiti

(Characters appearing in the novel are underlined)

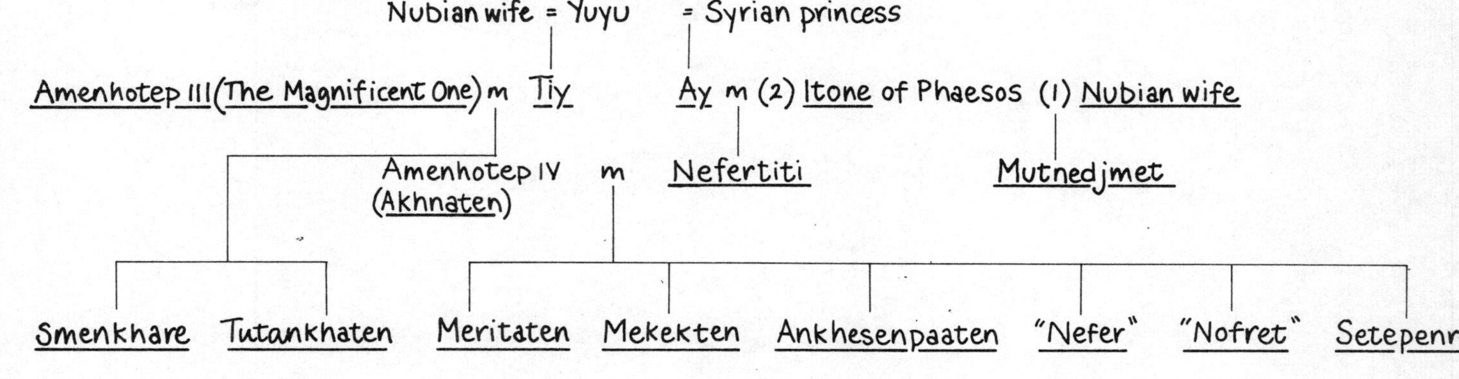

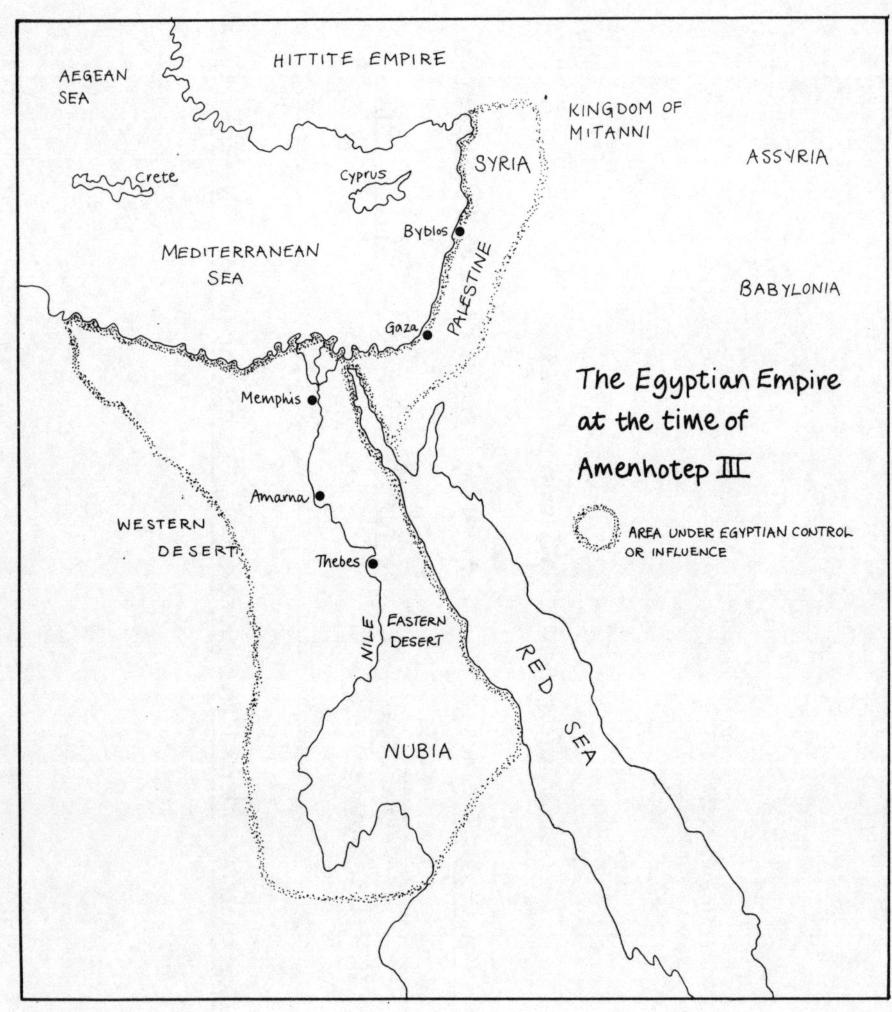
HITTITE EMPIRE
AEGEAN SEA
KINGDOM OF MITANNI
ASSYRIA
Crete
Cyprus
SYRIA
Byblos
MEDITERRANEAN SEA
PALESTINE
BABYLONIA
Gaza
The Egyptian Empire at the time of Amenhotep III
Memphis
Amarna
WESTERN DESERT
AREA UNDER EGYPTIAN CONTROL OR INFLUENCE
Thebes
NILE
EASTERN DESERT
RED SEA
NUBIA

PROLOGUE
Eos

Chapter One
Eos

I was born among shattered towns, and they say the city where I spent most of my life is already almost a ruin.

The gods had destroyed much of the island of Crete in my grandmother's girlhood. No one had slept for days on end that summer because of a great roaring noise to the north. Then came a booming sound so violent that people thought the world was being torn apart; the noise itself was enough to bring the upper storeys of palaces toppling down and men saw an appalling sight, the sea creeping away from the land as if that land were accursed. And then, again from the north, darkness, and a rain of hot dust. Finally, with another roar that threatened to engulf the world, the sea came racing, hissing back, gathered up in one immense, towering wave; how high no one could say, for it crashed down on the northern coast in the darkness that had already brought terror enough. All that people knew was that another darkness, a foaming wall of it, a great curling crest, dimly discernible, inescapable, travelling at enormous speed, fell on Crete and destroyed it.

Men had been too happy in Crete.

No one will ever know how many people died. Town upon town, palace upon palace are only names today. It was a destruction complete enough to satisfy even the most angry deity. The richest, most populous part of the island lay shattered; over all the rest lay a heavy layer of ash that poisoned the land.

The Cretans who died when the buildings crashed down, or the wall of sea rushed in were the fortunate ones; theirs was a quick death, not the slow dying by starvation and disease that was the fate of those still alive when the darkness lifted. Few survived the first terrible autumn and winter. And the next spring could bring little hope to those who still remained stubbornly alive. For almost a generation fields, orchards, vineyards remained uncultivable. And there was a sickness, no ordinary sickness, in the very air; poisoning humans as it blighted plants.

Crete, which for so long had seemed blessed by the gods, had become an accursed land.

And men showed little more pity than heaven had done.

For many years Athens, an insignificant, backward state on the Achaean mainland, had resentfully paid tribute to Crete. When they learned that the land of the hated overlords was now defenceless, that the fleets which for centuries had made the sea a Cretan lake, had vanished in the general destruction, the Athenians, brave as hyenas, sent an expedition to the island of which they had been so jealous for so long. Easy enough for bronze-clad warriors to make starving survivors their subjects, but Crete was not the rich prize they had anticipated and scarcely an easy place to live in. The anger of the gods had been shown too clearly for comfort, and there were too many ghosts of the unburied dead. So the newcomers, tall, fair, grey-eyed men, walked more warily than conquerers usually do. They propitiated the gods as best they might; tried, too, to propitiate the angry, vengeful dead. A man might have seized land, raped a woman — but often, especially if she were the heiress, he married her later.

My grandmother, Hellotis, was the only daughter of the King of Phaestos. In the spring before the destruction she had become royal priestess of the Mother-Goddess. One of the invading Athenian chieftains found her hiding in the ruins of her father's palace. All that was left to her of her old life was a little ivory and gold statuette of herself showing her aloof in her gorgeous priestess' robes, the long, flounced skirt, the golden diadem, the open bodice showing very round breasts, high and firm above the tiny waist. When the landless Athenian adventurer found her, she was starving, wearing rags, in no condition to put up any opposition to being taken.

But, afterwards, there was marriage. She gave birth to a delicate daughter, Itone, then coughed her own life away. Her husband sent back to Achaea for a second wife, who bore him healthy sons, but it would seem that in his heart he never forgot the girl he had found hiding in the ruins of a palace, for he gave his daughter all the tenderness he had not shown her mother until it was too late to mend matters.

I have frequently thought of my grandmother. My nurse, Ariaea, often told me how in that spring evening, the royal priestess, had crouched vainly in the ruins like a terrified fawn trying to escape the hunter, and how, while his companions laughed and shouted, the tall, fair man had walked inexorably towards her, bent, caught her by the wrist, dragged her out of hiding.

For mâny years I saw it all through the eyes of the watching Ariaea. She, too, had hidden, trembling, behind shattered masonry, watching in helpless despair as the tall figure of the man went steadily up to the last poor refuge of the dead King's daughter.

Later the time came when I would imagine the man as his prey must have seen him, coming relentlessly closer, with that curious stiff-legged walk of the male animal bent on rape. But that is the kind of detail no one ever tells you; it is something a woman only learns for herself.

Ariaea never called herself more than a servant, my nurse. Now I think that in the old Crete she had been far more than this. She told me that I must hate my Athenian grandfather, the despoiler and ravisher through whom the loathed barbarian blood flowed in my veins, to be glad that he was dead, dead before I was born. Now I am sorry I never knew him. Ariaea hated him for what he had done to the royal priestess of the Lady and, at that time, I was too young to ask, "But might *she* not have forgiven him — in time? Or even loved him, a little?" For if woman can be the most implacable of animals, she can also be the most inexplicably forgiving.

My grandfather's death came about partly because of his love for his daughter. He hoped to find her a husband in mainland Achaea, away from the poisoned air of Crete, and set out for his old home (a little village outside Athens, named Colonos) to arrange this. But he sailed too early in the year; a sudden storm sprang up, and his ship, with all she carried, was lost. His widow married the captain of the guard at Phaestos, and ruled on behalf of her young sons. Her stepdaughter, Itone, she had never liked; her husband showed the girl too much affection. But more important still, in the eyes of the people of Phaestos, she was the heiress. So her stepmother decided Itone's husband must be someone not only not living in Crete, but someone extremely unlikely ever to return to Crete to enforce his wife's claims.

It was at this time that an Egyptian Pharaoh, for the first time for many years, sent an ambassador to Crete. There were few craftsmen left in Crete now; all the island really had to export was valour, the bands of Achaeans from the mainland who had found Crete so disappointing a conquest. Pharaoh wanted mercenaries for his garrisons in Syria, and ships to bring them in. For such an important mission, he sent as his ambassador the young half-brother of his Great Wife.

At this my step mother saw her opportunity. When the Egyptian visited what remained of Phaestos, she suggested to him marriage with her stepdaughter. He was then about twenty years old; the girl, because she was a type of woman to which he was unaccustomed, might, for that very reason, have attracted so young a man. So my mother, weeping, became the wife of an Egyptian nobleman.

There was, of course, a feeling of outrage in the native Cretan part of the household — yet nothing as intense as might be expected. This was because my mother in looks took so much after her father; she had fair hair, grey eyes and was tall for a woman. Also her nature was as un-Cretan as her looks.

My youthful father consummated his marriage, brought his other, official, business to a possibly more satisfactory conclusion and returned to Egypt. But my mother, already pregnant, was too ill to accompany him. He would send for her, he said, when the child was born in the following spring. But after my birth (I was born at dawn, so they called me Eos) my mother's ill-health was permanent, and she stayed, with me, at Phaestos. So far as people knew, her husband had forgotten her — and me. But a child cannot forget her father, even if she has never seen him. Some instinct told me never to mention him at all to my mother. All I learned from her half-brothers was that he had a sneering — and quite hairless — face.

My mother lived until I was seven years old. I spent many hours in her room looking northwards towards the long ridge of Mount Ida, sometimes cloud-encircled, always snow-covered. That is what I chiefly remember of Crete. Then there was the mist, and the noise of rain falling in autumn. And spring, when the first brilliant splash of scarlet anemones lit up a corner of field and orchard, and soon the bare, knotted vines became covered in soft green, and streams began to gush noisily down the hillside. There was always the sound of water in Crete. And I remember the great trees covering the mountains — cedar and oak, cypress and fir and goats leaping about the crags; grass wet after dew or rain, small aromatic herbs, patches of iris and crocus and the tang of the sea. All these things I was never again to see or hear or feel or smell after being taken from the island of my birth.

I saw so much because, especially in the spring, my mother's three half-brothers would take me with them up into the mountains. They had always hated their sister's marriage they had been too young to prevent. They petted and spoiled me and raged among themselves against Egypt and the Egyptians.

On one thing they were emphatic. *I* should not marry a

foreigner. They should see to it, for they were reaching the age when they could assert themselves. My love from my mother's brothers angered Ariaea, to whom they could never be more than Achaean barbarians, members of the race not only themselves usurping on earth, but worshipping a petty heavenly tyrant, Zeus, who had usurped the powers of the Lady of All Things, the Mother, the Moon Goddess. All Achaeans were hateful, shameless, brutal, intent on the degradation of goddess and woman alike. "It is for the *Lady* to take what lovers, consorts she chooses, for her *pleasure*!" I knew what a lover was – Ariaea loved *me*. She was too angry to explain what a consort might be. Because of the word "pleasure", I thought it must be something to eat.

True worship, Ariaea instructed me, was entirely dominated by The Lady, with female helpers or Priestesses, she said, who were assisted by votaries, women who adored The Lady and revered her priestesses. What had men – true Cretan men – worshipped, then? The Earth-Shaker, the Bull of the Sea – whom the Achaeans called Poseidon. All of course, in the name of the Lady.

Ariaea looked at me sombrely. "And your great-grandfather – your *royal* great-grandfather – as everyone knew, was sacrificing to Poseidon when he died. Even the barbarians know that. That's why they won't go near the ruins."

In the shrine-room just inside the west wall of the palace, my great-grandfather and his three sons had stood before the red-burnished inlaid offering table with the double axe on it, the triton-shell used as a ritual trumpet and the bull-rhyton. And then the red pillars and the cypress-beamed roofs had crashed down on them, every man of the Phaestos kingly line. Human flesh and bone is less durable than much of what is fashioned by the like human hands. The bull's head remained unshattered among the royal débris – and when all that was to be found of my great-grandfather and his sons were a few bones, a herdsman crept among the ruins one night, and brought it out intact. The men used it in their secret ceremonies, Ariaea said. One night, indeed, she took me out of the palace, and three men brought it to us, together with a bunch of poppies which they asked me to make into a wreath and place on the great head for some ceremony they intended to carry out. The moonlight was strong enough for me to see it quite clearly; it was made of dark serpentine, with horns of gold and eyes of rock crystal. The strength of the head and throat!

"What will they do tomorrow?" I asked Ariaea, after they had gone.

''They're going to try to catch a wild bull,'' she said.

I was puzzled. ''But why come to *me*?'' I began to laugh. ''I shouldn't be much good, because I'm so little and not at all strong.''

''Being strong has nothing to do with it,'' said Ariaea. ''A bull's the most difficult animal in the world to capture by force.''

Next day she took me to a cave on the hillside and drew from a cavity in the wall two golden drinking cups. ''They were the King's,'' she said. ''What things they could, the people saved, to keep for better days.'' The cups were battered, but the scenes shown on them were still clearly discernible. One showed an attempt to ensnare a bull by force — an unsuccessful attempt. The would-be snarers lay bleeding, gashed by the triumphant beast. But the other cup showed the bull — beguiled by a gentle, beautiful-eyed cow — standing as if entranced while they netted him, tethered him.

The Achaeans, worshipping their stupid male gods, knew little of the religion practised by the people they had conquered — or perhaps it is truer to say they were allowed to know little. The moon, said Ariaea, ruled the lives of women — let men worship what and whom they pleased. Some, for example, were fools enough to worship the sun — even claim the sun was more powerful than the moon, although the moon was constant, never growing dimmer as the year wore on. ''But,'' I objected, ''sometimes she is of different shapes — even of sizes, thin, round, thin again.''

''It's because she's a woman,'' said Ariaea. ''Maiden, mother, old woman. All in twenty-eight days — that in itself shows she's a woman!''

One night not long after this, Ariaea took me to a meadow, and stood with me beneath an oak tree. Men brought a great white bull over to us. Ariaea told me to touch the bull's horns. I was not afraid — his strength, in fact, delighted me. But when I said this as she took me away, Ariaea was displeased. ''You don't love bulls,'' she said.

''Doesn't he belong to The Lady?'' I asked.

''Ah, yes, but the men say that above all bulls are sacred to the Earth-Shaker, Poseidon — that's why they're sacrificed to him. You touched him to show the domination of The Lady!''

There was another night when Ariaea took me down to the sea-shore. There is a headland close to Phaestos where in the south-westerly gales the great rollers came driving in on to a small reef. All the day I had watched them foaming in, brilliant in the sun. But at night the wind dropped, and the sea was calm enough for Ariaea, naked, to wade out some distance into the water with me in her arms. Behind us, on the shore, people were singing. And then, far out across the bay, under the starlight, green and white fire flashed through the waves, and in a great joyous curve, a line of dolphins shot through the water, to leap about us, more like birds than fish, streaming drops of blue and silver, to lie, rocking in the great ripples, watching us with dark dolphin eyes, smiling the dolphin smile.

Ariaea said I must tell no one of these midnight excursions, and until now I have kept my word. I remained puzzled, however, as to why I should keep it all a secret from my mother — and why had it not happened to her.

I asked Ariaea about this second point. She replied with contempt — the tone of her voice was unmistakable, even though her actual words left me no more enlightened. "These things are not for her. She lacks the capacity."

"What's capacity?" I asked, after a moment.

"It's possessed by every royal priestess of the Lady," Ariaea said, still angrily. "It makes her — as the Lady herself should be — importuned, *supplicated* by men." Since I knew the meaning of neither "importuned" nor "supplicated", I was scarcely enlightened by this, but I stored the words in my memory for further elucidation when Ariaea was not so angry. Were they, possibly, I wondered a rather roundabout way of saying *married*? Cautiously I asked Ariaea if the Lady had a husband.

"No!" she said, angrier than ever. "Haven't I told you before? For her pleasure, she has lovers, consorts who do what is necessary for renewal, then die in the spring."

So a consort couldn't be something to eat! My lip quivered; I didn't like being so stupid that Ariaea was angry with me, and apparently I kept asking the wrong things. But, noticing my distress, she swooped down on me, fierce as a hen-hawk with her chick, and caught me in her arms. "Don't cry, my darling princess; don't cry, my baby! I become angry with you because I have to tell you these things hurriedly, in secret, show you to the people in secret, whereas — oh, listen carefully, my little priestess, and try to understand. The Lady is the Goddess of All Things, the Mother; she makes all things that live and grow, but there are certain beasts who belong to her specially because on their bodies they show her emblem — the sickle moon. Think of the stag with its antlers, the bull with his horns — "

"I liked the white bull, Ariaea!"

"That's my darling! Never be afraid of him — he's your beast!"

"But I would like to meet the great beast again in a meadow in the sunlight — must I go to him only in the darkness?"

I asked plaintively. Was it all part of the need to keep everything secret?

"Only partly," said Ariaea. "The Lady deliberately chooses to manifest herself chiefly at night, dimly, as the Moon. Darkness — and not the sun these stupid barbarians talk about as the elder brother of the moon — is the source of life and death. Most people die at night. Most children are born at night. And certainly most children are begotten then!" She sat looking at me searchingly. "When you are a little older," she said, "I will tell you of the begetting of children, and the finger of the Lady that moves inside all true women and you must never forget this, my little princess. As the royal priestess you are not only the intermediary with the Lady, you are her symbol of *fertility*." (But, I thought, bewilderedly, one talked of a field being fertile. Or — or an orchard.) "You'll take young, strong, men to make you fertile — " (But fields were made fertile by rain and sun!) " — but they will never be your equal — they'll be ruled by you!"

A false light dawned on me. I should inherit an estate when I was a little older. And to make it fertile, I should have to employ farmers to tend the fields. And they would be my — what was the word Agenor sometimes used? *Tenants*, that was it. I looked up earnestly into Ariaea's solemn face.

"It will be important to choose the right men, won't it? But I'll try," I said. At this she wept and kissed me.

I saw little of my step-grandmother, but remember her as being tall, with a high colour, red-gold hair, bright dresses, many golden combs. I saw more of her second husband; younger than she was, he was thick set and heavy faced for an Achaean. He used to caress and kiss me when he met me alone, which was often. When he smiled his forehead wrinkled and his teeth gleamed in his beard; he looked like a dog about to bite. Although he gave me presents, I disliked him, and so did his stepsons. They kept making plans as to how they might get rid of him. Finally they agreed the only thing to do was to turn his own weapon, marriage, against him. Agenor, the eldest, was twenty. He would go in search of a wife — rather, not so much a wife, as a father-in-law with troops to spare. His brothers would accompany him; Cleitos was nearly nineteen; "I can start looking about," he said vaguely.

"Are you going to get married too?" I asked Metion, who was only seventeen, in real if vague distress. He had always played with me more than the others, given me a baby hare as a present, a pet bird, taken me to see the first flower buds on the wild pear-tree.

''No!'' he said, very emphatically.

Cleitos burst out laughing. ''But never fear, little one, he plans to get married one day!'' he said.

Although they did not tell their mother their real motive for going away, (saying they wanted to buy new horses) they had expected opposition from her. Instead, they found none. They talked of this a little among themselves, but not much; they were too glad to have found it all so easy. And they were too young to think it might all be *too* easy.

So in the spring, just after my seventh birthday, as soon as the sailing season opened, they left Phaestos. A few days after, Staphylos turned up, a cousin on my mother's side, the first Cretan relative I had ever met. I was excited when Ariaea told me he had come; I had heard so much of my Cretan male relatives, handsome, tapering-waisted; among the ruins one or two walls still stood showing them in all their slender beauty. We had believed that those who survived the earthquake and the tidal wave had been killed when the raiders came in the following spring, yet now it seemed some had escaped and the son of one of these had returned.

I was, however, greatly disappointed when I saw my distant cousin, Staphylos. There was no elegance about him whatsoever; he was a stumpy, squat man. And he was not at all handsome. He had a coarse skin and an underlip he thrust out a great deal. Although he was young, his hair was already sparse. His hands were ugly, scarred, calloused; to a child expecting so much, he came as a great disappointment. I fear that, being so young, I showed it, and that is one of the reasons he has never liked me.

Chapter Two
Staphylos

Many years later I was able to read Eos' account of her early life. Since the child was prejudiced against me from the start, I had better make some attempt to state my own case before her narrative continues.

My name, she said, is Staphylos. This is true enough. But I was in no way related to her; no royal Minoan blood flowed in my veins. Which largely accounts for the unprincely appearance she found so disappointing.

All men are self-centred; the survivors of a great disaster are, necessarily perhaps, more self-centred than most, only your own private tragedy matters. After the Cretan catastrophe those who remained in the shattered island believed that only a few, a very few, had escaped. But not every city was shattered as Phaestos had been, not every ship in the considerable Cretan fleets was destroyed, and men got away. Some went to mainland Achaea, some south to Egypt, and many, like my father, eastwards to Rhodes, Cypros, or, as in Father's case, to the coast of Asia — so many to Asia, in fact, that the name given by the Egyptians to these refugees — Peleset — is gradually being applied to the entire region of their settlement, Philistia, Palestine, they are beginning to call it now.

My father landed in the pleasant city of Ascalon. Like the rest of his compatriots he found life there not altogether uncongenial. The Goddess, of course, is worshipped there under the name Ashtoreth,* although they house her in a large temple, and

* Even the Achaeans, in their inevitably muddled fashion, are beginning to worship the Lady (to some limited extent). In their usurping way, indeed, they are beginning to accept her as their own (provided she knows her — minor — place!) One Achaean colony, I knew, in Cypros, a day's sail from Ascalon, have made complete fools of themselves. The Achaeans are the most lubberly linguists in the world; their mispronunciations of foreign names have to be heard to be believed. Unable to get their tongues round "Ashtoreth", they have settled for "Aphrodite". And, the Achaean word for foam being *aphros*, the fools have begun to concoct the stupidest stories of the Goddess' origin.

rather oddly give her eunuch-priests as well as fertility-priestesses. But otherwise it is not too difficult to accept this particular form of her worship.

Father had been one of the royal sculptors in Cnossos; Ascalon might be a pleasant enough city, but he would undoubtedly have done better for himself in a large state with a monarchy demanding frequent portrayals in stone. But, of course, refugees can't be choosers. And Father, if he had been a vegetable, would have been the kind averse to too much transplanting. One up-rooting was enough for him. The Goddess had sent him to Ascalon; in Ascalon he would stay.

He married the squat, ugly daughter of a local petty land-owner. So I am not one of the slim, tapering-waisted princes Eos yearned to see; I am wholly, alas, a Syrian peasant in body. It has its advantages, of course. Eos might have added that I have the broad shoulders, the strong arms and hands of a peasant. Without these physical attributes, I should be unable to be a sculptor. But I am, I think, wholly Cretan in mind.

Why did I claim to be related to the last King of Phaestos? And how did I acquire the background knowledge to be accepted as a relative? In the ship in which Father fled to Ascalon there was indeed, such a personage — a princeling lucky enough to be visiting Cnossos at the time of the disaster. But not altogether lucky; when the upper storey of the palace was brought down, he had a foot crushed. It was Father who managed to tug the pile of stone off the shattered foot, and who carried him down to the ship. And as a result was lumbered with this lame protegé for life.

Life as a prince is about the most inadequate of preparations for the life of a refugee. All that you are trained for is fighting. With a crushed foot, a fighting career is out of the question. Not that I think Prince Tectamos would have advanced far in the military profession; in character he was a poor, weak creature, and *stupid.* Father was a devout man; after experiences you would have thought would destroy all faith in any deity, he still believed in the Goddess. She had chosen him to save Tectamos. She would therefore hold him responsible for Tectamos' well-being for the rest of the life owed to him. So for the rest of his life, he lived on us. Father never showed the slightest resentment. He was delighted to share all he possessed with his guest, his wife included, if Tectamos had been so inclined. But all Tectamos did was talk — talk of the glories of Cnossos and Phaestos. All my childhood memories were dominated by two sounds — Father chipping and hammering away, and Tectamos talking as garrulously as a man can only when he is eaten up by self-pity. And I listened — my God, I listened! — so that my fingers were constantly bandaged because of ill-judged blows of my chisel — hence the scars that so disgusted our little royal priestess.

Father rarely had the time or breath for reminiscence, but sometimes on a spring evening he would bring in a jug of as good a wine as he could afford, and would join in Tectamos' nostalgic garrulity. Inevitably, as they became progressively more maudlin, they became eloquent on the loveliness of the royal priestesses of the Mother Goddess. Never had there been such women for rousing masculine desire. The bared, glorious breasts, the very white skins, the long, dark, curling, perfumed hair, the tiny waists, the graceful limbs, the gliding walk. . . I thought, pityingly, that the old fools exaggerated. No women could be so alluring. No women could be so totally unconscious of their allure.

And while, during the spring evenings, Tectamos babbled of the palace at Phaestos in general, as the night drew on, he would talk particularly of his cousin Hellotis, fifteen years old when the darkness had come to Crete, newly made royal priestess of the Mother Goddess, more beautiful than any man who had not seen her could conceive.

When I was twenty-two, Father died. Much to my surprise — and not too secret delight — Tectamos died a few days later. I think that, stupid as he was, he realized he would get no support or sustenance from me, and he more or less willed himself to die.

Father's legacy to me was skill in shaping stone, Tectamos' no more than extensive knowledge of the divinely royal family at Phaestos. Of material goods I had few, and I wanted more — *how* I wanted more — as they can be wanted only by an unattractive, clumsy youth, with all youth's desire (desire so hotly felt it seemed a need to me) for some things an ugly, awkward man can achieve only through wealth. But you did not become wealthy as a sculptor in Ascalon. I used to think bitterly of the riches of the palace at Phaestos, as described by Tectamos, the gold, the silver, the ivory. One evening it occurred to me (remember I was young, then!) that some of those treasures must still be there — buried in the palace ruins. We knew that the barbarian conquerors were afraid to go too close to those ruins. The diadem and necklace of his cousin, the royal priestess Hellotis, alone, would supply wealth enough. . .

That night I dreamed I was scrabbling among the ashes and the little bones that had once been Hellotis for gold, the necklaces, the ear-rings she had been wearing when the roof of her father's palace crushed the life out of her. And as I fumbled for a pendant of gold lilies that once had lain between the round, warm, living breasts, a feeling of almost intolerable grief and loss swept over me. "If you were still alive," I said, the tears running down my cheeks, "if you were still alive, I would rather find *you* alive than all the treasures of Crete."

But in the morning, though shaken by the dream, I stuck to my resolve — I would go treasure-hunting. To Crete's new overlords I should declare myself truly a craftsman looking for employment, but to what Cretans still survived about Phaestos — and who, I could be sure, would not take kindly to a stranger roaming about the ruined palace — I should be the son of Tectamos, Tectamos of the royal house, who had married in exile.

So I sailed to Crete in the spring, by way of Cypros and Rhodes. First to Cnossos. That was a depressing business. Cnossos had become a barbarian citadel, militarism had come to the peaceful unwalled cities my father had known.

Gratefully I journeyed to Phaestos, forty miles away, making the slow, laborious ascent over the mountains by a road winding between snow-clad peaks. And when I had crossed the backbone of Crete, and began to make the descent to the south, I cried out in surprise. For I was coming down to the richness, the fertility Tectamos had talked of. Through the incredibly clear air — the whole landscape was suffused with light — I could see the green of vineyards, the silver of olive groves. Phaestos *blossomed*.

I finished the lengthy descent equally dusty and bewildered.

A peasant agreed readily enough to give me lodging for the night. If I did not look a native-born Cretan, equally I did not look like one of the Achaean conquerors. And that evening I learned with amazement that although the last King of Phaestos had been crushed to death, one member of the royal house had survived. That very Hellotis mourned in his cups by Tectamos, had survived to be plucked out of the rubble of her home by an Achaean invader, and, eventually, married to him. But she was dead enough now, dead after childbirth, but she had left a daughter, still living here in Phaestos, married years before to a young Egyptian nobleman, herself the mother of a child by him.

You may imagine my agitation at this extraordinary news. Nowadays I am able to conceal my feelings pretty well; then I could not. But my excitement, consternation — I did not know which I felt the more — helped in a fashion. My hosts noticed it. And so, in apparent confusion, I "betrayed" my identity. I was the son of Tectamos — he might be remembered — to hear such things of a kinswoman, whom we had thought dead when the palace was destroyed. . .

One of the family slipped out. Within the hour he had returned with an elderly woman with blazing black eyes whom they addressed as Ariaea, once priestess-attendant to Hellotis, then nurse to her daughter, Itone, nurse now to Itone's daughter. She stared at me with suspicion; no one could be less like Tectamos, who, almond-eyed, slender, with a wealth of dark curling hair, silver bracelets on his wrists, silver and pearl ear-rings in his ears, the blue and gold sheath nowadays called the "Libyan" covering his genitals, must have been elegant enough, but, on the other hand, surely only a member of Tectamos' family could know all the details that slipped out convincingly, but not, I think, glibly, in my account of my "father"?

Eventually she said abruptly that on the following day she would take me to see the daughter of the legendary Hellotis.

If I dreamed that night, it was not of female *bones*. My disappointment next morning was, therefore, profound. The daughter of Hellotis was a poor, fair creature. Yet if I tried, diplomatically, to hide my disappointment from Ariaea, she did not attempt to conceal her own look of grim satisfaction as the hour I spent with my "cousin" limped past. I found her attitude bewildering. My God, I wish my bewildered state had been allowed to go on a little longer! For as we left the palace, Ariaea seized my arm and announced with some emotion that obviously the Mother-Goddess herself had sent me. She began to drag me up to the old palace ruins, and the words tumbled out. My "cousin's" stepmother was plotting something now that her sons had left Phaestos. I had come at the precise moment to save her. I must take her away — not, of course, out of Crete, because if the heiress accompanied her husband overseas she lost all claims to her lands —

"Husband?" I said blankly.

"You will marry her, of course, her kinsman — "

"But the Egyptian — " (No ordinary Egyptian, but, I had learned, the brother-in-law of Pharaoh himself!)

"Not Itone!" snapped Ariaea. "The *child*."

We were among the ruins now, the ruins where I had planned to come alone, stealthily, in search of treasure. The intolerable Ariaea gave me a final push forward. "Go straight ahead now," she said, and stood back.

I went forward.

A child, a girl child, was gravely playing a game in a garden of lilies. She raised her arms side-ways, bending them at the elbows. Then she brought her hands forward up to her chest, cupping them as if to hold tiny, non-existent breasts. She brought her right hand on up to her left shoulder, let the left hand drop to her right hip, the praying position. Then she raised both hands to the level of her head, on which she wore a crown of lilies.

It was a blazingly hot, windless day. The heat in that little garden enclosed in ruins should have been oppressive. It was not. All one was conscious of was freshness, as if on a spring night, and fragrance. As I watched, there was a rustling in the air, and two doves, after circling round the child's head, fluttered down on to her hands. Freshness and whiteness — the dazzling white of the doves, the white light of the sun, the white of the lilies, the white of the child's dress and body.

The child said nothing for the moment, but stood regarding me calmly. Ariaea had moved forward to stand behind her. Over the lily-crowned, small dark head the black eyes blazed triumphantly at me. "*Now*!" they said. "*Now* you understand."

Understand indeed. I understood that the child was a priestess — because the dark tendrils of her hair were fastened in the special sacred knot. And I understood what aspect of the Goddess she symbolised now — because of the doves fluttering about her. For certain birds are sacred to The Lady in Her aspect of goddess of sexual love and beauty — swallows, sparrows, swans — above all, doves.

Aloud Ariaea said prosaically, "Well, I've brought your mother's cousin to you."

The great, slightly tilted eyes were startled. She had not expected her mother's cousin to look like me. I could guess what stories Ariaea had told her of the dead princes of Phaestos, who lay somewhere deep beneath the ruins in which we stood. But this was a polite child. She said in her clear little voice she hoped I liked Phaestos. I said who would not like Phaestos? Did she realize how different it was from the rest of Crete, so rich and fertile?

She looked surprised. "It has been like this all my life."

She meant she had always known it like this. But again Ariaea's eyes blazed with triumph. The child's statement could be taken in another way. "Since I was born, it has been like this." The brilliant, menacing eyes told me that the land had become fertile again seven years before, in the spring when the child was born.

We talked a little of other things; I can remember nothing of what was said. She was glowing, spontaneous, a little nervous, childlike; at the same time she was graceful, oddly elegant in one so young. And, without the slightest pert precocity in her you were never unconscious of the fact that one day she would become a most exquisite woman.

And from the child, who gave that incredible impression of surface calm, yet beneath seemed to be quivering with excitement and eagerness, one went back to the mother, anxious, tearful, pallid, passive.

The violence of the fury aroused in me by this poor weak creature was amazing. She was as convinced as the child's nurse that, in the absence of her half-brothers, her stepmother was planning some move against herself and her daughter, but all she did was weep, and wring her surprisingly long-fingered hands.

Really, the whole business was ludicrously simple — Itone's stepfather was the key to the situation. He commanded the bodyguard. And he was — how shall I put it? — favourably disposed to the child, as Ariaea told me as she shepherded me warily away from her nursling. We had taken refuge in a clump of trees when a great hulk of a man came along the road. "Eos!" he called cautiously. "Little darling!" He grinned into the sun. He had an odd way of smiling, wrinkling his forehead as the teeth shone wolfishly in his tawny beard.

"She's safe — those animals are afraid of the ruins, even by daylight," muttered Ariaea. "And even if he found her — no real danger yet. But once her breasts begin to form. . ."

"Yes," I said — to myself.

"I've always known that in about five years' time, almost every man who sees her. . ." began Ariaea. "You should see Itone's half-brothers. They want her always with them. She's too young for the two oldest — they can't wait, they're off to look for wives with the right kind of father. But the youngest, Metion — *he'd* wait. He's said as much. But his mother's planning something now — I know. That's why the Lady sent you here."

But I had another plan. A good one — obviating the need for me to play an active part. Based on this famous mother-love one hears so much about. When I was smuggled back into Itone's quarters, I appraised her unobtrusively, but carefully. A poor, sapless thing, indeed, but with a certain pallid beauty, a feeble gracefulness. Such alone, the sheer attraction of opposites, might possess its appeal for the burly tawny-bearded captain of the guard.

I chose my words carefully. I did not suggest for a moment that she should invite the captain of the guard into her bed; I merely said that she was beautiful, men often talked freely to beautiful women who seemed interested in them. Of course, he might not be aware of what his wife was plotting, but it would be something to know if he were being kept in the dark.

But Itone almost fainted at the thought. It would not merely be a matter of talking. He would touch her, put a hand to her breast . . . She wailed at the thought.

Ariaea hustled me out, her face almost vicious with contempt. "It was a good plan," she said in a low, furious voice. "If you're a woman these days, your body's your only weapon. If I were in her place, I'd paint my face, perfume my breasts, and have him tonight. But *she* — !"

I myself had begun to have vague sympathy for the Egyptian husband. It must have been like trying to fecundate a waterfall. I left and when Itone, the weakly thing whose grandfather had been Priest-King of Phaestos, and whose father, barbarian though he was, must undoubtedly have possessed courage, heard Ariaea returning, she ran away. Afraid of reproaches from her nurse, she ran out of the palace, and hid. It was as simple as that.

I have said it was a blistering hot day, the kind when you can expect thunderstorms. No one who has not experienced a Cretan thunderstorm can appreciate its suddenness, its ferocity. The poor frightened wretch, cowering in some thicket, was buffeted and drenched. At last she ventured back. Within a few days she was dead. Few other women would have died so easily; for her, death was the ideal escape.

Tending her mistress kept Ariaea from watching me; I contemplated making a break for it, but speedily gave up the idea. Every native-born Cretan in the Phaestos area knew of me now, the hero-deliverer. I was still under surveillance. And not, alas, by the native-born Cretans alone. My prowls in the region of the ruins at night, without Ariaea's adroit shepherding, were observed by residents in the new palace. Not, unfortunately, by the guards. If they had seized me, and brought me before their commander, I could have spoken to him man to man — possibly with success. I could have assured him that I was not involved in any plan for spiriting the child away; I was quite content to leave her here, to be initiated by him at the appropriate time into the pains and pleasures of womanhood. But instead I was grabbed by two of the servants the step-grandmother had brought from her home, and was duly hauled into her presence.

She was about a head taller than I was, and massively built in proportion. Grey eyes like flint. She made it clear from the start that I had been seized because she didn't know what I was up to, but that was now immaterial, since she had merely to set eyes on me to know me for a gutless coward who would do anything to save his miserable skin. And what she intended me to do was take Eos to her father in Egypt. She really hated that seven year old. Doubtless, she would have preferred to have the child's throat cut, but she possessed just enough sense to guess the reaction to this, both from the native Cretans, and, possibly, from divine avengers. But she imagined that if the child were sent to her father in Egypt, the Cretans would accept the accomplished fact — and the gods would not be angry. Already, she explained to me, she had sent a messenger to Eos' father, announcing Itone's death and stressing his daughter's beauty. The messenger had returned. Let the child be sent to Egypt with a reliable escort. Her father himself would receive her at the Nile Delta; he was going to Syria on Pharaoh's business, but — with Pharaoh's permission — he would wait a little at the Delta on his return. But it was up to the people at Phaestos to get the child so far.

A Phoenician ship would come to Phaestos in two days' time. It would sail the moment the child was on board. I could either take Eos to Egypt or have my throat cut that night. And then she said, "You'll be paid when the brat's safely delivered — the captain of the Phoenician ship will give you these when you've handed her over. They belonged to my first husband's first wife, but I don't like them!"

And she handed me a small leather bag. I spilt the contents out into my shaking palm. A diadem, ear-rings, a pendant of golden lilies, alike in every detail to those of my dream. I vomited. She thought I vomited through fear, and laughed.

I could well have vomited through fear on a dozen occasions during the next forty-eight hours. Consider the danger to which that stupid, spiteful bitch exposed me! I was to take away from Crete the last royal heiress, who appeared to all who saw her as the reincarnation of the semi-divine priestesses of the past. If they had known, the people would have torn me limb from limb.

I had made my plans for Eos' 'rescue'. I would take her by ship to Cnossos (we should not put in at Cnossos at all) there we would disembark, and take to hiding. Ariaea agreed to set off herself over the mountains, taking her sister's grandchild with her. When Eos' disappearance was discovered, the hunt, inevitably set in motion by the Captain of the Guard, would follow the nurse — travelling with a child — whom they would assume to be Eos. I don't know how long Ariaea stayed on in Cnossos before she realised how she had been fooled. All that I have learned is that eventually she returned to Phaestos, living in hiding, waiting for her chance until the day when she came upon the child's stepmother alone. She slowly cut the woman's throat, then hanged herself.

The Captain of the Guard however, did not mourn for long. No use licking his lips now at the thought of beauty to be ravished in the future; instead he made use of the services of slave-girls. One day Phaestos will pass to one of his bastards. He seized it for himself, of course. The three rightful heirs, his stepsons, have, for all I know, remained landless wanderers to this day.

Ariaea had told me I could find her nursling at a spot, where, miraculously unshattered, stood one of the pairs of stone bull's horns of consecration that on the palace roof had seemed to pierce the sky. Feeling like Hades himself* I approached my youthful Persephone as she sat tranquilly among the grey-white stones.

She was gathering flowers, the scarlet anemones they say originally sprang from the blood of the beautiful Adonis when he died on the Syrian mountains outside Byblos. She had woven and placed on her head a garland of poppies, the flowers offered to, and worn by The Lady as goddess of death. I told myself angrily I was a stupid bastard to think so gloomily; I was merely taking a motherless child to her father. I was acting solely in her interests. One day she would be grateful to me!

I remember butterflies playing about the small dark shining head with its scarlet garland, a white dove circling above her. It was another warm, windless day — there was thunder in the distance, the great bull of the sea was bellowing.

My shadow fell clean across her white dress. "Ariaea has told you what we're doing to keep you safe. Will you come with me now?" I asked.

On the journey she was puzzled because we were taking longer to reach Cnossos than she had expected. "Where is Ariaea? Where is Ariaea?" she asked excitedly when we finally landed, not at Cnossos, but at Rhodes. "When do we go ashore?"

It was then I told her I was taking her to her father, in Egypt. She gave a little gasp, but apart from that received the information in utter silence. She did not shed a tear. It was only much later that night that she crept into my arms, and clung to me — because, enemy though I might be, I was the only familiar thing in the new nightmare life. "Please keep me with you, and let us go ashore at one of the other places we must stop at before the ship reaches Egypt! You are my cousin."

"I am no relation at all to you," I said loudly.

The eyes of a stricken doe regarded me mournfully. So bringing her aboard the ship had not been the first deceit. She

* It may seem surprising that a Cretan should make use of one of the childish stories the Achaeans tell of their essentially simple-minded deities. Because the stories *are* so elementary, they lend themselves easily to the description of simple situations.

wept then — even at that age she wept beautifully. She said she was frightened, she did not want to go to Egypt, they did dreadful things to your body when you died there; when her mother had died, the servants had said how glad they were she hadn't died in Egypt. *She* would die very soon in Egypt, she was sure, she didn't want those dreadful things to be done to her body. . . Well, if I had listened to her, how should I have lived, how *long* should I have lived? Pharaoh's brother-in-law might not have taken any interest in her over the past seven years, but, having made arrangements to receive her, he would not take kindly to being tricked. And at the Nile Delta I should receive my reward — literally the treasure of my dreams. So I refused myself the chance of becoming an active participant in her life, condemned myself to be nothing more than an onlooker.

After she had clung, sobbing, to me the night we left Rhodes, she said very little. I saw the glowing, sparkling, brilliant child deliberately forcing passivity on herself. But it was not like her mother's passivity. That had been the passivity of apathy, inertia, the negativeness arising from lack of emotion, passion. The passivity of the child was the passivity of anticipation.

As I have said, she spoke little to me, particularly after we had left Byblos, and she realized there was no longer any hope of escape. But she would sit looking at me — when I could not escape the gaze of the great dark eyes — and in my mind I would hear a low, gentle voice, more the voice of a woman than a child, pleading for mercy, even the briefest respite, begging me not to condemn her to the life she dreaded. Her air of forlornness, of desolation, even desecration, increased every day.

One can outrage without laying a finger on the body. I had violated the child's spirit.

And so, we came to Egypt. The approach is not beautiful. Long before we saw the actual shore, the blue of the sea was stained with brown mud, which became denser as the ship approached the great river. Then we saw a long, flat coastline, palm trees, and, eventually, smelled Egypt — swamps and sweat, and the reek of straw and dung fires. The child stood beside me with no expression on her face. That caused me some anxiety — I naturally wanted her to appear to her best advantage so that her father would be grateful to me for bringing him such an attractive daughter — and show his gratitude. Fortunately, the bone structure of her face was so exquisite that even complete lack of animation could not mar her beauty.

Before the day was out, I learned from whom she inherited a great deal of that beauty. It was, I imagine, all she inherited from her father. For Ay, the Pharaoh's brother-in-law, whatever his character (and he was cowardly, careerist and miserly) was about the most extraordinarily handsome man I have ever seen. One interesting side-result of foreign conquests is that the victorious troops take home with them the most beautiful women prisoners as wives or concubines and thus in Egypt there was a gradual refinement of the rather heavy native type of face. Later I heard that Eos, through her father, had had a Syrian grandmother, captured during one of the campaigns of Amenhotep II.

In the silent child I had brought to the Nile Delta there was a final flowering of all the astonishing beauty of those two exquisite, fragile women in Syria and in Crete. And it was not merely that she inherited all their astounding loveliness; there was a kind of witchcraft about her that laid a spell on you, so that when you looked at her — even when, in the future, on the most stately of occasions, in the most formal surroundings — you were immediately in your mind carried back to the battlefield, the burning city, the shattered ruins. Briefly, you thought of one thing only, and never envisaged the gradual approach. If you wished to be poetic, you thought of the flower, the fruit to be plucked harshly, the stem to be snapped. If you were not poetic, you simply thought of uncomplicated rape.

Chapter Three
Eos

I can describe in detail enough what happened on that first journey up the Nile, but even now I cannot — will not — do the same in recalling the voyage from Phaestos to Egypt, because during that journey I had still hoped that Staphylos, who had said he was a kinsman, but who was not, might still have pity on me. At Rhodes, Cypros, Byblos, he *might* have said in his abrupt way that we were going no further; every time we approached a port, every time even that he spoke to me, I had hoped he would say, "I've changed my mind." My heart beat so fast it almost choked me.

But once Staphylos had led me to the tall slender man in the white linen robe, sitting under the great awning, I gave up all hope. I accepted there was no escape now; I could only submit, as a wild bird, after days spent fluttering against the bars, submits to being caged eternally. All my life was to be spent in this harsh, cruel country, beneath the intolerable sun, among dark-skinned people, who worshipped gods with animals' heads, and who did dreadful things to your body when you were dead.

Father spoke my language, a little. He told me that he had sent orders to his household to find a Cretan servant to take care of me; Cretans who had fled to Egypt after the great destruction were glad of any employment. But as soon as I could speak Egyptian, of course, my Cretan nurse must go.

Father's boat was immeasurably finer than the vessel bringing me from Crete. It had a cabin roofed against the fierce sunlight, but open at the sides to let in the breeze, and here Father sat and looked hard at me, and I, bitch-puppy presented to new owner, stood and looked frightenedly at the master on whom her future depended. He was as handsome as Staphylos was ugly, as splendid as Staphylos was shabby; still young, not yet thirty, but I did not think of him as young, possibly because of his magnificence. He wore a robe of white linen, and a heavy black wig. He had heavy gold bracelets on his arms, and round his neck a great golden collar. His eyes were the most brilliant I have ever seen.

He smiled suddenly, carefully took me on his knee, and kissed me, a cool, smooth kiss, like his cheek. It was odd to feel that hairless cheek; I remembered the bristling tawny beard of my step-grandmother's husband. And Father did not smell as I had thought all grown men did — he smelled very pleasant indeed, scenting his body with orris-root, I learned later.

"You are beautiful," Father said, but he did not say it quickly, warmly, as if he spoke in affection; he said it thoughtfully, consideringly, coolly — as he had kissed me. "We must see you don't lose that pale skin," he said, half absently. "You mustn't go out too much in the sun."

It took us nine days to reach Thebes, Father's home. Each morning that pitiless sun rose early, and continued to shine mercilessly for hour after hour; yellow, glaring, sending down a constant blast of burning air, as if there were some great oven in the sky, and someone had stupidly opened the door.

"Is it always sunny?" I asked Father.

"Always," he said. Slowly he explained to me that there was never any rain, or snow, or hail, or thunder, or lightning, never any real mist, except a little sometimes at dawn on the river. He could talk to me of these things because he had travelled to Crete and Asia where they happened, but most Egyptians had no idea that such weather existed; there were accordingly no words for them in the Egyptian language.

Only the pitiless sun, then.

And the flat land baking beneath it. A land, I thought childishly, frozen in heat.

While we were not too far from the sea, a little breeze followed us, but soon that dropped. Now the sails could not be used; the rowers had to unship their oars and set to work. It was exhausting work for them, a continuous hard pull upstream, against the current. They were naked to the waist, sweating as they bent to their heavy oars to the beat of a great gong hanging astern, the gong which seemed to boom in my heart, *Goodbye, goodbye. . .*

It was strange that every body I saw now would be the colour of bronze. Only my body was different. I wondered why this did not anger Father, why he went on looking at me in a pleased way. "I think you must be like my mother," he said, more than once. Yet there was a strangeness in his manner. He would sit looking searchingly at me, and yet he did not really seem to see me. He was thinking of something else, smiling as he thought of something else.

Yet I learned later that when he received the letter from Crete, his first reaction had been to disregard it. There would have been no reply but for a quarrel with his chief wife; I never knew the cause, except that in some way it involved their daughter, Mutnedjmet. In a rage, Father had crashed his fist on the table, and exclaimed, "I have another daughter, a *beautiful* daughter, remember!" He read his wife part of the letter. "I will send for her tonight!" he shouted. Which was scarcely calculated to make my stepmother feel kindly towards me.

Every evening the boat moored at the quayside of some provincial town; I was surprised by this — surely Father wanted to get back to his home as quickly as possible? I did not like to ask him the reason, but the captain of the vessel spoke a little Achaean, and I turned to him. He said no captain would sail at night because of sandbanks. I was still comparatively at liberty in these first days in Egypt, and — when Father was ashore being received by local dignitaries — I had more or less a free run of the boat. When the captain had ended his deferential explanation and turned away, I saw one of the rowers shaking his head. I discovered that he spoke a little Achaean. The rest of the crew regarded him as simple-minded — and it was this simplicity, I think, that made him talk to me as he did.

I went to stand at the side of the boat, looking across the water, so slow-flowing it seemed oily, towards the bank where Father's reception continued. The heat pressed down, there was a little breeze, but it came from the south and it was hot and dry. It might flutter my dress momentarily, ruffle my hair, but it made my skin prickle unpleasantly, it caught at my throat, made it difficult to speak, to swallow.

The rower who wished me well muttered, "He wouldn't sail at night in any case, because that's when the dead walk." Now my skin prickled for another reason, something else caused the choking sensation in my throat. He saw my terror, and tried clumsily to reassure me. *I* should be safe at night, ashore in a strong house with thick walls and a solid roof. *She* couldn't get at me there.

"She?" I whispered, flinching. The demon who preyed on little ones, the female demon, face turned backward, who stole the breath of sleeping children.

"All shapelessness she is — " he said stammering, reliving the terrors of childhood in a riverside hut made of reeds, no protection there against the demon, but *I* should be safe enough in a great house with thick walls, so he could tell me. "Bad things always happen at night, but as I love life and hate death they can't to you, being so close to The One." No, he reassured me, I should not have to lie sleepless at night, staring into darkness, straining terrified eyes for the patch of deeper darkness, flowing, melting, except for the head twisted round on the neck – no night terrors for me, being so closely related to The One!

But, of course, after that I did not sleep at night, although because of the oppressive heat I was always very tired when we went ashore in the evening.

At Memphis stood the tombs of the ancient kings of Egypt. Some of them were two thousand years old. This increased my terrors. This was the land where they did dreadful things to your body after your death. Had they built the stone mountains to make sure the mutilated bodies did not come out after dark? But I said nothing. Instead, childishly, I tried to belittle these things which terrified me. I would shrink them, vulgarize them in my mind. That outer skin (of dazzling limestone, I know now) made them shine white, glittering. Why, I thought, they look like great mounds of white flour. The mounds cooks patted into shape to make wheaten cakes. "Pyramids," I said to myself.

"What's that?" asked Father. Fortunately 'pyramid' the Achaean word for wheaten cake was not one which had come his way, and without waiting for an answer he launched into one of his instructive lectures. The first unifier of Egypt, Hore-aha, had joined the two lands together,and built a new capital, Memphis, the White Walled Fortress, at the spot where the narrow river-valley widened out into the fertile plain. "Hore-aha means *Fighting Hawk*," continued Father. All the great founders of Egyptian civilization were called Sons of the Hawk.

It might be expected that after this I had fresh nightmares of giant fighting-hawks, but I did not. The hawk may be a cruel bird, but there is a kind of fierce inevitability about his cruelty, and apart from this he is noble, kingly. In fact, when darkness fell, I began to concentrate hard on thinking of a titanic fighting hawk – *he* would rout any female demon! And after our stay at Memphis, the Fighting-Hawk as a defender was reinforced, not by a creature conceived only in my imagination but by a splendid beast I saw with my very eyes.

We were fortunate in arriving at Memphis at this particular time, said Father; once a year Apis, the sacred bull, was led round the white walls so that the fields would be fertile. So there we were, a few hours later, at the forefront of the crowd, when the huge male creature, black, except for a white triangle on his brow, was led solemnly past us. I was entranced. How big and handsome and glossy he was! As he neared us, he halted, looked at me with moody, brilliant eyes, reviewed me ruminatively. In the silence I heard his rasping breath. I put out a hand, touched him shyly, where the great neck met the shoulder, traced the outline of an eagle on his back. He was vast, godlike, power and terror incarnate, and I loved him. I felt my heart pounding with excitement at the touch, the very sight of him.

Father started to say something; Apis-bull began to paw the ground at this, and his attendant priests hurriedly led him away. He bellowed angrily. I was close to tears. "I don't want him to go — he's so strong and splendid! He dropped his head to let me touch him!" (But I had enough sense to keep unspoken the chief cause of my emotion — I felt at home with the bull because he reminded me of Crete — and surely we must be dedicated together to the service of The Lady?) Vaguely I was aware that about us people were murmuring, but all I felt was grief because Apis-bull and I were parted. Father was looking at me with even more calculation than usual.

"You weren't afraid of him — why?" he asked.

My real reason, of course, was that once another great beast, but white this time, had stood placidly awaiting me, beneath the oak tree in the meadow.

"He offers himself to his goddess," Ariaea had said pleasedly. But I could not tell Father this — Ariaea had forbidden it. So instead, I said it was because, through my mother, I was of the old Cretan blood. For once Father listened to me quite intently as I told him how Europa, my ancestress, the daughter of the King of Tyre, had seen in a meadow a splendid bull, dazzling white, except for a black star between his horns. He was a gentle beast, and let her play with him, put a garland of flowers about his horns, mount his back. But then suddenly he had raced into the waves.

"And he swam with her to Crete, and, they say, ravished her there. . .," I ended rather lamely. I did not know the meaning of ravished, but it was the word unfailingly used — "in a willow thicket, or some people say under a plane tree, and then gave her a gold necklace, to make her beauty immortal." Wistfully I stared after Apis-bull, going further and further away from me, rending the air with his bellows of protest. If only I could mount on his back, and he could plunge with me into the Nile, swim out to sea, across to Crete, I shouldn't mind at all the incomprehensible thing he would then proceed to do in a willow thicket or under a plane tree.

"As a *bull*?" Father said, shattering my dream.

"Oh, no, once in Crete he took a human form, at least as much as he could, being Zeus." From the look on his face, Father had heard about Zeus. "And then Europa had three sons, who became the three kings of Crete, and I'm descended from one of them."

"I have heard of this barbarian god, Zeus," said Father, "but few other men in Egypt will know of him. You mustn't talk about such things again. And the Apis-bull is quite different." Apis-bull, as described by Father, was a far more complicated beast than Zeus-bull had been. There was a god called Ptah, the god of Memphis. He had inseminated a virgin heifer in the form of celestial fire, and the result was Apis-bull. I was dreadfully confused. Inseminated meant the sowing of seed. Which one did into the *earth*. And fire? How uncomfortable for the poor virgin heifer!

Father went on talking. Part of what he said I could understand — and approve of. The bull was the symbol of strength — Ah, *yes!* All those beautiful muscles in his great shoulders that rippled so deliciously! — because of his creative energy. That I didn't understand, so Father hurriedly explained. "People worship him because he has such wonderful power to make new life." Yes, that I understood. A bull was taken to a meadow full of beautiful-eyed cows, and some time later dear little calves were frisking around.

Priests were talking excitedly to Father. "He stopped before her, looked at her — she touched him, without fear!"

"It will, of course," said Father smoothly, "be passed on to the highest quarters?"

"Oh, indeed, indeed! Such a manifestation!"

Father translated all this to me as the priests stared hard at the small piece of absolute foreignness to whom Apis-bull had shown such unprecedented favour; I did not like to ask what a manifestation was. Then Father took my hand and, priests bowing, led me past the murmuring crowd.

After this encounter, although I did not think Father was a man who was usually patient with children, he readily answered any question I put, and seemed pleased to hear them. Thus, when we came to another city, Abydos, and he went ashore, he explained carefully to me when he came back that he had gone to make an offering at the tomb of Osiris, and gave me some explanation of who Osiris was. I could not understand it all, but gathered that Osiris had been a god-king who had been murdered, but restored to life by the efforts of his devoted wife Isis. Father bought for me a statuette, a woman, seated, with a child on her knee — Isis and her son, he said. At least, I thought, with an immense surge of relief, not *all* their gods had animal heads.

Although the next deity brought to my notice was animal-headed enough. We stopped at a city called Dendera, the city of Hathor, said Father, goddess of beauty, love, life, joy. She was usually shown with a cow's horns, suckling the king.

Nine days after the commencement of the journey up-river, we landed at that most immense of cities, Thebes. The sun was setting. Servants and guards waited at the quayside. A groom stood by a gilded chariot. The guards cleared the way for us; to my amazement the dark-skinned crowds touched their foreheads to the dust as we passed.

We came to a high outer wall, a lodge, a porter running out. I was dreadfully tired, and Father, noticing my lagging step, picked me up in his arms. I clung to him; now that my life among strangers was truly beginning, this strange man's body, smooth, orris-scented, was the only thing remotely approaching the familiar left to me.

"Daddy," I began, timidly, placatingly.

But he was not listening. Instead he was saying exasperatedly, "And I'd quite forgotten — we must find a name for you."

"I already have a name," said the bewildered bitch-puppy with a new owner.

He made a little clicking noise in irritation. "That's no use, it's foreign, you must forget it. We must find an Egyptian name for you." He was carrying me along a passage. "What did your mother say when you were born? Of course you don't know, do you? But that's how names are decided upon in Egypt."

We were in an immense many-columned hall — at least at the time it seemed immense to me. The lights — and, even worse, the shadows — showed statues of giant cats, a man with a vulture's head. Oblivious of my terrified eyes, Father grumbled, "I should have left word, instructions. Someone should have made a note of the first thing she said."

We had come to a room lit with alabaster lamps, full of furniture, splendid almost beyond belief. A big, dark-skinned woman sat on a couch covered with rich embroidery. This, I guessed, was my stepmother, Father's chief wife. She looked at me with intense dislike. "So," she said sardonically, staring at the pallid, puny thing held in her husband's arms, "the beautiful one has come!"

I, of course, could not understand a word she had said, but Father, possibly to anger her, took it all at face value. He said to me, "If we don't know how your mother greeted you, we know how your stepmother has greeted you. So we have a name for you after all." And he repeated slowly, two or three times, so that I should be able to say it, the Egyptian words which henceforward would be my name. *The beautiful one has come.* Nefertiti.

THE MAGNIFICENT ONE

Chapter Four
Nefertiti

Pharaoh's harem was always known as "The House of the Isolated", so strict was the seclusion in which his concubines were kept. Even a foreign princess, on entering it, was lost to the world. The seclusion was little less complete in the house of a notable subject like Father, although in ordinary households a harem was simply the quarters where women went about their duties, not a place of confinement, isolation.

Isolation from *men*. One was drowned with women.

At the best it was boring — all talk of children, talk of pregnancy, embroidering, weaving, dressing each other's hair, chattering about cosmetics, looking in mirrors, occasionally dancing, occasionally playing musical instruments. And eating. If you seek obsessions with rich food, heady wine, go to a harem!

At its worst, it was all intrigue and quarrelling — recriminations, tears, frenzies of rage, demands, provocations, jealousies. Jealousies aroused sometimes if Father seemed to show a preference for one woman over another. But often there were jealousies of another kind. Bored women fell in love. You could see them contemplating each other, feeling each other's breasts, exchanging kisses. I could never understand the attraction. A harem swamps one's eyes and senses with acres — so it appears — of soft, naked, highly perfumed female flesh. (And not only perfumed flesh. It is an Egyptian custom to set cones of greasy perfumed incense on the hair; the slowly melting grease eventually bathes head and shoulders in a sweet stickiness that always threatened to turn my stomach.)

Another aspect of my new life I found shocking was the constant attendance of eunuchs. I had never met such creatures before, and, at first, was chiefly repelled in the physical sense. Fat fingers. Bodies that were rolls of quivering flesh. High-pitched voices.

"What are they?" I whispered.

"Unmen," I was told — and there were jokes I could not understand. But other facts concerning the Unmen I comprehended soon enough. Although they were servile — how they grovelled before Father! — there was an arrogance about them. And they hated women.

The Egyptian custom of taking several wives was, of course, something else which shocked me, but when I was able to talk to the other members of the harem, and — unwisely, I realize now — said that men of my mother's race had only one wife at a time, I received the derisive response, "They must be a race of beggars! Can't they afford more than one wife?" Perhaps the people who said this spoke more truly than they knew. Polygamy's chief value, if any, is that it carries with it a certain economic prestige. You measure a man's wealth by the number of his wives.

Of course, all depends on the kind of husband to whom they are given, but, in certain cases, the real gainers from polygamy are women. If one has a clumsy husband, a brutal husband, a feeble yet insatiable husband — then one blesses the institution, for the burden of enduring his attentions is shared. I know I was to be grateful for it!

And there is another point which might well shake male complacency, but for the fact that the master of any harem seems to regard himself as so immeasurably superior to his 'possessions'. The point is one of capability. For these possessions can talk, compare, *criticise*. A skilled and virile master, therefore, might be able to bask in the warmth of rapturous feminine admiration, but if an owner not so well endowed knew the comments exchanged by the best qualified of witnesses as to his impotence, lack of expertise, he might be driven to join the ranks of eunuchs to which his chattels scornfully relegated him.

From which it may be surmised that although I could not understand what his harem said about Father, I gathered clearly enough that there was a distinct lack of enthusiasm. "I wonder why he bothers," was the usual comment. But I have since thought that Father's pronounced lack of interest was really due to the fact that the only person for whom he felt any real warmth was himself.

Most afternoons Father would take me into the garden, and press on with what I suppose was my Egyptianisation. Once or twice I found what he said very interesting, but most of the time I found my mind wandering. It was hard to concentrate in the mid-day heat of the Egyptian sun.

"Nefertiti!" Father – snappish. "What are you thinking?"

"I was looking at your hand," I said, my eyes fixed on the slender fingers. Father possessed a female hunting cat, a beautiful creature, who, not long after my coming, had given birth to four kittens which my Aunt Tiy had immediately expressed a wish to possess. The kittens, therefore, Father had taken from the mother cat and carried to the palace.

The mother cat had cried dreadfully for a day or two, but then seemed to have accepted her loss. "They always do," Father had said complacently. "Animals soon forget things." But months later, without warning – indeed, after coming up to him with every appearance of affection – she had suddenly flown at his face. He had managed to save his eyes by flinging up his hand, but that hand bled deeply for a very long time.

The scratches did eventually, however, heal well, but not completely. If you looked hard, there was a tiny scar along the top of the thumb, a faint roughness if Father touched you. But Father seemed quite oblivious of it. "That's all over and done with," he said firmly.

I might be only a girl and seven years old, but Father, it seemed, had great plans for me, mostly stemming from my encounter with Apis-bull. I must have a tutor – and, after the day when Father came upon me, idly and unwisely scratching in the dust with a stick he had been delighted. "So you already write the Cretan language easily enough!"

Next day I was presented with a scribal palette, reed brush, and the appallingly difficult, even more appallingly dull reading and writing lessons began. I copied endless texts, mostly gloomy accounts of the time a thousand years before when chaos had come to Egypt, when the first golden age had vanished in hunger and lawlessness, for there was no strong Pharaoh. Mornings I spent with my writing-master; in the afternoon, if Father were not at home, my elderly tutor Ptah-Nekhen instructed me in Egyptian history.

Before the present Pharaoh's family saved Egypt, the country had been tormented for decades by savage rulers from the east, the Hyksos, the Shepherd Kings, so called because of their once nomadic way of life and not because of any tender concern for their people. They had ravished (I still did not know what the word meant) they had burned, they had slaughtered . . . it had all happened a long time before, but Ptah-Nekhen regarded the invasion by the Hyksos as a bitter personal outrage – so did most Egyptians. Previously they had been unused to foreign invasion, and worse, conquest – the memory endured, rankling still, particularly in the Delta and the North, where the brutal alien grip had been firmest. Memphis had suffered hideously.

"Didn't they come to Thebes, then? Why not?" I asked.

Looking rather embarrassed, Ptah-Nekhen said that Thebes had been of little consequence at the time — it was only after Theban princes began the overthrow of the Hyksos . . . Hurriedly he burst into glowing praises of the Theban saviours, particularly the most god-like of all, Thutmosis III, who had finally set the boundaries of the Egyptian Empire as far apart as the sandy wastes beyond Wadi Halfa and the banks of the Euphrates.

"So because of what's been done by The One's family, the days of the Hyksos won't return?"

"Never!"

"But why did the Hyksos find it so *easy*?" I asked tactlessly.

"They had an unfair advantage — they used horses and chariots, which at the time were unknown here," said Ptah-Nekhen hastily. "It was only because of this that the defences the gods gave Egypt were broken." He went on to explain how Egypt, that long thin thread of green, was protected by dreadful wastes of desert.

It was not very interesting. I wished I had someone like Ariaea to explain things — *she* had made every plain and mountain about Phaestos come alive for me. I was drowsy; it was still early enough in the afternoon for the sky to be a sky of brass. "Do the people tell stories about the river and the desert?" I asked sleepily. Ptah-Nekhen was a little offended, but startled enough by the question to answer it.

"Oh, yes. They say the Nile valley is Isis — the rich earth, if you like. She can be made fruitful only by the Nile — that's Osiris, of course, in their story. But she's always threatened by the desert — all aridity, perversity. And that's Set, who murdered Osiris, desired his wife, and persecuted her for nine months — the evil days, the people called them."

Father himself also instructed me in Egyptian religion — rather he attempted to cram my totally unreceptive mind with all possible information on the Egyptian pantheon — and confused me dreadfully, for like so many very clever people he had no idea how to make what he said intelligible to a child. Once the chief god had been Re, the sun, but now ram-headed Amen, the god of Thebes itself, ruled supreme; Amen who had led the invincible warrior — Pharaoh, Thutmosis III, great-grandfather of the present god-king, to victory in Syria. (I was becoming very bored indeed with Thutmosis!) Then there was ibis-headed Thoth, Lord of Wisdom, cat-headed Bast, cow-headed Hathor, jackal-headed Anubis — even if Father's voice had not droned on so boringly, I could never have accepted what he said. How could I accept such monstrous creatures?

Not that they had ever existed, of course. For there were not many gods! There was only one true deity, the moon-goddess, queen of the mountains, animals, sea — all living things, all life! Men were not divine! Sometimes a man was temporarily associated with The Lady, but he was of utterly negligible importance, a lover condescended to by The Lady with a kind of divine contempt.

But I had sense enough never to voice my mental revolt, and would sit looking earnestly at Father. This did not require a great effort — he was so outstandingly handsome. Father, I was to find soon enough, was pompous, unlikeable, treacherous, despicable — but he had exquisite taste, and he loved beauty. Because of this sincere love of beauty, I suppose it followed logically enough that he loved himself better than anyone else in the world, and arrayed his narrow, graceful body in the most consummate manner.

All of which brings me to what I, without conceit, gradually came to believe was Father's chief motive for giving me such lengthy private tuition. There was an amazing physical resemblance between us. I had become aware of this during the journey up the Nile, when we had gone ashore each evening to spend the night at the local governor's house. Each time the governor's wife had said — so Father translated to me — that I was the most beautiful of children and with a look at Father so eloquent it needed no translating — "Of course, she resembles you so much!"

Father, in other words, kept me with him for hours, because staring at me he could admire the god he truly worshipped, less blatantly than if he had kept taking covert glances at his reflected image in a bronze mirror.

I don't think my stepmother realized this; *she*, after all, did not see any beauty in me whatsoever. I was nothing more than a freak in her eyes — a thin white body, sheltering behind a cloud, a curtain of curling, dark brown hair and not the oiled black of her hair or her own daughter.

My hair, in fact, provoked her first outburst of hostility towards me. The day after my arrival she gave orders that my long hair should be cut short; it is the fashion for girl-children in Egypt to have shaven heads, but for one side lock. When I realized why slaves were advancing on me with shears, I had wept, and struggled; Ariaea had told me that it was all-important I should wear my long hair tied in a special knot. This, the chief reason for my wild resistance, I could not voice, but there was another reason, too, and this I could sob out. Not, in this case, that there was any need for explanation on my part — the whole harem had been noisily amused by my shocked, frightened glances at the nakedness in which girls of my age lived. I could do nothing to make them clothe me, but at least my long hair, stretching almost to my knees, provided a screen behind which I could hide the body whose whiteness again evoked laughing derision.

"Why is she crying?" demanded Father, striding up.

"*This* girl never cries!" My stepmother answered contemptuously. But for some reason this same oddity on my part seemed to please Father.

"Don't cut her hair!" he shouted. "Never cut her hair!" So much I could gather from an outflung slender hand, angrily flashing dark eyes, but the rest of the argument was largely incomprehensible, although, from fairly constant repetition, I soon knew it well enough, Father giving orders for the care of my hair, my skin, my stepmother shrieking that this was enough to make every hippo along the Nile Valley dislocate its jaws in laughter — so great a man concerning himself with women's ploys. Merely because at *Memphis*. . .! (Being part-Nubian, she despised Northern beliefs.)

But he paid no heed to what she said; he would call the women slaves together and threaten dreadful punishment if my eyes became sore, my skin cracked because of the heat and the dryness and dust.

My stepmother's dislike of me increased. She could not claim that Father was over-fond of me — affection had no place in Father's scheme of things — but he had plans for me, whereas all his energies should be devoted to promoting the interests of *her* daughter.

Sometimes when he was in the middle of a pompous discourse, Father would abruptly lift me on to his knee, give me figs to eat or a caraway cake, and twist a tendril of my hair about his finger. "My mother must have had hair like this," he would say. I did not tell him that all the women of old Crete had had hair like mine; by this time I knew that anything in me that pleased him he attributed solely to himself. But more often, alas, he was displeased by something — some *things* I still lacked. Holding me on his knee, clasped rather uncomfortably against the great gold pectoral of Nekhnet, the Vulture goddess that was his favourite ornament, he would say irritably, "When in God's name are your paps going to appear? There's nothing at all there yet!", putting his long, elegant fingers to the two dark pink small beads perceptible only because of their colour.

This fruitless prospecting on Father's part usually occurred — incongruously it seemed to me at the time — when he was talking to me of the incarnate god, Pharaoh. Heralds preceded him with the cry, "Earth, beware! Your god comes!" and people flung themselves face downwards in the dust. It was certain death to touch him by mistake. And I must never, never call him Pharaoh – that was the barbarian name for him. The god-king's own subjects always called him "The One" or "The One who Lives in the Great House", and since Per-o was the Egyptian name for Great House the thick-witted barbarians called the House's occupant Pharaoh. *I* must always speak of the Lord of the Two Lands or Master of the North and South.

"Or The One?" I asked. No. This particular god-king, because of the splendour of his reign, was always called "The Magnificent One".

But since the gods of Egypt were false, I refused to be overawed by the god-king – who in any case, had married a human, my father's sister, my own relative. Once or twice when Father was not moody because my chest remained obstinately flat, I asked him what my Aunt Tiy was like. I really meant in character, but all that he would reply, shortly, was that she did not look like him at all.

She did not.

It was fitting, I suppose, that our first meeting should take place when I was in disgrace.

It had been one of the days when unhappiness choked me. My stepmother, who kept a wary, unsympathetic eye on me, asked me angrily why I was so discontented and sullen. I tried to stammer out that everything was so different from the life I had been used to. Unwisely – but I was only eight years old and still desperately lonely after almost a year in Egypt – I tried to tell her about the freedom of my old life, how my mother's brothers had taken me up into the hills. She shrieked with affected horror, and so, dutifully, did the women surrounding her. "By *men*?" By boys, I said, puzzled, and gave her their ages, tears in my eyes all the while, because, as time passed, I was finding it increasingly hard to remember how they looked. The grief this roused in me – and, of course, my youth and still incomplete command of Egyptian – made it difficult to follow what she was saying; I could only gather that she was suggesting that in the hills they had done strange things. "But why should they do those things to me?" I asked, staring. "They loved me!" At this she burst out laughing, and all the other women burst out laughing too.

But next moment she was affecting to be serious. "Your father must know of this!" she said unpleasantly. "*This* may make him alter his plans!" And she swept off in search of him, telling a slave to bring me along behind. Father was irritated at being disturbed, but he got rid of his secretaries when he saw his wife was in a rage, and after he had listened to her for only a few minutes, his rage exceeded hers — and was considerably more genuine.

"You stupid malicious bitch — you don't believe a word of it! You know their ways aren't ours — their girls don't marry until they're fourteen — even older. And even if you believed it, there's one sure way to find out if she's been interfered with." Then he shouted in sudden fury, "But you're not to touch her — like that! Neither you nor any of your hags are to touch her — like that! I'll find out by talking to her! Nefertiti, come here!"

Frightened, bewildered, I stood before him. "Did any of your mother's brothers — " and he reeled off all that *she* had said, and again I repeated in bewilderment, that they would never do such strange things, because they loved me. "Get out!" Father said in rage to the slave who had brought me.

I think my stepmother would have gone too, had it not been for the fact that at that moment there was a blare of trumpets outside, shouts of, "Life! Health! Prosperity!" and most of the household seemed to come running in panic. My Aunt Tiy had chosen this moment to make a surprise visit.

In a flash the anger on the faces before me changed to bland and respectful delight. Father started giving orders for the reception of his sister as if he were planning a major campaign; my stepmother hissed at the slave who had hauled me along in disgrace, "Bring my daughter here, immediately!" Then next moment, she and Father, the picture of connubial affection, went out side by side to greet The Magnificent One's Great Wife, leaving me quite alone, and equally forgotten.

I had no idea what to do, but decided to stay; I should like to see the human aunt who had married a god. A nurse ran in with Mutnedjmet, moon-faced and thick-lipped — somehow they had contrived to find time to put her into her newest dress, fix heavy gold ear-rings in her ears, fasten a gold collar about her neck, a lotus bud in the lock at the side of her shaven head.

"What do we do when she comes?" I asked my half-sister.

"I'm not telling you," she said, giggling. "I expect you'll make all kinds of mistakes."

Mutnedjmet was being stupid, as usual. I would simply watch her and do whatever she did.

A deep, harsh, imperious voice outside; Father's answering, deferential; my stepmother's, submissive. Then with a swirl of movement, they were all flooding into the room, attendants, my stepmother, Father — my aunt Tiy. Mutnedjmet fell flat on her face. I did likewise.

The deep, harsh, imperious voice. "Tell the younger one to

get up."

"Nefertiti — " (Father, cautioning, warning.)

I scrambled up and took my first look at my Aunt Tiy.

There were to be more than twenty years of — at the best — distrust and dislike between us. That distrust and dislike, I think, came like the spark from the friction of two pieces of wood from the moment we set eyes on each other. Yet I think my description of Tiy is accurate enough — dark skin, almost with the purplish colour of grapes, a heavy, sullen mouth, extraordinary protruding lips, almost ape-like, always suggesting to me later a gross licentiousness. There was little that was gracious or graceful about her. Her eyes were always arrogant; she walked badly, her breasts, like great over-ripe fruit, swaying as she moved. But she had enormous physical vitality, and she was capable of assuming a heady surface gaiety. She was, I suppose, precisely the type likely first to attract, then to dominate a weak, sensual, man sated with beautiful women, and so this woman of inexorable will, who had climbed to the throne from a non-royal family, could arrogate to herself more prerogatives than had been given to any royal wife on the throne of Egypt before her.

I must have looked drained of life as I stood there — drained of life in contrast with all the other women surrounding me, Tiy herself, enormously formidable physically, in any case, and blazing with gold. Behind me my stepmother, dark-skinned too, always almost top-heavy with bright jewellery at wrist and arm and throat. Even my stepsister, as dark as her mother, wore ear-rings and a gold collar. And, in the centre of them, the target of their inimical gaze, myself, puny, unformed, brittle.

And no friendly looks from Father, of course! Anxiety for the success of his own schemes made his face and eyes hard as stone as he stared at the small, unreliable piece of humanity on which so much was to depend.

"Come closer," said my aunt.

I went closer. Her body was drenched with strong, musky perfume. I was very frightened. But then — to my surprise, Father's delight, my stepmother's chagrin — she smiled. She was pleased by what she saw, for what she saw, she believed, would never challenge her physically or mentally. She said to Father in a disdainful way which later I learned was her usual way of addressing him, "Yes. She might do." Then, realizing — for she was a very shrewd woman — that she had enabled him to score over my stepmother, she added carelessly, "Or, of course, the other one."

Chapter Five
Nefertiti

After this I was sent away. Mutnedjmet remained. Presumably plans were being made for her too. I never learned what those plans might be, but after my aunt's visit, Mutnedjmet was sent to attend some of my history lessons. Even when Ptah-Nekhen was not droning on about the exploits of Thutmosis III, my sister found lessons unutterably boring. Her idea of interest, happiness, was playing for hours with the cosmetics on her mother's dressing-table. Her greatest treat was being given permission to use the cosmetics — to paint her upper eyelid black with galena, or pine-soot soaked into goose-grease, the lower lid green with malachite, to colour her lips with red ochre, her nails and the soles of her feet with intricate designs in henna*

All so much more congenial to Mutnedjmet than Ptah-Nekhen's never-ending account of the Hyksos, and the salvation that had eventually come from Upper Egypt — indeed, more than salvation, for "when the evil men were driven out, our armies pursued them into their own countries, conquering all Syria, building fortresses. Never again shall Egypt fall to foreign invasion!"

"So," Ptah-Nekhen concluded triumphantly, "The Magnificent One today rules over the greatest empire known to the world."

* This is a silly custom which has arisen among Egyptian women. Originally henna was used to calm down fevers — a paste was applied to hands and feet to cool them. Now a healing device has become a recipe for beauty. Some women, I have heard, even apply henna to their breasts. When I was older I myself often had cream perfume rubbed into the soles of my feet which, slowly becoming volatile, gave a faint, almost *imperceptible* fragrance, but I would never let henna be used.

And I sat and secretly mourned the simplicity, the naturalness of the lost life, within sight of the sea and mountains, the pet hare I could fondle, the smallness of life on that finite island, so far removed from this vast land bounded by deserts.

And I still could not accept the gods of Egypt. Isis, perhaps; the others, no. But even Isis could not fit in with what Ariaea had taught me, for the Mother-Goddess did not have a single husband, she had many lovers. Everything in Egypt seemed inverted; where there should be one goddess to many men, here was one man to many women, particularly if you were the god-king himself.

I had now seen that god-king — from a distance, when Father had taken me to see him sacrificing at the vast temple of Amen with its door overlaid with gold, and inlaid with lapis-lazuli and precious stones; the floor inside, Father said, was made of silver.

Theban temples still amazed me; there had been no temples in Crete, but even if there had, I should still have been stupefied both by the size and the colour of those of the Egyptian capital. They were so bright that they hurt the eye — enormous figures of men and gods, painted blue, green, orange, red against a background of dazzling white, gold flagstaffs flying scarlet pennants. And the size of them! They were not so much temples as great, arrogant fortresses built by the warrior Pharaohs as strongholds of the gods, especially Amen the Conqueror. They were new, smooth, sleek, gleaming — like Thebes itself, Amen's city. Highways lined with alabaster chapels and rows of sphinxes connected them until finally one arrived at the great temple of all, built by the present Pharaoh, with two great* statues of himself outside as tall as ten men. I studied them with some interest; this, then, was the husband of my Aunt Tiy, this upright, majestic, calm being, as detached from human follies as he was serene.

Eventually he himself came, to the music of flutes, viols and harps, the silver blare of trumpets, to his heralds' warning shout, to the answering shouts of the crowds before they flung themselves face downwards in the dust — "Life! Prosperity! Health to The Magnificent One, Lord of Lords! King of the North and South! Son of Re!" I tried to snatch a glance at him (being small, I could delay my prostration a little) but the great ostrich feather fans held over him partially screened him from view. My only impression was of a head almost weighed down by the splendid regalia it bore, the *Atef* crown, the tall conical White

* The height of each was 64 feet.

Crown of Upper Egypt, flanked by sweeping feathers, ram's horns, sacred snakes. And, beside him, my Aunt Tiy, jewels and dark skin flashing in the sun.

"There is a golden image in the sanctuary," said Father in a low voice when we stood again. He went on to describe the ceremonies — The One going alone with hawk-masked, ibis-masked priests further and further into the veiled, shrouded, most sacred part of the temple, into silence broken only by soft chanting, darkness lit only fitfully by torches, where he confronted a golden face dimly seen through wreaths of incense, his fellow god, Amen.

When they came out again, the great fans still obscured The Magnificent One's face, but now I had eyes for other members of the royal party; there was also a young man — at least, I thought he was a young man, for he wore a man's white pleated kilt, but from the thin, sloping shoulders and the wide hips he seemed more like a woman. Perhaps it was just as well I did not know that my aunt and Father — in that order — had chosen me as the possible wife of this individual whose sex I could not determine. As he came out of the temple, I thought he had the thinnest legs I had ever seen on anyone, male or female.

"Who is that?" I whispered to Father (after our second prostration). "The — the person with the thin legs?"

He looked at me in sudden — what? "Keep your voice down, and don't say such things. It's The Magnificent One's son — Amenhotep."

"Oh," I said. "His *son*. Are — are your sure, Father?"

Presumably Father — Amenhotep's uncle, after all — knew. Presumably he was angry with me for doubting him. Certainly he was staring down at me with a strange expression in his brilliant eyes.

Mutnedjmet now had a small army of attendants to prepare her for marriage; Father entrusted me to a partially deaf old woman who had come from Syria with his mother, and was renowned for her skill in the arts of beauty. Here, perhaps, was the only human being (beside himself) who was devoted to Father. Deafness left her in such isolation that she had no knowledge of his unhandsome character; all she knew was what her eyes told her that facially he resembled his mother, the Syrian captive-princess, and now Father had passed on that likeness to me! Deafness might have cut off Naya from most of the intrigues surrounding her; I never knew exactly what battle she thought was waging when she took charge of me, but of one thing she was certain — the grand-daughter of her beloved lost princess had as rival a girl of pronounced Nubian looks, and whatever the prize of *this* battle, the descendant of her dead mistress should win it.

Meanwhile, no Egyptian woman being interested in me, no one stopped my heretical attachment to the few oils perfumed only with the pure scent of flowers — acacia, rosemary, sweet flag, mimosa — above all, the pale blue oil of lilies that made me remember Ariaea and the enclosed garden in the ruins. Father, hawk-eyed, noticed it, of course, but was uncharacteristically indulgent to my eccentricity.

Although I saw far less of Father now; he spent a great deal of time at the Court. Still, he managed to take a brief look at me each day, eyeing me discontentedly on each occasion. "Give her time, give her time," said Naya angrily.

When he could manage it, Father also continued his lectures to me. Not so much, now, to my relief, about the gods of Egypt, as about the importance of the Nile, which dwindled in the summer to a ditch of reddish, slimy water between land hard-baked, cracked with heat. "I know," I said once, brightly, "but no one ever worries! Ptah-Nekhen has told me why." Pharaoh, the God-King, travelled annually to the northern border where the waters first began to rise, threw into the river a scroll reminding his brother, the Nile-God, of the treaty between them, getting his promise that the waters would soon come down into the valley again. And within weeks they would. First they were red, then green. Finally the waters crept over the land, villages became islands in a sea of muddy water. At the end of the next month, the waters began to subside; another month and sowers, singing, went over the sea of black mud, scattering grain. The seeds germinated rapidly; within a week or two a green haze of shoots hid the mud flats.

Father, when I repeated all this to him, eyed me moodily. "Yes," he said, after a moment, "it's quite true that all depends on The One. As, indeed, all the people believe." Sometimes — although very rarely — the fact that he was addressing a face so much like his own made him speak with the frankness he might use when talking to his reflection in a mirror. On this occasion, however, his tone, rather than his words, was expressive.

"Don't *you* believe it, Father?" I asked, surprised into boldness. Father promptly promulgated one of the chief articles of his political creed.

"What actually happens isn't so important, as what the people *think* happens," he said half-absently, then, rousing himself, "They also believe that *other* activities of The One cause the Nile to flood, the corn to grow." He began to grumble in Syrian to Naya, who could lip read very well. The tone of his voice was unmistakable. So was her inevitable response – "Give her time!"

Father reverted to Egyptian, so that I should be fully aware of the enormity of the crime it seemed I was in danger of perpetrating – proving a disappointment to him. "Look!" he growled, seizing me and fingering my relevant parts despairingly. "*She still has no breasts*!"

"Your mother had no paps when she was the little one's age!" replied Naya sturdily. "But later – Ah, the full moons of delight, the wonder of Syria! And *firm*! Your father," she continued furiously, "never had any complaints, I can tell you! He couldn't keep his hands off them!"

She spoke in the penetrating tones of the deaf; Father, alarmed, clapped a hand over her mouth. With the other he tweaked away at me discontentedly. "And her nipples are the wrong colour," he groaned.

"Nipples," said Naya tartly, "can be painted, can't they?"

"If she ever has any," said Father morosely. "You must start stroking them, drawing them out." His elegant fingers set an example; I found it quite pleasant.

"Oh!" said Naya. "You go off and help govern that damned Egyptian Empire that made your mother's life a misery, and leave *me* to look after the little one's nipples. They'll be like your mother's, I tell you! Beautiful. So *prominent*! Fairly *stabbing* away!" Father, still looking disbelieving, gave me two sharp valedictory tweaks of admonition, and went off to help govern the Egyptian Empire so detested by Naya who, to my intense grief, died a month later. Now there was no one to champion me – or hearten Father.

And Mutnedjmet's physical development meanwhile continued to surge on. One morning her mother was wild with delight. Overnight, Mutnedjmet had "become a woman". When I learned what this momentous event consisted of, I felt not the slightest envy, looked forward to the prospect of it befalling me not at all. (So this was how the moon ruled one's life!) But the harem rang with congratulations. My sister was a *woman*. "Ah, the Nubian blood!" said her mother, excitedly sending news of what had happened to my Aunt Tiy. My aunt, probably to aggravate Father, who, she knew, preferred another daughter as candidate, replied that she thought it was time that her son made the acquaintance of his cousin.

One of the reasons that, years later, I hated ceremonial so much was the fact that I knew what a tedious yet hysterical business it could be to receive Pharaoh, or his consort, or a member of his family.

The visit was to take place in the late afternoon. All day the frenzy rose; Mutnedjmet, making her own experiments in eye make-up, sat scowling and fretting in the garden. I sat quietly rejoicing in the fact that I was not involved in all the commotion — indeed, I had been told pointedly by my stepmother to keep out of the way.

And then he came too soon.

He came when my half-sister was still in the garden painting her eyes, while I obligingly held up her mirror for her. My stepmother ran into the garden, green-faced with panic under her dark skin, as hysterical as if a fresh band of Hyksos were battering on the outer door. "He's *come*!" she screamed. "He's *come*!" And, snatching at her daughter's wrist, dragged her away as if the first savage bent on ravishment was about to bound out from between the flowering shrubs. I sat on, infinitely contented that I had no part in the mad confusion. In fact, as I sat there by the pool, lifting my face to the sky, I held up my arms in silent gratitude to the Goddess for letting Mutnedjmet become a woman before me.

It was while I was in this possibly absurd position that I heard a nervous clearing of the throat. My eyes flashed round, and there, a few feet from me, stood our cousin.

"I said," he stammered, "I would wait in the garden. I like gardens, I — Who are you?"

"I am Nefertiti," I said.

"I am Amenhotep," he said awkwardly.

At close quarters Amenhotep looked even stranger than at a distance. Since coming to Egypt, I had seen few men — my father, tutors, men at a distance when I was taken out, those un-men, the eunuchs — but I knew that the proportion of his body was all wrong. The upper part was lean, the lower part swollen, like that of a pregnant woman. And then, while his hips and upper thighs were swollen too, below the knees his legs were as spindly as a starving beggar's. Cadaverous leanness, elongation, flimsiness of body, a long, solemn drooping profile, giving an odd impression of colourlessness despite the dark skin, or did I think of colourlessness because he looked so sickly?

We sat beside the pool. Great, brilliant butterflies hovered about us. He would not talk, but sat staring. Since it had been drilled into my head that I should keep out of the way, I felt I myself should not talk too much.

"Nefertiti," he said, suddenly touching very gently the inner side of my wrist, "Nefertiti, when you are a little older, I am going to marry you."

I stared at him. "Are you sure? But everyone thought it would be Mutnedjmet."

"No, my mother said it might be you, and now I know it must."

"Are you sure?" I repeated. "She's developed all over; I haven't started. They say that's what matters."

He looked embarrassed again, but said, "Not always. Other things matter."

"What things?"

"Your hair," he said. "Your eyes. Your sweet breath. The whiteness of you. White is the colour of hope — did you know that?"

To hear such things at nine and a half may very well lead to a fit of giggles. But I kept my face serious and said, "But because I'm white I don't look Egyptian. Isn't that undesirable?"

"I don't think so. Perhaps it's because I've been out of Egypt for a year or two."

"Where have you been?" The question shot out like an arrow from a bow. Perhaps he had been to Crete. To Phaestos.

But he had been only in Syria, with his father's mother's relatives, chiefly, but he had also travelled further to the east. Yet even this was something. "Then you will know about rain and snow and mountains!" I said. That, at the time, seemed infinitely more important than the fact that a few moments before he had said that one day he was going to marry me.

I pass over any description of the violent scenes that took place before my stepmother and half-sister accepted that Nefertiti, face unpainted, in her straight white dress (with straight white body inside it) was the chosen bride of the future Pharaoh.

But there was also the present Pharaoh to consider. After a few months had passed I, now aged ten, was taken by Father to the Great Palace at Malkata to be inspected. I was laboriously instructed in the proper etiquette to follow. You kissed the ground in front of The One — or, as a great favour, the thong of his sandal. When given permission to rise you should embark on elaborate praises of him before saying anything else. . .

I listened as if in an unhappy dream. For my stepmother the night before, in order to quench any feeling of anticipatory triumph I might have, had explained with brutal frankness what would happen to me when I married Amenhotep. I should be hurt — possibly a great deal. "But why should he want to hurt me? I haven't done anything wrong! And he's told me he likes me." (In the months since our first conversation I had seen him three or four times). "He likes talking to me."

"He won't be doing much talking to you after you're married," my stepmother said. "I've told you what he'll do." And she described the process again, very succinctly.

"I don't believe you. He's not like that. He's kind. He'd never do anything horrible like that. He's gentle. That – that's like two dogs fighting." I burst out crying. "I don't want him to do that to me! I don't want *anyone* ever to do that to me!"

"Save your tears until it's happened," said my stepmother maliciously. "Then you'll have need to cry."

"I don't believe it will happen," I said obstinately. "You made it up to frighten me. You've never liked me, and you wanted your own daughter to marry him. You love her as much as you hate me – you'd never want *that* to happen to her! It's not like that at all!"

Each Pharaoh on succession wants to build a new palace for himself; the newest palace, built at Malkata, called the House of Rejoicing, was huge, rambling, and almost indescribably luxurious. Pharaoh's very furniture was silver and gold (which may have been magnificent; it was certainly hideously uncomfortable.) Against such a background, a myriad of courtiers, soldiers, priests, gold, which seemed everywhere, I found myself clinging bewilderedly to Father's hand. Father took me first to his sister, who would perform the presentation. She viewed me with her usual contemptuous satisfaction. No physical or mental challenge from *this*. "She knows what's expected of her?" (She always treated me as a deaf and dumb half-wit, and never spoke directly to me.) "Well, of course, if The Magnificent One's so inclined, he may cut the ceremony short – "

To my great relief The Magnificent One was so inclined. And the presentation did not, as I had dreaded, take place in one of the great official rooms, for The Magnificent One, already an ailing man, spent a great deal of time in a smaller private room overlooking a garden.

As with his wife, I find it difficult now to record accurately my first impression of The Magnificent One. Looking back, I remember someone who could be irascible, capricious, melancholy, yet he never lost the ability to hold men to him. Overweight, prematurely aged, he was still capable of a wonderful charm – when he smiled and his face was animated, though his thickening body remained slouched inertly in a chair, you were suddenly aware of a vanished golden grace. When I had been taken to my aunt's apartments she had with her Amenhotep's two brothers, a baby, Tutankhaten, and Smenkhare, four or five years younger than I was. He was an extremely handsome little boy – and equally badly behaved, and the slightly slanting, laughing eyes, and the line of cheek and brow gave an indication of what The Magnificent One had been like when he had been young.

But as far as I can remember, my first impression of The Magnificent One was one of dejection and fatigue. His cheeks, for all his thickening body, were hollow, his eyelids heavy as if anxiety weighed them down.

I had duly prostrated myself, and a kindly voice told me to get up.

"I told you she'd do," said my aunt.

The weary, disillusioned eyes rested on me with a sudden flicker of interest. "Yes, she's a dainty thing. Too good for him, I'd say. Come here, child. Yes, I think definitely wasted on him."

It may have been a spontaneous remark; it may all have been part of a plan thought out in advance. At only ten years old I was aware of the hostility – no, more than hostility, *repugnance* – the two felt for each other.

It was hot in the room. One symptom of his illness was that he always felt cold, and there were braziers burning in the four corners.

"Almost," said The Magnificent One, "I'm inclined to change our plans. I've a good mind to have her for myself."

My Aunt Tiy exclaimed, "No! I'll never permit it!"

The Magnificent One shouted at her with sudden and furious authority, "Remember that I raised you from nothing, and can crush you into nothingness again. Remember that if you like your diversions, then I can have mine!"

She was suddenly terrified; but she spat back, "An old man – and a child!"

His voice was deadly. "My plaything would be more natural than yours."

They had both forgotten me, and I was glad of it. I wanted to creep away – but did not know where to go. I was as frightened as my aunt, but at least she knew why she was frightened, and I didn't. She had quite forgotten me. She muttered, "Do as you wish," and went away, leaving me alone with him. He sat staring after her for a long time. Suddenly I found I was crying. I tried to cry quietly, but he heard me, and looked down at me with a completely changed expression.

"I didn't mean to upset you, little one," he said. "What a pretty thing you are – you can cry and still look delicious. Not many women can do that. And white as milk, soft as milk, but smelling of milk and lilies. Well, what are we going to do about you? Would you like to come to me instead of to Amenhotep?"

I asked nervously what would my father say?

The Magnificent One grinned with real amusement. "A good question. What will that hero do? Opt to please me — or his sister? Which of us scares him most? Come and sit on my knee, and let's consider. Would you like some fruit? And here's some wine."

Physically, sitting on The Magnificent One's knee made for great discomfort. He wore a great gold pectoral of Horus, the Hawk, and on the arm he put about me were three heavy gold bracelets, one decorated with turquoise, one with lapis-lazuli, one with chalcedon. But mentally I felt at ease. The Magnificent One liked me, more — and more *genuinely* — than Father did.

The wine in the golden cup was stronger than anything I had been used to; I felt a little dizzy, and hoped I should not be sick. The Magnificent One drained his own golden cup. "Yes, little Nefertiti, I like you. Because of which, it's not for mere selfish reasons that I think you'd be better off with me than with *him.* But I can't tell you why — you wouldn't understand. How old are you? Ten? No, you wouldn't understand. . ."

He had given me fruit to eat. I was concentrating on eating as quietly as one can eat fruit; no doubt court etiquette decreed dreadful punishments for anyone daring to be a noisy eater in The One's presence.

"Yes," decided The Magnificent One, suddenly caressing me, "I'll have you for myself — but we'll keep it a secret for a time."

"May I tell Father?" I asked.

He began to laugh. "Yes, tell him by all means. Interesting to see how he'll react. Now we'd better get you back to him, but she's gone, and I'm not going to send for any of her women — let her sweat wondering how long I kept you with me. In fact, I'll keep you here a little longer, and then send you off with a military escort. Sit here on a cushion at my feet. You're going to see a young man going back to frontier duty, and very glad of it." He called, "Horemheb!"

From another door a young officer strode into the room, very soldierly, well turned out, saluting with a snap.

"You," said The Magnificent One, "are an ungrateful young hound. Chafing so visibly at being here that I myself feel physical discomfort — "

"Majesty," came the unmoved response.

"I've never known anyone able to convey so much inarticulate insolence in an impersonal voice. After all these years — in case you don't know, child, it's the custom to bring to the court a selection of boys born at the same time as the heir to the throne — we haven't been able to tame you, have we?''

''Majesty, there's a crying need for men on the frontier! Your ancestors won an Empire; *we* must defend it!'' And here the resonant voice was anything but impersonal. ''With the incidents in North Syria, the Hittites on the move. . .''

''What are you expecting me to do? Put on my blue war-helmet, get a couple of fellows to hoist me into a chariot, and. . .''

''Majesty, I know you can't come in person. But — your *representative* — ''

''And you should know *that's* impossible too,'' the Magnificent One shouted, but the rage in his voice was not directed at the officer before him who now looked meaningly at me. (It never had been, even a child could grasp that the Magnificent One liked the Captain of Chariotry very much indeed).

The Magnificent One now followed the direction of the angry, brilliant eyes. ''Poor child'', he said. ''Cornered between a terrible old man and a terrible young man. Well, Horemheb, take your leave of me now, then escort the Lady Nefertiti back to her father — you know who he is?''

Horemheb nodded, but his silence unmistakably conveyed a feeling of near-derision. But this did not worry me, I only hoped his leave-taking would not be prolonged. I felt distinctly queasy.

The Magnificent One was right; he was a terrible young man. As he stalked alongside me, taking me back to Father, I found him completely intimidating, for all his youth and the smooth black hair that shone in the sunlight. (Being a soldier, he did not wear a wig). His face, with its taut line of jaw, the straight, blunt nose, was oddly emotionless for one who was only Amenhotep's age. And he was not at all gratified by his charge; he strode along in grim silence — I had almost to run to keep up with him. He had very strong legs (I thought suddenly of Amenhotep's, so thin, unmuscular). Strength, in fact, was his most intimidating characteristic; the average Egyptian is broad-shouldered, slender-waisted, square-chinned, firm-mouthed, with a broad forehead, eyes set wide apart, with muscular arms and legs, and the Son of the Hawk, for that was the meaning of his name, possessed all these to a superlative degree.

In such circumstances, I think one of the bravest acts of my life was to touch his hard hand, and say, apologetically, ''I am sorry, but I feel sick''.

Immediately he became human. ''You can't be sick here!'' he said wrathfully, only to add, as he caught sight of my face, ''But you could, too!'' He picked me up and hurriedly bundled me round two or three corners into a little deserted sunlit courtyard where a fountain played. ''Don't say he gave you some of his strong wine to drink!'' he said, with the Egyptian clicking noise of disgust. ''Still, fresh air's probably all you need.''

I was half-sorry, half-glad when he set me down. Being carried by him was a strange experience. His shoulders were so broad, and the muscles in his arms were like bronze cords, cords that were alive – I was scared, repelled, yet I wanted to touch them, timidly.

He sat me on the rim of the fountain, took a corner of my dress, dampened it, and briskly wiped my face with it. ''That should do the trick'', he said.

I was impressed by his air of tremendous efficiency – although at the time I should not have used that precise word. And he was young. And quite magnificent in his military dress. It was, of course, the first time since coming to Egypt that I had encountered the essential male. All that I thought at the time was that no one could ever doubt *He* was a man, which made life beautifully simple.

And suddenly the pleasure I had felt when the Magnificent One had announced, ''I'll have you for myself'', had gone. I told myself it was because, married to him or his son, I should find Tiy always there and she disliked me. Also the Magnificent One, much as I liked him, was obviously given to fits of melancholy – if it came to that, I remembered suddenly, Amenhotep, when he had last talked to me, had suddenly started talking about enemies and persecution, all in an outburst of self-pity that had frightened and antagonised me so much that I had, until this moment, done my best to forget it. The tall officer of chariots looming over me did not seem likely ever to be sorry for himself.

I blurted out, ''How many wives have you?''

''How many – ?'' He had been looking impatiently about him, but now he gazed down at me in amazement, all his impassivity gone. My spirits rose; when he was not grim, he was distinctly handsome. But then they plummeted. ''What a strange child you are!'' he rapped out repressively. ''Being a soldier, I've no time for wives at present.''

''Would you like to marry me?''

''Would I – ? No, I would not,'' he said promptly. ''Apart from everything else, you are only a small girl with no breasts.''

How often Father had complained about my lack of breasts, and what little significance *his* anger had had for me. And how eager to please I was now! ''They will grow!'' I said eagerly. ''To be quite large. It's my barbarian blood that delays everything for me. And. . ." how speedily this impatient stranger made me forget my promise to Pharaoh! " – *The Magnificent One* wants to marry me!"

"He's a middle-aged man," came the discouraging response. "Middle-aged men often prefer small, unformed girls. *I don't*!"

"I would prefer you to The One or Amenhotep."

"You really must not say such extraordinary things," he said severely. "You could get yourself or me into bad trouble."

I sighed. "I think you are very cruel. Life will be so complicated for me if I marry either of them."

"My life," he returned briefly, "will be very short if it's known you've said such things to me. You must not talk again like this, ever, to anyone."

"You're the only person I've met so far I'd *like* to marry."

"It is not for any girl, and particularly for a girl in your kind of family, to like or not like whom she marries. That's a matter to be decided by The One and her father."

"I'm growing," I said hopefully. "In a few years – "

"In a few years," he said with sudden feeling, "with any luck, I shall still be far away from here."

"You're going to the frontier," I said.

The statuesque face, which could give such an impression of harshness, heaviness, was transfigured. "Yes, to the frontier! To the north. Away from this damned city."

"Don't you like Thebes?"

"Thebes? That was a little up-river village when Memphis was the capital. I'm from Memphis, but my mother's family came from even further north – Avaris. This isn't *my* Egypt. Now let's get you back to your father."

This time he did not offer to carry me. I was half-relieved, half-disappointed. Neither did he speak to me. In this case my disappointment was total. I should have liked very much to talk to him of my chief memory of Memphis – the splendid, menacing Apis-bull.

Chapter Six
Nefertiti

A royal concubine, if the divine son of Re sleeps with her only once, is favoured above all women, so to become a royal wife is the supreme honour. Yet Father, although he aped rapturous acquiescence, was anything but pleased by the news that *The Magnificent One* intended to marry me himself – although perhaps only I, young though I was, realized it. I thought I knew the reason; I had grasped quite clearly that The Magnificent One did not like Father; vain though Father was, he was too intelligent not to know this too! How much better if I were to become the wife of the sickly and, therefore, presumably easily-led Heir!

But, his good humour reviving, Father remembered he had another daughter. If my introduction to The Magnificent One had been too successful, Mutnedjmet might always marry her cousin. However, the good humour did not last long. Perhaps when he was summoned before The Magnificent One, Father rattled about a little too obviously in his sandals in a somewhat excessive demonstration of loyal obedience combined with helpfulness – this may appear fanciful, but over the years I learned to accept as a physical fact that when he was in the throes of a fidelity he always chose to make obvious, he *quivered*. Whatever the reason, when he put forward his idea of Mudnedjmet for her cousin, since The Magnificent One had deigned to bestow undreamed of honour upon the family by taking me for himself, The Magnificent One replied curtly, "No, I'm playing fair by my son. If I take a future wife from *him*, *he* can have a future wife from me. It's about time one or other of my allies sent me a daughter or sister to be my wife. Amenhotep can have *her* as his Great Wife. As for this other daughter of yours – first wife of some nobleman or other, a chief priestess?"

The Magnificent One, in fact, knew very well which foreign ally was due to send a daughter to him. Very soon, Tadukhipa, the daughter of Tushratta of Mitanni, would arrive. (Mitanni had always been Egypt's ally against the loathed Hittites, crouching in the northern mountains like so many wild beasts prepared to spring). But there was a good reason for The Magnificent One's vagueness; he hoped Tadukhipa's father would lend him his miraculous statue of the goddess Ishtar the Great, mistress of love and war — the statue of Ishtar in her first capacity reputedly had remarkable powers. The King of Mitanni in the past had steadfastly refused the loan even to someone doubly a kinsman — The Magnificent One's mother had been a princess of Mitanni, while earlier on in the reign he had married Tushratta's sister, Gilukhipa, now dead.

The marriage to Takukhipa, his niece by marriage, arranged years before, and almost forgotten by The Magnificent One, now became something he demanded should be brought forward. So I became The Magnificent One's youngest wife within a few weeks of our first meeting, but I felt that all this exchanging of wives was hard on the unfortunate Tadukhipa — also, without any thought of vanity on my part, on Amenhotep. With regard to him, I had enough boldness to ask, as I sat on my husband's knee, "Won't he *mind*, Lord of the Two Lands?"

"Mind?" said The Magnificent One. "Why should he? He can talk to her about Asiatic religions — that should please him."

"But," I persisted — being very spoiled by my husband, "I'm not being conceited, truly, but isn't it one thing to have a wife you've seen and another to have a wife you haven't?"

He laughed at me. "Oh, he knows her well enough! He was at her father's court for months on end."

"When he went to Syria?"

"Oh, you've heard about that, have you? Who told you?"

Suddenly I became very much aware that this usually easy-going man was The One.

"He did," I said in a scared voice.

"And what did he tell you about the trip?" His tone frightened me very much indeed.

"Only that," I managed to stammer, "that he'd been to Syria and stayed with his grandmother's relatives." Close to tears, I whispered, "I didn't mean to make you angry, Master of the North and South." After a moment's furious silence, my husband's face assumed the familiar look, all amused affection.

"You don't make me angry, little dove."

"I will try," I said earnestly, placatingly, "never to cause you trouble.''

''Now *that* I don't want,'' said The Magnificent One; ''I want you to cause me a hell of a lot of pain one day.''

''Oh, *no*, Lord of the Two Lands!''

''Oh, *yes*, Beautiful One, a tightness, an aching about the loins — that's what you're going to give me one day — ''

''Shall I be able to make it better?'' I asked, trembling in anticipatory contrition.

''Oh, yes, pet — *only* you can make it better. You'll hurt me — then I'll hurt you — but we'll enjoy hurting each other, I promise you!'' Some of the things he said to me were as incomprehensible as Father's discourses on religion, but definitely if inexplicably far less boring.

The vast House of Rejoicing, more a city than a palace, bewildered and amazed me, leaving me hungrier than ever for the simplicity, the littleness of Crete. From all the tales I had heard of my great-grandfather's court at Phaestos, even his cousin's at Cnossos, I knew that, for all their luxury and sophistication, they had never been a hundredth as glittering, as sumptuous, as glaringly splendid, as this court at Malkata. There was gold everywhere — every plate and drinking cup was of gold, furniture was of gold (and very uncomfortable), Pharaoh's chariot was of gold, the very royal barge, the *Splendour of Aten* was gold-plated. Small wonder that foreign visitors went away with the impression that for Pharaoh grains of gold were as ordinary dust for mere mortals.

My husband might be The Magnificent One, but he no longer took much part in the glittering court life, leaving that to be enjoyed by my aunt. (His last public duty had been his ritual annual visit to the northern border before the Nile was due to flood). Often he would sit with me on a balcony covered with rugs and brightly coloured cushions, staring at the changing colours of the cliffs, which came very close to the palace built on the very edge of the desert.

Most of the time, we sat in silence, but one evening, as the swallows dipped and swooped about us, my husband asked me why I looked so sad. I said the birds reminded me of Crete. If you are constantly in the company of another person, this companionship can, as it were, open up a window in the breast, enabling each to read something of what lies in the heart of the other. ''Little dove,'' my husband said after a moment, ''I know what you'd like me to do — have a fleet fitted out, to take you home. My young Memphis bull, that restless, fretting young devil, Horemheb, would jump at the chance of action. But I want you here. Soon, if that blasted brother-in-law of mine can bring himself to part with his damned miraculous idol, and it works, I'll marry you properly.'' He drew me on to his knee. ''Do you know,'' he said, ''I'd lost all interest in women until one day my brother-in-law brings to me his daughter, a little thing all calm eyes and pale innocence and no breasts, but all woman already, although *she* didn't know it. Soon enough you'll be setting red-hot coals glowing between men's loins — and not much longer, my pet, and I'll be able to give you other things than Crete to think about.''

I repeated this later to Kat-Senet (a village woman, The Magnificent One's childhood nursemaid, whom he had appointed to look after me); I always repeated to her The Magnificent One's more incomprehensible remarks in the hope of elucidation. She was delighted. So, after all these years, The One's interest was reviving — and in her charge. She had been even more delighted, because, more and more, instead of having me sitting on cushions at his feet, he took me on to his knee; and passed his hands, as delicate as Father's, over my body. ''But not before anyone?'' she said after a moment, her expression changing. No, I said, not before anyone. I looked at her thoughtfully. So The One's interest in me carried certain dangers.

The Magnificent One might have lost his interest in women, but the royal harem remained vast. One alone of Pharaoh's wives, Gilukhipa, aunt of Tadukhipa, had arrived a quarter of a century before with three hundred and seventeen women attendants. Mitanni was not so powerful a state as it had been twenty years before, but for this very reason, Tadukhipa, if she ever came to Egypt, would bring with her a dowry and retinue equal to, if not excelling, that of her aunt.

The Magnificent One had never had any liking for the wives he acquired for diplomatic reasons only; there was, I remember, a moon-faced Babylonian princess whose very name he kept forgetting. Even when her brother, the King of Babylon, asked after her health — never, significantly, her happiness — his repeated requests were ignored for so long that there was nearly a diplomatic incident.

I, aged ten, said one day to the prematurely aged man of forty-eight, as I sat on his knee, ''If we have daughters, will you promise they will never be sent abroad?'' He had looked at me in some astonishment

''Egyptian princesses never marry foreigners, pet — didn't you know?'' he said. He went on to explain the reasons for this. There was the Egyptian feeling of superiority — no foreign king, however powerful, was a fit husband for the daughter of

Pharaoh — so, at any rate, was the custom in those days. There was also, of course, the reason that an Egyptian princess might have rights as heiress.

I have thought since that this very fact — that up to the end of his reign, no Egyptian princess had ever married a foreign ruler — had much to do with the neglectful treatment accorded to The Magnificent One's foreign wives. Most Egyptians are not imaginative people, and the cruelty they showed these unfortunate princesses was to a certain extent the cruelty arising from sheer lack of imagination. Would I myself have felt any sympathy for the poor foreigners if I myself had not been snatched away from Crete? But whatever the reason, I have often thought with pity of the foreign girls brought with such splendour from their homes to become — nothing. During childhood they had been spoiled and indulged as only royal children can be. Their sense of importance was increased by the knowledge that they were being haggled over — although that term would never be used. Suffice it to say that a father, with a daughter to dispose of as advantageously as possible, would extol her looks and virtues, display her proudly before foreign ambassadors, enhancing the poor wretch's sense of self-importance. And then the fine clothes and the brilliant retinue and the strong escort, for it is guarding something very precious, and the honours and prostrations on the long journey south, for this is Pharaoh's bride. And then the alien country, the alien gods, the first sight of the stranger, the foreigner who is to be your husband. And this man tears your maidenhead within hours of first setting eyes on you. And the single act of your defloration is supposedly sufficient to secure your happiness — even blessedness.

Moreover, being a virgin you cannot even tell if you are satisfying him; you cannot speak his language, and you lack the experience to interpret the panting of the body, heavy on yours, which is all the intercourse other than the merely sexual there can be between you.

If you are a slave-girl summoned to your master's bed, at least you know he is impelled by something as urgent as lust; if you are a foreign princess, nine times out of ten you know this strange man is defiling your flesh for a reason no more compelling than the dryness of the sheet of papyrus on which the terms haggled over by himself and your father had finally been written down.

None of the foreign wives, princesses though they might be, ever challenged the supremacy of the non-royal wife, Tiy. They were all terrified of her. *She* moved about palace and capital freely; they lived in the utmost seclusion. No one took any interest in them. It might have been different if they had become the mothers of heirs for The Magnificent One, but their children, if not still-born, had all died when very young. Whispered reasons were given for this; I do not think they were fanciful. The harem was very much a place of fear.

I don't know how much The Magnificent One was aware of this; that he was not entirely deaf and blind he demonstrated in the amount of care he devoted to my safety. In addition to some twenty-odd attendants, he gave me a human watchdog, Kat-Senet. She was about sixty then, and looked older. Although she had spent nearly fifty years at court, she still remained to an extraordinary degree essentially a village woman. She scorned the elaborate dishes offered by royal cooks, and stuck to the traditional food of the poor — fried fish, bread, beer and garlic — garlic, indeed she revered so much that she always wore a garlic necklace to ward off all diseases, and hung one about my own neck, too, until I protested — and so did The Magnificent One. So she contented herself with making me wear a necklace of sweetly scented melilot. She refused obstinately to wear her hair — or a wig — in the fashionable short style copied flatteringly from Tiy's naturally short Nubian coiffure. This refusal to conform to courtly fashion was due to her hostility to Tiy. And it was because of this hostility, I am convinced, that The Magnificent One chose her to watch over me. And she did, to the last moment of her life.

Kat-Senet tasted all the food set before me, slept on a mat at the side of my bed, watched with foreboding as well as anticipation for the first sign that I had become a woman. "It will be then," she muttered, "that we can really expect trouble." In such discouraging circumstances, I approached puberty.

In my pretty bedroom (the ceiling was painted with white doves fluttering across a blue sky) cautiously, hopefully, I at last questioned Kat-Senet. Surely my stepmother, who disliked me, had told me all these things only to frighten me? Alas, Kat-Senet confirmed what I had encouraged myself to think of as malicious invention, but at least she threw in a little allegory to make the truth less brutal. Woman was the field in which man sowed his seed. Man was the creator; woman merely carried and nourished the seed he planted in her.

The Princess Tadukhipa arrived, with an even larger retinue than that which had attended her aunt. The Magnificent One inspected her, then conferred man to man with her father's ambassadors. They hurried back to Mitanni with an urgent message; The Magnificent One was afire to consummate the marriage, but because of the unfortunate state of his health . . . If the miraculous idol of Ishtar were in his possession for only one day, one might hope . . . Until the marriage was consummated, it was no marriage. The King of Mitanni reluctantly sent the idol. Meanwhile Tadukhipa's status was that of The Magnificent One's niece by marriage.

I, that other niece of his by marriage, remembering my own forlorn arrival in Egypt, wanted to make overtures of friendship; I asked The Magnificent One if I might visit the quarters assigned to her, but at first he was more interested in other things.

"When are these paps of yours going to start budding?" he demanded, inspecting my nipples as he did every day. (I never resented the inspection, as I had resented Father's nagging queries). Hopefully, I repeated my request. "She'll be happy enough with Amenhotep," said The Magnificent One firmly. "They've plenty in common, as you'll see."

I seized on one all-important fact. "Then I can see her?"

"On one condition. You don't tell her she's going to marry Amenhotep. I'm not taking any chances with that idol! But *first*, my pet. . ." Stupid father, I thought complacently. My husband seemed to *like* the light colour of my nipples!

The moment I set eyes on Tadukhipa, I knew what my husband had meant by, "They've plenty in common, as you'll see". As I saw, indeed. For Amenhotep's strange looks, the excessively long thin face, the drooping features, the body unnaturally lean down to the waist, were obviously physical characteristics he had inherited from hs Mitannian grandmother. Tadukhipa and he might have been brother and sister, even twins. It was not merely the duplication of features, there was the same bloodlessness, giving that greyish tinge to the skin that made it, in moments of emotion, seem ashen.

How can I remember so much of Tadukhipa's appearance after so long? Partly because of the resemblance of Amenhotep. But, above all, I saw, after Tadukhipa's own death, her features developing, year by year, in a face in which I searched desperately, during those same years, for some likeness to myself.

Tadukhipa, much to my relief, did not choose to talk much of The Magnificent One. "The wreck of a fine man, I think," she said dispassionately. "He must have been very handsome once. But I don't like men much."

Yet, in the next breath she began to talk of a man she obviously adored. And she went on talking about him — her father, the King of Mitanni. "If only," she said, weeping suddenly and, to my amazement, half-unconsciously touching parts of her body, "*we* had the Egyptian custom — fathers marrying daughters —

instead of that *stupid* occasional practice of . . . ''

But I had given up listening. Instead, I was thinking I did not envy her because she loved her father. At least, parting from mine had caused me no grief whatsoever. Not, of course, to be strictly accurate, that I *had* parted finally from mine. I wished I had. When I saw him — when The Magnificent One received him — he was so dreadfully effusive he embarrassed me. As for Kat-Senet, she detested him. He was always bribing eunuchs, he never asked her direct, to find out whether I was still a virgin or if the moon had taken possession of my body; he stalked down such information like a cat stalking a bird. Kat-Senet was furious. It was nothing to do with *him* — I was The Magnificent One's property. She said as much to her nursling, adding, ''And this little one's too good to be his daughter!''

The Magnificent One was amused; audiences were over, he was relaxing with me sitting on his lap as he played with me. He had such fine hands, long-fingered, slim-wristed. ''Well,'' he said, ''be glad she's his daughter in one respect. He's damned good-looking — she gets that from him.''

''Nothing else, though! There's no real blood in that one's veins!''

''And there is in hers? I agree.'' He did one or two of the things he had discovered made me wriggle, and laughed. ''Well, his reports are always so damned boring, we'll have a little fun with him next time he comes.''

So at Father's next audience, The Magnificent One waited until he was well-launched on an account of the latest tribute to be expected from Nubia, then challenged him brusquely as to his bribery of eunuchs. Father almost fainted, but, recovering, still prostrate on the ground, made a typically flowery speech. He loved me. He wanted only to know when he might start thanking the gods because I had received the supreme happiness of yielding my virginity to The One.

The Magnificent One decided to embarrass Father by plain speaking. ''Don't talk like a fool. What girl *enjoys* losing her virginity? It's a damned painful business at first. Not that later — '' Before Father's brilliant, bulging eyes, he lifted me on to his lap. '' — when she's acquired a pair of little paps, bouncing prettily when she walks, she won't be happy to know she's the wife of The Living Falcon, The Strong Bull himself — ''

Momentarily I was far away to the north, watching Apis-bull, splendid, massive, head down, regarding me. . .Before me, Father apologised obsequiously, expressed pious hopes that I should prove a veritable Hathor of love and fruitfulness.

''I don't doubt it,'' said The Magnificent One. ''Such a pretty little calf she is — '' alluding to the fact that Hathor is often depicted as a cow, symbol of fertility. ''*And* in Hathor's other form too,'' he continued after a moment. ''Don't we all know that Hathor as the moon drove men mad? Although I wish she'd hurry up and manifest herself in the goddess' other aspect, *obvious* suckler of Kings,'' he added, laughing, caressing me. I kissed him with spontaneous affection, and, to my amazement caught Father looking at us with ill-disguised resentment. Because I had never treated him like that, I thought. Well, how could I? He had never *liked* me! Tadukhipa, I reflected, might say she disliked all men except her father; if she had my father, she'd dislike the lot!

''About my daughter's paps, Lord of the Two Lands,'' said Father with an obvious effort.

''Oh, get up, man! All right, let's shelve the Nubian tribute for the time being, and discuss something more interesting. . . *two* things more interesting. . .''

''I assure you,'' said Father solemnly, coming closer, ''that when they start to develop, you won't be disappointed. On my head be it!''

''There, pet, do you hear? If two pomegranates don't start growing here soon, your father'll be shorter by a head!'

Father persevered. ''She's like my mother, it seems — and *her* nurse said her paps were late in coming, but when they did — ''

The fact that persistent breastlessness on my part might condemn Father to decapitation did not trouble me at all; on the other hand, I *did* want to acquire a pair of these apparently all-important appendages because The Magnificent One fretted for such a development. So I piped up to my husband, ''She said *his* father had no complaints — he couldn't keep his hands off them!''

The Magnificent One shouted with laughter. ''What — old Yuya? Old Sobersides, my father-in-law — austerity itself? Reaching out all the time for 'em, was he? I don't believe it!''

''Truly, Lord of the Two Lands, she *did* say so!'' I assured him.

The Magnificent One suddenly became aware that Father was standing almost within touching distance of me. ''All very well to keep bringing *your* side of the family into it,'' he observed. ''*Your* mother. . .how in the hell do I know what a girl in your father's harem looked like? What's more to the point, what was my little *dove's* mother like?'' While Father, taken aback, was trying, only too obviously, to remember, my husband observed maliciously, ''You can't say you couldn't keep your hands off *her*! The wonder is you left the Beautiful One inside her! On her, into her, then back to Thebes fast enough for you, and never a backward glance."

"I can't show you what her mother was like, Lord of the Two Lands, but *her* mother...There was a little statue of her — ivory — the Keftiu* always had figures of their royal priestesses — I brought it back — in the Treasury now — ". So the statue was sent for, and Father reverted, gratefully, to his report on Nubian tribute.

The Magnificent One listened half-absently, played with me anything but absently. Of course, I thought, it was safe for him to do it before my own father — if I had possessed breasts, they would have been swelling with triumph at this moment — *now* not-so-clever Father could see that The Magnificent One didn't object at all to the colour of my nipples! I stole a look under my lashes at Father — to find that *he*, while droning on about the tribute, was staring at me under lowered lids. And beneath the obsequiousness, he seethed with anger. Why? Because, I supposed, he'd relinquished a possession and he was miserly by nature. The Magnificent One could send his hands in roving expeditions — investigations. Father couldn't — and resented it. How he wanted to touch me too! Once I had been *his* to prod and poke, however disconsolately. Now, would he have been so resentful if Amenhotep —

I suddenly realised I should not have enjoyed Amenhotep doing these things to me at all. I was still pondering on this when the ivory statuette was brought in. So *this* was what my grandmother had looked like!

"By God, I never saw this before!" said my husband. Father reminded him he had been hunting lions when he (Father) had come back from Crete. "So I was! It all comes back to me. By God, little dove, if you turn out to be like her, it'll *all* come back to me!" The Magnificent One's elegant fingers moved with anticipatory pleasure over the two very prominent ivory globes. "Left bare — eh! Just as well, *this* pair would burst out of any covering when — God, the capacity's there. And she, your wife's mother, was a royal priestess, you say?"

"The King's daughter, particularly an only daughter, was always — " Father was beginning when another thought occurred to my husband.

"King's daughter! Why in God's name didn't Minos follow our sensible custom — marry his own girl? *Particularly if she looked like this*! Wouldn't you, in his place?"

Father, with uncharacteristic hardihood, suggested they

* Cretans.

might revert to his report on Nubian tribute. He took a step backwards. I was sorry. I had liked having the two good-looking men staring so hard at me. In mutual hostility.

During the period I spent at the House of Rejoicing — one cannot call it marriage, rather a lull between the major upheavals of my life — The Magnificent One did not, of course, spend his entire time in isolation. Seated on a chair of state, looking remote and aloof, like the two great statues he had had built outside the temple at Karnat, he regularly received ministers. But there was really no point to the audiences.

Ministers saw their first duty as keeping their ailing ruler free from care. A stubborn young officer of chariotry might blurt out unpalatable facts concerning the situation in Syria; older, more wordly-wise courtiers spoke soothingly of Egyptian conquests so firmly consolidated that diplomacy with perfect adequacy might replace warfare in dealing with Egypt's neighbours. So, I gathered, they had spoken throughout most of the reign. This was the time to *enjoy* the unparallelled achievements of The Magnificent One's predecessors; they by their victories had won for their successor the leisure to savour Egypt's supremacy in the world, and the incalculable wealth that poured into Thebes as a result of that power. With such quantities of gold to back Egyptian diplomacy, what need was there of chariots?

What else did I notice, sitting silent, unobserved on the chair The Magnificent One had had specially made for me (adorned with lotus, and ending like all royal furniture, in feet carved like lions' paws?). I saw that the privileges enjoyed by the Nubians at court was exceptional. Nubian influence had begun two generations previously; my stepmother's father had been one of the many Nubians to achieve high office. And now, with Pharaoh's Great Wife a woman who stressed her Nubian descent, they were at the pinnacle of their power.

This, of course, caused bitter resentment. The 'union' of Upper and Lower Egypt had always been more apparent than real. Between the inhabitants of the two regions there was great rivalry. The Northerners were a proud race, never forgetting that it was on their territory that Egyptian power and civilization had begun; Memphis was far older than upstart Thebes. The rulers of Upper Egypt might talk of 'unifying' the Two Lands; the royal palace might have its symbolic double door; many Northerners thought in terms of conquest rather than unification — and conquest after they had been decimated by the Hyksos.

But if the lighter-skinned Northerners had only grudgingly accepted the supremacy of Upper Egypt, judge how they detested the fact that the country's government now seemed to have fallen into the hands of the Nubians – the Nubians who, in the days of the decline of the earlier dynasties, had not only broken away from Egypt, but allied themselves with the abhorred Hyksos!

Approaching eleven years old, I could not know all this. But I saw and heard enough to gain a fairly accurate general impression. In the palace gardens I saw incident after incident – faces (a few) of angry bronze confronting faces (many) of sneering ebony. I would hear voices with a northern accent blaming Nubian influence for military inactivity where Syria was concerned. And these northern voices also asked was it not equally significant and ominous that the armies on the frontier, such as they were, were composed largely of Northerners with a sprinkling of men from Upper Egypt, but here in Thebes the royal guards were almost exclusively Nubians?

The miraculous idol of Ishtar arrived from Mitanni. The Magnificent One was delighted; nothing could be more opportune – at last my nipples were sprouting! Almost immediately Tadukhipa was married to Amenhotep. At eleven years old children can be callous enough; by the time the idol arrived I was rather glad to see her go. I had felt like this for some months, because she began to show too much affection towards me. She ordered her women to watch when Kat-Senet left her mat beside my bed in the early morning, and then she would come to visit me. She kept asking me to feel her breasts, oddly flaccid and drooping for one so young, and express admiration for them, she all the while stroking and investigating the tender area around my own small buds. I had become accustomed to The Magnificent One doing this, very frequently indeed now – and with ever-increasing approval and interest – indeed, I enjoyed it, sometimes wriggling with a pleasure that delighted him (an odd pleasure experienced chiefly by other parts of my body) even when he explored the painful little core that was growing behind them, but I did not like Tadukhipa doing it at all, and said so, pushing her hands away in disgust. At first she was angry, and said this was far preferable to what The Magnificent One would do to us both one day; then she cried, and said she loved me, and wanted to give all she possessed, and even though this included a dress given her by the King of Babylon, of a soft, shining material called silk, her offer did not strike me as being generous, as it meant she wished to possess me entirely in return.

A few days after her marriage, she came to visit me. The greyish tinge of her face seemed every more pronounced. "What is it like – being married?" I asked in a whisper.

She replied, her eyes fixed on my face, "That's what I came to tell you. He hurt me and went on hurting me. I cried and asked him to stop, but he wouldn't. And it hurt to walk afterwards. That's what being married is like." She burst into tears then, and I, too late, perhaps, kissed her pitifully; an eleven-year old attempting to comfort a twelve-year old.

Or was there something other than pity in my attitude — a condescension, a complacency? A feeling that *this* would not happen to me? For I was quite calm when I thought of the consummation of my own marriage; the eventual arrival of the statue of Ishtar had roused interest in me, but no apprehension. I think this calmness was largely due to my husband's attitude to me. He regarded me as a small, cherished pet animal; such an attitude was more than acceptable to an eleven-year old. Such an attitude, if it comes to that, might well be happily welcome to the majority of maturer wives, since so many men show to prized mares and bitches far more consideration than they feel for their two-legged female possessions.

With me sitting on his knee, The Magnificent One would discuss with Kat-Senet the technicalities of my physical development much as I had seen him, when he was well enough to move about, discussing with grooms or kennelmen the progress of a prized foal or a puppy, running his hands appraisingly over me in the same way, testing my potentialities, with Kat-Senet watching appovingly. And I would, possibly still wriggling slightly, listen, tranquilly enough, as they discussed the actual technicalities of consummation. The Magnificent One, being genuinely fond of me, wanted to make the process as painless as possible.

Kat-Senet greatly enjoyed all these conferences, even the problems they posed. For all Egyptians believe that the white-skinned women from outside Asia and Africa have particularly tough maidenheads. (A belief, I imagine, which arises from the fact that Cretan and Achaean women do not readily submit to a system of polygamy and concubinage. They resist, even struggle violently, which makes their defloration difficult.) So The Magnificent One and Kat-Senet had their long discussions as to how she could best prepare me — and afterwards, of course, take me away and soothe me. "I wish," I said to Kat-Senet when we were alone, "that you could be there all the time." She had, after all, been there all the time when I had had a touch of fever, a stomach upset. She clucked disapprovingly at me, at a loss for words at the suggestion that a mere human should be present when the God-King. . . ? Yet when it came to giving me practical advice she forgot my husband's divinity easily enough.

"He'll be heavy, of course. He'll hurt you.* You'll cry. But he'll be kind to you afterwards, and I'll come for you, and look after you, my little Beautiful One, and find something to take the soreness away."

There were other technical discussions of a different nature. It was some years since The Magnificent One had shown any interest in a woman. Such a revival of interest carried with it dangers for its object unspecified then, apparent enough now. The child plaything of an impotent Pharaoh had her uses; she was a diversion in more senses than one. But if Pharaoh ceased to be impotent, planted his seed in her childish womb. . .

The Magnificent One eventually ordered the secret construction of a door between his bedroom and a room untenanted since Tadukhipa's aunt had briefly occupied it years before. Entrance to it had hitherto been through corridor and ante-room. Once the moon-goddess had taken control of me and the statue of Ishtar had restored to full strength what Kat-Senet always referred to as The Magnificent One's pride, I should be brought at night across the garden to long-dead Gilukhipa's bedroom and the Magnificent One would come through the secret door and make a woman of me.

And I heard it all calmly. I was fond of The Magnificent One. If he wanted to do odd things to me, I accepted it, particularly as they would gratify him. And Kat-Senet talked of the practicalities in precisely the same way as she had discussed the childish ailments from which I had recovered speedily enough. Consummation of marriage therefore seemed to me to be very much like those brief fits of malaise — not very pleasant, but something you got over soon enough.

The Magnificent One might not be unselfish enough to send me back to Crete, but otherwise his growing affection for me was probably the least selfish emotion of his life. His discussions, consultations with Kat-Senet increased, lengthened. He would say "Talk to her, prepare her in every way — it stands to reason that a woman will know better than any man what will give pleasure to another woman, however young!" If he was not a wise ruler for Egypt, he was very wise in his treatment of me.

* Although Kat-Senet prepared my body in so many ways for marriage, one feature of marital initiation was not possible in my case, since I was to be the bride of the Pharaoh. More fortunate virgins might have their maidenheads manipulated, stretched, by kindly mothers, nurses, wise women, a midwife, but such consideration could not be give to me. I must be left wholly intact for the God-King. But The Magnificent One, I had no doubt, would be skilful, experienced enough, and also liked me sufficiently to show a fair amount of self-control and patience.

So Kat-Senet talked to me, explaining that if I were prepared for, eager to receive The Magnificent One, what Egyptians call rather sentimentally the gate of love would lengthen, broaden out so that I should find less and less difficulty in accommodating my husband. "The very entrance will draw back to welcome him!", said Kat-Senet ecstatically.

"*Really*, Kat-Senet?" I asked dubiously.

"Really, Beautiful One! Only be *happy* to give The One the hospitality that's his due, and it will be so easy — it's when," she went on, to my immense confusion, "a woman's unwilling that she becomes nothing more than one of those nasty dried-up desert gullies, and is hurt, hurt, hurt, but otherwise, why, then you're *moist*, like the Nile at sowing-time — and as long as these little muscles don't get stiff", she continued, gently, lovingly stroking, fondling, manipulating. "I'll do this every day, Beautiful One, to enlarge your gate of love — "

I giggled. "More like *lips* than a gate!"

"Well," said Kat-Senet severely, "whatever you choose to call it, see that it *welcomes* The One, and don't have any silly nervousness — "

The Magnificent One asked me amusedly next day if I was enjoying taking lessons from Kat-Senet. "Yes, I am," I said, after a moment's thought.

"So did I," he said laughing. "So did I."

I eyed him cautiously from under my lashes. "But — but, Lord of the Two Lands," I said, "she — she couldn't give you the same lessons as she is giving me. She — she couldn't *do* the same things because — " A false light broke in me: "Does — does a man have a gate of love too?"

The Magnificent One roared with delighted laughter. "Not even if he's The One, sweetheart! Although I don't know whether you've just spoken the most damnable blasphemy and treason! No, my pet, the man has to do all the — the breaking and entering, but a boy may need a little help and encouragement — and that's what Kat-Senet did for me when I was fourteen, and she — *how* old were you?" he demanded of Kat-Senet who had come hurrying up, hearing his laughter.

"How old was I *when*?" she demanded crossly. "That's not the way The One should behave!"

"That's what you said to me at the time," he said, grinning. "This isn't the way The One should behave — up against the garden wall, wasn't it?"

"Such talk!" said Kat-Senet, in her usual fashion.

"But then you taught me how a *man* should behave, didn't you? And the lessons went on for quite a time, didn't they —

and you liked giving them!'' He slapped her affectionately across the buttocks. ''You give the little one as good a grounding as you gave me, and. . .''

''You shouldn't say such things before her!'' she scolded. But I was enchanted. It seemed to me absolutely fitting that Kat-Senet, who had been The One's tutor, should now teach me, and I said as much. How glad I was that The One had taken me away from Amenhotep; I don't know who had instructed *him*, but it couldn't have been dear Kat-Senet.

Chapter Seven
Nefertiti

When I look back on this period I do so with a double feeling of guilt. Guilt towards Tadukhipa, and also guilt because during this time The Magnficent One gave to these secret discussions and plans concerning me the attention that should have been given to matters of empire. Some years later I said as much, remorsefully, to Kat-Senet. She disagreed angrily. If the statue of Ishtar had done its work, if I had become a woman *in time*, The Magnificent One, roused from his lethargy, would have had abundant energy to deal with all Egypt's problems, she said. Men being so oddly constituted, she may have been right.

But at the time, I felt no guilt at all. I had, it is true, once felt some towards Tadukhipa, but that had been before I had met her and she had antagonised me. Now, if sometimes, inexplicably, the long-nosed face, so old in a child, appeared in my thoughts, I banished it in the complacent belief that really I had robbed her of nothing. The Magnificent One had never shown the slightest interest in her. If she had been his wife, he wouldn't have had *her* daily with him, discussed her so earnestly with her equivalent of a Kat-Senet, he wouldn't play with *her* breasts, even though already hers were almost — I tried to think of the right word one day when I sat on The Magnificent One's knee, and — how cruel a child can be! — asked him to help me.

He burst out laughing. "Why in God's name think of *her* now?" Kat-Senet shook her head disapprovingly at me. But The Magnificent One was amused. "Oh yes," he said, "when she came I had to feel her breasts — for form's sake, so that I could tell her father's ambassadors I was mad to get into bed with her. Pendulous is the word you want, my pet, pendulous. And she is a virgin still! Loose, shapeless, pendulous." He held a brief technical conversation with Kat-Senet over my head. ''Yet Amenhotep got into bed with her right away, didn't he?'' he concluded.

''She didn't like it,'' I said. ''She told me.''

''Well,'' said The Magnificent One, ''aren't you grateful to me for saving you from that?'' He began to caress me. I wriggled. ''That's more than *she's* ever done done with Amenhotep,'' said The Magnificent One. Again he addressed Kat-Senet. ''This one will be different, won't she? Jig, jig, jig, she'll go, up and down, a real credit to you.''

I could think only of a toy I had once possessed, a row of wooden dancing dwarfs on a platform, made to jog up and down by pulling a string, but Kat-Senet glowed with pride. In Egypt if you are the mother of a son, your highest ambition is that he will acquit himself well in Pharaoh's service in the field; if you are the mother of a daughter, that she will acquit herself well in Pharaoh's service in his bed. And if you are a girl-child brought to his harem, the status of your nurse depends largely on such accomplishments as you show in that respect.

That day I might be said to have surpassed even Kat-Senet's highest expectations. Something very odd was happening. As I sat squirming on The Magnificent One's knee, something seemed to be squirming under me. Like a little animal. And in response to the little animal stirring beneath me, something faint, warm, vaguely pleasant, although there was an odd soreness about it, stirred inside *me*. I gasped, and looked at my husband with enquiring eyes. I had never seen him so excited. ''By God!'' he said. ''She's done it! *Done* it!'' He started to kiss me with strange violence. But Kat-Senet swooped down and picked me up.

''*No*, Lord of the Two Lands! She's too young! If you don't wait until her moon-courses begin, you'll damage her health!'' She was very much *his* former nursemaid now. After a moment's furious silence, The Magnificent One nodded.

''I suppose you're right. She's too small and undeveloped for it yet — that barbarian blood in her, of course. But — by God — '' And suddenly he burst out laughing. ''Look at her, all innocent bewilderment and enquiry, when what she's done to me, for me. . .You'd better take her away before I — ''

I was indeed bewildered. ''Are you angry?'' I asked my husband worriedly. ''What have I done wrong? I'm sorry — I won't do it again — '' Contritely, I pressed a kiss on his cheek.

''Oh, take her away!'' he said, still laughing.

As Kat-Senet hustled me towards the door, I looked back. The One sat staring after us, the half-rueful amazement still on his face. I could not shake off the feeling that I was to blame (although for something I could not understand at all). So I wriggled free from Kat-Senet, ran back to my husband, prostrated myself in the proper way, and said humbly, "I — I didn't know it would be like that, Lord of the Two Lands — *growing*, I mean, and I know I'm very little, but I'll *try*." And I ended formally with the words Kat-Senet had told me I must say when The One laid his body heavily on mine. "May I be a fertile and productive field for the Master of the North and South." (This was why, she explained to me later, The One couldn't do anything to me until I had become a woman.) But The One, it seemed, had different ideas. He tickled my neck.

"Your fertility doesn't matter," he said, laughing, "But you'll be ploughed often enough, little as you undoubtedly are, my pet. Get up." I got up, quite tranquilly, and gave him the passionless kiss of childhood with genuine fondness. "Take her away, you old killjoy," he said to Kat-Senet, "but I warn you, next time this happens, *bang*, I'm going inside her, whatever you say. And she'll like it, won't you, pet?"

"If it pleases you," I said, sincerely. But doubts still lingered. "Is the One truly not angry with me?" I asked when alone with Kat-Senet.

"No!" she said in wild excitement. "No! It's *proud* again with him! You've made it *proud* again!" She threw herself on her knees before the little statue of Hathor, the Love Goddess which she made me (with silent reservations) worship daily. My reservations were even stronger when it came to worshipping the second object of her devotions, Min, the ugly and, to my innocent eyes, dreadfully mis-shapen god of fertility, for all Kat-Senet's impatient explanation, "But I've told you, the pride of a man *stands up*!"

Well, I was fond of my husband, he was fond of me — above all, it was intensely gratifying to be told by Kat-Senet that I, a child, had, without trying, apparently achieved more than all the doctors' efforts and the attempts over several years of more mature members of The Magnificent One's harem had been able to manage. Quite calmly, almost pleasurably, I reviewed what had occurred. It was as if I had revived, released — I didn't know quite which — a strange little animal, but a friendly little animal. (And somewhere within me, it seemed, another little animal was located. Was *that* what Ariaea had meant when she talked of the Goddess' finger inside women?) The Magnificent One's little animal which, according to my husband and Kat-Senet, wished me well, was also capable of hurting me. Well, so did pet animals, often, without meaning to. This was to be my own rather unpredictable pet animal. I viewed the future with equanimity.

But Kat-Senet was frowning. "But he mustn't talk!" she said fiercely to herself. "If he starts boasting that it's come back to him. . ."

But he must have. (To whom? To *Father*? Only to Father, surely — the obvious confidant.) Men, said Kat-Senet resignedly, frequently did. Next morning The Magnificent One looked sickly, said little. (But why should Father betray the secret? Hadn't he sworn he looked forward eagerly to the consummation of my marriage?) Within three days my husband had to take to his bed. The idol of Ishtar might have proved its miraculous power, but other magic seemed stronger. The rapid decline in The Magnificent One's health seemed to loosen Kat-Senet's tongue; she talked darkly of Nubian counter-spells, hinted more than once that The Magnificent One's premature ageing years before had been due to stuff administered to him by his Chief Wife that not only harmed the body, but paralysed the will. Kat-Senet was dreadfully anxious on my behalf — what would happen to me if my husband died?

After he had fallen ill, I saw The Magnificent One only once more. We heard that he complained even more so now that he always felt cold. Kat-Senet believed there was one sovereign remedy for this; his youngest wife must be introduced into his bed, warm his body with her own. There were, of course, difficulties. Now that he was so ill, my Aunt Tiy was nearly always watching him. But even Tiy had to sleep occasionally.

I was more than willing to do all I could to help my dear Magnificent One, but a little embarrassed. "I'll have to go into his bed *naked* before people? I don't want eunuchs looking at me naked!"

"What an odd barbarian child you still can be," said Kat-Senet in amazement. "Eunuchs are the very people you *shouldn't* worry about!"

"Soldiers would be different," I said. I was thinking of the fretting young Memphis bull. I shouldn't mind if he were there, because he simply wouldn't bother to look at me at all. Clothed or naked. *I don't like small girls.*

Eunuchs did. But there was no point in trying to explain what I meant to Kat-Senet, who was telling me vigorously I was capable of very wicked thoughts sometimes. In any case, the rebuke was deserved. Here I was, thinking of arms like bundles of bronze cords and long, strong legs, when my only thought should be of The Magnificent One, who was so ill —

"Oh, I'll stand between you and the rest of them when you

get in beside him,'' said Kat-Senet, watching my dreaming face with uncomprehending, irritated affection, ''but, after that — no silly shyness, mind!''

''Why should I be shy?'' I asked in amazement. ''I — I press myself to The Magnificent One as close as I can — ''

She was contrite. ''Yes, that's my darling, that's my Beautiful One.''

As indeed I did. A hurried awakening at midnight, Kat-Senet whispering, ''She's gone.'' Blurred drowsiness, reminding me of those other midnight excursions with Ariaea. A darkened, stuffy room. There were other people about us, but Kat-Senet interposed herself solidly between me and their gaze as she whipped my dress over my head, and lifted the coverlet.

The Magnificent One stirred, smiled. ''Well, Nefertiti,'' he whispered, ''this is a sad come-down from what I'd intended.''

I kissed his cheek, and earnestly pressed myself against him, clinging close to the familiar heavy body. They had said he might not recover; I was just old enough to understand what it would mean never to see him again, to touch him. I clung to him now with a feeling of incredulity. There had always been women in my life to love — my mother, Ariaea, Naya, Kat-Senet — but The Magnificent One had been the only man.I clutched at him desperately; he understood my grief, and, I think, was touched. In my childish way I loved him sincerely, and so did Kat-Senet, the very young and the very old. He was cynical and realistic enough to doubt all other protestations of affection. ''Little one,'' he said, ''I'll get better.'' With his cold, elegant hands he caressed me, necessarily more gentle than usual.

''I will make you warm, Lord of the Two Lands,'' I whispered.

''Little one, in a year or two you'll melt the Sphinx itself, if you set your mind to it. Even now — '' He was so pleased to have me with him, I wriggled with pleasure. And the little animal answered me. Faintly, almost shyly, but I could not be mistaken. The Magnificent One laughed weakly. ''Nefertiti, are you trying to rape me?''

''No, Master of the North and South, I'm trying to keep you warm'', I said earnestly. The Magnificent One put his hands, those very elegant hands that I admired so much, ringless now, but warmer now too, gently about my buttocks, and pressed me even more closely to him than I could press myself. ''I do love you, Lord of the Two Lands,'' I whispered vehemently.

''I know, my pet, and I'm trying to show you a little of how I feel about you.'' The little animal was growing bolder, trying to —

I giggled faintly. ''It tickles.''

The Magnificent One's mouth twitched. "People have been thrown to the crocodiles for lesser blasphemies."

"It — it's trying to — "

"But it can't, alas. Not yet. Let me get my damned strength back." But he sounded quite pleased, and he was warmer, and the little probing, friendly thing, like a baby's wavering finger, I thought sentimentally, was pleasant and companionable. So we lay contentedly, The Magnificent One and I, whispering to each other occasionally, stimulating each other gently — although I was too young at the time to realise it. I don't know what the watchers made of it; I had long since stopped being aware of them. All that I was conscious of was the belief that so long as I was with The Magnificent One, husband/father, he could not die. I suppose the watchers duly noted one fact; that I was very fond of him, that he was very fond of me, that *once* I became a woman impregnating me should be easy enough for him.

Someone came in hurriedly and whispered. Kat-Senet plucked me away from my husband — and I wept bitterly, went on weeping as I was hurried through the greyness to my own room, sobbing supplication all the while. "When can I go to him again? I did him good, I *know*!" But I never went to him again.

A few hours later I was roused again from sleep, but not by Kat-Senet. Far more roughly. By a horrible grinding pain, and sudden realisation that there was blood about me, trickling from me. Was I bleeding to death? Terrified, I screamed for Kat-Senet. Her first reaction was incomprehensible. "But he didn't" she cried. "He *couldn't*! Or — or could he?" She began to bathe me, soothe me — and investigate.

Hers was the first general reaction. That The Magnificent One had, miraculously, before at least a dozen pairs of watching eyes, and with the minimum of movement or exertion, contrived to deflower me, after all. The news spread — mine now being a body royal by marriage. My apartments were invaded by hordes of inquisitive, congratulatory courtiers. They were not, of course, permitted to see me — I was rigorously confined to my bedroom — but through all my misery of sickness and pain and bewilderment, I could hear the eternal buzzing of voices, like blow-flies on a dunghill. And above them all, at one point, Father's, shrill — with eagerness. "Did The Magnificent One effect the full penetration?"

No, said Kat-Senet stolidly, my maidenhead was still intact. That had been her first concern. But I had undoubtedly become a woman. "But", she added proudly, "it's a step in the right direction." I heard no reply from Father; I imagined he had rushed off to tell his cronies. But I, now at eleven years old, a woman, bit my knuckles to prevent myself from screaming as I pondered on certain conclusions. So this was that essential condition I must attain before I could conceive; childbirth, therefore, was inextricably linked with this essentially messy, animal business. I began to cry — on my own account. But later I wept on my husband's account. Not even Kat-Senet suggested that I should be taken to him now — at least for four to five days. Any virgin during her monthly loss of blood was a receptacle of all kinds of evil magic, and a virgin on the *first* occasion. . .

"But I wouldn't hurt him! I love him dearly! I — I couldn't help him *that* way — I wouldn't want to — to be close to anyone. This is so *horrible*. But can't I just see him, from a distance?"

"No."

"But he'll wonder why I don't come."

"Oh, he'll know — have no fear of that! I'll tell him myself. And he'll be so glad to hear it. Now, *next* time he sees you, and he's strong again, he'll be able to — "

It was ironical that The Magnificent One managed to cling on to life until a few days after I technically became a woman, and so was then physically capable of performing a wifely function. Kat-Senet, who held a special position in his household, went to kneel beside him, to whisper the momentous news — "Nefertiti is a woman."

"Ah," he said, "that will make me better sooner than all the potions and incantations of the damned doctors." Indeed, for a day or two he actually seemed to improve. Kat-Senet was delighted.

"Not long to wait now," she said. "You'll soon catch up with that long-nosed wretch from Mitanni." For Tadukhipa was several months pregnant. The women of Pharaoh's harem, when I was in their company, spoke of this as the most natural condition, the happiest condition, for any female, whatever her age, to find herself in. But there were times when I went in quietly, or unexpectedly, and I would catch, "I never saw such narrow hips on a girl", or "both of them with such long heads" — and the heads of the speakers themselves would shake in unison.

I did not see her during her pregnancy. She sent me a message saying she did not wish to be seen, above all, by me. And then I myself had become a woman — and, for the time being, forgot about Tadukhipa, until I heard someone saying that the King of Mitanni had been killed in a palace revolt, and that Tadukhipa's brother had called in the Hittites to help him in the civil war that now seemed imminent. "Poor Tadukhipa", I said. Poor Tadukhipa indeed — eight months pregnant in a foreign country, and hearing of the murder of the father she adored.

And yet perhaps the news of her father's death was merciful. The child she carried was too big for her; at eight months it killed her. It would have killed her even more cruelly if she had carried it to full term.

She sent for me when she was dying. It was a dreadfully public way to die. Animals creep away into darkness and solitude and die in decent dignity; in Egypt they pride themselves on the fact they they are a kindly people who do not torture their criminals and traitors in public for hours on end as they do in certain Asian states. They reserve such treatment only for their queens and princesses! When they took me into Tadukhipa's bedroom it was crowded with people watching avidly the centre of the room, savouring the obscene spectacle of the wretched morsel of royalty, kneeling, writhing, sometimes whimpering, often shrieking like the animal in pain she was reduced to, driven almost insane by the savage ordeal she must endure in public.

The Court Physician chanted incantations enough, placed amulets enough on her swollen belly when her long labour began, but when the midwife, squatting behind, finally drew out the child, it was dead, and Tadukhipa herself was dying. It was only then that they let her lie on a bed, and I was permitted to go across to her and take her hand. It felt cold, clammy, scarcely human. Eyes that were scarcely human glared up at me from a face like dead ash. "Nefertiti, Nefertiti, to be a woman is a dreadful thing," groaned Tadukhipa, aged thirteen, and died.

The women surrounding us had only begun, somewhat perfunctorily, to wail, when the thin noise they made was almost drowned by a shriller, infintely piercing throbbing sound of immeasurably greater volume, coming from outside Amenhotep's palace. The Magnificent One, my husband, dead, was being mourned by thousand upon thousand of voices. He had died shortly before Tadukhipa. Therefore it might be said that the first event of Amenhotep's reign was the death of his wife after a still-born child had been wrenched from her — hardly the most propitious of omens. He had been in the room, of course — I had not noticed him as I took Tadukhipa's hand, but now, like a field of corn when a strong wind blows through it, every person in the room, except myself, was bowing, prostrating before him as he stood gloomily staring down at his dead wife.

I did not lie flat on my face because, although dreadfully confused by the rapid course of events and, in any case, quite stupid with the shock of what had happened to Tadukhipa, I kept one thought steadily uppermost in my mind. I would not release my clasp on the poor dead hand I had taken when she was still living. She should not be abandoned. So Amenhotep and I were the only two people still on our feet in that crowded room with the terrible smell of blood and sickness. Across the prostrate bodies — how ludicrous they looked — our eyes met. 'He will be angry,' I thought. 'I should be lying down too, but I won't let go her hand yet.' But instead his sombre faced cleared.

''Nefertiti!' he said. ''You are not to go back to the House of Rejoicing. You will stay here.'' His eyes gleamed. ''When the period of mourning is over, you will marry me after all!'' As he awkwardly made his way towards me, having to step between the dozens of little mounds of prostrate bodies, I thought, as I stood clasping the hand of his wife dead in childbirth, that this was scarcely an auspicious moment to proclaim a forthcoming marriage.

The same circumstances should have left me almost prostrate with horror on the eve of that marriage, but the marriage could not take place until the period of mourning — seventy days — was over and The Magnificent One rested in the splendid tomb he had built for himself, and at eleven years old one forgets horror quickly, and seventy days can be a very long time. And, of course, recollections of dead Tadukhipa became blurred by the genuine grief I felt for my kindly, indulgent dead husband. Possibly my tears for him were stimulated by Kat-Senet's desperate mourning. She had really loved her nursling; I noticed that his death had made her suddenly seem a very old woman.

But even bereavement can have its ludicrous side. The wildest exhibition of grief from Kat-Senet came when she related to me what was being done to my late husband's body. I tried hard not to listen.

She told me that when I followed The Magnificent One's corpse to the tomb, I must feel prouder than any other member of the harem because *I* had begun the process of restoring his manhood. ''Perhaps I should have let him have you that day after all,'' she said, sobbing noisily, ''when he was *ready*. Then, at least. . .'' She explained that if The Magnificent One had indeed been allowed to take my virginity, I, although left among the living, might have remained his favourite wife, wherever he was. With tears rolling down her wrinkled cheeks she described how this was possible; between my husband's legs the priests and embalmers, possibly at this very moment, were replacing his bandaged genital organ in a state of erection. ''Oh, my poor baby'' she sobbed, ''how eager he was to rip through your tight little maidenhead that day — and I took you from him! And now he will never be able to do it!'' And I should have to marry Amenhotep. Kat-Senet wept afresh at this thought.

But I did not follow my husband's body to the Valley of the King's; Amenhotep would not permit it. I had not been his father's wife, he said — the marriage had never been consummated. He sent for Kat-Senet one day, and questioned her rigorously as to my intactness. I think she would have lied if there had been any hope of being believed, but all the harem knew the precise date when my moon-courses began, and it was not royal custom to consummate a marriage without the possibility of that marriage becoming speedily fruitful. So Kat-Senet replied as sullenly as one dares to a god-king, that I was indeed a virgin. Amenhotep apparently was delighted — but Kat-Senet, as his father's loving nurse, was always suspect to him. So the day afterwards all the etiquette of royal mourning was disregarded. Tiy herself and a half a dozen of her Nubian women came to probe my shocked, shrinking body — Tiy hurt me, and I think intended to — and at the end of it reported to Amenhotep that I was indeed a virgin, and a very tense, immature one at that. I managed to remain stiffly silent while they were there, but afterwards wept bitterly with pain and humiliation. Kat-Senet did what she could to comfort me. "At least, if he knows you're a virgin, he'll be gentler than if — " she began, but I interrupted her, my teeth chattering.

"Did you hear what they said — when they laughed so much?" They said, "This will be another one, too, to scream like a horse. Did — did Tadukhipa scream then?"

Kat-Senet compressed her lips. "So they say. But she was a poor creature."

"Oh!" I wept. "I wish you hadn't taken me from The Magnificent One that day when — when you say he wanted so much to become my husband! Oh, I wish he weren't dead! Because *this* isn't going to be like what it would have been like with him, is it!"

No, said Kat-Senet, wild with contrition. My becoming Amenhotep's wife was going to be a very public and formal affair indeed. She told me the details. Every night two eunuchs would undress him and escort him to my bedroom. Then they would sit outside the door until morning.

"Oh!" I sobbed. "It would have been so different with you bringing me secretly to The Magnificent One, then taking me away again and giving me something to rid me of the soreness."

I suppose it was significant that we both concentrated on the preliminaries to the act, and not on the act itself. I suppose it was also significant that I wept so much after The Magnificent One's death — as if I knew in my heart that soon the tears would be frozen within me for year after year.

Yet despite Kat-Senet's all too imperfectly concealed forebodings, and my own conviction that being Amenhotep's wife would be very different from being the wife to his father, I was, at eleven years old still amazingly resilient. And on the eve of my second marriage, my stupid imagination ran away with me again...

I can remember with complete clarity that day before my marriage to Amenhotep. In the morning, everyone being very busy, I was left alone in the garden for an hour. I lay on my back on the grass, and stared at the sky; it was still just — but barely just — early enough to be able to do this without being blinded by the sun. There was even a gentle breeze rippling across my body — like a caress. But then the breeze died away, and I was conscious only of the heat of the sun, soon too strong for comfort, but I suddenly did not want to move away from its probing rays. Drowsily I remembered what Ariaea had said once, contemptuously. "The Achaeans pretend that the Earth is the Mother-Goddess, and the Sky is a God. The sky faces downwards, the Earth faces upwards to him." So that was what my grey-eyed Achaean grandfather had believed. It was strange how I thought of him at that moment.

This is marriage, I thought. Sky — sun in sky — looking down on Earth, giving herself unquestionably although the sun, which pours life into the fertile body beneath him, can be cruel, can scorch, can kill. The sun poured on down. Almost I could imagine the rays were spears striking at me. I closed my dazzled eyes and lay drowsily in the heat, arms outspread on either side — after slipping down the shoulder straps of my dress. I lay open-breasted, open-armed, almost, I could imagine in that piercing radiance, open-bodied. I felt as if my small breasts, the lotus-buds, Kat-Senet called them, would unfold to the warmth as if they were the flowers themselves, to be bruised. Yes, I understood now what people meant when they talked of consummation of marriage as bruising the breasts of virginity, and — Oh, Goddess, I *wanted* them to be bruised — like this. For what I felt now was something far more violent than a gradual unfolding. The hot, stabbing streams of the sun's heat on my naked skin seemed to have penetrated my body itself, were in my very blood, I could feel them throbbing in my veins, my heart was pounding — yet with it all I felt a delicious languor, lassitude.

And now the strength of the sun seemed gathered up into one gigantic spear point driven into me. I gasped, but whether in pain or rapture I did not know. My eyes flashed open. And sight of the sun was blotted out. There was a man's face between me and the light, he was looking down at me, I could not distinguish his features because they were shadowed, yet I knew the expression on that face, although I had never seen such an expression on a man's face before. It was an expression of mastery. I was weak, I was lost, I knew pain — and — oh Mother-Goddess, I was *happy*!

"Beautiful One!" cried Kat-Senet, shaking my shoulder. "Beautiful One! What stupidity — to fall asleep here in the sun!" Angrily she hustled me inside, rubbed oil on my face and body. "If you've burned the skin — *now*, with all that's going to happen tomorrow!"

My eyes were still blinded by the sun, my head ached, my body smarted. But I was still happy as she clucked over me exasperatedly. Now I really knew what was going to happen tomorrow. All that they had told me was wrong.

But what they had told me was right, after all. Except that, in what seemed to me to be the worst of bad dreams, I stubbornly would not let myself cry — but he did. And then, when it was over, he began — interminably — to talk. At the time I was glad. Better that he should talk than inflict fresh exhausting and painful new experiences upon me. But later I thought it was strange that all he talked about was his hatred of his father.

So I underwent that other essential preliminary to childbirth. I bled for weeks afterwards. Yet some might say I was amply rewarded. "I'm sorry," he said at one point when I stiffened and gasped with pain. "You're so little, so young. But tomorrow I'm going to have you proclaimed as my Great Queen. Anything you want then shall be yours." But what I wanted then even he, greatest one on earth, could not grant me. What I was crying out in my heart, as the clumsy thrusting went on, was that Tadukhipa should be alive still, to share this dreadful burden of marriage with me, so that I might be spared a little of this lacerating beastliness.

But even Tadukhipa, alive, could not have shared one further misery to be inflicted on me, for only one — blessed — girl might undergo it. Amenhotep might have told me that I should be his Great Wife, but not even he, at his point, was prepared to flout precedent until one fact about me had been established. For in The One lives the human part of that power which causes the overflow of the Nile so that crops grow plentifully along its banks; he is the immediate *agency* for this. The virtue, the power, residing in him is, of course, that of fertility. It is therefore vital that his potency should be proved in the most practical way — and the utmost care is taken that his Great Wife should not be barren. Even Amenhotep would never have proclaimed me his Great Wife if he had believed he could never beget children on me.

But, according to Egyptian belief, there is one sure way of verifying this. The morning after our marriage, Tiy and her Nubian attendants laid hold of my body again. "So," said Tiy, "you've lost that tight little virginity of yours, have you?" I stared back at her in frozen silence. "Well," she said, laughing, "let's set *his* mind – and the minds of all Egyptians – at rest!" They took a clove of garlic and inserted it – very roughly – inside me, laughing because I was still bleeding. I screamed inwardly, but disappointed them by outwardly remaining silent.

Somehow, before evening fell, Kat-Senet managed to come briefly to me. I wept then. "Oh, Kat-Senet, if you had been here, you would not have let them treat me so!" We were, miraculously alone, but even to her I would not talk of the night's happenings, only of what Tiy and her women had done to me.

"I know, my lily, it's always done," she said.

"But you didn't tell me – when I was married to The Magnificent One – that it would happen."

"It wouldn't – with him. He didn't mean you to be his Great Wife, so wasn't particularly concerned about your having children. But *this* One – " She was half-laughing, half-crying. She was proud because at only eleven her charge might have been Queen, but regretted it was queen to this Pharaoh. "He has to know you can conceive," she said rapidly, "and this is the way. Has he given you jewels yet, my dove?" Amenhotep had; there on a table stood a very ornate jewel box, all jasper and malachite. Kat-Senet bustled across and hid beneath the glittering pile I had been too wretched to investigate – another clove of garlic.

"Oh, why are you doing that?" I whispered, flinching. "Are they going to do it once *again*?"

"No, my lotus, but listen. No one must know it's there – that can be managed because no one will dare touch your jewellery box unless you order her to. Tomorrow, my little Beautiful One, the moment The One has left you – " Did she notice how I flinched again? "you must eat that clove of garlic, because almost immediately after The One has left you, the doctors will come to you – "

"Oh, Kat-Senet, Kat-Senet, *why*?"

"If your breath smells of garlic, they'll know you can conceive," said Kat-Senet. "That's the test."

If I had been less stupefied with misery next morning, I should have realised my way of escape lay in *not* following her commands, but rape, even if not for the first time, leaves you a scared animal, and while I could remember that Kat-Senet, who was the only person I loved now in Egypt, had given me this instruction, I was too dazed to remember why. So I chewed the garlic clove — and a few moments later Pen-tu declared I could conceive, and before the day was out I was officially proclaimed Great Queen.

Most fortunate of women — at eleven years old.

THE REIGN OF AKHNATEN

Chapter Eight
Nefertiti

The spoilation of a virgin is, I suppose, always necessarily a cruel and brutal business, and I have no doubt that I myself was at fault. Again, to some extent necessarily so, since I could scarcely be expected to exercise a skill I had never yet had to use, and, in which, it seemed throughout our married life, I was entirely lacking. Worse — when I realised what was being done to me, I struggled against my god-husband (instead of lying acquiescent, a fixed expression of bliss on my painted face). Possibly because he was hurting me atrociously, and so I was struggling against the infliction of pain. But also, I think, because my mind as well as my body was in revolt. Suddenly, the virginity which I had been placidly content to surrender to The Magnificent One seemed the most prized of possessions, which I could not bear to lose. Didn't he realise, I sobbed in my mind, that entering me was difficult because the Goddess had made my maidenhead so hard to stretch, so thick, to protect me from this dreadful intrusion because I was too young for it, or even — I was almost out of my mind with pain and revulsion — she had made it like this *for this occasion because she did not think Amenhotep in particular should do this to me*? My body was a fortress, and she had set a guardian at the gate.

So I struggled. This was not only my husband, but divine-Pharaoh, but what was being inflicted on me seemed mere brutal lust — no, more than this, for young though I was, I sensed that the ravaging of my body went beyond simple clumsiness on his part, ignorance on mine. He kept gasping that he had married me because I seemed so untouched, innocent, yet his only wish seemed to be to gratify the desire I roused in him, and yet this appeared to make him feel ashamed, even terrified. He took what pleasure he could from me as quickly as possible. And then, abruptly, although physically remaining dreadfully close to me, mentally he became quite remote. For this unbearable process of being made a wife, incomprehensibly involved more than one kind of hatred. Not only my own sick loathing, but Amenhotep's hatred of his dead father; this seemed the only explanation for the transformation between the day-time Amenhotep who treated me kindly and gently, and the stranger in the dark who lay heavily across me, stretched and tore me, treated *me* as more than a stranger, as an enemy, so that marriage at night-time was like a battle, always a losing battle for me, and who then, afterwards, cried and muttered about how he hated his father. I felt it was an extra unfairness that all this ludicrous and disgusting business that I had once found impossible to credit, should be done to me not even because Amenhotep disliked *me* — but because he disliked his father and wanted to prove something to his father's spirit.

I should have hated it less if Amenhotep had said to me, "These things have to be done because we are the King and Queen, and these are the grotesque preliminaries to the children we must have for Egypt." This, at least, would have been logical. And there might then have grown up a feeling of comradeship, we were undertaking an unpleasant obligation together as soldiers might. Sharing, partnership, even if never equality. But, instead, what partnership there was for him seemed to be with an unseen third person.

This is a stupid, muddled description, but a terrified child, revolted physically, wretched, wakeful, felt only confusion when, night after night, her husband began to mutter in his sleep not to her, but about her. He talked to me a great deal about his father and how he hated him, but did not address *him* in his sleep. Then there was no hostility in his voice, only guilt — and an almost fawning desire to placate. I used to be extremely frightened, thinking he was addressing a god who was angry with him for some reason. But then I realised it was not for *some* reason. It was because of me. "She is so beautiful," he would say. "She is innocent. I could truly love her if you would let me."

Understandable, I think, that I should be frightened on hearing this mumbled, time and time again, night after night; Amenhotep trying to appease a god who was angry with him because he wanted to love me. So was not the god even more angry with *me*? I used to wonder desolately what I, only eleven years old, had done to make the girl detest my marriage to him; I was so insignificant a person. I was not at all challenging like my Aunt Tiy — *she* had even had herself pictured as a Sphinx.

I should explain perhaps what a Sphinx is. It is quite unlike other Egyptian gods who have human bodies and animal heads; the Sphinx has a human head on an animal body, that of a lion. The most famous Sphinx is the Great Sphinx, outside Memphis. It has the face of the great Pharaoh Chephren who ruled centuries ago — Sphinxes always had the faces of Pharaohs — and the body of a reclining lion.

Still, having Amenhotep beside me, muttering guiltily in his sleep, was infinitely preferable to having Amenhotep so clumsily awake. Kat-Senet, in one of our brief moments alone, had assured me that as time passed, he would hurt me less — "He'll be familiar with your body, know better what to do." But although he used it enough, Amenhotep never seemed to know my body. I had thought at the beginning that he was unused to such a poor, unformed thing as I was, and that when he realised I was so much younger and smaller than the other women he had had, he would be gentler. But he never was. What happened after the ceremonial disrobing and anointing never progressed beyond an animal business, a bungling ravishment, wild, clumsy, with myself at the end of it a huddled, wretched thing of flesh that silently whimpered to be put down like any other savaged animal.

". . .Queen of Egypt, too!" Kat-Senet would say, administering doses of camomile to rid me of my silly nervous state. "Isn't that what every other woman would give her eyes for? Dear Isis, why aren't you thanking her for your good fortune? Think of what you'd have had to put up with if you'd been in Babylon or any one of those nasty foreign places where every girl has to give up her virginity to the goddess Ishtar — such tales I've heard from the foreigners here, there the poor soul has to sit until a man — *any* man, mind you! — throws a silver coin in her lap. 'I take you in the name of the goddess!' he says, and does it too, then and there, and no chances of refusal on her part!"

"But it would happen only once!" I stammered. "Then she could forget it — and him. It wouldn't go on with him — night after night."

Kat-Senet also told me that when I had borne children it would all be easier. It was never easier. He would take me again before the birth wounds were healed; my body was always torn when the child left it.

Such were the nights. In the days tradition took hold of me. My body was never my own, even by day — waking, rising, bathing — always attended, preceded, followed, I was a performing animal rather than a human being. No individuality was permitted to me. A Queen, for example, must always smell in a certain way — rather, different areas of her must smell in a certain way. There were different perfumes for different parts of the body — twelve, all told: hair, eyes, cheeks, breasts, arms, hands, shoulders, ears, lips, throat, belly, inner thighs. And they were heavy scents. Against this, at least, I rebelled. Heavy scents I had always detested. "I shall speak to The One," I said. By day, when Amenhotep was kind and gentle and talked to me, he often told me that my body was naturally fragrant — so I asked, could I not use only the lightest flower perfumes that I loved? He said with sudden violence, "Of course you can do what you like! That's why I was determined to marry you — you're so different from other women." More gently he continued, "You're not happy, are you, Nefertiti?"

I shook my head, but had enough intelligence not to say that it was the nights I detested chiefly. He said restlessly, "I'm not happy here, either. I can't be myself here."

"Are you going to build another palace?"

"I don't mean only The House of Rejoicing, I mean Thebes itself. I hate it!" With growing excitement he said that surely if one were Pharaoh, one could live where one wished to live, could cut one's self off from the past, completely.

I said dubiously, "I don't think anyone, even The One, can ever cut himself off from the past altogether," but he was not listening.

There were, I suppose, material benefits enough accruing from being Queen of Egypt. All the resources of Empire as far as jewellery was concerned were mine — agate, amethyst, rock crystal, chalcedonyx, red and green jasper from the Eastern desert, malachite and turquoise from Sinai, lapis-lazuli from western Asia, mother of pearl from Nubia, all the gold in the world it seemed. I bathed in water on which floated blue lotus blossoms, I rode in a palanquin that had on it my hieroglyphics in gold, I slept — fitfully — in a bed of sycamore wood covered with gold plaques incised with a pattern of pomegranates. But would I have not surrendered the entire cascade of jewellery, lain on the muddy ground, walked on bare, bleeding feet if in return I might have slept *alone*? But every night Pharaoh came to his wife's bedroom, after two eunuchs, quivering masses of obscene obesity, had undressed him ceremoniously, the two eunuchs sat on guard outside the door, on many heavy chairs especially made for them, stools and ordinary chairs broke under their grossness. Even now I write irrelevantly of the chairs specially made for those two eunuchs as if I am still trying to delay the entrance into the room of the husband ceremoniously disrobed by them now, gigglingly guarding the door while he comes across to the bed of sycamore wood (sycamore is sacred to the love goddess Hathor) covered with gold plates incised with a pattern of pomegranates — pomegranates which symbolise both sexual desire and fertility.

Well, the sycamore wood of the bed might not transform me into a priestess of love, but the carved pomegranates must have been more effective. Or was it the ritual magic of those words I had to say every time Amenhotep put his body over mine — "May I prove a profitable and fertile field for my lord?" I was fertile enough. Only once I had to go through agonies of embarrassment to explain to my husband why he would not be able to have the use of my body that night — and then I was pregnant. I gave birth to our first child just over ten months after our marriage.

Despite the grotesque garlic-test, at first it seemed incredible to me that a body so inwardly shrinking, so outwardly unresponsive should conceive, although I had been told frequently enough that I was no more than the passive receptacle for my husband's seed. For it was incredible to me that so immature a womb, that had so recently sprung to life, should be ready to receive that seed. Sometimes I would link the ease with which I, a child, became pregnant, with the strange mutterings I heard each night. Was he possessed by a god? Was that the explanation? But if so, why did the god dislike me so much?

But I did not ask the last question for long. If any god dislikes a woman, the best divine vengeance is to make her bear a child — at twelve years old. A child pregnant at twelve is grotesque. My nipples scarcely protruded from tiny conical breasts. After five months of much nausea and bewilderment, I found the skin of my belly becoming taut over the swelling womb which crept higher and higher up to the rib cage. I could scarcely support this bloated body on my thin childish legs; I lurched as I walked, to keep my balance I had to throw my narrow shoulders back and strut ludicrously.

Now I knew why Tadukhipa had not wanted me to see her — like this. Should I die, as Tadukhipa had died? If this were henceforward to be my life, I wanted to die.

I now fell into the hands — flabby hands, often slippery with sweat — of the court doctor Pentu. That immature body of mine, the breasts that scarcely existed, were subjected to the most elaborate preparations — sponging and stroking, much rubbing of oil, such careful manipulation, such squeezing, such drawing-out, such bathings with warm water and wine. But there was never the slightest possibility that I should ever be able to suckle the child. At the time this did not cause me great anxiety. The child would die, I should die, as Tadukhipa and her child had done. But later. . .

Later, I thought with bitter inner tears that if I had not been so young, if I had been able to suckle my first child, if her first knowledge of me, that knowledge which extended over months, had been of a soft warm breast giving her sustenance, I think she might have loved me. If they had given her to me immediately after birth, so that I could have held her in love, naked flesh to naked flesh, whispering to her, in the years to come my touch and my voice might have been tolerable to her.

There is a saying common among women, laughing without much humour, 'nine months' pain for five minutes' pleasure'. There was as little pleasure for me in the conception of my children as there was in the carrying and the birth. Eventually, Amenhotep became angry with me because I was cold, unresponsive. What else could he expect of a child of eleven in the first terrified months of marriage? What else could he expect of a child of twelve, thirteen, fourteen, fifteen, sixteen, lying remembering the last pregnancy when the child, forcing its way out of me, stretched and tore at me as its father had done on those first nights of defloration? I do not think I am a great coward where pain is concerned, but I was young, little, unformed, and the size of the child is not mercifully scaled down to the size of the mother. Look at any painting — if any survive — of the children I bore him. They were all like him. They all had his elongated skull, that elongated skull that had killed Tadukhipa, and which kept me threshing for hours like a frightened mare foaling, wave after wave of pain, voices saying, "The head is not advancing," myself writhing, sweating, exhausted, but never exhausted enough to become unconcious.

Kat-Senet, on the rare occasions when she could talk privately to me, had sought to reassure me. The gods themselves would help me. Already Khnum Khnemesh had seen to the formation of the child in my womb, fashioning the body on his divine potter's wheel at the moment of conception. And there was Meshkhent, the goddess of childbirth — she would appear beside me at the precise moment of delivery, having brought me relief in my labour pains. (But she had not helped Tadukhipa. . .) And then Renemet, the nursing goddess, would come to me, to preside over the suckling. . .But none of them ever came to *my* assistance.

All that was true in what Kat-Senet had told me, was that since I was so small, Pentu would try to bring on the labour pains by boiling bran, and putting it on a cloth on my belly, and then, when the pains had started, I should be made to kneel, crouching on two bricks, one midwife in front of me, a second behind me, supporting me; a third would draw the child out. No god or goddess rendered me the slightest assistance, either in the shaping of the child or in the time it took to leave me. I myself might be Queen-Goddess, but I gave birth in the obscene agony of all female animals — and lacking the privacy into which a female animal drags herself. For I think I could have borne it more easily if, as I asked, they had covered my face from prying eyes, but this was never permitted, and so my womanhood was outraged again.

Worst of all, I think, worse even than the pain and the fear, was the loneliness of that ordeal before that multitude of eyes. Was this how criminals felt when they were punished in public? Useless to close my eyes and imagine they were not there; the eyes had murmuring voices, and muskily perfumed bodies that sweated with excitement at the spectacle before them. So I kept my eyes open. I was unable to stare accusingly at Amenhotep, because *he* always kept his face buried in his hands, weeping and moaning. So instead I kept my eyes fixed on Father. He — wherever his increasing duties might take him for the other eight or nine months — was always there when a child was born to me. Not, oddly enough, in the forefront of the gathering, watching my performance with a proprietorial eye — Mutnedjmet, married, widowed soon enough, always occupied *that* position, staring, I suppose with all the fascinated disgust, the envy mingled with gratitude, of the childless women — no, Father always stood in the background, near the door, in the shadows. He was quite unmistakable, tall, elegant as he attended the supremely inelegant mess of childbirth. I knew it was him, although his face was a distant blur except for the glitter of his eyes. I don't know what expression was in those eyes, but I knew he correctly read the message in mine. "*You* handed me over to this."

So, when the pain did not make all logical thought quite impossible, I knelt looking at Father, and wondering why on this occasion above all others, he chose comparative obscurity? After all, here I was, the heifer he had bred, proving her ability to calve. Why did he always stand just inside the door as if he wished to escape yet could not bear to leave? Eventually, I hit on a solution. I was fertile enough — yet produced only daughters. And, I thought, Father must find the disappointment of not being a grandfather to a future Pharaoh particularly hard to bear.

But there was a limit to the time during which I could escape from my physical throes by pondering on Father's motives. Soon enough I was no more than an animal screaming soundlessly for hour after hour. But eventually, when I was convinced my body would burst because the great bulging head could not be shifted, hands pressing on my belly, a tearing sensation — could not people *hear* the sound of tearing? — other hands groping between my legs, and then a measure of physical relief with the cessation of the most rending physical pain, and a greater measure of mental relief as I whispered, "Can I be — covered, now?" and they let me lie on a bed and drew a sheet over my body to hide it from the staring eyes, that weary animal's body, quivering with the pain of exhaustion.

Perhaps the most incredible fact of all is that both the child and I survived — six times.

Amenhotep was doubly more fortunate than I; he cried more easily than I could; he could also forget the pregnancies and childbirths more easily. As I have said, as the years passed, he began more and more to reproach me because, although he had done these things so often to me now, I remained as unaroused as I had been on our wedding night. I did try. There were occasions when I genuinely tried to show him love. And then, when I put up my hand to caress his face, stroke his hair, I would feel the length of his head, I would remember those other heads being forced from the very opening he was now. . .

He said I was still and cold as a corpse. I know now that I was not a good wife to him, the right wife for him. I was too young to play the woman's part, too ignorant to aid him when he needed help. I know now he had been determined to marry me because I was so very different from what he was trying to escape. But if I had not been so different, I might have helped him more. As it was, in those first years of marriage, when the battle might have been won if he had had a woman to turn to, I had little chance of becoming a woman. For six years, I was a child giving birth to children, with no time in between to attain womanhood.

My first child — like all the others — was a girl. I was worried because she was so solemn and unsmiling and old looking. Kat-Senet laughed at me; "All babies look old when they're born," she said. But Meritaten — I gave her a pet name, Mayati, but when she grew older she said only one person, and that not myself, should use it — went on looking old and solemn and unsmiling. I loved her dearly. Perhaps at the time it was nothing deeper than the love of a child for a new doll, but it was as real an emotion as I was capable of feeling at twelve years old. I sang to my baby at sunset, the Cretan songs Ariaea had sung to me, played with her throughout the day, scrutinised the little face time and time again for some resemblance to myself, but could never, for all my wishfulness, find any. She was all her father's daughter. If she resembled any woman she resembled her father's first wife, and this frightened me. Only the Mother Goddess knows the inner tears of contrition I shed, remembering my cruelty to Tadukhipa,

But my second child, Meketaten, gurgled and held out her hands to me when she was a baby, loved me as she grew older. I have always thought this was because, even though I could not feed her myself, at least I could choose the woman who did. My Aunt Tiy had again provided the wet-nurse, another Nubian from her own household, but just before I gave birth to Meketaten, this woman fell ill with fever, and I had my chance. Amenhotep, of course, had an immense harem, which supplied him with ample compensation during my pregnancies and the days in the month when I was no use to him. There was a Syrian girl, about twelve years older than I was, who had already had several children by him, all still-born. She was a gentle, simple creature, with a lightish skin and curious elongated breasts; Amenhotep had brought her back with him when he had visited Syria years before. Our lives — hers and mine — were beginning to follow a set pattern; he slept with her when I became pregnant, so that when I was having a child she was in the middle of pregnancy. By the time she gave birth to the child, I myself was pregnant again. But three months before Meketaten was born, the Syrian girl gave birth to a child that lived, although it was sickly. She was delighted. But the child did not survive for long, and died only a few days before my own child was due to be born. The mother's grief was dreadful; she howled like a dog. I sent for her — I was in no condition to go to her — and she came to me, stifling her sobs as best she could.

I took her hand and looked up at her earnestly. "Will you suckle my baby when it is born?" I was desperate to find a wet-nurse before my Aunt Tiy found a substitute for the Nubian woman, and had a childish, no doubt fantastic, idea that if my second child associated a pale and not a dark breast with motherhood, it might love *me*, although the breast from which it sucked had not been mine. But I think I also was honestly, if fumblingly, trying to help the poor Syrian, although she did not understand what I meant until I pointed first to my breast, then to hers. (She still did not talk Egyptian very well although she had lived in Thebes for years). Then she caught my hand and kissed it. Her name was Mekten. I called the child she fed Meketaten; it was close enough to please the girl who nurtured her. Meketaten was the gentlest of my children; I have always thought that she drank in gentleness with her wet-nurse's milk. And was it because Mekten, I think, loved me, and smiled in welcome whenever she saw me, that Meketaten loved me, too?

That was one of the more tranquil periods of my early married life, when I used to watch my baby, if not feeding from me, at least content at the breast of someone who loved me. Meketaten was a pretty child. Soon enough I was wistfully trying to find something of myself in her, but never succeeding. But one day, when Mekten, the baby and I were sitting peacefully together, I gave a sudden exclamation. In Meketaten's face I had at last traced a resemblance to someone I knew. My mother. Black hair in place of yellow, brown eyes instead of grey, dark skin, not white, yet feature for feature — yes, the resemblance was there. My exclamation had made Mekten look at me in surprise. I tried to explain to her that there was a resemblance between Meketaten and my mother. Her expression changed to alarm, fear. She shook her head vigorously.

"No. No. Never!" she said. I stared at her, amazed by the sudden vehemence, even hostility in one so placid and amiable.

"But you have never seen my mother!" I said in bewilderment. Eventually I realised she thought I had meant Meketaten was like Amenhotep's mother. I laughed and shook my head. "No," I said, pointing at myself, "*my* mother." Her face cleared then, but after a moment clouded again. She began to try to tell me something, but in her agitation her poor command of Egyptian was lost completely, and I would not let her go on, for fear she became upset, both for her own sake, and the baby's.

I was now sufficiently recovered from Meketaten's birth to have Amenhotep across me, then beside me each night again.

My third child was Ankhesenpaaten. I was very distressed at the time of her birth; Mekten died suddenly. They said there had always been a weakness in her; later, when Meketaten proved to be so delicate a child, I was reproached for having given her so sickly a nurse. But I do not think now that she died naturally, I believe orders were given for her death. The friendship that had grown up between us had been noted; it was necessary that I should be isolated. It was also thought necessary at the time that Mekten should not be able to talk to me.

They said she died of fever. Certainly as she lay dying, fever had burned the flesh from her face, dried her lips so that they had begun to flake. Against all protest and opposition — against even Amenhotep's stated wishes — I sat beside her although she knew no one now. Her dark eyes were open and staring, but I hoped that if in her mind she saw anything it was the sea and the hills of her own Syria.

"Come away," they said to me again. "To all intents and purposes she's dead." True, the flesh was now stretched so tightly over the bones that the still face might have been no more than a skull. But the voice of the heart still beat feebly in the wrist I held, and I would not leave her. I was glad of this, because just before she died she recovered consciousness, and looked up at me with love and recognition in her eyes. I put my free hand to her poor burning cheek.

She moved her head slightly so that she could kiss it. "Be careful," the dry lips said, with infinite difficulty. And then she was dead.

"There!" they said, hustling me away, "She herself saw the danger of your staying with her!"

Ankhesenpaaten was born that night. I myself fell into fever after her birth; I had no choice as to *her* foster-mother. Tiy took complete charge of her — and when I was well enough to take my child into my own arms, and once again searched the little features for some resemblance to myself, I almost cried out. Meritaten was like her father, Meketaten like my own dead mother — but Ankhesenpaaten's mouth and eyes were incontestably the mouth and eyes of her other, paternal grandmother.

These were the three children to whom I gave birth at Malkata. Within a few months after Ankhesenpaaten's birth, I was pregnant again, but before the child was born, we had left Thebes. Although I had never liked Thebes, I should have preferred to see our leave-taking delayed until my fourth child had been born. None of my pregnancies were easy; this was harder than most.

Since becoming pregnant, I had seen little of Amenhotep. It was not that he neglected me; he was not in Thebes at all, he was sailing great distances in the royal barge, unusual for him because hitherto he had rarely stirred from the capital — unlike the Pharaohs of the past, who, when not incapacitated by age or sickness, campaigned in the summer and in the winter journeyed from end to end of the Nile Valley, conferring with the local governors. But Amenhotep had stayed in Thebes, arguing, so I vaguely understood, in an increasingly acrimonious manner with the local priesthood; he had never, it seemed, forgiven them for some oracular pronouncement years before.

But now he returned, his haggard cheeks unusually flushed, his eyes burning. When I saw him I thought he too was in a fever. But it was the fever of excitement. "I want you," he said, "to come with me to the Council meeting tomorrow."

"You want *me* to come?" The prospect left me apprehensive

and wretched. I had never before attended a meeting of the Royal Council — had, indeed, never dreamed of doing so. And I had no wish to establish a precedent now. At close on fifteen I was not so physically grotesque in pregnancy as I had been at eleven, but I still did not want strange men looking at me when I was over six months advanced. But he insisted. It was all-important that I should be there, all the more essential because I *was* pregnant.

So, very nervously, I accompanied him next morning. To any dispassionate observer, I must have looked absurd, a child dressed in adult clothes and regalia, with a pillow stuffed over her stomach to provide broad humour. They had elaborately painted my face, but, because of my condition, at least I was spared wearing one of the heavier crowns, simply a ceremonial wig and plumes. I was extremely confused and embarrassed; I stood beside Amenhotep, my eyes fixed on the ground, hardly listening at first to what he was saying, concentrating solely on wishing he would say what he had to say as quickly as possible, so that I could go. But then I became conscious of a very unusual sound, gasps, even cries of astonishment. Ignorant though I might be, I realised that such was not the usual punctuation to one of Pharaoh's orations. Therefore what Amenhotep was saying must be very surprising indeed. I began to listen.

He was talking excitedly of a crescent of land half-way between Thebes and Memphis. "I went ashore and spent the night in my royal tent, then drove in my royal chariot to a part where the sun's rays told me I should fix the boundary. No man advised me to go there. No, it was the Aten himself, my father, who urged me to build this horizon city!" By this time his voice was quite frenzied. "Look at my queen!" he continued. "You can see that she is far advanced in pregnancy. Our next child will be born in the new capital of Egypt!"

With this, he took my hand and stalked out. I waddled heavily beside him in a state of desperate confusion. "We're leaving Thebes?" I whispered when we were out of earshot.

"I've always told you how much I hate this place," he said, "how I've longed to get away!"

"But not now," I said desperately. "I mean, not yet. Not until I've had my baby. I mean — where shall I have the child? It's been a difficult pregnancy — am I to have the baby in a tent? I don't know if I can even stand the journey. I may lose it — "

"If you lose it," he said impatiently, "we can have others."

Chapter Nine
Nefertiti

In the ten years that followed, the more sycophantic courtiers — and they were nearly all sycophants — were frequently to congratulate me earnestly on the happiness I must have felt, indeed, the privileged blessedness, to have been The One's constant companion when he was working out the principles of the religious revelation accorded to him alone.

I would smile, and murmur the non-committal reply expected of a queen. The truthful answer would have been that during this period I was pregnant most of the time, and still a child. I was so imprisoned, trapped by my body, that the intricacies of new religious thinking were the matters least likely to occupy my mind. All my energies were occupied in preparing for, or recovering from, childbirth. Even if this had not been the case, I don't suppose I should have been any more aware of what was going on. In those days there was an invisible but quite impenetrable veil of secrecy screening not only Pharaoh's harem, but Pharaoh's queen from the outside world. And if the outside world could not see within that veil, so Pharaoh's queen could not see out.

Now, as we came away from the Council, after brushing aside my protests with the airy rejoinder that if I lost this child, we could have others, Amenhotep informed me furiously that certain priests were saying evil things about him. That was the reason he had decided to abandon Thebes. The break with Amen would be complete. He would found a new capital in the desert. He. . .

I interrupted him with, "What evil things do they say about you?"

He did not reply.

"Is it because you show such favour to the Aten?" I said after a moment's awkward silence.

Amenhotep often talked excitedly to me of the Aten, the sun; usually in the afternoon, when even the lizards seemed exhausted. I did not say, watching one of the little panting creatures, that a times the sun seemed to threaten life; I did not repeat what Ariaea had told me concerning the Mother-Goddess and the *moon*. Instead I would try to make Meritaten smile, or sing to Meketaten one of the songs Ariaea had sung to me and Amenhotep would say, ''Nefertiti, are you listening?'' and I would say, ''Yes, of course. You are saying that now the priesthood of Amen has arrogated to itself much of the worship that should go to the Aten alone,'' and he would smile, pacified, and go on with his talk.

And I would ask myself secretly how any woman could truly worship the sun? For Ariaea had spoken the truth years before. Any woman knows that for her the heavens hold a sole authoritative ruler. Virgin or whore, wife or widow, blissfully happy or wretched to the point of despair, she knows it is the moon which inexorably, inescapably governs her body from childhood to middle age. The barbarian Achaeans show themselves superior in intelligence to the Egyptians in this respect at least; they divide the year into months. Whereas the Egyptian priests long ago divided the year into *dekans*, thirty-six successive periods of ten days each, fixed by certain stars. So a male Pharaoh, I would think ironically at certain phases of the moon, decrees worship of the sun, male priests divide the year according to the stars — and women of every race on earth, whatever their masters ordain, secretly divide the year by the waxing and waning of the omnipotent moon.

I had never seen Amenhotep so excitable as he was on that journey we took northwards from Thebes. I lay wretchedly on cushions; the child quickened sluggishly inside me, Kat-Senet squatted behind me, looking worried. Amenhotep, oblivious of my whey-face, said, ''This idea should appeal to you Nefertiti — the new city as an *island*! A little holy island where we can be quite cut off from the rest of the world, from the past!''

He had frequently repeated to me what a marvellous thing it would be to cut yourself off from the past, but this idea of cutting himself off from the rest of the world was entirely new. For all my physical misery I began to say that if you were The One this was surely the one thing you should not do, when a voice said gruffly, warningly, '''Majesty; *don't cross him*.''

The speaker was Parennefer, whose position in Amenhotep's entourage is difficult to explain. There were two strands to it. As a child he had been extremely delicate and had been served by Parennefer. Amenhotep was always very conscious of that sickly childhood; frequently in proclamations he would describe himself as "he who has survived" — and as time passed he came to add "to live long." Then there was the period spent away from Egypt, in Mitanni and other parts of Asia. I had never been able to discover exactly why he had been sent away. However, I had gleaned one fact. He had gone with an extremely small retinue, which left me to conclude — inescapably — that he had been sent away in semi-disgrace at least. I had gained a distinct impression that the members of that small retinue had volunteered to accompany the prince, and the chief of them had been Parennefer — another reason for gratitude on Amenhotep's part.

So this was the Parennefer who whispered to me not to cross my husband. I said nothing, but at dawn, I told Kat-Senet to bring Parennefer to me. Dawn was the time of the day above all others that found Amenhotep lost in meditation. It was also the time of day when I — well, liked him best is too cold a term, perhaps, and cannot, in any case, convey the feeling I always had that the Amenhotep of the darkness, who plundered the body of an unwilling child as mercilessly as he was capable of was quite a different person from the Amenhotep of the hours of daylight, who viewed every living thing with tenderness, who had already forbidden any form of human sacrifice throughout the empire and who would not hunt for pleasure any living creature, for all were equally God-made.

I think these are the qualities I may remember longest about him; I can recollect them now, away from him, in tranquillity. And I am now old enough,and have gained sufficient experience, to realise that the other Amenhotep, the frantically grasping and clutching Amenhotep, who frightened and revolted the child he married, was himself nothing more than a child afraid of the dark. One day he himself was to confess this fear of darkness to me. But I was still too young and ignorant to know that so much of cruelty springs from fear.

Throughout the days of our marriage I remained a child. I did not become a woman until other men taught me to be one, so I could only help him as a woman, made a woman by those other men, at our last conscious meeting. I could have been a good wife to him — when it was too late.

I knew that at dawn Amenhotep would be so absorbed in watching the sun rise in the eastern sky he would not notice Parennefer talking to me.

If one is afflicted with pregnancy one might as well exploit that condition as much as possible. I said rapidly to Parennefer now, "Since I am carrying a royal child, I too should not be crossed. What is the reason why I should not cross The One?"

After a few moments' silence, he told me. I knew, of course, that Amenhotep had been so delicate as a child he had not been expected to live? He had suffered from convulsions. At first it had been thought that these were the childish kind, that he would outgrow them, but when they had continued, it had to be accepted that he had the falling sickness. Did I know what that was?

I said slowly I had only heard of it.

"He falls down with a loud cry. He is quite rigid, teeth clenched, head drawn back. You have to ensure he doesn't bite his tongue. This stage doesn't last long. Then the limbs jerk, the eyes roll. Sometimes blood-flecked foam comes from his mouth. And then he falls into a deep sleep, sometimes lasting for hours, and when he wakes he remembers nothing."

"I didn't know," I said. "No one told me."

Perhaps they had felt there was no need to tell me, said Parennefer. Amenhotep had not had a convulsion for years. Ever since he had gone away to Syria.

"Why should you think the sickness will return?"

Because in the past the sickness had occurred when he was excited, agitated — as he has become in the past weeks.

"What causes it?"

He shrugged. "Some people say it is being possessed by a god."

"You don't believe that."

"It runs in families," he began, but after this, I had stopped listening to what he said. In a flash all my anxieties changed direction. Might my children inherit the disease? This thought was still obsessing me when in due course we came to a point almost half-way between Thebes and the sea, where the limestone cliffs lining the east bank seemed to swing away some three miles inland, continuing so for five or six miles. I was glad we had reached the place where Amenhotep had decided to set up his holy city — for it meant that soon we could turn and go back to Thebes. I was oppressed by fears that the child would be prematurely born. And how the last stages of pregnancy dull the imagination! Along the river's edge I saw a narrow strip of land where a few peasants grew a little corn; Amenhotep talked of palaces for us, mansions for the courtiers. Behind it stretched the smooth expanses of desert; Amenhotep talked of royal pleasure-parks, great temples. Sand and gravel sloped up to the cliffs. "Roads and causeways — can't you see the chariots rattling along?"

"Please, Mother-Goddess," I prayed, "let us go back soon —

because I'm afraid the child will be prematurely born." I stared desperately down at the brown swirling water. "Please don't let my baby, don't let any of my babies, inherit the falling sickness."

"Are you seeing what I see in the water?" asked Amenhotep, that other child — with a new toy in the making. "Reflections of the quays, the temples, the palaces?" He caught my hands. "I'll have the most beautiful trees brought from Asia to give you shade, Nefertiti, but there'll be no shade in the *temples*, they'll lie open to the Aten, not like those dark caves they call temples in Thebes!" The rippling water increased my feeling of dizziness; desperately I stared now at the firm half-moon of cliff-tops. He followed my gaze. "I've already had great boundary stones set up there so that everyone will know and respect the limits of my city — my city remote from all contaminating influences, Nefertiti, my holy city built on clean soil — "

"It will be very splendid," I said carefully. "Very splendid. Can we go back to Thebes now, please? I think the baby will come early."

It took some time for him to gather what I was saying — and, by the time he did, what I was saying had altered significantly. "I think the baby is coming early," I said with some difficulty.

He was ecstatic then. "What a marvellous omen for the new city!"

Yet when after hours in which any mental image of pain, suffering, danger of death had been surpassed, I eventually held our fourth daughter to my inadequate breast and looked down at the poor small thing, I could not see in the dark, wrinkled little face anything propitious. Weakly, premature — with a poor chance of survival, I thought, sick at heart. She breathed with difficulty, cried like a mewing kitten, but Amenhotep was jubilant. "We shall call her Neferneferuaten," he announced. Such a lengthy name for such a tiny creature, I thought; I shall call her, simply, Nefer.

I had nearly died in that premature childbirth, yet in a way the premature childbirth saved me some degrees of agony, for the bones in Nefer's long head were soft, flexible. She nearly died, but was saved because at the spot where they carried me ashore there had been a peasant's cottage, and the peasant-wife, nursing her own child, had milk to spare. Amenhotep was delighted with everything. He issued proclamations, set up commemorative tablets. An enthusiast, of course, always assumes that those close to him share his fervour. So proclamations and tablets all asserted that the Queen, hearing what The One intended, had insisted, although far gone in pregnancy, on accompanying him to see for herself the site of the holy city in the crescent formed by the cliffs. And her time came upon her while she actually looked for the first time at the site of the City of the Horizon. . .

It sounded very pretty. It sounded very simple — almost as if I stepped lightly ashore and proceeded to lay an egg with all the businesslike promptness of a hen.

It was not so simple or pretty in reality. I was ill for weeks afterwards, and poor Nefer always, I thought, bore the appearance of the premature baby, that wizened, aged look of the youngest of things. Her face, I used to think anxiously, was never really childlike — or was it merely the expression in her eyes, particularly her expression when she looked at me? For she resented her appearance — and blamed me for it. If I had not insisted on going to see the site of the City of the Horizon myself, as the memorial tablets stated, she would not have been born prematurely.

"Neferneferuaten," said Amenhotep.

I was anxiously contemplating my three-day old, prematurely-born child. Was her cry any stronger? She should still be safe, secure inside me, not struggling to breathe — no wonder she cried, if only so weakly. The waxiness of her wrinkled skin —

"Neferneferuaten."

I roused myself. "Yes, *Fair is the goodness of the Aten* — I think it is a beautiful name."

But he was frowning. "Perhaps you should have it."

"I?" I stared at him. "I'm a little old to be renamed."

His frown deepened. "But I *told* you — only all you seemed to want to do was look at the child. Didn't you even hear what I said before that?"

"I was worried," I said apologetically. "Her breathing seemed to falter. . .What had you said?"

"That I'm changing my own name. I don't intend to go on bearing *his* name — I mean," he corrected himself abruptly, "I don't mean to go on bearing the name of the local god of Thebes."

I should explain that Amenhotep means 'Amen is in peace'.

"I shall call myself Akhnaten."

"*Aten is satisfied*," I translated to myself. Aloud I said, "You will not be angry with me if sometimes I forget to call you that at first? I should like," I went on, still apologetically, "to go on being called Nefertiti. My name has been changed once already."

Little Nefer wailed suddenly. I hurriedly began to soothe her. My husband's face softened. ''If you like,'' he said, kissing my cheek. ''Akhnaten and Nefertiti, then.''

Chapter Ten
Nefertiti

But even the Pharaoh, favourite son of a god or God himself, cannot wave his sceptre and expect a new capital to spring up overnight in the desert. It had been an error to make the announcement — and then to have to stay on in Thebes for month after month, but Akhnaten — it took me almost as long to call him by his new name as it took the builders to construct his city — did not possess a calculating nature. Neither did he possess a patient nature. The waiting fretted his nerves — so, for the first time I saw the falling sickness for myself.

It was just as Parennefer had described it, but mere words were no real preparation for the reality: the livid face, the staring eyes, the great pants of breath foul as that of a wild beast. And I had to teach myself to identify, and dread, the symptoms of an impending attack. Akhnaten dominated by the feeling that his surroundings were hostile, Akhnaten suspicious, seeing persecution, betrayal everywhere — these were the symptoms he showed while we were still in Thebes — and who will ever know, I wondered painfully, how much his hatred of his father and the Amen priests was really due to his sickness? And then at Amarna there was that other symptom, swinging to the other extreme, the excitement, the exaltation, the elation, the feeling of omnipotence, god-head. And again I wondered how much of his religious ecstasy was really due to his sickness. . .

He spent a great deal of time with me — partly I knew, because it was not pleasant to go about Thebes to be confronted with purely formal obeisances, and scowling faces. But he had another reason. The priesthood dominated, among so much else, all the arts in Egypt. That grip too, must be broken — radically. As a boy he had been fascinated by the marvellous objects sent to his ancestors from Crete; now he questioned me about the old art of the island. I could remember little, and that only ruins, but here and there I had seen a wall brightly painted with butterflies, birds, dancers.

''Cretan artists never came to Egypt in the past!'' Akhnaten said angrily. ''The artistic conventions laid down by the priests crushed them. But everything will be different now. I'll send for them from wherever they've taken refuge!''

It was a little later that same afternoon that I first saw an attack of falling sickness. It had been a happy day. The children had been playing with us; he had Meketaten on his knee when a minister — an elderly man, brother of the High Priest of Amen — was received in audience. Akhnaten would not let me go, or the children; he even kept Meketaten bouncing up and down on his knee as he spoke. The minister could not entirely disguise his scandalised expression. ''You had better get used to this kind of thing,'' said Akhnaten. ''This is how all Egypt will soon get used to seeing its king — with his family!'' Almost before the man had gone, he was turning to me, his eyes glowing with another new idea. The sun was beginning to set now. I sat with Nefer in my arms, and the warm golden light falling about me. ''Parennefer,'' said Akhnaten, ''remarked to me the other day that while I could expect trouble from the priests of Amen because I was attacking their privileges, the ordinary people might be unhappy if they ever thought I was depriving them of Isis, Osiris and the child, Horus — that's what they can understand, he said, *a family*.''

Remembering how the only divinity of Egypt's terrifying pantheon who had raised any response in my childish heart had been Isis, her child in her arms, I said that Parennefer was right.

''Well!'' said Akhnaten enthusiastically, ''they will have myself, you and our children, won't they?''

Later that evening, and when we were alone together in the garden in the dark, he harked back to the idea of us as a divine family. Because he was in so good, even excellent, a mood — and because of all his talk of the family — I summoned up the courage to ask him the question I had wanted to put to him from the moment he had spoken of leaving Thebes. ''Will your mother, or brothers, come with us?''

I could not see his face, but his very silence had something frightening in it. ''No,'' he said, eventually, slowly, and in a thick kind of voice. ''No. She is — entirely against the idea''. And then the words began to run into one another. ''No! She's not coming! No! She's not coming!'' And then the cry, the scream, that Parennefer had described to me, but he had not said how high it was, how shrill it was, how unhuman it was, how it seemed to last for a very long time, before it became a whimper, and then silence, and then the fall, and I groped in the dusk for his face, and called for help, and courtiers came with torches, and there was Pen-tu, and eventually Akhnaten fell into the deep sleep described by Parennefer, and awoke remembering nothing — but I remembered everything.

Akhnaten spent most of his time with me now; he could tell himself that this was elected seclusion with his wife and family. It was a pleasant method of self-deception. His mood was forward-looking, a joyous indulgence in daydreams of the glories of the new capital, the acceptance not only in Egypt but throughout Syria and Nubia of the religion of Aten, revealed to him alone by God. But our existence together was really imprisonment. As it was to end, with us isolated, beleaguered. As I was to remember with silent, unshed tears at that ending. Yet that first isolation was serene enough. For the first time I conceived in tranquillity — and partly a tranquillity he could not guess at. His mother would not be coming with us when we left Thebes — it was only now, in that knowledge, that I could admit to myself the obscure dread, hatred, I felt for her.

Akhnaten called his new capital city Akhetaten — the City of the Horizon of Aten. Now, if men cannot avoid speaking of it, they call it the accursed city. I shall simply call it by its geographical location — Amarna.

The birth of our fifth child was imminent when we left the House of Rejoicing. This time I did not protest. Akhnaten thought of a capital without a past — free from the shadow of Amen; I thought of a home with a future, free from the shadow of Tiy. Our palace — the first of the palaces — was completed — just. Our bedrooms were on the eastern side, so that the rays of the rising sun shone directly through the windows. The children's nurseries were in a separate six-roomed suite to the south-east of the building. That is all I really remember of our first days in Amarna, the children's nurseries, the family altar close to my bedroom where I prayed inarticulately but fervently to undesignated deities, and then my bedroom, the walls inlaid with faience plates showing lotus buds, and the sweating, fleshy hands of Pen-tu moving from breasts to belly, and finally the familiar ordeal before the watching eyes, and the familiar response to my gasping question — "A daughter, Majesty."

Akhnaten called her Neferneferure. I called her Nofret, for she was so sweet. She was little and fragile and sickly, as they all were, except Ankhesenpaaten. I was sixteen; I thought I might be able to feed her. She came to my breast readily enough, seeming to grasp for it with wavering fingers, and for a whole day I suckled her and we were both happy, so happy. She curled her little toes, suckled beautifully. But then the milk stopped flowing. They say this happens sometimes if a mother is over-anxious. And I was over-anxious. How I yearned to be able to feed a child at last! But I could not go on suckling Nofret. Yet she loved me, although I cheated her cruelly, smearing honey and date juice on my nipples so that her little lips would tug at them. She knew me at an incredibly early age, my voice, my hands — she rarely slept well, but I could soothe her as no one else could. When I held her in my arms and sang the Cretan Swallow Song to her, she would lie watching me with loving dark eyes. She was *mine*.

I had asked Akhnaten if, since we were to make our own way of life here at Amarna, I might bear our child in privacy. But he had refused. This was a divine, royal child. Such births could not take place secretly. He looked at me with kindly, affectionate eyes, and said to me gently, "You're too sensitive in this matter."

'Before the next time', I thought, 'I'll talk to him, try to make him understand how I feel.' But years were to pass before there was a 'next time'. There was one very good reason for this. Akhnaten no longer slept much with me and, when he did — well, perhaps it was because we both tacitly accepted the fact that I was frigid and unresponsive, found no pleasure in the marital act — he would talk to me, and rarely did anything else.

But — oh, how I gloried in the nights when I slept alone! To be able to sleep blissfully, for hours on end — how rarely I had been able to do so for years! I was seventeen — and I could sleep alone, unharassed by that essentially alien thing, a man's body. For such it was to me. For years I had shared Akhnaten's bed, for years he had forced his body inside mine, and with each year the shivering repugnance had increased.

Father, who of course was constantly in Amarna, filling — with, I must admit, a great deal of efficiency — a variety of posts, inevitably got to know what had happened. He had not lost his good ear for harem gossip, cultivating particularly the friendship of the eunuchs, who had sat outside my bedroom. Handsomer than ever at forty, he came to see me, and after a period of silence, came to the point. Did Akhnaten *never* sleep with me now? If not, why? He asked this with great urgency, and, without awaiting my reply subjected me to the kind of detailed questions on my attitudes during copulation that a baffled stockbreeder might put to an unserviced heifer, if heifers could talk. I suppose it was because I was so astonished at this that I felt no real resentment, although I did not answer his questions.

"It's a threat to your status!" muttered Father (meaning of course his own). "If he doesn't come to you, he'll go to someone else. Perhaps regularly!"

I did not mind Akhnaten's going each night to his current favourite — a fat Ethiopian whose breasts were so large she seemed top-heavy, because it meant I could sleep alone. But how to explain this to any man, above all to Father, who, I thought, would have slept with a she-bear if this were necessary for advancement?

I dreamed of Amarna the other night. . .I was looking down on it from a great height, and it seemed like a toy city built to delight children. There was the principal street, the royal road, the King's Way. There at the southern end stood Maru-Aten, our pleasure palace, with the lake, the great entrance pavilion, with columned halls and throne room. There was the Temple, which we entered daily to the singing and playing of Akhnaten's cherished choir of blind musicians — ivory flutes, jewelled harps. There, between Maru-Aten and the Great Temple, was the Great Palace, with its terraced gardens, and the pavilion they called the Queen's Pavilion. And there, on the bridge spanning the road was the Window of Appearance, where Akhnaten displayed himself in splendour, and threw down gold to his faithful followers. And there I was beside him, a doll-queen, and below all the doll-courtiers, wooden faces carved in the proper expressions of loyalty, adoration — Pentu, Chief Physician, Apy, the Royal Scribe, Tutu, the Foreign Minister. Above all, Father — at that time Commander of Chariots. The other wooden figures were stiffly immobile; Father's wooden limbs were jointed, articulated, rightly so, for I was seeing the re-enactment of the ceremony when Akhnaten gave him the Golden Collar. The excitement, the bustle of Father then — all faithfully reproduced in the jerking wooden toy. His arms quivered with pride — and, presumably, loyalty.

Not that Father was unique. It was royal gold that had drawn most of those who followed Akhnaten to Amarna; it was gold that kept them there — and how they cherished their precious fetters!

Whatever Father's private opinion of me might be, in public no parent ever treated a daughter with greater love and honour. The spoken word, swept away by the wind, was too ephemeral for him, he said. Almost immediately on arrival at Amarna he had commenced building the most ornate tomb in the new capital, and on the walls of it he set down an expression of paternal love which greatly touched the gullible Akhnaten.

This was the loving homage offered to me by Father: —

Lady of Grace, sweet of love, Mistress of the South and North, fair of face, gay with the two plumes, beloved of the living Aten, the Chief Wife of the King, whom he loves, Lady of the Two Lands, great of love, Nefertiti, living for ever and ever. . .
Akhnaten, when Father proudly led us to the inscription, was so greatly impressed that he ordered these should be my official titles, inscribed on all boundary stones. I myself felt that Father's heart had been more sincerely engaged in another composition, not pointed out to us — an essay in autobiography. ''*I was eminent*,'' I read with some amusement, ''*possessing character, successful in opportunities, contented in disposition, kindly, following His Majesty, according as he commanded. The end thereof was an old age in peace. . .*''

Father, noticing how my notice was taken, and my amusement roused, hastily directed Akhnaten's attention elsewhere. On one wall of the tomb he had had inscribed a hymn that Akhnaten had composed. Aten, it ran, would live on ''till the swan be black and the raven white, till the mountains rise up and move away, and the water flows uphill.'' Father repeated this aloud now, in a hushed, reverent voice. Tears trickled slowly from his magnificent eyes. It was so beautiful, he said.

Chapter Eleven
Nefertiti

Meanwhile Akhnaten's religious fervour, or fury, increased. I devoted myself to the children, but even the nurseries were not free from religious debate; with ferocious denunciations, their father would interrupt a scene when I crawled on the floor, dragging a wheeled animal with nodding head before the baby Nofret, denunciations not only of Amen now, but of all other Egyptian gods. Nofret, usually the most sweet-tempered of children, would justifiably cry because the angry voice interrupted her game; Meritaten, who was old enough, partially, to understand what her father was saying, would sit staring, silent. I worried a great deal about Meritaten because of her sullenness, her silences which were alternated with bursts of wild screaming and destructiveness. Kat-Senet suggested that if her hands were kept occupied, there would be less tearing and breaking, and eventually she learned to weave badly, for she would never concentrate.

I worried, too, about Ankhesenpaaten, the liveliest of my children. Even now, when I think of her, it is as if my heart has turned to ice-water in my breast. She was always greedy, greedy for pleasure, self indulgence. This may seem the harshest of judgements to pass on a child, and my own child, but I saw that childish face coarsened, almost bloated with greed so many times that my love for her was irretrievably tainted by anxiety and suspicion.

Akhnaten's ministers gained their posts and held them because they flattered, conformed. Outside Amarna all was corruption, chaos, famine — this was the time people were to call the Years of the Hyena. In Syria matters were even worse. No one but Tutu, the Foreign Minister, will ever know how many reports he delayed, even destroyed — I think eventually he himself lost count.

Yet all inkling of what was happening in Syria could not be kept from Akhnaten. When despatches went unanswered, desperate commanders and governors sent men they could ill spare to speak to Pharaoh, if it were possible. These messengers appeared among the glittering, perfumed, luxurious society of Amarna like men from another world. The note they introduced was harsh, discordant. Travel-stained, haggard-faced, they leaped off their ships at the quay, dismounted from dust-coated chariots, strode through the idling inhabitants whom such haste offended, laid unavailing siege to officials who smiled disbelievingly or contemptuously at their urgency. Even when they had had time to bathe, and change their clothes, they still stood out from those about them because they so signally lacked the general air of comfortable complacency. They were impatient, urgent, incredulous, despairing. I suppose they alone were alive, conscious, free from the unreal trance of life in Amarna. But no one ever spoke of them to Akhnaten. Any mention of them angered him. In loud voices, shattering the tranquility of his capital, they spoke of matters which defiled one of the very concepts of the creed of the Atenist. They spoke of war, violence. Such intruders, invaders of the dream city must be denied existence.

Perhaps the only courtier in whom I possessed any real confidence was May, a big, middle-aged man who had once held high military rank and now was the Chancellor. He differed from the majority of courtiers in two respects — he was a Northerner and he was not one of Akhnaten's "new men", owing everything to royal favour; instead he came from the old nobility of the Memphis region. The reason why Akhnaten kept him on in office after his father's death could only have been that May had a reputation for great industry and efficiency, and even Akhnaten must have accepted that while fervent (or apparently fervent) adherence to the new creed was most important, expertise in administration also had its occasional benefits. Inevitably, May was an isolated figure at Amarna. Birth alone would tend to keep him aloof from the new men, who found him arrogant; disliking equally his habitual taciturnity and his occasional speech, which could be brusque and tactless.

I myself did not think May had any respect for me — after all, I was the daughter of the man who embodied all that he most disliked. But — with the exception of Parennefer — he was the only surly straightforward dog in that court of cats who would rub themselves against you ingratiatingly to get what they wanted, dab at you with velvet paws in play, yet in those paws were sheathed the rending claws, and the eyes of the cats were shallow. A dog cannot sheathe his claws; there they are — plain for all to see. And once or twice, meeting me by chance alone, save for Kat-Senet, or holding Nofret in my arms, May would walk beside me through the garden or along the colonnade, saying nothing, obviously deep in thought, but from time to time he would stand still, and look at me as if he were about to say something — but he never did. . .

He had spent the earlier part of his life as a soldier, and never forgot it. This must have been the reason he stayed on in the most uncongenial of surroundings — he would do his best to ensure that Syria and the garrisons of Syria, should not be forgotten. When Akhnaten had begun to rule, he had not stood alone in urging that Syria should be defended. Adding their voices to his had been the fighting generals of previous reigns. Unfortunately, these were few, and all were old, the last major campaign, having been fought in Nubia when Akhnaten was three or four years old. To my distress, Akhnaten was unkind, even cruel, to these increasingly frail old men. Once when two of them, very old indeed, old enough to have taken part in the real fighting in Asia, before his father's accession, spoke to him in twittering, breathless voices of the need to hold cities and strongholds that were names from my history lessons — Megiddo, Byblos, Jerusalem — he turned on them brutally, shouting at them that they were survivors from a barbaric past who were over-long in dying. They looked at him with bewildered, rheumy eyes, slowly, painfully, made obeisance and began to grope their way out.

"How could you be so cruel to them?" I asked in a low voice later.

He turned on me. "They talked of war. War must be only a *word* now."

"They weren't talking of war. They talked of peace. They said Syria had known under Egyptian rule a peace never before experienced, but that peace is threatened now. Yet all that's needed, they said, to prevent untold misery, is — is a display of force." Strange how in those days I fumbled for the proper military phrase.

Akhnaten was very angry. The generals were senile bigots. If they could or would let themselves understand the creed of Aten, they would realise that geneal acceptance of this would make all wars unnecessary. He spoke at length on universal brotherhood. And then he added, even more angrily, "Can't they see I'm going to unite all Syria even closer to Egypt by the ties of one common, universal religion, the religion of love?"

He had shown little love to those frail survivors from the past, I thought unhappily.

And above the queries, the doubts, the uncertainties, the divine sun poured down incessantly from a blue, cloudless sky. The shadows were always ink black. There was rarely a breath of wind. Easy enough in such circumstances, perhaps, to believe in the Aten as the supreme god; but, oh, how the heat and the airlessness imposed by that god stultified thought! Later, self-pitying, self-exculpating, I would tell myself, that in another climate I might not have been so stupid.

May was disgraced when we had been at Amarna for seven years; I suppose the wonder is that he lasted so long. His dismissal followed a scene at the North Palace, a place I have not so far described in any detail, because we rarely used the actual apartments. When we went there, it was to see some new addition to the collection of rare animals Akhnaten was assembling in the garden, as on this particular occasion when some foreign ruler had sent him a rare white fawn. We took Meritaten; she liked to be with us when we drove together through the streets, and Akhnaten encouraged her to come since he always wanted to stress the idea of the divine trinity. But on this occasion I wished she had not been with us; she was in one of her perverse, destructive moods. She had with her a little goad, with which she prodded the rumps of the horses. Akhnaten, never a good driver, had difficulty in controlling them; we swerved, jolted; he lost his temper; he had come out immediately after our mid-day meal; he was shaken up by the drive; his digestion, never strong, suffered. So an afternoon which began badly, ended disastrously.

When we reached the North Palace, Akhnaten, in a rage, and feeling sorry for himself, went off to his retiring room. He said he had a headache. Certainly, it had been appallingly hot on the short journey; the reflected yellow glare of the sun had beaten about us from the road surface and the surrounding buildings. Left with Meritaten, I told the attendants to take her to the great aquarium; she was angry, she wanted to see the white fawn, or at least to visit the aviary, but I was afraid that in her present mood she might hurt the young creature, or the birds; the fish in their tank should be safe. I told the attendants to go with her. Such ceremony pleased her — and I longed for solitude. I too had something of a headache.

The garden was large. There were groves of figs and sycamores, thickets of scented blossom, climbing vines, some cedars. Easy enough for me to lose myself there. Easy enough for me to remain unobserved when I heard two men striding along the path, and the angry voices drew nearer.

". . .asked for an audience this afternoon, and was granted it. But then, I suppose, he forgot." It was May's voice.

The other voice, deeper, said something about the Council.

"Council? When does the Council meet? He has no interest in government; it is a struggle to get him to give a moment's hearing to the most important. . ."

In great embarrassment I retreated silently among the groves of trees, but the voices followed me. The deeper, younger — *familiar*? — voice, very earnest,". . .last wish that you should lose favour on my behalf. . .the matter can wait for a day or so, until your next regular audience; he's more likely. . .

"Regular audience? I don't have a regular audience. The only man who can count on being received daily is the Chief Priest of the Aten."

"We can't afford to lose our only spokesman at court."

"You said the matter can wait. It can't. It's not this one isolated case. The entire question must come to a head. Without a show of strength *now*. . .

The answering voice was derisive. "A *show of strength*? From this *woman's* city? I came here still sweating from travelling fast on no easy road, my armour'd never seemed heavier, my weapons clumsier — and it's all flower gardens and love songs and harps tinkling and curled hair and scented carcasses — and in Kadesh and Simyra, Byblos and Jerusalem, the Egyptian garrisons are *moving out*, moving out from where they've been for century upon century, whole generations haven't known a time when they haven't been there. . ."

The voices receded into the distance. I sat close to tears, although I could not have said precisely why this was so, particularly since I so very rarely let myself weep. I realised I must be there if the audience were given. The younger man would do nothing to control his anger, and the effect on Akhnaten. . . There had been no attack of the falling sickness since we had come to Amarna, but I dared take no chances.

May and his companion met Akhnaten before his headache had left him — when he was coming to look for me to say he was going back to the Palace, to send for Pentu. And if he had decided to go home too soon, Meritaten refused to go home until it was too late. She flew into one of her furies. Her screams of rage could be heard all over the garden. It was in these unpropitious circumstances — the poor little white doe cowering frightenedly in my arms while Akhnaten clutched his head and complained of the weight of the crown he always wore, the blue leather *khepresh*, ironically the war helmet, against a background of howls from the unseen Meritaten, that two tall figures skirted a balustrade almost hidden by climbing vines and with a soldier's tread defiantly unmuted by courtly etiquette, strode to confront him.

It was one of the occasions when Akhnaten, in his heart, must have cursed his practice of informality. I recognised May's companion, even though I could not for the moment remember his name. The voice had indeed been familiar. It was the Officer of the Chariots who had been angry with me on my first meeting with The Magnificent One. Akhnaten, of course, recognised him at once; hadn't his father said they had been brought up together? So there was no need for formal presentation.

In a way he looked much older than his actual age. There was a bitterness about him; his eyes were unsmiling in a stern face even when he went through the ritual prostration. Well, it made a change from the eternally beaming faces exuding the desire to please. I bent my head, and caressed the white fawn, told myself to be deaf to the actual angry words, yet remain alert to the note in Akhnaten's voice that might herald a return of his sickness. I was not altogether successful. Again I heard the names of towns — Kadesh, Byblos, Jerusalem, Simyra, the names of kings — repetition of two in particular, Ribaddi, the faithful King of Byblos, Aziru of the Amorites who, May insisted, was a traitor.

Akhnaten flew into a rage at this, began to quote letters expressing the most fervent loyalty.

"All ending, I have no doubt, with requests for more gold," said the deep voice.

There was a thudding of feet of the path. Meritaten ran up, screaming she did not want to go home. The terrified white fawn bounded away. I put my arms about my daughter, telling her in a low voice that she must be quiet.

"Action's essential, Majesty, rapid action. . ."

"Ever since the murder of the King of Mitanni. . ."

". . .Aziru is the creature of the Hittites. They encourage him to revolt against us now; later he can be dealt with. . ."

"Don't sit listening to this man!" shouted Meritaten. "You're not listening to *me*, Mother! I want the white fawn!" I put my hand to her lips in an effort to silence the shrill sound. She promptly bit me.

He was talking about Byblos. Byblos was one of the places where I had hoped Staphylos might take me ashore instead of bringing me to Egypt — I had never forgotten the name. Apparently Byblos now was threatened by Aziru.

"Ribaddi's sent appeal after appeal for help to drive the

bastard away. . .''

Despite myself, I gasped. Over Meritaten's angry head I received a cold dismissive glance. ''I apologise for bringing the language of the camp into Her Majesty's garden,'' he said with no trace of apology in his voice.

So if Staphylos had listened to my pleas, I should now be living in a city threatened with destruction. Married, I supposed, with children.

''One might even say that if Ribaddi had any sense he'd save his skin by allying himself with Aziru. But he's a poor fool of a loyalist, so he and his will go down.'' This thought seemed to provoke such rage in him that he fell silent, and May took up the argument.

I realised with a sudden shock that I had not been listening to any of Akhnaten's replies, although my motive for being present had been to strain my ears for any warning note in his voice. I had even been deaf to Meritaten's screams. That was as well, perhaps. Finding herself ignored, she was reduced to whining, ''Why are you listening to those men? Why don't you listen to *me*?''

May had finished speaking. The other voice took up the. . . the what? Complaint? Indictment, rather, for the tone was harsh, imperious.

''The work of generations is being undone. Worse — the lives of thousands who died to give peace to Syria were lost for nothing. And once anarchy's let loose, you can't stop it at a convenient frontier post at Suez. We'll see it soon in Egypt itself if it's not checked in Syria.''

Now I was looking towards Akhnaten, dreading the agitation, the loud cry, the fall. But he was not listening. Had he really been listening at any point? He was staring at the sun, beginning to sink towards the western cliffs. ''Almost,'' he said petulantly, ''you made me late for the evening service.'' He turned to me. ''We must go — quickly.''

''I don't want to go,'' said Meritaten monotonously. ''I haven't played with the white fawn yet.''

Akhnaten grabbed her by the shoulder and propelled her away. She began to scream, ''I want my goad! I want my goad!''

''I'll get it,'' I said and turned back. I thought the little glade was deserted; there was the goad. I hurriedly kicked it into a flowering thicket. From the other side I heard a voice saying, ''. . .and someone should strangle that child. She bit her mother's hand to the bone — did you notice? And *she* made not a sound.''

Then they had gone too. I followed Akhnaten. ''I can't find it,''

I said to Meritaten, hiding my hand from her father, although I really did not think he would notice. He was intent on reaching the temple in time, to obtain The Aten's blessing before the light faded. I knew now that he was always afraid of the darkness. "Who was the man who came with May?" I asked when we were in the chariot.

"The commander of the frontier troops," he said without much interest. "A Northerner, of course, since May was so friendly towards him. From Memphis – his father was *nomarch** there. His name is Horemheb."

Of course. His heavy gold collar had had a hawk motif. Son of the hawk. The same ruthless sense of purpose. Owing allegiance to no one. A very angry bird of prey, with all the falcon's cruelty.

"What he said. . ." I began tentatively.

"When I realised what he meant to say," said Akhnaten, "I stopped listening. It has all been said before."

I said with a gladness I tried to keep out of my voice, "And you're not angry with May?"

"But I am," said Akhnaten. "He deliberately detained me. As I said to him, he almost made me late for the evening service."

May was dismissed a few days later. He must have seen the disgrace coming. A few hours before he was sent from court, he met me in the garden of the Great Palace – but not, I think, by chance – and walked beside me, silently after the initial greeting, as he had done in the past. And then he stopped – as in the past – but this time he actually spoke. "This may be the last time I speak to you, Majesty. Perhaps it's just as well. One often remembers better what is said at a leave-taking. May I accompany you to the pavilion? But say nothing until we can be sure we are alone."

And when we were alone, and I looked timidly up to him, he said in a low urgent voice, "You must listen to the advice from someone who has learned – reluctantly, at first – to admire you. It is brief. Because you've achieved great beauty, because the people have been allowed to see that great beauty – and your goodness – you must ape indifference, passivity, stupidity even, where matters of State are concerned."

"I never tried to interfere. . ." I began bewilderedly.

"No, Majesty, because you've rarely had the outside world breaking in on you, have you? But the other day, you were listening intently enough."

"I was afraid The One might have one of his attacks."

"You weren't looking at The One," said May brusquely.

* Governor.

"Now for your own sake, Majesty, go on occupying yourself only with your children. If ever such a scene is likely to be repeated, excuse yourself at the beginning, say in a loud voice, 'Such things don't concern me.' Make clear your complete lack of interest. And there is something more, Lady of Grace, touching your. . . security; at present the threat is at a distance, but. . ."

There was a light step on the path outside. Father, looking very splendid, the great vulture-pectoral flashing in the sun, came up to us. "A summons from The One," he said softly to May.

"I was expecting it," May replied unemotionally. There had always been hostility between them, but never so great as now. May turned to me, made as if to take my hand to kiss it. But Father was up the steps, between us. "If only," May said harshly to him, "I could be sure you'd put yourself between her and danger when she is in real need of protection."

"The One is waiting for you!" said Father. "And you know the reason."

May disregarded him, looked past him towards me. "This, I fear, must be my leave-taking, Lady of Grace."

"No!" I said with a passion of distress that bewildered me.

"May Isis protect you," he said very deliberately, giving me a soldier's salute, and not the courtier's prostration, before he turned away.

I stared after the powerful figure, going steadily, irrevocably farther and farther away. Beside me Father talked angrily. I did not hear him. "How bright the sun is," I said mechanically, to explain a hand going up to shield my eyes. But surely I should be feeling only relief — once May had gone, there would be no one left to introduce into Akhnaten's presence any further disturbing element I dreaded because. . .

"How long was he alone with you? *How long*? What did he say?" Father suddenly gripping my wrist — Father's face, close to mine, reminding me — why, reminding me over so many years of the face of the Captain of the Guard at Phaestos, the wrinkled upperlip, the. . .I wrenched my hand free.

"My head aches," I said, hurrying down the steps, "and you should be at the Council too — enjoying yourself!" If my head ached, so, suddenly did my breasts; they were as heavy, as tender as in the days preceding the moon-sickness. But it was too soon for me to be prey to that. In any case, in Amarna one acknowledged only the power of the sun.

I never did see May again. When he was disgraced, he went back to his estate between Memphis and the Delta. A few days after his arrival, he went out wildfowling in the marshes, alone. He did not come home that evening, and when his household took torches and anxiously searched for him, they found him lying face downwards in the mud. Drowned. In very shallow water. In Amarna the courtiers said the unfortunate wretch, unable to endure his disgrace, had committed suicide. May was a resolute man, but it takes an uncommon degree of resolution to keep yourself lying face downwards in shallow muddy water until you are dead.

It was Father who told me what had happened. He came to break the news to me, brutally, the moment he heard it — in the evening. "Did you know his estate?" he said. "We passed it one afternoon sailing upstream when you first came to Egypt — although possibly you were asleep."

But, of course, I had never slept; I had been too afraid of the monsters lurking in the river. "Did they — the creatures of Sebekh — attack him?" I asked, and the horror in my voice could not be mistaken.

"No," he said, "his carcass is still intact. He is still an entire man, if that's what's worrying you!"

I dreamed of the creatures of Sebekh that night. I was drowning in foulness, it was in my mouth and hair and nostrils, and eyes, and before me crouched one of the creatures of Sebekh, one of those bigger monsters kept in a sacred pool and adorned with precious stones.

But I was the victim of more than one kind of recurring nightmare in those days following May's disgrace. In the other dream I was a child again, terrified by the demon that came by night. I was imprisoned in a rocky cave, and, knowing that soon the demon would come, to rend and tear, I tried, weeping, with the weighted feet of nightmare, to escape through a passage so narrow and sloping I bled as I struggled upwards and the demon came in pursuit. In the distance ahead of me I could see light, and as I drew closer I could hear wings beating outside. "You think the fighting hawk will save you?" shrieked the demon, reaching out a claw. "He'll rend at your womb with beak and talons!" And I knew this was the truth, but now I was running swiftly, joyfully, to the pain awaiting me in the sun. But always at the very moment that I came out into the warmth and the light, and the wingbeat grew louder, I awoke. And I wept, saying, "I am so lonely."

Chapter Twelve
Nefertiti

Akhnaten had indeed brought artists and sculptors from Crete and elsewhere to Amarna. He liked talking to them — I say talking to rather than *with* them because he did most of the speaking. He constantly lectured them about the need for Truth in all their work. Truth as opposed to convention. We were to be shown exactly as the Aten had created us.

He invited sculptors to come to the Palace to be instructed by him; I, however, invited another kind of artist to instruct *me*. One day when we were visiting a Cretan sculptor's workshop, a youngish stranger stood bowing in a corner. From his slight build he was scarcely a sculptor. I asked him if he were a poet.

"No," he said, embarrassed, and with an accent I told myself hurriedly I could not identify, "more a stitcher of songs." I then asked him from which Achaean town he came from. He told me, with an odd mixture of deprecation and pride, that his city was not as yet well known. It was called Athens, I would not have heard of it, and he did not even live in Athens itself. He lived outside, in a village called Colonos.

"Colonos!" I said. "My mother's father came from Colonos! And her brothers!" In wild hope I asked him if he had heard of them. He had not. I said with the old hopelessness, "It's a long time — fifteen years — since they left Crete." I told myself that it was absurd that I, the Queen of Egypt, should feel such unhappiness; if I went on talking to this poet — what was his name? Sophronicos, that was it — I was plunging into foolishness, a fathomless marsh of stupidity from which I might never be able to extricate myself.

But I heard my voice asking, "Will you come to me at the Palace — frequently — and talk to me of my grandfather's people?"

May's advice must have been unnecessary I thought to myself. With my husband I talked little. It was not merely that Akhnaten's conversations with me were fewer and shorter, increasingly they lacked depth and content. Yet while our private communication dwindled to extinction like the Nile in mid-summer, he not only demanded that I should appear in public with him even more frequently than before, but during these public appearances, he demonstrated affection for me in a way that made me hot with shame. He began, when we drove about together, or stood, or sat, at public functions to feel and fondle my breasts, his arm flung about my shoulders. I hated it. I suppose his purpose — for a reason I could not understand — was to give the impression that he was still in love with me. He was not. He never had been.

I would often lie awake in the quiet bright stillness of the morning wondering why he wanted our marriage, which lacked so much, to appear so ecstatic. And then with a sigh, I resigned myself to the entry of my attendants — which meant my surrender to the stupefying splendour — above all, the stupefying boredom of Court ritual; first each foot bathed by two noble-women in perfumed water in a bowl of alabaster, rubbed with fragrant oil, while others prepared my bath — the Cretan-style bath I had insisted upon — with sacred blue lotus-blossoms floating on the surface of the water. Obsequious voices asked if Divine Majesty might choose to use her writing palette this day? This was necessary since the very ink I used had to be freshly perfumed each morning, and I was required to say which herbal fragrance I preferred as the tips of those plants I chose must be picked just before the buds opened.

Then the women would put necklaces, bracelets and anklets upon me, an elaborate head-dress, gold, carnelian, lapis-lazuli, place an ostrich-feather fan in my hand — and I myself donned the serene mask that to some extent, I think, concealed the real woman, shivering with nerves, fear and embarrassment. Oh, the emptiness of this existence of endless appearances as Queen Goddess — and really being never anything more than Queen Doll! Yet May had advised me to be nothing more, and he, I knew, had wished me well.

Sophronicos would soon be leaving. I think he was disappointed by what he had found in Egypt. He had come primarily because of legendary Thebes, golden Thebes, Thebes of the Hundred Gates as the Achaeans called it. But Thebes' grandeur had departed, and Amarna, I suspected, was too new, too raw, to catch at his poet's imagination. He said, however, that he would return — but first he wanted to visit the famous cities of Syria before they were swallowed up by war.

Seized by a sudden thought, I said to him, "I want you to do something for me. When you visit the coastal cities of Asia, look among the Achaean and Cretan communities there for someone called. . ."

I was nearly twenty-three and very childish.

From time to time Akhnaten's two brothers had sailed down from Thebes to visit us, yet their mother had never come to Amarna. But then, in the twelfth year of our marriage, she came. She would stay, said Akhnaten, for good. Once the palace being built for her was complete, she would come.

I tried to reason myself out of the intense depression, almost dread, which this news gave me. I had some success by day, none by night. I dreamed once that I was being driven by Akhnaten to view the palace being built for his mother. I wept to see the swift progress. "Why are you crying?" he asked angrily. "You've never cried before!"

"They are building my tomb," I said.

In reality he himself went many times to see the progress being made, but the speed with which the building was erected seemed to give him no pleasure. He would drive there to stand unblinking, the bright rays of his god streaming mercilessly, vertically down on his head, and he would come back, his eyes fevered, staring, his shoulders drooping. Then there was a delay. Because of the desire for haste, the builders had been told to use the nearest stone supply, but the limestone from the cliffs that surrounded the city was of such poor quality, porous, crumbling easily, that the use of this had to be abandoned, and Tiy's Palace, like the other buildings of Amarna, had to be made with mud bricks faced with stone.

I thought the delay would anger Akhnaten but his reaction was not rage, even though I could not decide precisely what it might be. Except that there was a wildness of desperation about it, and that he suddenly resumed coming to my bed, night after night — and except for the first night of all, night after night, whatever he sought, I failed to give him. I was all tense flesh, tense muscle, my bleakness of despair afterwards worse than ever, despair for him too, for after the first night he could no longer penetrate me, although he tried — Goddess, he tried! More than ever before I was not enough of a woman for him; I was only a husk of a woman, as our marriage was only a husk of a marriage. I said to him, despairingly, "You must tell me what I do that's wrong." He began to try to tell me something, but it was so wild and incoherent and desperate that all it amounted to was that *she* had always been so excited, whereas I — and then he began weeping, at intervals reproaching me bitterly because I never wept. And there was enough to weep for. For him and myself. Then he would seize me and in silence now would inflict on me moments of clumsy nightmare, defilement of the flesh, worse even than the wild thrusting that had once left me bleeding night after night.

Yet on the first night he had returned to my bed, he had driven deep enough. I found I was pregnant again. But before I could be sure of this, Tiy had come to Thebes and after this Akhnaten never came to me again.

Just about the time that I realised I might be pregnant, Meketaten, as the Egyptians put it, became a woman. I looked at the childish face, and was suddenly almost sick with fear. And it was the first time that this had happened to one of my daughters. Meritaten's moon-courses had not begun, although she was older than Meketaten.

Akhnaten, of course, had to be told. I asked him placatingly — Oh, Mother-Goddess, how placatingly! — if, although I knew the Egyptian custom was otherwise, any marriage for her might be delayed until she was at least fourteen years old. He said I should not forget that she was royal. His heresy extended to only a few royal practices.

I told myself that whoever married her would find it easy to be kind to her. She was such a gentle thing whose only desire was to please.

And then Tiy arrived.

She had not changed since I had last seen her; the eyes were the same, the lips. She wore vivid yellow, and more jewellery and regalia than I had ever seen carried on one woman's person. We entertained her at dinner on the day of her arrival; a simple family meal, said Akhnaten, his mother, ourselves and our two elder daughters. So I wore no jewellery, had my hair up under a simple cap, with only the gold cobra at the front to show that I was wife of the Pharaoh. Akhnaten himself wore the simplest of insignia. But Tiy wore the double plumes of empire and the horned disc of sovereignty.

The eating arrangement ordered by Akhnaten was unconventional. He sat facing his mother; I, not beside him, but behind him, almost as if he were trying to screen me from her. Well, I was glad of the protection, defence, however unconscious. She had given me a hard, inimical look at our first greeting, had begun, "Smenkhare told me. . ." and then lapsed into sullen uncommunicativeness. If she had changed little between mid forties and early fifties, I suppose the change in me, from fifteen to twenty-three, was necessarily more marked. She did not like what she saw, and made her dislike obvious. Even the children could sense it — at least one of them could. While Meritaten ate stolidly, Meketaten got up and came to stand beside me, her arm about my waist, her head on my shoulder. She stared at her grandmother with wide, frightened eyes. Tiy stared implacably back. Akhnaten made stilted conversation. Typically, he had summoned artists to immortalise the scene and when they had gone, mother and son began to discuss matters of state. I contributed nothing, talking in a low voice to Meketaten, but I could not help hearing what Tiy said in her harsh voice. The present Comander-in-Chief was a sick man. A replacement should be made. "Who?" asked Akhnaten, without much interest.

"Mother," whispered Meketaten, her soft lips close to my cheek, "is she coming to live here for ever and ever?"

". . .your father used to call him his young Memphis bull. . ." Tiy was saying.

"Why has she come now, Mother?"

". . .Well, no doubt he was insolent, but how much of what he said was put into his mouth by the dead brute May?" Tiy's face was very animated. "And better to have him here, under your eye, for months on end, than to leave him up on the frontier. From all accounts he's repeatedly disobeyed orders. Have him here. Clip his wings."

"How can you clip the wings of a bull?" whispered Meketaten (but not quietly enough, for Tiy's angry stare was on her).

It was the most wretched of my pregnancies. In the last months Tiy had the three older children to stay with her at her palace, less, I thought, because she wanted their companionship than because she wanted to deprive me of it. Akhnaten spent a great deal of time there too.

I was very ill before the baby was born. Father brought Mutnedjmet to the Palace. She had been married twice now, to elderly noblemen who had died not long afterwards. Both marriages had been childless. She said she longed to be with my younger children, since I was too ill to be with them much. At times I could read her mind with great accuracy; she was thinking, covertly scrutinising my sickly appearance, that if I died in childbirth, she might marry Akhnaten after all.

But I did not die in childbirth, although I nearly did. And the child was another weakly daughter. She was named Setepenre. When Akhnaten came to visit me, his first words concerned neither her nor me. Meritaten, he said, would marry Smenkhare.

"Your mother wants it," I said.

"So do I. After all, she is the heiress."

"Would it have made any difference if this new baby had

been a son?''

He said nothing.

''I asked, ''Don't you want to see her?''

He took her awkwardly, briefly. There had been a time when he had ordered sculptors to show him dandling Meketaten on his knee, caressing her. But no longer.

It was some weeks before the doctors said I was well enough for the other children to come back to me. Meritaten was triumphant; even to live in the same building as the handsome Smenkhare had been bliss for her. But Mekataten looked dreadful. Tiy had been harsh with her, I thought. Well, she should see how her mother rejoiced to have her home. I said I should give a little feast for them. Each child had beside her chair her own individual little table piled high with the delicacies I knew were her favourites, quails, roast goose, cucumbers, melons, figs. I even ordered a little, a very little, of their father's best wine, had the wine jars set on stands and decorated with wet garlands of lotus to keep the wine cool, just as if this were an adult party.

Meketaten still looked unwell. She said the smell of the flowers made her feel sick. I had Setepenre in my arms; I had thought Meketaten might like to play with the new baby, as she had loved playing with Nofret. But when I asked her if she would like to take her sister in her arms, she winced. ''No, I'm clumsy, I might drop her.''

''She keeps droppings things all the time these days,'' said Ankhesenpaaten, greedily eating roast goose.

Nofret at least came to play with her sister. ''Is she like me, mother? Isn't she little? Look, she's waking up.''

But she was not. The irritability, the restlessness, the twitching of the eyelids and hands presaged what I had always dreaded in my children. The eyes were partly open, but only the whites showed, and now the twitchings had spread to the whole body. The baby face grimaced, the neck was thrown back, the tiny fists clenched.

The attack went on for almost half an hour; then she lapsed into a stupor. At some point I was dimly aware of commotion in a far corner of the room, of voices saying Meketaten had fainted. ''She's feeling sick again,'' came Ankhesenpaaten's shrill voice. ''She's always feeling sick these days.'' My poor Meketaten, I thought, the most sensitive of them all — why hadn't people taken the children away the moment I ordered it? The sight of the baby in convulsions. . . And I thought I was angry then!

A few hours later, when Setepenre had recovered — temporarily — I was able to concentrate on Meketaten again. My first instinct was to go to her at once, but then I hesitated. I was worn out physically – and looked it. Better for her not to see me like this. And first, too, I must rid my eyes of the anxiety that would haunt me so long as Setepenre lived. So I bathed and changed my dress,and had a cup filled with the wine from the ill-fated feast – the lotus garlands had all withered now I noticed – and, as I began to sip it, I sent for Pentu, whom I had told to go to Meketaten once the danger to Setepenre had passed.

I looked at him earnestly when he came in, for I was anxious and frightened about Meketaten. "How is my daughter?" I asked quickly.

He said she had recovered from the faint.

"But what caused the faint?" I asked. "Was it. . .was it some inherited weakness?"

He shook his head. He was looking at me intently. There was no pity in his look, only a kind of curiosity.

"She is growing fast," I told myself, choking down the wine. "That's what it is." I finished drinking, and the moment I put the cup down, Pentu told me that Meketaten was pregnant.

I stared at him. "You're insane. She's only a child herself. Pregnant? By whom? Who would dare? The One's daughter. . ." And then I found that I was repeating the last three words and fighting down nausea and faintness as if I, too, were in Meketaten's state, my darling Meketaten, The One's daughter.

It had happened before, but this was my Meketaten.

In a toneless voice I told Pentu to go. I know I sat for a time with my hands covering my face, but have no idea how long. I know that as I sat there I trembled with cold, that I kept telling myself to think what I must do for Meketaten, but I could not think, the cold that shook my body seemed to have crept into my brain, numbing it. Almost I could think that my heart had ceased to beat. I found the tears were trickling through my fingers. I was weeping, I who never wept. I must not let the others see me like this, or even hear my sobs. And I must find the strength now to comfort my daughter, to sustain her in the months that lay ahead of us.

I bathed my eyes and made my way to her room. I thanked whatever gods there were – if indeed there were any – for the practice I had had in drawing the mask of aloof indifference over my face. I did not think anyone noticed how, as I came to the door, I halted momentarily, hand against the lintel, summoning up every grain of courage and strength there was in me so that I might comfort her.

"I said I didn't want it to happen, Mother, because I thought it would grieve you, but they said a mother didn't matter, all that did was that I was daughter of a King, and this was what happened to the daughter of a King."

Tiy, I knew, lay in bed late every morning. So I rose early and intercepted Akhnaten alone, as he contemplated — in his proprietorial way — the rising of the sun, the first stirrings of the birds. He listened unmoved to my frantic outcry. These things were permissible to a King.

"Years ago," I whispered, "you were so delighted with the statue showing you embracing her as a child. Wouldn't it be even more delightful now to have a statue carved showing you. . . I can't even say it!"

He repeated that such things were permissible to a King. He continued that I must accept this. As my predecessors had done.

"You mean my betters," I said. "*She* put the idea into your mind, didn't she? To hurt me."

He denied this angrily.

"You are blind, blind!" I cried. But the cold, deadly hatred that almost choked me was not directed at him. One day, I prayed, I should be able to hurt Tiy as she had hurt me.

All my old horror of Egyptian customs revived. Sophronicos had gone — and when I remembered the errand with which I had entrusted him, my flesh crawled — but there were other Achaeans and Cretans who would see incest as incest whoever the participants might be. When I was not with Meketaten, I would go to their workshops, and sit watching them, never saying much — what was there to say? — but feeling comfort merely in hearing the unEgyptian voices.

But most of the time I spent with Meketaten. If it may seem surprising that I was allowed to be so much with her, a grotesque kind of treaty had been made. At some point in the dawn interview with Akhnaten, I had cried out that I would never appear with him in public again. This had made no impression on him at the time, but a few days later, so I gathered, Mahu, the Chief of Police, in an audience had asked innocently enough when the people would be able to see me once more at the great ceremonies. "They look for her Majesty eagerly. . ." Apparently the need for a facade of a happy marriage still remained. So I drove my bargain. I reappeared in public, I would sit in our apartments with him and the children when audiences were granted — and I would look after Meketaten.

But with all the love in the world even I, her mother, could not look after her enough. She had conceived about three months before I learned of her condition; hysteria threatened to possess me when I reflected that at one point she and I had been pregnant at the same time, I was to have her for six months more before she gave birth to a still-born child and died herself.

Death was a fact that Akhnaten for years had refused to recognise. Now his own daughter was dead — and his wife knelt with the dark head in her arms and looked at him accusingly and said, "You have done this thing." I don't know whether he remembered this. He ordered artists to portray a very different scene — himself tenderly leading me from the death chamber while I rent the air with my cries.

Meketaten's body, or what the embalmers left of it, was buried in the tomb Akhnaten had had built for himself, and me, and our children. You reach it by penetrating a desolate, rocky ravine which opens up the great line of cliffs to the east of Amarna. The building of the tomb was not complete when Meketaten was buried there, but Akhnaten's own sarcophagus had been installed, pink granite, with figures of myself at the four corners, instead of the conventional guardian goddesses.

I wished they had put Meketaten there so that my image, at least, might continue to watch over her.

Chapter Thirteen
Staphylos

I had always intended that my first brief excursion to Egypt should be my last. Further visits held no prospect of advantage to me, and I had thought that the payment I received from the child's step-grandmother seemed to offer security for life. Moralists would rejoice to know that this was an illusion. For the coastal strip of Syria, which had offered a haven to the refugees from Crete a generation before, was now producing its own pathetic streams of the wretched dispossessed. The Egyptian Empire — rather the Egyptian peace — was falling apart like a piece of unbaked clay. The Hittites were on the move in the north, wandering tribes, the Hebrews, in the south. In comparison with these two collections of savages, the Achaeans who had taken over Crete seemed the acme of civilization and decency. And what did Egypt do? One cannot accuse her of doing too little too late. She did nothing at all. The pity was that, at the beginning of the wretched business, not much would have been needed. No one was required to emulate the achievements of the great soldier-Pharaohs of the dynasty — *they* had done their work so well that the mere appearance of an Egyptian Army with a figurehead Pharaoh would have made all the difference. But the army never came, Pharaoh never came — Pharaoh instead sent vast quantities of gold to uncertain allies (with predictable consequences) and absorbed himself with passionate frenzy in the religious revolution he was foisting on an unwilling country.

Ascalon was as yet not threatened directly; the various enemies of Egypt were concentrating their efforts against Byblos to the north. Byblos held out staunchly, but there is a limit to human courage and endurance. Everyone knew that without help from Egypt, Byblos would eventually go. And once Byblos had gone. . .

It behoved any sensible man to take stock of the situation.

The question was where to go.

The Achaeans on the mainland, I had heard, were even more narrowly martial in their outlook than their relatives who had gone to crete. True, it seemed there were exceptions. One day a wandering rhapsodist/minstrel/bard — I forget what he termed himself — sought me out. His name was Sophronicos. He came from a tiny stagnant backwater of a place I had never heard of, but for all that seemed reasonably civilized.

Then one day, just before he was leaving Ascalon, he said, "Why don't you come back with me to Egypt?"

I shrugged. I could not very well explain to him that because of a seven year old child, who might very well be dead by this time, for years I had tried to forget that Egypt existed. Sophronicos began to speak animatedly. Amenho — no, Akhnaten he called himself nowadays, of course, might seem to us poor despairing wretches in Syria a bad Pharaoh, the priests of Amen might detest him, but he was generosity itself to painters and sculptors — in his new capital the houses and studios allocated to them stood in the finest quarters and so on. I listened with growing interest. It seemed as if Akhnaten were carrying out an artistic as well as a religious revolution. Hitherto, Egyptian art had been all uniformity, monotony, strictly controlled by the priesthood. An artist was little more than a copyist of the standard models.

But now, according to Sophronicos, matters were different. So I fell in with his proposal; I too would go to Amarna.

But long before I reached there, I had begun to regret my decision. Because, I asked myself, what did I gain by a (still hypothetical) freedom from control if the people I was required to carve roused such little enthusiasm in me? I refer, of course, to the women of Egypt. The men are not a bad-looking lot, tallish — thought not usually as tall as Achaeans — with good, broad shoulders, flat bellies, slim hips, well developed limbs. I saw at least two army officers I should dearly have loved as models — but they, alas, possessing what might be called a shrinking frontier obsession, had no use for Amarna and anyone who chose to live there.

But the women!

And, of course, I preferred women as my subjects. Only a woman's body offers the real challenge, followed, with any luck, by the real satisfaction of making hard stone seem soft, the sweeping curve of the hip, the line of the thigh, the near-impossibility of showing in stone the shadows on the flesh.

I, of course, had been nurtured on a dream. You know my dream; the priestesses of Crete, the white skin, the tiny waist, the curving hips, the long, loose dark hair with a stray lock touching caressingly the round firm breasts. And the face above matching the body in delicacy, allure. . .

Well, here I was surrounded by another breed of woman. Broad shoulders, thick ankles, flat chests, large hands, clumsy feet, features as roughly hewn as their husband's, but lacking the expression you saw with a man. Lifeless, vacant, sulky. Large noses. A tendency to receding chins.

Sophronicos watched my growing depression with something one might almost construe as amusement. He said there were occasional variants, reminding me that the foreign conquests of Pharaoh's ancestors had meant some leavening of the uncommonly heavy female dough. We were standing in Memphis in a deserted temple of Amen containing sculptures of Pharaoh's mother and wife installed before the religious revolution. The mother was all thick lips and udders rather than breasts. The profile of the wife, God help her, duplicated that of Pharaoh himself. They looked a pair of physically degenerate twins. I said morosely I wished I'd stayed away until the foreign yeast had made the dough considerably lighter.

But I was not so self-centred as to be obsessed solely by my own professional problems. Or perhaps the growing murmur of discontent only added another anxiety. To be — possibly — cosseted by Pharaoh at Amarna might be all very well as short-term policy, but if the country turned against Pharaoh, better for me if I had never come.

Because the country was beginning to seethe with unrest. Gently, almost imperceptibly at present, but who knew when it would all boil over? Sophronicos wasn't practical in these matters. As we approached Amarna, his face was beginning to assume an expression I can only describe as bedazzled. Perhaps his muse was taking possession; I could hardly get a word out of him. So I began to talk to other travellers; you were constantly coming up against Cretan or even Achaean immigrants. And what they said didn't make for comfortable hearing. The old capital, Thebes, was deserted now. The quays were empty — all trade, and what tribute still came to Pharaoh went to Amarna. There were tens of thousands workless, facing starvation. In the great temples weeds grew in the warm pink stone court-yards, dogs scavenged. And if you travelled in the villages, there were swarms of dispossessed priests on the move. I remember a youngish Cretan trader saying in a low voice as the brown water surged past, "Egyptians may be arrogant to foreigners, but normally they're the easiest people in the world to govern. But if they're afraid of Pharaoh, they're equally afraid of their priests. If the river doesn't flood this year. . .''

I said with feeling, ''I begin to wonder what I've let myself in for.''

He and his elderly companion looked at me and laughed. Then the older man said, ''Do what we're doing. Make what you can in double quick time, then get out!''

You may judge, therefore, that the sight of Amarna next morning did not fill me with any joyous anticipation. I must say I found myself giving a gasp of unwilling admiration at the size of the undertaking. Everywhere you saw palaces, temples, mansions, pink and white buildings, the green of gardens. How much soil, how much water had been brought here to make the desert bloom?

To a god-king all was possible. You could construct those incredible tombs at Memphis, or build a new city. But while you could direct the people's hands, could you direct their hearts?

Moralising thus, I went ashore.

I had not been so naive as to come to Amarna not knowing whether I should find employment there; before leaving Ascalon I had gone to the local Egyptian military governor for a letter of commendation. He was pleased to oblige; I had carved a statue of his wife (a Syrian, thank God) that had delighted him. I had sent these letters ahead while we spent a few days in Memphis, and had received a reply from no less a person than the master-sculptor Tuthmosis welcoming me cordially. There was a groom with a chariot waiting for me — and Sophronicos had been quite right in what he had told me. The house and studio provided for me were luxurious beyond my dreams.

Luxury and splendour, in fact, seemed the only fit words to describe Amarna, at first. After you had lived there even only a short time, you realised how essentially shoddy it all was — not surprising, when you consider the frantic haste with which it was put up. If you took a good look at what appeared to be limestone, you would find it was mud-brick whitewashed to look like stone. Masonry was rubble with a stone facing.

It was, in fact, all facade.

And you had a shrewd idea that the facade was not limited to the buildings. Nearly every face among the courtiers and officials was false.

But Pharaoh, convinced that all was well in his wonder-city, led a happy, carefree life, from all accounts.

I was taken to a studio and shown a piece of work being done for Mahu, the Chief of Police — there was the Pharaoh, in his chariot with his wife and child, masterfully controlling his horses with one hand, while fondling, remarkably intimately, the wife who so strongly resembled him. The ease with which he controlled the beasts was all the more remarkable since his child was prodding the nearest rump with a goad.

The elderly artist stood beside me, his face impassive as I praised the work. Later I said to Phereclos, the Achaean who had taken me to the studio, that this particular craftsman had seemed almost sullen. "Oh, take no notice of him," was the reply. "He's of the old school. When you've time to study his work, you'll find there are some of the new standards to which he won't conform."

And next day, Phereclos continued, I might see for myself the physical embodiment of Aten; some kind of ceremony — what precisely I could not gather — was to take place outside the great entrance pavilion of Maru-Aten, the royal pleasure palace to the south of the city. At some point after that, I would no doubt be summoned to meet Pharaoh himself.

Yet I was late joining the crowd outside the pavilion. I had been so fascinated by this extraordinary creation of a city mushrooming up as if by magic from six and a half miles of desert, that it was only when I heard a roar of voices in the distance that I realised the royal procession had started. Sophronicos had vanished early that morning. He mooned, yet was exalted. I concluded his muse had him by the throat.

I set off at a run, thanking my own gods for the fact that outside Egypt it was winter, and even in Egypt the heat was less blistering than usual.

There was the crowd. . .the personal bodyguards of Pharaoh, all Nubians. And, on a raised dais, God-King himself — scrawny-chested, swollen bellied and thighed. My heart sank. To hack stone into *his* likeness. . . He moved slightly, and just beyond him I saw what made my heart sink even further. Beyond him stood so consummate a carving of a woman that I thought, 'There's no place for me here! With that I could never compete.' As the gods may judge me, when I first set eyes on the Queen of Egypt, I did not think her a living woman at all.

You may think that even the mild Egyptian winter sun had crazed my brain, but my error was not as insane as it may seem. Outside Egypt it had been difficult to work out Pharaoh's religious beliefs; I knew the Egyptians had a habit of depicting their gods with animal heads, that, for example (from a visit to the Egyptian temple in Ascalon) their love-goddess had the head of a cow. So my immediate reaction now was to be pleased — for aesthetic reasons — that Akhnaten had broken with tradition so that this statue of the love-goddess standing beyond him had a human head. Obviously the Goddess of love, although,

I thought, Pharaoh had let tradition be so far observed as to allow the goddess to be shown as royalty — carrying on that head enough weight of gold, lapis-lazuli and cornelian to break the average neck, but wearing very little on the body, a finely pleated, almost transparent dress that left the breasts bare.

Obviously the statue of a goddess because of the very lightness of the skin, the pale colour making it stand out against the background of Egyptians and Nubians like ivory against bronze or ebony.

Or was it a statue of alabaster?

Another reason why I was so sure I was looking at a statue was the fact that, except for the eyes (and God knows they had little need of it) the face was delicately tinted rather than painted as Egyptian women paint their faces. The lips were deeply red, but not garishly so. Whoever carved this must have gone overseas for his model. Yet the sculptor, despite his skill, had been unable to bring the statue to life. Or was it supposed to be that of the goddess in a trance, unawakened, still dreaming?

A long slim neck and throat. Fragile shoulders with the sheen of pearls — whatever medium the sculptor had chosen, the whole statue had that pearly sheen, the glimmering translucence of the interior of a rare shell. Exquisite arms, hanging straight at the sides, ending in small delicate hands. Graceful slender legs, ending in small, most beautiful feet, one with an anklet of malachite set in lapis-lazuli, thrust a little before the other. Gently curving thighs and hips, so gently curved, in fact, that from the small, shapely feet to the stem-like waist, one saw the virginal slenderness of a young palm tree. But between the slender waist and the slim neck. . .

I am a sculptor. I should regard women's bodies as mere stock-in-trade, view the statue of a beautiful woman with no more passionate interest than, say, a fruitseller views a competitor's produce. At this point Pharaoh, as if following my line of thought, began to embrace the statue. When he pressed his fingers, hard, about one of those — let me try to be dispassionate — possibly slightly over-heavy spheres, the statue blushed!

It was a startlingly beautiful blush, storming up from the breasts, covering her shoulders, streaming over the face although the face itself remained absolutely expressionless, just as the body remained motionless.

So not a statue.

The queen?

The queen who, on the carvings I had seen, looked like the twin of her husband?

But after this, purely masculine reactions disrupted thought.

She seemed to play tricks with your eyes. As she stood motionless, as she was to go on standing motionless for hours, in that hot windless Egyptian air, you had the impression of movement, an invisible breeze pressing her dress against her. Was it the right foot thrust forward that gave you the idea? She stood absolutely still, her face a beautiful passive mask, but for the great shining dark eyes, you would think her asleep. You had the almost frightening feeling that here, too, you were encountering another facade in Amarna, but there would be no rubbie or mud-brick behind this facade — if you could penetrate beyond it.

And in my mind, two thoughts, connected, like little intertwined writhing snakes. Why had I told myself that the sculptor must have gone overseas for his model?

Because I had believed he had taken as that model not a living woman but a statuette, one of the dead priestesses of Cete.

And why was it suddenly so alarming to me that she had blushed? Because of fools like damned Sophronicos, who, like all other Achaean minstrels, invariably used certain stock adjectives. The dawn for them is always blushing. The dawn. *Eos*. . .

Reluctantly I had to accept the inexorable fact. Before me, queen-goddess of Egypt, stood Eos, the child who seventeen years before had looked on me as her betrayer.

I have often thought since, that I was a lunatic not to have got out of Amarna then and there. Staphylos the man did indeed think of running — as soon as possible. It was that fool Staphylos, the aspiring sculptor, who decided to stay.

My first thought had been to slip away that night. But I must not rouse suspicion — I must go on touring the workshops of other artists in the company of Phereclos, as cynical as only a rootless man can be. He echoed what the merchants had said coming up-river — it couldn't last. But *while* it lasted, life was pleasant enough — with the exception of a few snags he would not tell me about, but which he said, ominously, would become clear enough in a day or two. Being resolved not to be in Amarna when the day or two had elapsed, this did not bother me greatly.

It was Phereclos who, after some prompting, took me back to the studio of the elderly sculptor who had made King and Queen almost indistinguishable figures. Once our host had ushered us into the studio, and retired grumpily, I stared again in some stupefaction. At my side, Phereclos, correctly interpreting my expression, grinned. "I told you — he's one of the old school," he said in a low voice. "The convention was that Pharaoh's wife must always look like Pharaoh. Well, now that you've seen her in one of her rare public appearances. . ."

We looked at each other.

"Hasn't *anyone* shown her as she is?" I stammered.

He grimaced. "They've tried. But all they produce are — masks. I don't mean dead, I mean *frozen*. 'No more lifeless formalized art!' Pharaoh decrees, and all the statues of his wife show — what? Smooth, polished skin, and exquisite bone structure, but no hint of movement, feeling, blood that courses." He shrugged and turned away. "Before we go, we had better express our thanks to our host. Briefly. A few years ago he married a young wife, and still resents any intrusions in the evenings."

As we crossed the courtyard to the old man's house, I was given proof of his dedication to marital duties — a small child running unsteadily across our path, so unsteadily that he tripped, fell, yelled. A nursemaid appeared, picked him up, carried him away. "Wait!" Phereclos called after her. "He's forgotten his toy!" but the child was shrieking so loudly she did not hear him. Phereclos went across and bent to pick up the play-thing, but, seeing it more closely, he straightened more sharply and let the thing lie. Intrigued, I too went across, and, in my turn, bent, then jerked up. The "toy" was a model chariot being driven — and driven badly — by an ape. An ape-child prodded the rumps of the horses. And the receding forehead of the charioteer was like the Pharaoh's and the melancholy face of the ape-child was the face of the eldest daughter I had seen standing behind her mother that morning (a regrettable, spindle-limbed, testimony to her mother's faithfulness to her husband).

"A toy?" I asked after a moment.

"Not designedly," Phereclos said.

"You've seen others?"

He nodded. "Several. Sometimes with variations. But always the apes — ugly, clumsy, ludicrous."

"Who's making them?" I asked. "This fellow here."

"I don't know. More than one person, I'd say, judging by the numbers produced. Come on, let's get out of here. Come back to my house."

This is where I should have made my excuses and scurried off to make preparations to get out of Amarna, out of Egypt in double-quick time. But I went with him. Partly, I suppose, because of the Cretan inquisitiveness that other races find so discerning. And also becuse of that damned professional ambition of mine. Others had tried to portray her. They couldn't. The beautiful mask. They couldn't even be sure there was anything behind it. But I knew that once, at least, there had been an ardent child — even if I couldn't show the woman she was not,

I could show the woman, whom but for me, she might have been. Outwardly politely enquiring as I walked beside Phereclos to his house, inwardly I boiled with — well, no more than lust, I supposed. Lust to show in stone the kind of woman she really was.

Years before she had begged me to keep her with me. Well, I should pay for that refusal for many years to come.

We sat in the garden of Phereclos' house, a jug of wine between us. It was almost dark now. Aten had vanished over the rim of the horizon. Phereclos said, "Don't expect variety in your work. All that you'll be expected to portray is the Pharaoh, whose mental quirks are matched only by his physical oddities, his wife, who has a facial bone structure equalled in magnificence only by the fleshy shapes of. . ."

"I know." The words jerked out of me.

From his voice he was grinning. "You too! We're all a bit obssessed by them — the foreigners, at least. But if superbly ornamental, they've scarcely proved useful. As any old Egyptian hag will wag her head and tell you, she couldn't feed her children. And of those, poor little bitches, all that needs to be said is that the model we saw tonight would not seem so shocking were there not so much truth in the caricature."

"About that model," I said slowly. "I noticed that only the father and child were caricatured there, not the mother."

"The Beautiful One is never caricatured. By the way, when we foreigners talk of her, for prudence sake, we call her *Despoina*. The Lady. And when we have to talk of him, we use a slang term. The Egyptians think we're talking of a fellow-barbarian, of course. We simply refer to Old Swollen-legs."

"I'll remember that." Old Swollen-Legs — in Achaean, Oedipos.

Next day Tuthmosis himself, a stocky, dark-skinned man, appeared at my house. He had spoken of me to Pharaoh and had been ordered to take me to the palace that afternoon.

The royal pair sat facing each other, he on a chair, she on a cushion on the floor. The two elder daughters stood between them, the two younger played on the floor, the baby sat on her mother's lap. All, of course, carefully posed, for the sun fell about them, struck across the floor.

"A charming scene," Tuthmosis was to say to me afterwards. I could not agree, although I had the sense to keep my mouth shut.

No doubt it was the influence of that damned model chariot, but the two children, playing on the floor in the cruelly bright rays of the sun, with their dark skins and receding foreheads had the appearance of two little apes. And their faces were not the faces of children at play – there was a look of animal melancholy about them, each mouth sagged at the corners, with two little lines running down. So, if it came to that, did their eldest sister's and baby's. The only child who escaped that old, melancholic look was the child Ankesenpaaten. She, I was told later, physically took after her grandmother Tiy – and no look of melancholy was ever discernible about Tiy!

The children were horrifying creatures. Their shaven heads, whose dreadfully elongated heads, their dark, skinny little bodies, with the swollen bellies one usually associates with starvation – the scrawny little necks seemed too weak to support those great heads, additionally weighed down by huge gold tasselled ear-rings that not only dragged down the ears out of all shape, but emphasised the dreadful disproportion of head, neck, trunk. The pathetic little brood were entirely their father's daughters, weak, sickly, deformed. All they lacked of him – so far – was the look of religious fanaticism that sharpened his narrow face all the more.

I shall not describe the appearance of Pharaoh at close quarters. I imagine it must have been a shock to any conservatively minded Egyptian being summoned before his sovereign, and finding that sovereign wearing a crown and little else. To an artist with some respect for beauty, the shock, in its way, was greater. And I shall not describe our conversation, consisting as it did largely of a monologue on Pharaoh's part on how I should best pursue my own trade.

Neither shall I describe the appearance of Pharaoh's wife except to say that she, at least, wore a flimsy dress, but no crown; instead she had her hair up under a kind of cap. And if his physical oddness seen at close quarters was, to say the least, disconcerting, so was her physical perfection. And if I do not describe our conversation it was because we had none. She acknowledged our ritual prostrations with a slight inclination of the head, but otherwise, except for an occasional, flickering sideways glance beneath the long dark fringes of her lashes, seemed absorbed in her children, particularly the wizened little thing that clutched with dark, near-skeletal hands at those superb pearly melon shapes that had never given her suck.

But did she recognise me?

Her voice when she spoke to the children, was low, tentative, almost shy, so soft that the words seemed to float on air.

Pharaoh's monologue to me was twice interrupted by visitors whom a less egotistic man would never have wanted alongside him in that cruelly bright sunshine. The new Commander-in-

Chief, General Horemheb, of quite enormous presence, the most formidable of men, with that kind of physical magnificence about him that the passage of time only enhances. How often I was to see those dark, untamed features, far removed from the crowd of courtiers above whom he towered, emanating hostility to all those who contributed to the butterfly world of Amarna.

Now, face taut, eyes watchful, Horemheb presented a report in a voice as deep as his chest. He realised he said, that he was offending against protocol, such reports should only come through the Foreign Minister, but his friend (the garrison commander of some obscure outpost) was desperate. The report was received querulously. Soldiers always liked to depict themselves as surrounded by seas of hostility. In any case, letters had been sent to the rulers Horemheb's friend complained about. "When an Asiatic knows that all he'll get is a polite note he'll go on doing as he chooses," said Horemheb in his oddly impersonal way. He kissed the ground before the God-King, and retreated without speaking another word. Had I been the God-King, to have such menacing virility retiring in sullen silence, I should find distinctly alarming. But Pharaoh, as the martial figure strode away, felt only relief that the unwelcome interruption to the important business of the day — his laying down of the laws of sculpture to me — had ended. As he had not bothered to conceal this feeling from Horemheb, the one look that most grimly authoritative of men cast in my direction had been one of ferocious hostility.

And Pharaoh's Queen? Had she never wondered what it would be like to be clasped in those almost excessively muscular arms? She seemed entirely absorbed in play with her sickly baby who, much to my private relief, had now given up tugging at her mother's breasts, and was tugging instead at her cap. When Horemheb was reading his friend's letter, the child actually succeeded in knocking the cap askew. A great wealth of dark curling hair tumbled down about the smooth pale shoulders. At that Horemheb gave his sovereign lady one look beneath his lowered lids, a look of not very well concealed, arrogant, contemptuous dislike which she was conscious of. She kept her own shadowed eyes lowered still; but for the even surge of her breasts, the little pulse beating in her throat, she might have been a statue, but — Ah, there was the betraying blush again! She was dreadfully embarrassed.

I thought — with a spurt of inward laughter — "Europa and her bull! Europa and her bull!"

But Pharaoh's wife could scarcely disregard the other visitor —

Pharaoh's own brother, Prince Smenkhare, nineteenish, beautiful, graceful, elegant, altogether the son of Amenhotep the Magnificent. And he knew he was beautiful and graceful and elegant! He carried a finely carved staff with him, and stood leaning negligently upon it. The little breeze that comes with the early evening fluttered his snowy robes. Meritaten, his eldest, ugliest niece, gazed at him in adoration. His brother addressed him half in irritation, half in affection. (Smenkhare, one gathered, did not take religion seriously enough; Phereclos told me later he devoted all his not inconsiderable energy to the pursuit of women.) Now here was another model I should like to have. A Hermes in bronze. But how to convey that glow of excitement? He didn't look at his sister-in-law from under lowered lids; he gazed at her boldly, with appreciation. She sat there in all that freshness of young motherhood, seemingly as unaware of this as she had been only too aware of Horemheb's hard hostile stare.

Smenkhare left, to the accompaniment of a wail of anguish from his eldest niece. She really howled — and looked quite appallingly ugly with her normally drooping mouth open in a square. Eventually the howls became articulate. "When can we be married?"

"Soon, soon," said her father hastily — obviously this was no new question. How old was she? Eleven? Twelve? But Egyptian girls mature early. And the superb Smenkhare? Would he have appreciated the, "Soon, soon?" I doubted it.

Meanwhile, Tuthmosis and I were being hustled off by the Pharaoh to a room in the same south-east block of the palace where he, himself, dabbled in painting. Theoretically speaking, a royal interest in art should, for an artist, be the most gratifying thing in the world. But it has drawbacks — my God, it has drawbacks! There is the tendency in the kingly amateur to impose his whims (thinly veiled as suggestions) on his professional employees.

At last we were graciously dismissed; servants began to usher us out. But an old woman intercepted us. The Queen wished to see me. "She will speak to you about your assignment with her," said Tuthmosis. He was only too eager to get out of the palace; Pharaoh's lecture on art he must have heard at least a dozen times, and he wanted to escape in case he was recalled for still another repetition.

So almost sick with apprehension — and anticipation — I followed the hag to a pavilion — the Queen's own pavilion, I was to discover — with a balustrade and columns ornamented with vines and convolvulus.

She stood quite alone there. She had put up her hair; her small head, as always, seemed to be tilted backward on the arched ivory throat, as if pulled by the dark perfumed weight. This last of the royal priestesses of Crete, steeped — there is no other word for it — in the allure of generations, of a beauty great enough to stop the heart. And the wave of unconscious sensuousness that flowed from her!

She addressed me in her mother's tongue, foreign-accented now, delicate, lilting. No nervousness now, as in the presence of the lowering Commander-in-Chief. "You need have no fear. I sent for you in a spirit of revenge, but not the kind of revenge that might occur to you."

I gazed at her blankly. "You sent for me? But I came because Sophronicos suggested it."

"I asked him, if he ever met you in Syria, to suggest to you that you should come to Egypt."

"Why?" I was insane enough to think for a moment that she harboured kindly thoughts of me. But she turned great, dark, disillusioned eyes on me and said, "I was — bored. I wanted you to see my apparent triumph. But things have now altered so much that if you wish to leave immediately, I'll do nothing to stop you."

She turned away. If with her every attitude was an attitude of grace, when she moved, every step seemed part of a solemn ritual...yet one felt it might — easily — become part of a dance.

I suppose it was inevitable that I should dream of her that night. To my mingled relief and regret on awaking, I myself was not directly involved, was merely a spectator. . .

Equally inevitably, I dreamed I was in Crete — not the island I had visited nearly twenty years before, but the real Crete before that brilliant, rich life died in a single night of terror. I had been summoned to the palace at Phaestos, walked nervously through ceremonial halls the walls of which were lined with thin slabs of alabaster to the room where Prince Tectamos awaited me. Long scented curls, embroidered, padded blue and gold sheath, jewelled belt, bracelets, collar, boots with gold-lipped tages — somewhere a man was concealed beneath the finery, very much a man in his own opinion, evidently, because he lisped to me that he wished me to carve a statue of the Earth-shaker. "I must say," tittered Tectamos, leaning on a finely carved staff, "one gets a bit tired at times by the over-powering femaleness of our religion, so I'm all gratitude towards the god a man can understand — and appreciate!"

I eyed him dubiously. His own virility was scarcely over-powering. (The sheath, I imagined, was very well padded and engineered!) And I must have some kind of model for the god of earthquakes, lord of land and sea, whose voice was to be heard in the thunder of the trembling of the ground, the great bull bellowing in the heavens, under the earth, destroying cities in his rage. Where in the hell could I find a model for the strong god of anger among the mincing elegants of Crete?

"I must go to Egypt," I said to myself. "I saw him today!"

And here I was, on the seashore, looking with all the anxious frustration of dreams for a non-existent ship. There was a surge in the water, the sun glittered on huge gilded horns above a great dark head, an enormous black bull coming to land with a naked girl sitting on his back, all grace, delicacy, melancholy, voluptuousnesss — my God, the subtle, exquisite emanations that came from her! As the bull splashed up on to the land, she slid from his back into the white foam at the water's edge — was she trying to escape? But no, she was all submissiveness, bowed beautiful head, with trailing hair, timid woodland thing that had been mastered. She walked dreamily beside the great brute — the languor of her, the tenderness of her breasts, the innocence of the pale face, the parted lips, the glimmering eyes! Where were they going? Into the willow thicket? "Don't go!" I shouted. "Don't go!" and began to run after them, dreading every moment to hear an appalled, appalling scream.

But when I heard a sound, it was the sound of laughter — woman's laughter. I burst through the willow thicket, and found myself in a room, a lamplit room with red pillars and white walls where Europa, laughing, danced with the bull. His head was down, he was, for the moment, quite still, yet terrifyingly ready to charge. And *she* laughed. Nothing of languor, melancholy in her now, she was all graceful, exquisite coquetry. "Come, come!" she called mockingly, tenderly, "Come to Europa, whom you thought you'd take! But she's taken you!"

And as he thundered forward, and the earth shook, and the scarlet pillars toppled about them and the lamps crashed down and golden flames shot up, she laughed, did a running hand-stand towards the furious brute, twisted her hands on his horns, up, up into the double somersault I had seen in a dozen ruined frescoes — my God, the fearsome contrast between the great dark shoulders and arrogant head and the pale, delicate body with the tight upward thrust of the jutting breasts on which the nipples stood so erect, and perhaps, even more fearsome, the similarity between the almost unbearable pleasure beast and woman manifested at that moment! And the potency of both living symbols of fertility! I awoke groaning half in regret, half in relief that such an intolerable ecstasy of violence, terror, death, passion, was not twisting my own loins.

Chapter Fourteen
Nefertiti

Setepenre died when she was not quite a year and a half old. To see a second child dying in convulsions is a dreadful thing, especially so small a child. She was tiny, helpless — now she was left alone to face the long, dreadful journey in the dark. All that I could do for her was to pray desperately to Isis to be a mother to my little one, to feed her, tend her — and permit my Meketaten to come to her sister and be a child again with her.

I remember wondering sometimes, fingering the gold rattle filled with pebbles, that I had secretly kept back from my baby's tomb, if whatever gods existed were punishing me for some offence of which I was ignorant.

Death was always in my thoughts. Sophronicos had told me there was sterility throughout Egypt. These were the years of bad harvests, the Years of the Hyena, but, he said, the barrenness of the fields extended to cattle, even women. He said there was pestilence too, so that along the whole length of the Nile Valley, people lamented that all Egypt was dying because the gods had turned their backs on the land. Because, I continued silently, when he faltered into embarrassed silence, the Pharaoh had turned his back on *them*.

The death of two children within little more than a year made me see Amarna, harsh white sunlight, harsh black shadow notwithstanding, through a grey mist of sorrow. All that cheered me was Nofret's devotion, and the fact that, not long after my baby died, Tiy left the city — for a time. She went to Nubia; hardly a year ever passed without one of those visits to her mother's country which seemed almost essential to her.

She had left before the New Year's Day Ceremony, because then the floods begin, or should begin. Otherwise she would inevitably have sat beside Akhnaten under a great canopy when the craftsmen came from their workshops with the gifts prepared over the past year for foreign rulers and favoured courtiers. Eventually Akhnaten came down from his throne to see the exhibition, followed by a small army of scribes, who noted down who was to be the recipient of each gift. The scribes, in fact, separated me from him. I wondered if I might leave. There was Father hopefully eyeing the more showy gifts; I had no wish to talk to *him*; he was angry with me for my grief over Setepenre. But as I turned away, I was confronted by someone equally unwelcome — Horemheb, detained in unwilling attendance for some days now. Surrounded by courtiers, and so having to make some kind of conversation, I asked him nervously if this were the first New Year's Day Ceremony he had attended. He said briefly he had attended several in the last reign. "The gifts were very different then. Mostly craftsmen made beautiful weapons. The Magnificent One before his illness, was interested in them. But now. . ." He shrugged and stared angrily across the room. Akhnaten was examining, with delighted exclamations, an obsidian vase set with gold, filled with a valuable unguent.

I was almost glad when Father drew close to greet me with reverent affection. To Horemheb he said, "How much longer do you stay in Amarna?"

"Not much longer — what I say in the Council is wasted breath," said Horemheb, bowing to me briefly, then turning on his heel.

"There he goes," said Father, with something very close to a giggle. "The would-be strong man of Egypt."

"Yet useful to have as a member of the family," I said. When Horemheb had been appointed Commander-in-Chief, Father had actually suggested he should marry Mutnedjmet. The matter, of course, had to be referred to Akhnaten, who really had no option but to speak to me about it. I had argued against the idea, because it was such a cold-blooded political alliance — both men disliked each other intensely.

Akhnaten had said quickly, "I had already more or less decided against it," meaning, I suppose, that his mother had decided against it. Yet apparently it had not been altogether a cold-blooded idea; Ankhesenpaaten had come running in one day to report with glee that Mutnedjmet had been screaming with rage. She wanted to marry Horemheb — so much!

Possibly because Tiy had left Amarna, Horemheb's words in the royal Council at last made some impression in Akhnaten's mind — although perhaps it was just as well that Horemheb himself had also left Amarna before the impression produced any tangible result. For, of course, it did not occur to Akhnaten to visit Syria in person. Instead, he organised a Pageant of Empire in a specially erected Hall of Foreign Tribute.

At the climax of the ceremony, Akhnaten would accept the tribute of the vassal kingdoms. Afterwards, he said, he would receive the ambassadors privately, and expound the new religion to them. For him this was the essential part of the days business.

The doll-queen was carried beside him through the street on the great state palanquin, borne by sweating courtiers who competed ferociously for the onerous honour. The four children followed us. Nofret had not liked the idea of a lengthy ceremony, with reason, for she tired easily, but had brightened when I told her there would be a show of animals at the end of the ceremony, and if a baby gazelle were among them, she might have it.

I, too, thought of the forthcoming event as an ordeal to be endured. I was – weary. I had slept badly – though alone. But I always slept badly these days. The stupidity of bringing Staphylos to Amarna – he himself provoked no reaction whatsoever, but the memories he evoked of the happiness he had destroyed, the impossible, childish dreams he revived of Agenor, Metion, quite faceless now, mere tall shapes, voices, but *rescuers*, taking me from this country I hated, back to innocent unknowing, to gushing streams, sea-birds crying, great breakers rushing in. . .

Of these things I would dream, and then I would awake. To find myself, inescapably, Queen of Egypt.

We had come to the Foreign Ministry. The priest walking before the palanquin sent up such clouds of incense from his censer that I had only a blurred sight of the Foreign Minister bowing low at the gate. Indeed, the smell of incense was so overpowering that, queen-goddess or not, I felt it would choke me. I bent to pick up one of the lotus flowers they had strewn about my feet – the scent, I thought, might relieve the incense fumes. But even as I bent, the smoke cleared a little, and I found to my amazement that I was staring down, but not too far down, into an impatient, angry face – the expression was so unmistakable, so jarring in its contrast with the eager, adoring faces about it that I would have noticed the man even if he had not been a head taller than any of those surrounding him, if his skin had not been so much fairer, if his eyes – they were a light grey, the colour of very early morning, the hour before daybreak. I had never seen eyes blazing with such hostility. No, I corrected myself, Horemheb looked at me often enough with that same antagonism. I was accustomed to it, accepted it. But this antagonism I could not accept because it gleamed from grey eyes that recalled to me almost unbearably my home, my childhood, the innocence that had been Eos. He might be the very age of Agenor, Metion, Cleitos. And he had a look of them!

But then I became angry. (How pride helps!) How *dare* he? How dare the police let him into the city — or let him stand on the processional route? He was dusty, travel-stained, wearing battered armour — everyone else was in holiday dress. But above all, he should have been debarred because of that face of violent bitterness, and those accusing, transfixing eyes. He did not look at Akhnaten like this — all the hostility was for me! I was never so much a piece of haughty royalty as in this last procession as Akhnaten's Great Wife; this, I raged silently to myself, was no way to look at a queen!

Nofret already looked tired when we reached the pavilion, so I cheated. I sent an attendant to find out if there were indeed a baby gazelle among the animals to be paraded. There was, and they brought it to her. That is how I always want to remember Nofret — the slow, dawning look of delight on her childish face, and then, even before she took the little soft thing into her arms, the way she ran to me and lifted her face to mine and kissed me in gratitude. This slight spontaneous scene seemed to create some favourable impression among the waiting foreign emissaries; as we took our places, Akhnaten put his arm about me, told me to lean against him, then up came his fingers to my nipples, pressing, squeezing.

Envoys from Asia and Africa, introduced by Father and other ministers, Father's eyes furious in an otherwise disciplined face. And now here were wrestlers, and dancers and acrobats performing to castanets and hand-clapping. But Akhnaten was not watching; he sat in the pavilion earnestly instructing the emissaries in the creed of Aten. I sat beside him, seeing dark faces, closed faces, deep or shallow eyes, equally impenetrable. Depressed, I looked away. At least, some amusement might be gained from watching the Nubian guards. Their vigilance had relaxed — like the children, they were giving their attention to the wrestlers and acrobats, and so they permitted the stranger to approach within earshot.

Akhnaten was repeating that this was a religion of love, for the Aten was the creator of all men. His hearers would have seen for themselves that the ceremony had been unique in one respect — slaves had been presented to him, but on his explicit orders they had not been cruelly bound, their arms forced into agonising positions — indeed, if this procession had been one of triumph following a war, there would have been no offering up of captured enemies as human sacrifices as had happened in the reigns of his ancestors – no, this was a custom he abhorred, there would never be any sacrifice of enemies in this reign.

"No," a voice said violently, "instead Your Majesty sacrifices your own subjects and most faithful allies."

At the entrance to the pavilion stood the stranger who had stood dusty, travel-stained in the crowd, and stared at me with enmity. The Nubian guards, startled, angry, were moving in on him with raised weapons. "Don't touch him!" cried Akhnaten, and, then as the man gave a gasp, then pitched forward, he cried, even more loudly, "Why did you touch him?"

"They didn't," I said in a whisper. I had seen the great rush of blood pouring from his chest before he collapsed. It was a dreadful wound.

I didn't want the children to see it, and told their attendants hastily to take them away. Poor Nofret went readily enough, clutching her pet gazelle, and very near to tears. Meritaten was inquisitive when she saw the blood, Ankhesenpaaten incredulous. "Look at the colour of the barbarian's hair!"

It was the colour of burnished bronze.

"There's no blood left in his face," said Meritaten. "It's all coming out of his chest."

"There won't be any need for Father to tell the soldiers to kill him," said Ankhesenpaaten, sounding disappointed. "I've never seen anyone being killed."

Nofret began to cry.

"Take them away!" I repeated angrily to their attendants and, as they left, two of them reluctantly, I said appalled to Akhnaten, "You're not going to have him killed, are you?"

He looked at me in amazement. "Certainly not. He's temporarily insane, poor fellow – these barbarians can't endure our sun. But what a beautiful animal he is!"

In much the same spirit as he amassed rare wild beasts at the North Palace, he had decided to "collect" the unconscious stranger. He must be taken to the Great Palace, nursed back to health.

"He speaks Egyptian," I said, "but if he's seriously ill, delirious, he'll talk his own language. We'd better tell one of the foreigners to go to him, to translate what he says – Sophronicos the poet, say."

"Or Staphylos. They could take it in turns." Akhnaten was delighted. He had forgotten what the stranger had said before collapsing; his only thought was that he *was* a stranger, of an unusual kind – to receive instruction. "As soon as they find out who he is, and what he is doing in Amarna, I want to know.''

His name was Acamas, and he came from Byblos. Acamas had been sent with desperate appeals for help. But this was all that Sophronicos reported at first. The messenger from Byblos was very ill indeed, and could say little. He had been attacked on the way south from the threatened city.

Akhnaten was as delighted with him as he had been with the panther presented by the Nubian envoys. The beast was sent to the royal menagerie and visited every morning; the man, bedded down in the Great Palace, was visited every afternoon. Akhnaten insisted that I should accompany him on one of these visits of inspection. I was very embarrassed and stared about the room as if I had never seen the furnishings before — anything to avoid looking at the latest human acquisition. A chest of gilded ebony, a chair of cedarwood, walls painted with lotus flowers and poppies, a ceiling on which great crimson butterflies hovered in a cloudless sky. 'How odd,' I thought, 'how embarrassment clears the sight. I've never seen a room with greater clarity.' And yet I should not have been able to do so. The narrow, grilled windows allowed in only a small amount of light. The gay colours should have been subdued, but they had never seemed to glow so intensely.

Brightest of all was the ray of sunlight which struck through a window at precisely the right angle to fall directly on the unconscious face of the messenger from Byblos.

He had an attack of fever when were there. He began to mutter restlessly — in Achaean. ''What is he saying?'' asked Akhnaten.

''He is talking about the sun, Majesty,'' said Staphylos. I had rarely seen Akhnaten so pleased. But the man from Byblos was not speaking of the benevolent sun Akhnaten worshipped — he was trudging across a waterless desert in heavy armour, lips cracked with thirst, this sun was scorching, pitiless, hateful.

But neither I, nor Staphylos, told Akhnaten this.

He began to toss so wildly, he threw back his bedclothes. I told our attendants to get a doctor quickly. Meanwhile Staphylos and Akhnaten, sculptor and royal instructor of sculptors, held a rapturous conversation over the twisting body. ''How tall and lean he is, all bone and muscle,'' said Staphylos.

''How strong and vigorous he must have been!'' said Akhnaten. But there was a note in Staphylos' voice missing in Akhnaten's, he, the professional sculptor, was less detached in his admiration.

'Is he in love with this man?' I asked myself. I had heard that such things happened with Achaeans, that their men could feel for each other an emotion far transcending in intensity any feeling they were capable of experiencing for a woman. Yet Staphylos was Cretan by race.

"He's burning," said Akhnaten, touching him with an appreciation that turned to panic. He turned to me. "Feel how he's burning!" I touched him with one finger.

"He's beginning to shake," I said.

"No, you're imagining it, it's your own hand that's shaking!" said Akhnaten.

Then to my great relief Pentu was with us.

Akhnaten, who had become suddenly terrified lest the Achaean should be inconsiderate enough to die (so many of the wild animals, after pacing up and down in their splendid cages for a time, lay down and obstinately refused to live) was relieved by the report that, while the barbarian was a difficult patient, he should live, nevertheless. He was determined to live, to get back to Byblos, with or without help.

"But how did he ever get to Byblos in the first place?" I asked Sophronicos idly some days later. "It's a long way from Achaea." We sat in the garden. A harpist played softly. At no great distance Nofret was picking cornflowers to make me a necklace.

Sophronicos nodded. "His father ruled a little kingdom by the sea, in the north-east, Lady of Grace, until the Dorians came down on it."

"The Dorians?"

"I don't suppose you've heard of them, Mistress of the North and South. They speak Achaean of a sort, but they're savages. harsh-voiced — they maim the language as they speak it. Long yellow hair. They have a foothold in the north; I pray to all the gods they'll get no further."

But I was listening only perfunctorily now. Meritaten had come into the garden, Meritaten in a bad temper. She had not seen Smenkhare for days. Yet — with a sudden feeling of shock — I realised that I was almost envious of her. Young as she was, she knew what it was like to love a man, even if the love were not returned.

Beside me, Sophronicos talked of a few survivors getting on board a ship, the ship being wrecked on the coast of Syria near Byblos, the King of Byblos, Ribaddi, showing great kindness to those surviving this second catastrophe.

". . .fifteen or sixteen years old at the time. The King treated him like a son. Now he's Captain of the Guard."

"How long ago did all this happen?"

"Seventeen or eighteen years ago, Mistress of the Two Lands."

At about the time that the vessel in which Staphylos was bringing me to Egypt had put in, briefly, to Byblos. Why couldn't we have sailed earlier or later in the year, in the bad season, so that we could have been ship-wrecked too? With any luck I should have been drowned.

"For these reasons he is intensely grateful to the King of Byblos and has resolved to share his fate."

Half unwillingly I asked, "Has he recovered consciousness enough to speak of Byblos to The One?"

"I took word to The One that he is completely conscious now. The One is to visit him this afternoon."

"To talk of help for Byblos?"

"No. He ordered slaves to carry the gaming set into Acamas' room. Until Acamas is recovered enough to talk about serious matters like religion, The One intends to teach him the game of *senet*."

Senet is a game in which pawns are moved on a chequered board according to the fall of a dice of small sticks, the surface of which are painted in different colours. The aim is to proceed to the opposite end of the board. Akhnaten always played a game or two with his brothers whenever they visited us. Tutankhaten, a slow, rather stupid little boy, invariably made mistakes, but they were honest mistakes, so Akhnaten kept his temper. It was different when Smenkhare condescended to play. He played brilliantly — but also cheated, quite needlessly, at every opportunity.

So the set — ebony, ivory, gold, silver — was carried ceremoniously to the bedside of Acamas, fretting, incredulous enough already. I was glad I was not there to see the grey eyes blazing with astonishment when his entertainment was introduced. Besides, I did not think Acamas would welcome a vist from a woman, or listening to what conversation I could make in the face of his contempt. I imagined there was room for women only in a corner of his life, and that for a specific, limited purpose. And particularly he would have no use for any woman connected — and who could be more closely connected than I was? — with the government here in Amarna. From what Sophronicos blurted out — and even more from his reticences, I gathered that Acamas thought of the administration as rotten, corrupt, cowardly. The same government that Akhnaten, less than ten years before, had declared would be essentially and eternally free from contamination or taint.

Sophronicos was still talking. ". . .he says he must be back in Byblos by the spring, whether he goes singly or with an army at his back. Aziru of the Amorites has been getting reinforcements throughout the winter — they say he's even getting Dorian spearmen."

"Dorians? In Syria?"

"They have frequent feuds. Brothers rule together, then quarrel. The loser goes overseas, acts as a mercenary until he's gathered enough troops to go back to seize power. Lady of Grace," Sophronicos continued, but with a change of tone as sudden as it was complete, "won't *you* accompany The One when he nexts visits Acamas? I'm afraid of an outburst. If you were there to divert The One's talk from religion. . ."

"To save the skin of an intolerant savage who dislikes me?" I asked angrily. I stood up to go away in a fury. But then I hesitated. If there were an outburst from the Achaean, the effect on Akhnaten might be disastrous. I said dully, "Very well, I'll go with The One. But don't let *him* know I speak his language," I continued, almost in panic. "If I must talk to him, it will be only in Egyptian. Tell Staphylos this too!"

Sophronicos agreed and kept his word, I know. Staphylos did not. For Staphylos, who must have always disliked me with the unquenchable animosity any wrong-doer feels towards his victim, now seemed to be viewing me with even greater spite. He was with Acamas, Acamas fully conscious, when I went into the room after Akhnaten.

Obsession creates insensitivity as to atmosphere. So, I suppose, does the condition of being born royal. Akhnaten always assumed his visits were as welcome as the sweet northern wind in the evening. Did Acamas wish to continue his *senet* lessons? Acamas, with an irony anyone not born in a palace would have detected, professed himself to be very stupid at learning; a demonstration by two skilled players. . .

Akhnaten nodded happily. "The Queen shall play with me — how fortunate she came today!"

"I'm not a skilled player. . ." I began but he brushed my protests aside. So we sat in the pool of sunlight, and played *senet*. It was true that I was not a skilled player, but I was deft enough to ensure, by a series of misreadings of the way the sticks fell, that Akhnaten won. If he won, he would go on playing. If he lost, he would abandon the game, and begin talking. So I cheated. And, Acamas, stupid pupil that he might profess himself to be, knew I was cheating. One unintentional glance, the briefest of glances, told me that. I felt my cheeks flaming. I I had forgotten Staphylos; I remembered him only when I heard a low voice speaking in Achaean to him — and, I thought, at me.

Akhnaten heard nothing. He had the enviable gift of being able to cut himself off mentally from everything except the task currently absorbing him.

"I ask for men. He says that when Aten-worship is adopted in Syria as it has been in Egypt – *as it has been in Egypt!* – all men will become brothers, and then there will be no more wars." And then with sudden rage, "He should travel about his Empire! Then he'd get other ideas about his benevolent sun."

A murmur from Staphylos – of caution? Muted caution, if so. For all his love for Acamas – and consequent concern for his safety, one supposed – he was delighted at the spectacle of my discomfiture. And he knew I could never tell Akhnaten what was being said.

Akhnaten had always been intrigued by physically splendid, mentally unfathomable animals. Hence his assiduous collection of such beasts. He had always done his best to make these beautiful, unpredictable creatures happy. He had not always been succesful in the past; with his new acquisition he met with no success at all. In his vexed concern, he began to seek me out, to discuss the problem – almost as much as he had come to talk to me at the beginning of our married life. And I remembered an incident of that period. In those early days of the reign, real tribute was still being sent to Pharaoh, from as far afield as Northern Achaea. A region there is called Thessaly. All that we knew of it was that it was mountainous and green and the people bred horses much bigger than anything we had seen in Egypt. And one of the petty rulers of Thessaly sent Akhnaten a great shining stallion. Akhnaten admired the horse's strength, swiftness, beauty; he used to rave about it to me like a little boy. He was worried because the stallion fretted and pined. He had a splendid stable built for it, with an elaborately carved manger. The stallion, trained war-horse, kicked down the confining doors. Finally, in the days when The One was sailing down the river, seeking the site for his divine city, I had taken one of the few independent actions of my life: I ordered that the stallion should be taken back to Thessaly, although I hated seing him go, he was so beautiful. But he had to have his freedom. I had awaited Akhnaten's return in some trepidation. But he now had a new obsession – the City of the Horizon. He scarcely noticed when I told him that the stallion had gone.

But in recalling the earlier incident, I had forgotten one method by which Akhnaten, in the days of his infatuation, had tried to make the stallion happy.

He came to me early one afternoon as I played with Nofret in the garden, and said, "Let's go to visit Acamas."

''Why?'' I asked unwillingly. It was beautiful in the garden, the end of the Egyptian winter, the beginning of spring.

Akhnaten looked more youthful than I had seen him for years. ''Because I think we shall see a miracle – Acamas looking happy!'' he said. I doubted it, but went with him, reluctantly. Otherwise he might vent his rage on Nofret. He showed no affection for her these days. Because she showed too much for me – and others saw it?

Acamas was striding up and down, restless as any caged thing. I waited for Akhnaten to tell him the surprise he had prepared, but I should have known my husband better, he was jealously hugging the secret to himself for a time. He began by chiding Acamas gently – he should go out more, sample the delights of the capital, ''But even if you're not really well enough yet to go about much,'' Akhnaten concluded, ''you're well enough to enjoy other pleasures, I hope?''

I had completely forgotten one of the devices by which he had tried to tame the stallion from Thessaly. The ebony black mares from. . .

''. . .Nubia. Presented to me at the Pageant of Empire.''

Four well-grown Nubian slave-girls came in. Everything had been done to enhance their attractions – including the trick I had always detested. Cones of greasy perfumed incense had been placed on their round, short-curled heads. Already the melting stuff bathed head and shoulders in sticky sweetness. But even more disgusting was the expression on their faces as they looked at their new master. They looked excited. At any moment I expected them to squeal with excitement.

I could not bear to look at them any longer. I turned to look at *him*.

No miracle to delight Akhnaten. No smile, no gratitude in the blazing eyes. He said in a low, furious voice, ''I asked for men, Majesty – and you give me *women*!''

Akhnaten's face crumpled in disappointment. So he had looked when the stallion from Thessaly had struck out at him with his heels.

Acamas' mounting rage left him now too angry to talk in anything but his own native tongue. ''When in the hell are you going to learn that there's more to ruling an empire than eternally squeezing your wife's paps in public?'' And when he found my appalled eyes on him – and I hated him then – he laughed and said, ''Well, is the Lady of Grace going to translate?''

''But I wanted to make you happy,'' cried Akhnaten, hurt, but not angry. One should be no more angry with a beautiful, incalculable barbarian than with a beautiful incalculable animal.

Acamas looked past me, at him then. He said, very formally, in Egyptian, "I regret that Nubian women are not to my taste, Majesty."

Then, even though his face was averted, I saw the sudden change in the expression. Behind me, a loud cry. Before I could turn completely, Akhnaten had pitched forward across the painted floor. The Nubian women began to scream. Acamas lifted Akhnaten and put him on the bed. All the signs were there — the rigidity, clenched hands, clenched teeth, head thrown back.

"You've killed him," I said. The limbs were jerking. The eyes rolled. Froth appeared between his lips.

"You mean," Acamas began incredulously, "that my — ingratitude. . ."

I wiped the bloodstained lips, tried to prise the teeth open. "You made him ill by refusing his gift. . ." I began, then — "*You've reopened your wound by lifting him*!" The blood was welling up through the linen bandages.

Pentu was with us, courtiers, slaves. Shocked, deferential voices asked questions.

"The foreigner's wound re-opened. The sight of the blood distressed The One. . ."

"Ah," Pentu said, "that would explain everything."

A very junior doctor, excluded from Pharaoh's side by his seniors, came over, made abeisance. Might he attend to the barbarian? I did not reply at once. My hesitancy puzzled him. He said that if the re-opened wound were not attended to — so much loss of blood — The One was so interested in the barbarian. . .

"Very well," I said shortly, not looking at him.

I walked beside Akhnaten as they carried him away, stayed with him until he was sleeping soundly. Then I said I would go to sit in the garden. "Why are you staring at me?" I asked Pentu.

He said, thick lids half hiding his eyes, that I appeared distressed. But all would be well. When his Majesty awoke he might possibly have a slight headache but nothing more. We knew he would remember nothing of what had happened. He wanted to give me some potion or other. I refused. Someone asked if I would like the princesses brought to me. "No, No!" I did not want them distressed.

"Your Majesty, as always, is very wise," Pentu said bowing.

I told him I wanted to be left alone in the garden. He bustled off. His face, his hands, his whole body was flabby — he disgusted me. The smell of greasy, cloying incense had disgusted me. And the look on the Nubians' faces. That excitement. . .

I walked towards the pavilion they always called the Queen's

Pavilion, my favourite because about it I had ordered to be planted those Cretan flowers and shrubs that could withstand the Egyptian sun. Their scent was *clean*. Here was a myrtle bush; I rubbed my hands against the fragrant leaves, lifted them to my face. This was the beginning of the Egyptian spring, so already the sweet smelling stars of the flowers, white, gold-centred, were beginning to appear. I broke off a spray. I had not done that since I had been a child in Crete. "You must learn, Ariaea had said, "to make your first bridal wreath." Which girl had been about to be married? I could not remember, even though, in an absurd attempt to jog my memory, I held the spray, scented flowers, scented leaves, to my face, and sat there in a little bower, trying to remember the child Eos.

A long shadow fell across the path. I looked up, my eyes widening. I clutched at the spray of myrtle as if it afforded some absurd protection, and said, "You should not be here."

The junior doctor, running up, misunderstood. "So I told him, Majesty. But he insisted."

"Take him back. He should never have been permitted to come to me!"

"I know, I know, Majesty," he wailed, wringing fat hands, "but he will have to rest a little, Majesty, to get the strength to return to his room. If you would graciously permit him to sit in your presence. . ."

"You must take him away from me quickly!"

"Yes, yes, as soon as I can — I'll get some wine to help him make the effort."

"Make haste, or I'll have you scourged."

He went off quickly enough, but he should have been running. Nesting birds sang in the thickets. The vines that made the bower gave a little shade against the afternoon sun.

"Did you know what was planned with the Nubian women, Majesty?"

"No!" I said violently. "No!"

"You didn't like it, did you?"

"No!"

His hair shone like burnished metal, but most of his face was in the shade. It did not help; there was nothing to conceal the hostility in his voice as he said, "Sophronicos is dazzled by you. He becomes eloquent on — what is it? — the bright rain of your tears. But why should the Queen of Egypt weep? Of course, he told me, two of your children died, and there was some difficulty in the flow of milk in your breasts to suckle them. Poor Majesty, how you've suffered! When my people were attacked, it was a winter's night. Do you know what winter's night is like in my land? Those who could get away took to the hills. Then we made our way as best we could down to the coast. In that flight there was a woman in childbirth at the roadside — and we couldn't stop for her — and new born babies, we took from dead mothers, starved to death before we got aboard ship. And that's what's been happening in Syria for years.

"When I've been taken to the Temple, I've watched you going through all the exhausting rites of the Chief Priestess of the Setting Sun, not a thought, an emotion behind that mask of a face. And I've thought of other women, standing on the walls of little cities in the evening, knowing that before the next night-fall, their men will be dead, and their children, and that they themselves will have been dragged out, raped, in the street. Is there a sense of humour, if no other feeling, behind the pretty mask, Majesty? Then this should amuse you? *You were our last hope.* Possibly you've never heard of Abdkhiba, the governor of Jerusalem? Well, you're not likely to hear any more of him after today — he held out as long as he could, and died when the city fell. He'd asked for troops, too. Before he died, he sent a last letter to Byblos. He'd a friend here at Amarna — May. I see you've heard of *him*. Usually accounted a man of sense, I believe, but a fool, nevertheless. Because he used to write to his closest friends, praising you. . ."

"The doctor is coming back," I said.

"So May was a fool, as I thought! He and his companion really never existed for you, did they? So, go away and perfume your hair and breasts with oil of lilies — then you won't catch the whiff of the blood running in the streets of little sunlit towns. I pray to whatever gods there may be that soon — very soon — this city is reduced to the ruins *he's* responsible for in Syria."

"Majesty. . ." The doctors arrived with wine and servants.

"Wait. Her Majesty may want you to bring — other attendants. Soldiers, perhaps."

'Now,' his eyes said, 'Have me arrested. Prove yourself Queen of Egypt in one respect at least. Order my execution.'

Those eyes would have been friendlier, less contemptuous if I had sent for the guards and demanded his death. But I said, "I have no orders," and walked away with bowed head and drooping shoulders.

Akhnaten remembered nothing of what had immediately preceded his attack, and accepted that it was the re-opening of Acamas' wound that was responsible. His infatuation continued a little longer, but now I always had a carefully invented excuse to avoid accompanying him. I also tried — unsuccessfully — to persuade him to send men and grain to Byblos. "Why are you taking this sudden interest in Syria?'' he asked excitedly — and for ''Syria'' he might as well have said ''things which don't concern you.''

I thought suddenly, 'I'm doing precisely what May told me not to do.'

But Akhnaten did not give Acamas what he wanted, except eventually one small concession. He allowed him to leave the Palace, and take up quarters in one of the city's barracks, with the understanding that when his wound was completely healed, he might return to Byblos. The infatuation, if not dead, was flickering low now. For Tiy had sent word that she would soon be returning. This was enough to account for my even worse sleeplessness, my misery, the feeling of hopelessness that oppressed me day and night. I dreaded Tiy's return as much as I longed for Acamas' departure.

I could not avoid hearing of him. I heard Mahu, the elderly police chief, talking to another minister — ''It's as if the men are infatuated by him!'' He was, it seemed, testing out his strength by going out with them on patrol. Well, they always liked a handsome officer. But from the men closest to him, I heard little directly.

One day poor, devoted Sophronicos began to talk in a muddled, embarrassed fashion; at the end of it I realised he had tried to give Acamas a favourable impression of me, had spoken of my childhood in Crete, which I had talked about to him, had even said that I had once been called Eos. Poor naive poet! His wretched face was eloquent enough as to his complete lack of success.

Sophronicos' admiration might one day result in a poem — the young warrior defending the doomed city; the admiration of the other foreigners in Amarna produced more material tokens of esteem. The armour worn in the desperate breakout and journey south was battered, riven. The foreigners decided he must be re-equipped before he went back at the beginning of spring to face the last onslaught. I have said how, after Meketaten's death, I would often go to their studios and workshops; now I had to time my visits carefully. I could not bear the thought of another confrontation, but one could not escape talk of him.

And there was one occasion when I had not timed my visit carefully enough. I sat in the studio of the sculptor Phereclos, and when a voice sounded outside, I sprang up, said hurriedly, not even mentioning a name, ''He'll probably speak of leaving Amarna, he may speak bitterly, he mustn't see me.''

''Hardly possible, Despoina,'' said Phereclos. ''You'll meet in the doorway.'' I pointed desperately to a curtained recess.

"Can't I go there?"

"It's a store-room," he said staring, "but, of course. . ." I flew for shelter like a hunted hare, dragging Kat-Senet with me.

"This is no way for the Queen of Egypt. . ." she began. But I raised my finger to my lips, and gazed imploringly at her. She settled herself resignedly on a block of undressed stone.

They talked of swords. He was dissatisfied with the weapon he had. Only an Achaean armourer could make the sword he wanted. The sword produced in Amarna was good enough for thrusting, but not stout enough for slashing.

"Why's slashing so important?" asked Phereclos.

A laugh. "It's your instinct when fighting to slash. Just stand back — there, you see, your natural blow sweeps round in part of a circle centred in your shoulder. They *teach* you to thrust, but when you're actually fighting, you forget a hell of a lot of acquired knowledge."

"There was an Achaean swordsmith in the Delta. . ."

"Yes, I've heard of him. He's good, from Argos. But there's no time — only Pharaoh could get the message through quickly enough, and pay enough for a rushed job. Can you see *this* Pharaoh. . .

Phereclos, no doubt hideously embarrassed, brought the conversation to a hurried close. When the sound of retreating footsteps had died away, I came out into the studio, and said to Phereclos, "If you'll find me a messenger, I'll give him the authority to use all royal resources to get to the Delta quickly. And take this to pay for the cost of it!" I was wearing a bracelet of gold inset with lapis-lazuli, shaped like blue lilies. "But he must never know what part I've had in it." He never did.

Let him go soon. Let me slip back into my old state of — of apathy, of mental numbness, of ignorance, surrounded only by shut-in faces that told me nothing. Let me sink back into safety.

Time leaped, yet lagged. The day of Tiy's return drew nearer; would he never go, would he never accept defeat, take no for an answer, was there no one to tell him that Pharaoh was now deaf to everything except the messages coming down river from his mother, coming closer, closer.

Until the afternoon came when she was so close that Akhnaten decided he would sail next morning to greet her when she was still three days distant. They would not return immediately to Amarna. At the point where they would meet, a temple of Aten was being constructed. Akhnten wanted to be there at the dedication. Once he would have wanted me to be there with him.

By the evening I thought I was sickening for a fever. My head throbbed, my breasts ached, from time to time my whole body shook. Kat-Senet vainly administered her camomile brews, her poppyhead poultices. My mirror showed a flushed face, brilliant eyes. Even Akhnaten, coming to tell me he was leaving next day, noticed my appearance. In a mixture of concern and irritation he asked me if I were ill. I said in a distracted manner, "I don't know. I think so."

"Have you sent for Pentu?"

"I don't want him. I don't want anyone to touch me. My body aches too much."

I had sent Kat-Senet away. I sat at my dressing-table taking off the heavy ornaments I had worn to the evening service. Suddenly I began to cry. Misery, fear, loneliness, all combined within an aching, suddenly burning, body. Seeing me in tears, Akhnaten stood staring, then exclaimed, "What is it?" He sounded scared. The wife who seldom if ever wept, sat sobbing, her head on her outspread arms. "You must be ill, very ill. I'll send for Pentu."

"No, *no*. I don't want him to touch me. I hate him."

He said awkwardly, "We both know you can't be pregnant. Is it the difficult time for you?"

"That was days ago."

He said agitatedly, "I've never seen you cry because of pain."

"I'm not crying because of pain."

"Why, then?"

"I'm frightened – I don't know of what, and I'm lonely – so lonely."

After a moment he said, "You have the children."

"Not all of them now." Suddenly I was running across the room to him, flinging my arms about him. "Please don't go tomorrow."

"I must," he said bleakly.

"I know you want to go," I faltered, "but can't you delay for one day?"

"I don't want to go," he said. "I have to go."

But I was still frightened, of what I did not know, that I could not appreciate the full significance of what he said. I only knew that he would be leaving me to meet *her*. I let my arms fall from about him, but I still stood with my head against his shoulder. "I'm sorry," I said dully, "and you'll want to go away from me now, of course. They will have prepared the girl you've chosen for tonight."

He said, "I want to stay with *you* tonight. You're different."

I thought, 'So I attract you only if I'm in the throes of fever.'

"Come to bed."

I felt sick. I wanted to scream, "Mekataten!" I know I cried out something inarticulate, and then the tears began again, flowing as if from a well. I thought this would alienate him; instead, it seemed to attract him, for suddenly he began to kiss me. "If you had always been like this," he muttered. (What a child of eleven?)

"If you were always like this. . ." (Then ask the doctors if they have some magic spell or potion not to cure, but to perpetuate fever.)

"Let me come with you tomorrow!"

"Part of the way." He drew me towards the bed.

How long was it since this happened last? It would be like coupling with a stranger. But there was to be no strangeness, only dreary familiarity. For me, that is. For him it was different. My body burned, trembled, instead of lying cool, inert. He was so excited he did not realise what had happened — rather what had not happened. If this had been our wedding night I should have remained a virgin. But I *cried out*, because this was infintely worse than being with a stranger. This was a fresh defilement of the flesh of my dead Meketaten. It was in realisation of this that I cried out — and left him triumphant, deluded after non-performance.

In the morning Akhnaten looked at me oddly. In his eyes there was more furtive guilt than rapture. "I hope I haven't made you pregnant," he said in a scarcely dynastic manner.

I was sure he would have liked to have broken his promise to let me go part of the way with him, but dreaded fresh storms of tears. He sent for Mahu. Mahu came in beaming unspoken congratulations. It must be all over the Palace now — The One had spent the night with me after all these months! But it was soon made clear that this conjugal felicity was not to continue. Mahu had imagined he had been summoned to discuss the plans for crowd control at the dedication of the new temple, for he, of course, would be in attendance. Instead he was questioned closely as to where I could leave the royal barge so that I should be off it well before nightfall. Akhnaten, I reflected, did not intend to be seduced by my tears a second time.

Mahu always assiduously tactful, chose to misinterpret this: Akhnaten's anxiety was all for my safety, that I should be back in Amarna before darkness fell. As Chief of Police he said, he knew every road approaching the capital. Close to the city they were almost as broad as those within Amarna itself, but further out they deteriorated rapidly, only marked with stones on prominent points.

Akhnaten cut him short. "At what point can the barge put in to. . ."

Mahu, as usual, all eagerness to please, named a police post that would be ideal. It had a garrison of sixty men – enough to provide Her Majesty with a sufficient escort.

"That will do," said Akhnaten shortly. He avoided looking at me. He went on avoiding looking at me as much as was possible even when we were in the comparatively straitened conditions of the royal barge. We sat side by side on silken cushions under the brightly coloured awning, but he played detestable *senet* with a succession of courtiers.

I sat watching the river gliding past us, the dark, sweating backs of the oarsmen. Except for the greater luxury of my surroundings, I found it strangely, unpleasantly, reminiscent of the journey upriver when I had first come to Egypt eighteen years before.

Before me on the deck rested my long-distance palanquin, with its linen panels. Akhnaten was taking no chances. *Why had I ever asked to come?*

In mid afternoon, Mahu came hurrying to inform Akhnaten that the police post was in sight. And there it was, a series of squat, white buildings, the garrison lined up long before we drew alongside, and there was someone who could never be mistaken for an Egyptian policeman. His appearance could mean only one thing. He was going. In one respect at least the Goddess was being kind to me.

He explained, coming aboard and saluting, that he had not previously taken his leave of The One because he had not known until mid-day how long The One would be absent. His own preparations would probably be completed, he would be on his way back to Byblos before The One had returned to Amarna. So he had come by jackal-tracks across the desert to. . .

Akhnaten said to him earnestly, "We shall meet again, and then you will admit you were wrong. No further attack will take place on Byblos. I have fresh assurances from Aziru – "

"Well then, Majesty", said Acamas, "my fine new armour will have been wasted."

"New armour?" The childlike Akhnaten had temporarily reappeared. "I should have liked to see it."

"It's in the chariot in which I came."

"Then bring it here."

As Acamas returned to the little quay, Mahu tried to combine deference and urgency in low voiced reminders that if Her Majesty were to return to Amarna before nightfall, now was the time. He was disregarded. Akhnaten had another toy to play with.

Acamas returned, burdened.

"Put it on," said Akhnaten. "I've never seen anyone wearing

full Achaean armour,'' and he watched in a kind of trance of pleasure. He had shown similar ecstasy over beautiful toy soldiers in Tutankhaten's collection. ''Let me feel the weight of that spear!'' He had to take two hands to it. ''You can't *use* it! If it comes to that, you can't fight wearing such a weight of armour — ''

Acamas said that conditions were not right for him to demonstrate how he used a spear, but he was quite willing to show his ability to fight in heavy armour — if any of His Majesty's retinue would take a sword and —

The captain of Akhnaten's guard sprang forward. ''I've always wanted to take on a man armed like you. I've always said such equipment must slow you down.''

''Try me!''

A kind of modified outcry from Mahu. ''If Her Majesty is to be back in Amarna — '' But no one paid heed to him. Every other man wanted to see how effortlessly such heavy weapons could be handled, they were excitedly clearing a space on the deck before the royal awning under which Akhnaten sat like an eager child, behind him Mahu chewing his lip in disapproval. And there was the clash of weapons, then, finally, the long bronze sword whistling through the air, slashing out, and suddenly thrust forward from the shoulder, in an amazing climax of effort, all the power of body and arm behind it, every muscle strained in it, yet despite the tautness of the body, the man himself seemed relaxed, not at the stretch — effortless. And smiling. His eyes had smiled all the time he fought.

At the last moment he dropped the sword-point. Calling on gods other than Aten — but even Akhnaten did not notice — the captain of the guard staggered back. ''You'd have had me,'' he gasped. ''*Had* me. Quicker than I was — carrying all that on your back.''

They gathered round, congratulating, lifting the weapons, examining them curiously. More minutes passed before Mahu said in disciplined anguish, ''Her Majesty's departure — it's too late now.''

And Akhnaten suddenly panicked. Surely no-one, seeing the way he was determined to dump me ashore, would have retained any shred of illusion as to the 'perfect marriage'?

''They'll never reach Amarna by nightfall,'' Mahu wailed.

''Men carrying a litter wouldn't. Chariots could.''

Akhnaten and Mahu, master and man, stared at the speaker with gratitude. Then Mahu said, dolefully, ''Half a dozen chariots here, but lightweight only, carrying a single man.''

''I came up from Amarna in a heavy chariot. If you're going

to make a decision, make it quickly. One of your patrols thought a sand-storm was threatening."

This information threw Mahu into lamentable indecision. Acamas said, "We could take four of your chariots as escort, two to turn back to set your minds at rest when we reach the half-way mark, the other to continue with us to Amarna."

So, hurriedly, I took my leave of my husband. Mahu escorted me to the chariot where Acamas, a red cloak covering his armour, already waited. Akhnaten did not even watch me go.

Chapter Fifteen
Nefertiti

It was a sultry evening. This affected my mood, leaving me nervous, apprehensive. And my head still ached, my hands still shook, my whole body still seemed feverish. Yes, I must be ill.

Meanwhile the man standing beside me said nothing whatsoever as he drove me swiftly, expertly, away from my husband. I supposed he would claim he was not being impolite, his attention being absorbed in urging the horses on as fast as possible, all the while scanning the horizon, from which the storm might come. Although even from him I would have welcomed a few words as some distraction from my growing feeling of physical misery. My flesh seemed unnaturally sensitive. Even the touch of the material of my dress, the finest, thinnest linen obtainable, was almost unbearable, especially across my breasts.

We reached the half-way mark. He gestured to two of the escort, who saluted, jerked their horses' heads round, and began careering back across the desert. So Mahu's mind would be set at rest, because the Queen was safe from the storm, and Akhnaten's mind would be set at rest because there was no possibility of his wife coming back to him.

I had scarcely been conscious of my surroundings, but now I suddenly realised that it had grown atrociously hot — and that great clouds of powdery sand were blowing across the valley. Banks of it were beginning to form across the track; they were still shifting, but once they stayed, every sign of the road would be obliterated, and we might be lost, left to suffocate in a sea of sand.

He shouted to the remaining escort, "I'm going to turn back — we can't endanger the Queen by carrying her into the storm.

Will you take the risk of trying to get through to Amarna to tell them what's happened?''

They nodded, saluted, plunged on into the growing darkness. Acamas turned the chariot and spoke with unexpected politeness to me. ''Have you ever been in a sandstorm, Lady of the Two Lands? This isn't too bad yet, but hold your cloak up to cover your eyes and mouth.'' Already the sand was stinging my face; I held my cloak up as ordered. I could breathe, but I was blind.

''Are you afraid, Mistress of the North and South?'' I heard him ask.

''No,'' I said.

''A Queen of Egypt, of course, is never afraid,'' he said, still politely. He added thoughtfully, ''A Queen of Egypt, of course, rarely has cause to be afraid.''

I wondered how he managed to guide the horses. For a moment I let my cloak drop a little. He was bending forward, urging them on — I could see little more than his profile against the gathering darkness, but he seemed to have that eagerness, that glow of excitement about him which I had noticed when I had seen him fighting.

The chariot jerked abruptly to a halt, almost flinging me against him. I let my cloak fall again. The wall of some building loomed up before us in the wild darkness. I asked in confusion, ''Where are we? We're nowhere near the river yet.''

''No, this is a newly constructed desert fort, fully provisioned, but not yet occupied,'' he said.

''Then what are we doing here?'' I asked in angry bewilderment.

''Doing, Lady of the Two Lands?'' he said, not bothering to look at me. ''Why the Mistress of the North and of the South will shortly share at least one experience with those many female subjects for whom she has never spared a thought — the experience of rape. It may enable her to take a less detached view of the Syrian problem.''

My first reaction had been sheer disbelief that this could be happening to me, that it must be the delirium of the fever that had been threatening me for days. But then I was aware that I was no longer in a fever, that, in all the atrocious heat, I suddenly felt as if my body had been plunged into ice-water. In dismay and terror, I clutched at any hope. ''They'll come looking for us.''

''Will they? Word went back to the river that we'd safely passed the half-way mark. Word's gone forward to the city that we've turned back. In Amarna, they'll think you're with Pharaoh; Pharaoh'll think you're at Amarna. No one will have any idea where you — more relevantly, where *we* really are."

"But — later — " I stammered.

"How much later? This kind of storm can blow for days. There'll be no communication between court and city."

I said, my teeth chattering, "The storm can't blow for ever. When they find out what's happened — "

For the first time there was feeling in his voice. "I shall have left for Syria. And you — you'll have experienced what thousands of decent, terrified women have felt, and that's all I'm interested in. *Get down*! Or do you want to be carried?"

Shock had left me almost paralysed, but the thought of touch, and what touch might provoke, made me force my rigid limbs to move. Stiffly I got down. He backed the chariot so that I was penned against the wall, unable to escape into the darkness, then freed the horses, who promptly trotted off to take shelter on the far side. "They, at least, needn't suffer," he said. "For you the same choice again — will you walk, or do I have to carry you?"

I walked, trying to ignore the tall, lean shape beside me, concentrating only on his weapons. Beside his sword, which I knew I could scarcely lift, he had a dagger. I could not hope to snatch at it now, when he was alert, but later, after the defilement of my flesh, he might be less on his guard, so there might be an opportunity to plunge the blade into that same defiled flesh.

There was a gateway, then steps. I climbed, his footfall steady behind me. There was sufficient light left for this, but at the top, before the door leading to the guardroom, I halted. "It's too dark here," I replied. "I can't see."

He came past me and kicked the door open. "There are lamps inside," he said. "I supervised it all a few days ago." He pushed me in before him, slammed the door shut behind us. It was a thick door, as the walls of the guardroom were thick. The noise of the sandstorm died away, and I stood in the darkness, listening to the sound of a lamp being kindled.

The lamplight showed a square room, not large, with a small window to the north. There were some jars of wine stacked along one wall, a rack for weapons, and a very broad, straw-covered ledge running along another wall. "Enough to sleep half a dozen men at a time," he said. "Do you want some wine?"

I nodded. Anything to gain time.

"Take off your cloak, and that absurd cap."

I obeyed. If, by some wild chance, I were given the opportunity to seize his dagger before he violated me, the cloak would be a hindrance. I took off the cap because otherwise he might do it. My hair fell about my shoulders.

He poured out two cups of wine. When he handed one to me, I managed to take it without our fingers touching. It was rough, strong stuff, but I drank it because it might warm my body a little. My hands were cold. Coldness meant clumsiness. The wine must be given time to warm and strengthen me. I said. "When did you plan this?"

"When that old fool, Mahu, decided against his better judgment that Pharaoh must be obeyed, even though you might be heading into a sandstorm. And how he tried to salve his conscience by deciding it was safe enough if you travelled without the usual escort! If I were you, in the future, I shouldn't rely solely on Mahu for your protection. No doubt he's well-meaning, but he's scarcely efficient."

He picked up my cloak, threw it over the straw, took off his own and dropped it over mine. My stomach contracted into a hard knot. So this was terror. It was quite different from what I had known with Akhnaten; then there had been only a feeling of sickness, bile rising in the throat, into the mouth. He took off his helmet. I could see all his face now, but was conscious only of the bright glint of his eyes. I said, "If you don't touch me, I will tell no one what you planned, I swear it."

"*Touch* you?" He was unslinging his sword, that I had provided for him, drawing it from the sheath. "If any sand's sifted through — " he said, examining it. "No, not a grain. What were you saying? Oh, yes — " He looked across at me, carefully inserted the tip of the sword into the sheath, than slammed the whole weapon home. My hand went up to my mouth. He burst out laughing. "I'm glad you get the allusion," he said. He put the sword in the weapon-rack, added the dagger to it. To reach the dagger I should have to get across the room — and past him.

"Going to help with the rest of the unarming?" he asked.

I stood mute.

He shrugged. "The choice is yours. If you help me, you'll save yourself a few bruises, and can go on hoping a little longer that your loyal Chief of Police will come charging to your rescue at the last moment. Otherwise, no point in wasting time in getting down to it."

I thought my heart would choke me, but I forced myself to go across to him, and silently began to unfasten the stiff buckles. But I could not prevent my hands from trembling, and he had to help me. "Now take off your dress," he said, but by this time my hands were shaking so much I could do nothing. He came to stand behind me. "I don't know whether you're being deliberately unhelpful, but I'll give you the benefit of the doubt. After all, I suppose you're not used to undressing yourself.

Let me see.'' He dragged the dress down from the shoulders. ''This is how Pharaoh likes to see you. And this is what Pharaoh likes to do – '' He grasped me to him, and I cried out. I had tried to prepare myself for pain of another kind, but not for the hardness of a man's strong body, the clasp of brutal arms, the grasp of impatient hands calloused by the use of sword and spear. Those hands were on my breasts now, and suddenly he whistled. ''Well, look at that! You're becoming quite a big girl now aren't you?'' I stared down with dilated eyes. Under his hands the breasts were swelling, the nipples hardening. I tried to bring my own hands up to protect them from him, but he had my arms pinioned at my sides. All I could do was move my head blindly from side to side, tears of shame pouring down my face, gasping out incoherent prayers for pity.

''Too late,'' he said. ''Now that we've had our fun with Upper Egypt . . . it's Lower Egypt's turn.'' He began to laugh. ''And the Delta, of course.'' He lifted me up, held me crushed against him, carried me over to the other wall, put me down, seized my shoulders and threw me back. ''Now we get down to essentials. And consider yourself lucky! You've only my unaided efforts to contend with – you're not being held down while a dozen men do what they like with you.''

And then only moments later there was a sound I could not recognise at first, it belonged to my childhood in Crete, a high, despairing scream of pain like a wounded sea bird. But it was a scream wrenched from my own throat at the deep, savage thrust with the whole power of his body behind it, as he drove into the vitals of his enemy.

''Mistress of the South and North, Lady of the Two Lands, you may now fairly add to your titles Nefertiti the Well and Truly Raped.''

I tried to move my head so that he could not see my face. But he could hear my desolate sobbing.

''Seeing it's the first time I've tried to rape a woman, I think I made a good job of it,'' he said, putting up a hand to take my chin so that I had to face him. ''I must say I got more out of it than I'd expected. I must make a habit of it.''

''Have you finished with me?'' I whispered.

''I told you, I must make a habit of it.''

''Please – please – '' I said, weeping. ''Hurt me any other way you like, I won't resist or cry out – I'd rather you killed me, rather than – ''

''Oh, for God's sake, stop acting as if you've never had a man before. How many years is it since *you* were a virgin? Still, by the time I've finished with you, *he'll* have to go a hell of a way and at the hell of a rate to catch up with me, won't he?'' His hand left my chin, began to move slowly down my throat. Like a trapped animal I tried to creep further under the straw beneath the protection of my cloak. ''That's not much of a defence,'' he said, and in almost a leisurely manner, pulled my cloak from me. Then, like a terrified animal unable to retreat any further, I could only lie motionless, staring up at him fixedly. The weapon-calloused hands began to move over me. ''Now who,'' he said smiling, ''would ever think that a mere barbarian could ever treat the Queen of Egypt so roughly?'' His mouth began to come down on mine; he had not kissed me before. I tried to push him away, I was sobbing with misery at the thought of his mouth on mine, but it descended inexorably, forcing my lips open, and my frantic hand rested on his head. The bronze hair that shone like metal was as soft as silk.

I could not scream now, but I still tried to struggle. This time he mastered me slowly, methodically, as he would have broken a rebellious mare. And I wondered, in a wildness of shame and misery and self-hatred why I had let him – why I was letting him – have the satisfaction of hearing me moaning, crying out, when, as no more than a child myself, I had somehow managed to endure childbirth silently – this was pain enough, but nothing like those rending agonies – if he would take his mouth from mine, I would be able to think clearly – *then* I would have given my soul to have had someone holding me – *he* was holding me now – the slow, as if reluctant passage of the child out of me – this urgent, increasingly rapid stabbing into me – weakly children – male violence – breasts that could not suckle – breasts as heavy and swollen now as if they teemed with milk, aching beneath the hard strength of him – I was moaning because when he pressed down on them, I thought they would burst, sending great jetting arcs of invisible milk spurting through the air as he moved away from me again after the last great convulsive drive.

Was I giving birth – or was I dying? I could feel my womb contracting, again, again, again – every muscle stiffened. A tremendous tremor shook my entire body, sending it arching up against him. Momentarily I lost consciousness. When my senses returned, his mouth had left mine, I knew he was staring at me, but I closed my eyes as a second shudder shook me, jerking me frantically closer to him again. ''You've killed me,'' I said faintly. I had heard of death agonies. Was this my death agony? My head fell back. He put me down quite gently, then bent over me, dominant rider with the wild, terrified, quivering thing he had tamed.

''No,'' he said quietly, touching my breasts. ''I haven't killed you. But I've surprised myself, and I think you've surprised yourself, too. Certainly you've surprised me.'' Then he lay down beside me with his face against my neck. He was laughing softly. Someone – not *I*? – was clinging to him, sobbing.

''Don't go from me! Don't leave me!''

''Not for some time at least, have no fear,'' he said, still laughing. ''That conquered territory of yours can enjoy the invader still – and bring him to battle again in due course.''

I timidly stroked the shining, bronze, silken hair; emboldened, took the hand at my breast, kissed it, put it back to cover my heart. ''Why did you laugh? Did I do something wrong?'' When he said nothing, I went on in a shamed voice, ''I know I'm cold, unresponsive – ''

''Unresponsive!'' He raised himself on his elbow, looked brilliant-eyed with laughter, down at me. ''Listen, my darling, you were being raped, fairly conclusively, weren't you – ''

''I shall tell no one.'' I said passionately, shyly touching his silken hair again.

'' – and at the end of it you proceed to have the most stupendous climax – something nine hundred and ninety-nine women in a thousand, if that, would never experience. And you lie there looking up at me, big-eyed, apologising for being unresponsive – '' He began to kiss me. I kissed him back in wild delight. ''You know what it meant, don't you?'' he whispered.

I said slowly, ''My body had realised, while I thought something unbearable was happening to me, that it was really – ecstatic.''

''Not the first time, my poor darling. You cried bitterly afterwards.'' He stroked my hair tenderly. ''I can't even say I'm sorry. It was marvellous for me right from the start.''

I carried his hands to my lips. ''When I'm really hurt, I don't cry. I made no sound in childbirth. But I think I must have cried because I thought you hated me, and I must have known I loved you.''

''Do you still think I hate you?'' he asked, caressing me. I shook my head. ''The second time was different because you kissed me. And you said you'd never raped a woman before. And I thought – hoped – that you wouldn't rape a woman unless you wanted her – a little.''

He kissed my throat. ''And you know now I want you – a little?''

I said, blushing, ''More than a little, I think.''

''You *know*, darling heart, no one could know better than you

— or I. And are you trying to tell me you hadn't suspected before that I wanted you?'' I shook my head. ''Little one, once I became honest with myself, stopped fighting fanatically against capture, I used to want you so much when he used to bring you to see me when I was sick, I'd have given a year of my life to have put out a hand and pulled the lily-breasted, lily-scented queen into bed with me.''

''It would have hurt your chest a great deal,'' I said, fingering the scar lovingly.

''Sweetheart, the pain in my chest would have been a great deal less than the pain I'd have given you! And if I hurt you again, My Lady of Grace, it's because I want you so. But other things will be different, won't they? And then we can sleep.''

''In each other's arms,'' I whispered.

''Yes, my darling, in each other's arms. But first will you open those arms to me now?''

''Willingly,'' I whispered. ''Oh, most willingly.''

He kissed me, caressed me, took me as gently as if I were indeed a virgin on my wedding night. But then as I lay trembling, yearning, begging for the strong embrace, the strength I gloried in, came the urgent possession, making me cry out in ecstasy. And eventually, his beloved head heavy on my breast, he slept, so happily, so completely, and I lay there with my arms holding him, marvelling at the sweetness of the body surrendered in love, surrendered to love, and thanking the Goddess for making me a woman — for this. For years I had thought she had cursed me, but now I knew I was blessed.

This was the Nefertiti who night after night, year after year, had lain indifferent, unresponsive, physically torn, penetrated; mentally, emotionally untouched. Had lain silent and still. Who now had been invaded, conquered, liberated. Who gasped with delight at the touch of a strong hand exploring her breasts, those breasts which rose to him unafraid, whose whole body rose to his unafraid, again and again, who trembled in uncontrollable delight — ah, such delight! — at the beginning of her conqueror-liberator's entry into her body, who cried out in almost intolerable ecstasy as the fierce rhythm of her subjection — liberation-raced to its climax, who trembled with desire at his every look, and clung to him in a shuddering convulsion of passion when the last great wave — not a dark roaring wave of terror as had overwhelmed Crete that night, but a great sunlit-white-crested wave of laughter, brilliant in the sun, such as I had seen dashing on the headland at Phaestos in the south-westerly gales — swept through both of us, mutual surrender, the extremity of delight, swept us together, made us one. And then the quiet drowsiness of naked, fulfilled love, eyes closed, but every other sense more intensely alive then ever before.

It should have been no surprise to me. For weeks if he had as much as moved a finger on the other side of the room, my body ached for his, trembled for his — and I had told myself I was in the throes of a fever. And had no inkling of his thoughts, except that intensity was there — and I had thought it the intensity of hatred. And now I knew every inch of that beloved body, had kissed it, caressed it, knew the full strength of it. . . He wanted to give me tenderness, I did not want his tenderness, there was no time for tenderness, I wanted to be seized, held, possessed in a passion so intense, so ruthless that it was almost unbearable — except that it would have been even more unbearable if it had ceased.

I was deaf to the storm raging outside, but his faintest whisper thundered in my heart and blood, I was blind to everything but the face above mine. Each time he took me, I had died a little, was taken out of, far beyond, ordinary experience, and then I had returned to a life more fiercely vibrant than I had ever known before. If, indeed, I had ever previously been alive.

The dust storm blew for three days.

Outside the window the sky was always dark. We kept lamps burning all the while — we wanted to see each other, we had so little time; we knew, although at first we did not speak of it, that soon we should be able to see each other only in the heart. When we were about to sleep, we would let the lamps go on burning so that immediately on waking each could see the other's beloved sleeping face. And then the other would stir, wake, and we could gaze on each other, myself looking up at the eyes that shone silver in their brightness, under the straight, almost frowning brows, the mouth that had once seemed so stern, the cheek so deliciously hard to the touch, the hair that gleamed like metal, but was as soft as silk, and he — he stared down at me naked in the lamplight, and that was why I had been born, why my breasts had been shaped, my lips, my quivering limbs, why the Goddess had been kind, after all, in making me a woman, so that he could take pleasure in looking at me, in caressing me, in possessing me. Lamplight, straw and a soldier's scarlet cloak, rough wine, dried fruit, the sound of the storm ever outside, but I rarely heard it, in the clamour of my heart, the surging of my blood. Hard, impatient hands, strong urgent body, muscular fettering arms that I kissed as they held me imprisoned, his eyes and his mouth and his hair and his voice whispering that I was his walled secret garden at dawn, with budding lilies covered with dew, I was his cool spring, his sweet ripening fruit.

But even as I lay in his arms in the act of love, I could no longer forget the thought, 'Soon he must leave me.' And then I would wish that the strong hands which had brought me such rapture might bring me death rather than that he should go from me. It would be easy enough for him to bring them up from my breasts to my throat — a little pain, perhaps, but only a little, brief pain compared with the long pain that I did not think I could endure. He could not take me with him to Byblos. Byblos, he was convinced, would fall, and he would die with it. But I — he condemned me to live on, *because I was a queen.*

In those three days and nights we had together he awoke not only my body, but my mind. By what he did to me he made me conscious of joys so exquisite that even now my heavy body trembles, is light and urgent at the remembrance of them; by what he said to me, he made me conscious of sentinels on the northern border, beleagured cities, little villages, women with dread in their hearts, men fighting against desperate odds, invaders from the desert who dashed out children's brains against walls, ripped up women with child. And he told me what he had seen in Egypt itself — people selling their own children into slavery, dying animals, death under the scorching sun.

If in his arms I felt I was one with the gods, when he left me, I could no longer continue a remote, withdrawn existence, for I knew now I was one with all living creatures. My life had never been my own; now it was less my own than ever before. I knew that when he left me to go north again something of him would remain within me, something more than the seed I prayed he had implanted in me. The beloved body might withdraw from mine, never be mine again, but the essence of him would always be part of me, would *be* me. "I am yours, I am you," I whispered to him as he slept in my arms for the last time. I bent to kiss his closed eyes, his hair. When I raised my head again I felt as if my heart had turned to ice within my breast. Staring over his sleeping face, I could see the little window that was scarcely more than a slit in the wall. And through the window there was dimness. I began to weep. My tears splashed on his face and roused him. I said, "Look at the window. It's growing light. The storm must have passed."

He washed my face as if I were a child. "Shall I dress you?" he said, and I nodded — I could not speak. But first he took me into his arms. "Your body fits into my arms as exactly as my sword fits into my hand. If we can meet again before I go back to Byblos — ''

I could speak then. ''We must,'' I said, carrying his hands to my lips.

''It may not be for days. All that we can be sure of is that it will be a hurried meeting, and so I may hurt you again. But it will only be because I want you so much.'' He smiled at me suddenly. ''When a man's been starved, his table manners may leave a good deal to be desired.''

I whispered. ''Do you think I shan't be starved too?''

''They also say,'' he said, carefully adjusting my cloak about me, ''that it's the most dangerous thing in the world to let a starving man have all he needs to satisfy his hunger. But we'll take the risk, shall we?''

''Any risk,'' I said.

And so, when the guardroom had been made to look as undisturbed as possible, it was time for us to go. I went with heartbreak. I stood in the doorway, looking back. ''Until we came here I did not know what happiness was,'' I said.

Chapter Sixteen
Staphylos

I had been finding life in Amarna increasingly frustrating, yet now found that, paradoxically, the absence of the very people who had contributed so much to this feeling, left existence dullness itself. With Nefertiti at the Palace, I could hope each morning that this would be the day when at last her face would show a little animation that I could try to convey in my work, while in the evening I could hope that this particular discussion would at least convince Acamas that it was absurd for a rootless man to feel allegiance to the point of self-sacrifice to a foreign city.

Physical discomfort added to mental unease. It was unbearably hot, and then for three days we saw little of the sun. The sky was an angry yellow, and to the north we could see what seemed like great dark clouds driving furiously down on us. A sandstorm, Phereclos, said. With luck it would blow itself out before it reached us. It did – just – but even so the atmosphere had been intolerable.

And it meant that Acamas' return would be delayed.

I heard that he had, indeed, started out, and would have got through had he not been ordered to escort Nefertiti to Amarna. Feeling he could take no chances with her safety in the storm, he had turned back, sending on two chariots with the news. Then there were confused stories of traces breaking, the beginning of an ordeal lasting three days, the Queen in fever – for days she had been the prey of intermittent fever – sheltering as best she could. Such was the news in the evening. In the morning I was amazed to receive a summons to the Palace.

An old blind harper sat in a corner playing some plangent tune. The scrawny child I could now identify as the Princess Nofret, clung to the Queen. She sat with her back to the light.

In my bad Egyptian I enquired cautiously after her health. ''I was in good hands,'' she said, and I immediately thought the fever could not have left her, because she sounded as if she were laughing. Hysteria must be very near. But to my relief she pulled herself together, and asked if I were more satisfied with the portrait bust. No? Then perhaps my skill might be greater if I worked in my own studio. She would visit me that afternoon.

As I stood trying to digest this, she said to her child, ''You're tired — they say you haven't slept for days. You must sleep now that I'm back.'' She turned to the two women in attendance. ''She must go to bed. I will come to her very shortly.'' The child was led out, wailing. Now there was only the old harpist, playing softly at the far end of the room, and ourselves. She plunged into rapid Achaean. ''You will find Acamas, and tell him I shall be at your house this afternoon. And you will see that all your servants stay in their own quarters, and that we have the garden and one room for our use, unobserved.''

I don't know which stunned me more, what she said, or the way she said it. It might have been Acamas himself rapping out orders. Where was the timidity, the hesitancy? Astonishment robbed me of utterance.

''Yes,'' she said, taking two paces forward, ''I am making use of your house as a place of assignation with a lover. And you will do what I ask — *order* — otherwise I shall find some other way of being with him, and then I shall tell him who it was who tricked a child of seven into coming to Egypt and who refused to listen to her when she begged you to let her stay in Byblos — Byblos where *he* was coming in that very year — ''

I mentally tried to dodge the great jagged rocks of verbal missile being hurled at me, but at first could have made no reply to save my life. For if what she said left me thunderstruck — Nefertiti calmly and resolutely talking of assignations with a lover — her face, now that she had taken those two steps forward, into the sunlight, stunned me! Colour ebbing, flooding, glowing. Great eyes dark, shining — no, sparkling as never before. There was tumult in her breasts, her whole body seemed to emanate warmth, life, triumph. It was my first sight of Nefertiti in love. It was also my first insight into the single-mindedness amounting to ruthlessness of Nefertiti in love. She was going to meet her lover, and I was to provide the meeting place. It was as simple as that.

And, my God, she looked a Queen of Egypt then! All was clear, unshadowed, brilliance, assurance, *splendour*!

I found Acamas in his quarters cleaning a sword that scarcely needed cleaning, and whistling under his breath. He should have looked exhausted — he looked exalted, damn him. I felt more exhausted than he seemed. In as detached a voice as I could manage, I said, "The Queen will be visiting my house this afternoon to sit for me — " My voice trailed away. How to continue? ' — to sit for me, and — well, what for you, you lucky bastard, looking ten foot tall and alive as an entire regiment of picked troops, slamming your sword into the sheath and — ' I could bear it no longer. "She told me to tell you. What happened?"

He laughed, sprang up, stretched his arms in triumph above his head — looking twenty foot tall now, damn him — and said, matter-of-factly, "I raped her. And then I started to rape her a second time. But then it stopped being a rape. And now I feel a bit of a god."

He looked and sounded every inch of a god, damn him, damn him, sempiternally damn him. To cut him down to size, I said I thought it would have been up to him to make arrangements for other — ah! - comings together.

He laughed again. "You don't know my girl." (And how the Mistress of Upper and Lower Egypt would have cried out with pleasure at the term, I knew even then.) "She insisted on doing it. And then, when the storm ended, although I'd thought up a few good excuses, it was she who decided the traces must have broken."

"You seem," I said sourly, "to have played a very passive part in all this."

His eyes blazed with amusement. "Do you think so? Ask her!"

As I plodded back across the city, feeling an old, old man, I reflected on the first words addressed to me by the Queen of Egypt. She had had me brought to Egypt in revenge, because she wanted me to see her apparent triumph; well, she was certainly avenging herself on me now, and this triumph was real enough. I still did not really believe that this was all happening, but I made preparations as if I were not participating in a particularly vivid dream or nightmare. I selected limestone, quartzite, nervously inspected the flowering shrubs in my garden, the essential furnishings of "the room" demanded by my royal guest. Where in the hell had they conducted their amours? huddled together on the floor of the chariot in the sandstorm? Well, here was a fairly comfortable couch for them, with my best embroideries. My best wine. Choice fruit. If he drank my wine, damn him, I hoped it choked him!

She came first, attended only by the old woman she always seemed to have with her. Not that even the crone remained long. She wanted, said her mistress, to visit my cook. I gave directions.

She went off, grinning. They were taking no chances; she would keep a sharp eye on my household all the afternoon. No possible chance of intervention from that quarter.

Her mistress turned coolly to me — women never cease to surprise me — those calm eyes concealing boiling emotions, hunger for physical passion. "We might as well make use of the waiting period. Shall I sit here?"

And suddenly I was almost agonisingly eager to start work. For it had happened! Surface tranquillity — but a woman at last alive, dreaming of a lover, she sat there, quite oblivious of me, waiting, calmly, because he would come, he had said he would come to her, and so she would wait for ever. She was back in her waking dream, *blushing* in her waking dream. Limestone, I thought. Painted limestone. Showing her dreaming, blushing in the dream.

And then the sound of footsteps, coming closer.

She was on her feet, eyes fixed on the door. He came in. She did not move towards him, but her hands came up, instinctively, I think, to cup her breasts as if offering them, the old sacred gesture of the goddess of the island of her birth. My God, there she stood, the ivory royal priestess, making the ancient invitation to. . . And he, the chosen one, was across from the door faster than I would have thought humanly possible. No wonder she gasped as he caught her in his arms. "My falcon! My hawk!" He was kissing her eyes, her throat, then lifting her up, turning to me.

"Where?" he asked.

"There is a room — " I began, but she interrupted with, "The garden. *In the sun.*"

Of me she had taken no notice, ever since he had appeared in the doorway. A pity, for I had prepared a short but pretty speech. My house, like my life, was at her disposal. (Only too true, alas). But she had all the terrifying single-mindedness of a woman madly in love. As she existed now only for one man, no other man existed for her. Meanwhile here the pair of them were, presenting me — briefly, as he carried her off — with a marvellous subject for my skill — the conquering god, the violated nymph, the male face proud, the female face hidden against him, his head high, hers drooping, his air of possession absolute, no attempt from her now — or ever again — to deny that possession.

Damn her, once — only hours before — she had seemed the most unrewarding, the most frustrating of subjects. Now she was offering me too much. This — with him. The woman dreaming of her lover. The ivory priestess making the ritual gesture of offering. And now yet a fourth. The woman in the presence of her lover, lifting her face to his, as she had when he had come across the room to her. . .

And I should be grateful to her for occupying my mind with thoughts of a purely professional nature. So I hammered away as best I could, but unfortunately I was not deaf, and Nefertiti was not dumb, and had gasped, "The garden. In the sun." And in the garden, in the sun, she was still gasping, and giving moans of pleasure, and more than once she cried out in ecstasy.

I hammered away as loudly as I could to drown her ardent testimonials, but my concentration was ruined for the day. The chips flew, but more than once I nearly stabbed myself with the chisel. And eventually, inevitably, I suppose, I stole out into the garden. To spy? Only partly. Above all, I wanted to see her vulnerable, accessible — debased, degraded, if you like. But I did not spy for long. I caught a sudden glimpse of her face, and turned back hurriedly. I had thought the transformation in her already great enough, but never in all my life, before or since, have I ever seen anything so magnificent and radiant as the transfiguration of that face in the moment of supreme, total surrender and ecstasy.

Chapter Seventeen
Nefertiti

The afternoon after we returned to Amarna, we met at Staphylos' house, and went together into the garden. His face came down over mine, blotting out the sun. It was what I had dreamed of, long before, on the day before my marriage. A face looking down on me, sky over earth, man and woman.

He loved me as deeply as any man of his race had ever loved a woman. But it is not the fashion of that race for a man ever to love a woman as much as a woman loves a man. In my thoughts there was no room for anyone or anything but him. My absorbing wish was to give him pleasure. He loved me, but if I ruled much of his thoughts, he never forgot Ribaddi, the white city of Byblos, the advancing enemy. If he took insane risks to come to me, he would have done even more to take help back to Syria. But never think I was not content with the love he gave me. Content? How inadequate the word is. Grateful? Again, inadequate to the point of idiocy. I gloried in his love, and in my heart a hundred times a day, I was on my knees to Heaven, thanking every deity to whom women have ever prayed, for what they had given me — unasked.

I permitted three people to know my secret. Staphylos, because his house would be a useful meeting-place. He was jealous, of course, because Acamas loved *me*, and also resentful because I did not do the obvious thing — use all means to keep Acamas in safety, in security in Amarna.

I asked Acamas to tell Sophronicos. It would help with the conveying of messages when we were parted. I could not trust Staphylos, of course, to do this — I was his rival — I knew this, although Acamas never did, never suspecting the feeling Staphylos had for him.

And Kat-Senet had to know. She was delighted. Her little

queen, she said, at last knew what it was like to be a woman. And with joy she would do all she could to assist my infidelity to my husband.

We had very little time left to us. Since he could obtain no help, he would go back north without it. We met for a few times at Staphylos' house – usually, after the first meeting, in the morning. In the afternoon he would openly come to me in the garden, and plead for help for Byblos. Only to be with each other, to look at each other, to speak with the eyes while our voices. . .

Once or twice at the beginning there were attendants at the entrance to the garden, but then I dismissed them, except for Kat-Senet, saying, "I have to be bored by his eternal talk of marauding Hebrews and Hittites – but there's no need for you to have to listen to it as well!" But even when only Kat-Senet was there, dozing in the sun on a distant seat, we were circumspect enough at first – by day; he would argue, demand, until we were approaching the pavilion itself, and the screen of flowering trees surrounding it, and only then he would catch me to him, and kiss my eyes and mouth and throat, then turn me gently so that I leaned against him, my head on his shoulder, my eyes closed, and his hands on my breasts. A few moments only, and then he would raise my hands and kiss them, gently, a few moments, no more, and then back into the sun, completing our walk, our conversation, and I would say loudly, with irritation breaking through queenly condescension, that when The One returned, I might speak to him, but all the time my heart was crying out, "Oh, my love, my love, I shall do it for you, but I shall half die with grief as I plead for you, because it will mean your leaving me."

And in the night he came to the pavilion, and stayed until just before dawn. Kat-Senet would keep watch. I suppose we were both recklessly foolhardy, but our meeting was *possible* – that was all that mattered. There were very few patrolling guards – there never had been, the double wall had made a large force unnecessary. There were now very few indeed, with Akhnaten away. I had often slept in the pavilion when not required in marital attendance on Akhnaten. And so our two bodies could become one body – there was never any separation now between our minds – and we could whisper together, and before he went away, I could kiss each scar on the beloved body, kiss his hands, trace each plane of his face with loving fingers, as if I did not already know every line of that face by heart! But I was new to love, and like a child, slow, stupid, yet eager to learn, I was afraid of forgetting.

Sometimes the intensity of my love left him troubled, half-remorseful. "Darling heart, I don't know what I've started," he said once.

In the morning, I asked Kat-Senet what he had meant. She cackled and said, "What you've never had, you never miss. But when he goes away, my dear little mistress, he'll leave you knowing for the first time what it's like to be — "

The wrinkled, loving face suddenly seemed to me the leering face of treachery. I stared at her in horror. "You mean that I shall want this — pleasure of the body so much, I should want someone else! How can you? How dare you!"

"It's always been there," said Kat-Senet. "This — capacity. The Magnificent One knew it, didn't he?"

I broke into angry tears, sobbing that I loved him so; surely the two people who loved me most realised my body would always be sacred, for him?

When we whispered together in each other's arms, it was not always of love. Any man can impregnate a woman's body; even if a man wished to do so — and most of them, I think, would not — few are capable of impregnating a woman's mind. If Acamas brought every part of my body to life, he also roused my mind. We both knew that Byblos was doomed, that when he left me, it would be never to return, but to hearten me he would now talk hopefully of the future. The battle was not yet lost. One day he would regain his kingdom. One day he would take me there. I should be his queen. "Tell me what I must do as your queen," I would whisper to him — and he taught me to be queen of that little city between the mountains and the sea, the little city I shall never set earthly eyes upon.

I persuaded him in one thing; to wait, after all, until Akhnaten came back. Akhnaten came back, refused to give help, while trying to persuade Acamas to stay in Amarna. Then he went back to Byblos — alone.

That is really all there is to say.

I remember that when we were last together, someone was playing a flute in the distance — a sweet, clear melody, and that he said that in Achaea shepherd-boys played on reed pipes with the same sweetness. And that one day, one night, we should hear that sound together, that after the Evening Star rose in the green sky to the left of the setting sun, the star of the Achaean love-goddess, we should be brought together again.

But I knew it could never happen. I had been named, not after the Evening Star, which brings men and women together to the bed of love, but — and this is what he had called me ever since we had first loved each other — after the dawn, the cruel dawn, red as blood, that dictates the parting of lovers.

And dawn came soon enough. Hardly had the moon gone down, the stars paled, disappearing into the blue-black sky, than that the same sky began to lighten in the east, to which he must return, lighten, grow crimson, and he kissed my eyes and mouth and hands and left me for ever.

Chapter Eighteen
Staphylos

It is given to few men to be present at the birth of a new religion; I may, I think, claim to be unique, in that I witnessed the birth of two.

One of the great differences between men and women is that if a man invents a religion, he proclaims it from the house-tops. But if a woman creates her own secret cult, she hugs it to her, as she would a lover.

I don't suppose it has ever happened before in the history of the world, and is extremely unlikely to happen in the future — a husband and wife almost simultaneously originating new faiths.

Acamas, of course, left her pregnant. Of course. He would. Brief though their intimacy might have been. But isn't that the way of the gods? Since I have settled in mainland Achaea, I have been able to study the rather childish Achaean religion further, and it abounds in stories of virgins who after one solitary encounter with a god give birth to heroes. Like all the best gods, Acamas did not pursue his amours in a decent bed. I am sure Nefertiti was convinced he made her pregnant the first night he spent with her; how god-like he must have appeared, grasping her to him against the howl of a sandstorm, and informing her that he was acting as he did, not because he remotely wanted to do these dreadful things to her, but because he was avenging those women raped on Syrian hillsides. I don't doubt he successfully persuaded himself that this was so — but it was an idea of sheer genius when it came to winning Nefertiti's adoring allegiance. Would her reaction, pure fanatical devotion, have been the same to whichever man finally took hold of her with real desire? I doubt it. Because any other man except Acamas, would have wanted a response from a willing mistress. So — a tentative approach. Nothing to shock or startle the gentle doe with her innocent, lambent eyes. Finger tips touching. A kiss on her hand, her brow — finally, and with immeasurable tenderness, her lips. All the while, *supplication.*

And such tactics would have got a man nowhere.

But Acamas crashed in like one of those savage hordes he was always talking about, and undoubtedly succeeded in giving her mental and physical hell for a time. But also, such being the nature of Nefertiti, satisfaction. And once she'd yielded, she reciprocated energetically enough, was capable of enduring any amount of pain, violence, indeed delighted in it. Her anxieties over the unlovely Meritaten had their irony. She never seemed to realise that it was from her that the girl inherited such capacity for boiling passion.

But I run ahead of my narrative. After Acamas left, I did not see her for weeks. I was glad. I anticipated floods of tears. And I had captured the Nefertiti I wanted to immortalise; I didn't want to see her now that the dream was broken. Sophronicos, however, went daily to the Great Palace. He, of course, had been ecstatic over the whole business. *He*, devout soul, had never aspired to coupling with a goddess; that these two marvellous beings should be in love was sublimely right, to him. I asked him if he had seen her. Yes, he said enthusiastically. Nothing could exceed her gentleness, placidity. It was he who had told me she was pregnant. From his description of her she sounded uncommonly like a very beautiful heifer in calf.

It never seemed to occur to the unworldly idiot that it was remarkable that Nefertiti should be allowed to go on enjoying a peaceful and public pregnancy. When eventually I saw her I questioned her as tactfully as I could. She was quite matter of fact about it. The Goddess, she said calmly, had contrived to allow her to bear Acamas' child with all the facilities the Egyptian court supplied because not long before her darling impregnated her, Akhnaten had spent the night with her — attracted, I suspect, by all the symptoms she was unwittingly showing of a woman madly in love.

Well and good, I thought, for the time being — but what if, when the child is born, there are grey eyes to be explained away, hair the colour of bronze? I found myself informing all and sundry that in Crete I had seen the Queen's mother, fair and grey-eyed, that the Queen's grandfather, I believed, had been fair and grey-eyed, I told the guileless Sophronicos that he had better start making it widely known that his native Colonos, birthplace of the Queen's maternal grandfather, abounded in grey-eyed inhabitants.

Shortly afterwards, I was bidden to present myself at the Palace, to be received by the old crone who was Nefertiti's watchdog. She grinned at me with toothless gums — I was early, she said reprovingly. The Lady of Grace had sent a summons to the Commander-in-Chief, briefly returned to Amarna, leaving next day for the frontier again.

A summons to Horemheb? I could not believe my ears. A profile of angry bronze. A frustrated man, carrying with him an atmosphere of violence, the frontier, conflict. As out of place in Amarna as a bull in a lily-garden. She had always been very nervous in his presence. It seemed unthinkable that, *pregnant*, she could send for him, brooding, bitter, restless. . .Yet send for him she had. Acamas, my friend, what have you started?

The crone, who did not like to have her mistress out of her sight for long, went back into the garden to maintain a discreet surveillance, unseen. Unbidden, I went after her. Yes, there they were, together, and — My God, Nefertiti was nervous! She clutched — absurdly — a fan of ostrich feathers. How they shook — and how he must have noticed it! The interview was coming to an end. He kissed her hand, briefly, with far less than the approved, courtier-like rapture. She, nervous to the point of ineptitude, forgot to take her hand from his, looked up at him wide-eyed. He saluted her formally, and came stalking away. His face had its usual shut-in look. An unusual face; emotionless, but not heavy. That lack of expression was not blankness, but an exercise in rigidly disciplined self-control. He tramped past us in his usual grim silence.

I prepared to make my own, no doubt far less impressive entrance, trying all the while to conceal my reluctance. For what in the hell could she want to talk to me about, save prattle about Acamas? Or about the child?

But I should not have forgotten that Acamas had those ideas about a king being Shepherd of his People. In his arms Nefertiti achieved two kinds of conception — his child, and the idea of herself as royal Shepherdess. For when I approached her, she said, quite simply. "You know that I haven't left Amarna for years. I don't know what is going on in Egypt. You always view matters without sentiment. Tell me what you saw when you came up the river."

In her pregnancy, those months when Queens of Egypt traditionally lay inert, like great bloated insects, as she herself, in earlier pregnancies had lain, she was acting in a revolutionary manner — voicing concern over what happened to the wives of soldiers sent to the frontier, what was happening to the refugees from Syria, what would happen to all ordinary Egyptians if the Nile floods were again insufficient.

At first I was flattered that my realistic opinion should be sought so earnestly; then – and the jarring blow to my self esteem! – I began to see the matter in a different light. The Beautiful One was also being a beautiful bitch. She was exacting a little belated revenge. If she had originally planned to bring me to Egypt because she had never forgiven me for bringing her here from Crete, how she hated me now because I could have taken her to Byblos at practically the same time Acamas was landing there! In all her life she was never so beautiful as in those first months after he became her lover – if you could see how I immortalised her in stone, you would not doubt me! – and so she obtained the subtlest of revenges. She kept me in attendance on her while she gloried in her pregnancy by another man. Well, I hope she was satisfied. And yet it was not all unallayed misery. I had always believed that the gradual swelling of a pregnant woman's body was unsightly to any average man except a devoted husband. She was different. For all my twinfold jealousy (what did *he* need of 'love' from a woman?) I found myself regarding her in the months that followed with the careful compassion, the anxiety, the tenderness that a man gives a beloved pet animal big with young.

She was left much to her own devices. Akhnaten, while not appearing to doubt his fathering of the child, seemed oddly furtive, almost ashamed of it. He spent most of his time with his mother in the great palace so recently built for her. This was foolish, for it made the people murmur – impossible to convey to anyone not living in Egypt during those feverish near-hysterical years of drought, misery, and the would-be shattering of the old beliefs, how much significance the people gave to the Queen's new pregnancy. And her husband did not seem to care – even more unforgivably – seemed to wish that it had never happened.

They are an extraordinary people, the Egyptians. They are obsessed by death as no other people I know, but they are also obsessed by birth, fertility, far beyond the preoccupations of any other farming folk. After a monarch has ruled a certain number of years, they hold a not too thinly disguised test of his physical powers, called the *Sed* festival. But, of course, what is most essential is that Pharaoh should be sexually potent – is it not one of his titles, the Bull? And there is only one way of showing this – by filling the womb of, preferably, his Queen. On Nefertiti's continuous fertility, it seemed, depended the fertility of Egypt. Well, when I had first come to Amarna, the outlook for Egyptian fertility seemed a poor one. No child for some years (when the real famine had started.) The children she had already borne stunted, sickly. Two of the children dying

(as the crops had failed.)

But now, against all hope, the Queen pregnant again — and splendidly so. The near-hysterical rejoicing throughout Egypt when this news spread, was Nefertiti's greatest safeguard. Who would dare harm the divine child — or its mother? Also, of course, a safeguard for Akhnaten too, if he had sense enough to realise it. In fact, if he had been a practical man, he would have seen to it that Nefertiti speedily became pregnant again after her delivery. If not by himself, by someone of rude muscular strength. I should not imagine that, despite his talk of the brotherhood of all men under the benevolence of the Aten, he would really relish the idea of a landless Achaean begetting children on the Egyptian Queen, but a crown official of some kind might be viewed differently — and here the man most obvious to beget a strong progeny leapt to the eye. The Bull of Memphis himself. Who, admittedly, stared at his Queen with such strong dislike. Well, he was used to obeying unpalatable orders, carrying them out efficiently, even if in his usual grimly impersonal manner.

Such ludicrous fantasies gave me my only amusement those days.

Not that I was the only person in Egypt to be obsessed by fantasy. Up and down the Nile Valley they were singing a song in possibly doubtful taste, the refrain being that the warmth and moistness of the filling royal womb represented the only chance of fertility along the river. In the villages, it was whispered, little carved wooden models were appearing — Nefertiti as Hathor, cow-goddess, suckler of Egypt, in a variety of postures. Often, naked, on all fours, she was hitched to a plough like an ox. You placed the little figure somewhere in secret on a handful of dried-up soil, and you prayed that the Queen's good swelling breasts and belly would fertilise your fields for you.

It was in reaction against such crudities that I found myself whittling away one day at a piece of ivory. One couldn't escape the prevalent mania for talk of Hathor, Hathor, Hathor, but my own inclinations were to think of that goddess as the elegant patroness of the delights of love rather than the uddered suckler. So I carved away, and the body began to emerge, slender, graceful, and here was the head-dress, the disc of the moon, the horns. . .

Phereclos strolled in; I couldn't hide the ivory in time, so offered it for inspection. I had heard, I said, that whores rather liked mirrors with the somewhat elongated body of Hathor as handle. Phereclos duly inspected then grinned. "Amazing how she's kept that head-dress on through all *that*!"

"That?"

"My God, as if you hadn't done it deliberately!" he said derisively. I stared, gaping, saw his point. The goddess was very much in the throes of the act of love — her arching back made it a *very* curving handle.

"I hadn't meant it that way!" I said. But I suppose I really had, and when he had gone, I completed the carving — the only part left unfinished was the face, and the face of course was the face I had seen upturned like an opening flower, when her whole body had been opening like a flower here in my own garden.

I fixed a bronze mirror to the handle — it really was a very skilled piece of work! — and showed it again to Phereclos.

His hand shot out, and grabbed it. For a moment there was silence, then a low whistle. "What imagination! Do you think that's what she'd be like — with the look of — of serene, smiling *expertise*? By God, I'll buy it from you! I'll have to hide the damned thing from my wife, but — My God! No need for you to dream of owning a Nubian gold-mine; turn out a few more like this, and every foreigner in Amarna will give you what you like for 'em. But for God's sake, don't let the Egyptians know! They take their royalty seriously!"

I turned out half a dozen more. I obtained definite satisfaction over arching the back, shaping. . .well, no need to go into details. I disliked selling the mirrors — the way the bastards ran their fingers and thumbs along the animal tokens of feminity. Yet appreciatively rather than lewdly. I don't think a single man among them meant to degrade Nefertiti by possessing this carving of her. It was just every man's dream — moon-pale loveliness, fixed, frozen, if you like, in ivory.

But next time I visited Phereclos, he was not smiling. "No more carving of a certain kind if you want — literally — to save your skin," he said curtly. Some fool had talked, or boastfully shown his possession to an Egyptian, and all hell was let loose, Egyptian officials taking studios apart, confiscating any ivories they found.

"Will *she* know?" I stammered, blenching. (For she would know that only *I* could have —)

"No, she won't know, she'd never be allowed to. And *he* doesn't know, either! But the order's gone out from some very high authority indeed, confiscate and destroy all copies, and impalement, at the best, for any vile brute found in possession of one. And so," concluded Phereclos reluctantly, "I'd better destroy mine." He took a hammer and speedily reduced it to fragments. "Goodbye, Lady of Grace. It was nice possessing you. I wish you might have the luck to get that look on your face one day! And if you do ever find out what the nasty foreigners have been up to, believe me, we all have great affection and admiration for you, Beautiful One, which we'd show, given a proper chance!" He turned to me warningly, "But no more ivory carvings of the Despoina, Staphylos! I don't think they're lucky!"

"All right," I said, and then my guts churning suddenly, "The high Egyptian authority — it wouldn't be Horemheb, would it?"

"Horemheb? Oh, no. He's still at the frontier, won't be back for a month or so, they say. Here, you'd better have a drink."

I drank with him, wondering all the time why I had been so terrified at the thought of Horemheb coming upon the carvings. So I went on thinking after I had returned to my own house. Anything to defer the moment when I too, for safety's sake, must destroy my own little piece of carved ivory, the best of the lot. . .But destroyed it had to be, although up to the moment the hammer came down on it, I tried to persuade myself it might be safe enough to keep it — I could always tell the 'high authority' it was a carving of a Cretan woman bull-dancer — yes, get rid of the head-dress, and. . .

No. It reminded me of the nightmare I'd had of her and the bull when I first came to Amarna.

Down came the hammer. And, I thought, sweeping up the mess, I should never know whether it had been carved in hate, or love. Possibly a mixture of both?

Chapter Nineteen
Nefertiti

Staphylos, I know, eagerly alert for any sign I had not truly loved his friend, found such evidence in the glowing physical appearance that befalls most pregnant animals. If he could have seen into my soul, *that* wore a shrivelled look of suffering. Even now when, very infrequently, I hear the name of Byblos, that soul dies a little.

I saw little of Akhnaten. When he came back to Amarna, he spent most of his time with his mother, but on one of these rare occasions when he came – to see the children – and I was sure of my condition, I sent the girls away, and said, "I'm pregnant." He did not doubt for a moment that he was the father – after all, the clumsy, clutching embrace, the seemingly guilt-ridden thrustings and plungings had been all part of the pattern that had made me pregnant six times before. But he had never previously shown such consternation at the news that I had conceived. Now his jaw dropped, and he stared at me with as much dismay as if he were, not a husband, and a royal husband with royal views as to the need for a good supply of heirs for the succession, but a lover confronted by a not much prized mistress with the most unwelcome news possible. So I thought at first. Later, recalling his appalled face, I imagined that such an expression might appear on the face of a priest of one of those religions which demand the dedication of manhood to the goddess – but this priest had momentarily lapsed with a human.

After this, he avoided me as much as possible – and when a meeting could not be avoided, he tried not to look at me, particularly when my pregnancy had become obvious.

At least Akhnaten's distinct lack of rapture – duly noted by courtiers' vigilant eyes – meant that on this occasion I was not so surrounded by doctors as I had been in the past. In fact, although Pentu paid me formal visits and prepared the same spells and incantations, I relied more on concoctions of herbs brewed by Kat-Senet. Pregnant women in her village had always drunk them; the peasant children of Egypt are strong and healthy, far more so than those born in the harems of palaces, said Kat-Senet. But she did more than brew potions, she encouraged me to go out of the Palace, let the people see me.

"It will give them hope, Beautiful One. Look at these big melon-breasts of yours — they'll teem with milk this time — so the Nile will flood! You're a promise of fertility to them, Beautiful One, their fields will yield crops again! Let them *see* you, and *hope*!"

So I went out, often, and let myself be seen. Certainly, if one excludes the mental torment, I had never known an easier pregnancy. And the child quickened to vigorous life.

I realised now that Kat-Senet had another reason for urging me to let myself be seen. In the people's devotion, she reasoned, lay my chief safety. Safety *then*, perhaps. But danger — afterwards.

I will not let myself recall the letters that came to me from Byblos, except to say that they were to me a glory indescribable — and an equally indescribable grief. In my own letters sent on by Sophronicos, I told him, not only of my love for him, but of what I was doing to put into practice those other lessons he had taught me. But I did not always give details, especially if those details showed me still the Nefertiti he first knew — uncertain, inept, very bad because of nerves and shyness in establishing any personal relationship — *betraying* him. Such as the time I summoned up all my courage, and talked to Horemheb, back briefly in Amarna, showing no pleasure whatsoever in his command, only an increase in the rage he suppressed with such difficulty. He had never liked me, had never really tried to conceal that scornful aversion. Yet in all Amarna he was the only person to whom I could turn, for he was the only person — rather, personage — who took any independent line. I thought I could trust him, for this sole reason. He would take a savage pleasure in secretly countering Akhnaten's wishes.

I could not have any woman except Kat-Senet in attendance to hear what I should say to him. I was dreadfully nervous. I had never previously spoken with him alone, as Queen. I kept my fan of ostrich feathers in my hands, to give them some employment. But my hands still shook so much, and the curling fronds shook so much, that I would have been better off without the fan.

I chose to see him in the garden. I thought that in the open air he would not seem so overpowering as in a room – however large. But when he came, I still stammered like a child. Yet, on reflection, not like a child. Suddenly – perhaps because here, too, I sat by a fountain – I remembered an episode I usually did my best to forget – our ludicrous first meeting fifteen years before. Well, the years that had passed had left us both mentally scarred, bruised, battered, the one by marriage, the other by the long retreat through Syria. His face and eyes were always bitter; so, I suppose, mine had been, on the occasions when the mask had slipped.

Another man – not through sympathy, but with the skill of the courtier – would have tried to help me to say what I wanted. He did not. He merely stood fixing me with the steady, powerful stare that always seemed so inimical. But I managed at length to say what I had planned. That I should have liked to leave Amarna and move about Egypt, to give what comfort I could to two kinds of people in particular, the sufferers from drought and pestilence and the refugees from Syria. But this was impossible.

At least he spared me any comment here.

I laboured on. But I should like to do what I could. I had estates, many estates, given me by The One in the first years of our marriage; I should like the revenues from these to be used for the benefit of the people in distress. It would have to be done in secret, of course. I had no idea as to the best way of doing this, or, indeed, the chief needs of the people, but he would know, and so, if I gave him full authority to –

He interrupted me then. "Why haven't you asked your father to do this? He's the obvious choice, and he's back in Amarna – no doubt because of your pregnancy."

I made no reply. Father had, indeed, made a brief return from Nubia – in his usual state of raging doubt. Should I let him down *again*?

"Am I to take it, then," he said in his impersonal way, "that I am being regarded as a – a substitute father. And why me?"

The first reason was simple. "Because I know a little of how you feel about Syria." After a moment I added in a low voice, "I can think of no one else to whom I can turn."

"Go on," he said grimly.

"And no one else would do anything he considered to be against The One's wishes."

"All right," he said. "I'll do it. Give me your authorisation."

I thanked him, then asked hesitantly when he was going back to the frontier. Soon, he said. "When you return, will you come to tell me what you have seen? About the women and children?"

He nodded, saluted stiffly, prepared to take his leave. Then he said abruptly. "You've surprised me today. This awareness of the dreadfulness of the world outside this artificial nightmare of a place. Surely that should be excluded from a queen's knowledge like the filthiest contagious disease?"

"All that I have done," I said wearily, "is show a little imagination where other women are concerned. And I don't deserve much credit for that. My father's mother was a Syrian captive. I've never been able to find out much about her — after all, she was simply one of many women in a harem — "

"You couldn't have asked the right people. I've heard veterans talking about her — she was beautiful. For which reason, of course, the jealous bitches in the harem would want her forgotten."

He sounded almost friendly, and I reacted as if I could not bear that he should think reasonably of me. "I still haven't really explained why you shouldn't give me too much credit for imagination. I expect you know that I was born in Crete, and lived there as a child. My grandmother was the daughter of a king ruling in the old Crete when it was destroyed. She was living among the ruins when invaders came from a small city on the Achaean mainland you'll never have heard of. She was only fifteen. The leader of the invaders married her — eventually — but I don't have to possess much imagination to understand what had happened to her first."

"Still," he said, "at least give yourself credit for remembering such things after so long a time, particularly since you've spent more than half your life in all the security of queenship."

"Of being Queen of Egypt. If I were queen of a little state in in Achaea, a city in Syria, it might be different. But you are right, of course. As Queen of Egypt, one is secure from what may befall most women — reasonably secure," I corrected myself — and suddenly I was miles away, long months away, for the Lady of Life, whose child-priestess I had once been, had sent a desert storm, had allowed me to free myself from the trammels of queenship. It must have been the Lady, for he had called me his priestess of love, and — Oh, Goddess, I remembered his arms about me, the sweet strength of his possession of what had been his from the moment I had been conceived in my own mother's womb. I could feel my body shaken by something more real than recollection, more a re-enactment, from their warmth I knew my cheeks were brilliant, from their wetness I knew my eyes were filled with tears of love and gratitude. In sleep a dream covering much, need last no more than seconds. And, waking, my dream now lasted no longer. " — reasonably secure," I finished the sentence, "For who knows what the Goddess may send?" And then I stared at Horemheb aghast. I had talked of 'the Goddess'. But he understood my dismay and only looked grimly amused.

"Don't be afraid, Majesty. Don't you trust me, even though reluctantly, because there's no one else? And I suppose it's permissible to talk of a goddess (whoever she may be) in the historical sense — the old benighted beliefs. Interesting enough, in their way. Gods of good — and gods of evil. With priests and priestesses, not always recognised by the world at large." He stood staring down at me. "A Queen of Egypt might reasonably expect security, but these are not reasonable times. Be on your guard, Majesty, yet don't be too afraid. Others may have thoughts for your safety."

I sat looking up at him with amazed eyes. "I don't understand what you mean. And when you talk of 'others', you mean yourself, don't you? But I've always known you neither respect nor like me."

"Well," he said easily, "since we're being honest, when have you had any liking for me? Let's put it this way, Majesty — you've turned to me because there's no one else.I may decide to protect you for a similarly negative reason."

He took my hand and kissed it briefly. His great palm had the hardness, the inner part of the fingers the callouses created by the constant use of weapons. I flushed, and took my hand away. He said nothing more, but saluted, and strode away.

He planned to protect me, yet he nearly killed me. He completely killed something infinitely dearer to me than my own life.

The letters from Byblos became shorter, ceased. The last said, "*We cannot get out now, being entirely surrounded. Their armies increase every day. They even have the same barbarians — Dorians — who drove out my own people, mercenaries who have come to join them to take part in the looting of the city.*"

Staphylos' ill-will towards me increased. He thought I should have been screeching, keening like a hired mourner. But Acamas had told me once that when a man receives his death blow, he rarely makes more than a very little noise.

I was nearly nine months pregnant. Akhnaten, whatever his own inclination, had to conform with general expectation now, and spend at least a little time with me. When we sat together, as we were doing in the Queen's Pavilion, there was no conversation between us — indeed, anyone coming into the garden would have imagined that Akhnaten was alone, not only because of the silence, but because he seemed as much averse to physical proximity to me as he was to any mental nearness. So while I half-sat, half-lay, drowsing in the shadowed interior of the Pavilion, he sat at the entrance, in the full glare of his beloved sun.

I slipped into a dream of Acamas, a silly dream, all wishfulness on my part, that I had been having for days now. Each time he was journeying; each time he was closer to me. And now it seemed to me that he was there with me in the shadows of the Pavilion itself. A voice shaking with anger shattered my dream. I was still so drowsy, so reluctant to leave the comfort of unreality that at first I tried to ignore it. People became enraged over such stupid things in Amarna: Precedence, priority — voices eternally whining like the sound of gnats. But this was a furiously angry voice. Not the kind of voice one usually heard in Pharaoh's presence. Not a voice, for I recognised it now, that I had ever previously heard expressing any emotion whatsoever.

Horemheb was back from the frontier far earlier than expected.

". . .they cut off the heads of the dead, and stuck them on posts before their kings' tents. They dragged the wounded to death behind their chariots. Then they hacked what was left of them to pieces and burned them in great pyres, all Byblos in one vast funeral pyre. . .that's what the new religion of peace and love brought to those who were loyal to Egypt. Not a man of the garrison escaped — "

I could hear Akhnaten moaning. I would not let myself make a sound. Somehow I must drag myself to the entrance.

They were both quite unaware of me: Akhnaten, his face buried in his hands, rocking his body as if in physical pain, Horemheb, his dark face usually so impassive, now working in bitter rage.

"The King — " he began, then stopped. "I will not tell you what they did to the King and those about him", he said. "But they burned them too — ultimately. And they scattered the ashes far and wide. Where is Ribaddi, Lord of the North and South? Dishonoured ashes scattered over the seashore of the city he defended so well."

I still had made no sound, but perhaps I moved suddenly, for as suddenly he was aware of me standing there, leaning against the entrance. I don't know how I looked, but he stared at me in consternation. Akhnaten did not look up; it was to him that I spoke, although I think Horemheb believed I was talking to him. "You have killed my child," I said as another pain seemed to tear me, and the great drops of cold sweat began to pour down my face. "I pray you have killed me too." Akhnaten had dropped his hands, was staring at me now, but he made no movement, and it was Horemheb who moved forward, and, though I tried to twist away from him, caught me before I fell.

The child was a boy, perfectly formed, and dead. I made them bring the little thing to me. My dark hair, pale, clear skin. I would not let myself lift the tiny lids to learn the colour of the eyes that had never opened. But I kissed, passionately, the tiny lips that had never parted to breathe, or to cry, or to suck at my breast. I held him to that breast all that night and all the following day. I screamed like a wounded beast when they tried to take him away from me. I could not believe that he was dead, although from the first he had been still and silent in my arms, and now he was quite cold. And even when I had to accept that he was dead, I still would not let them take him from me. I knew what they would do with my dead baby, dead Acamas' child and mine. And I knew what I must do. I said that if they would leave me alone with Kat-Senet that night, I would put him in the gilded cradle that had been prepared for him. I could read the expression in their eyes. Even when I fell asleep through sheer grief and exhaustion, they could not take him from me when I clasped him to me so closely, but if he were in his cradle. . .In an hour or two they would creep in and snatch him up, carry him away for the obscenity of preserving his body.

So they smiled, and agreed.

Kat-Senet sat weeping. I lay dry-eyed, reserving what strength remained to me for a task other than tears. She gave me one of her herbal potions to drink; I made her swear to me that it was not narcotic, and she kissed my hands, assuring me, sobbing, that it only gave some relief from pain and fever, so I drank it, and then she went to sit in a dark corner so that the sight of her tears would not distress me. She too was grieving, exhausted and old. Soon enough she was asleep.

It was difficult enough even to stand, far less walk at first; I moved slowly, clinging to pieces of furniture, too slowly, so at the end I crawled. But I was able to drag myself up, to take him from his cradle, and kiss him for the last time, the little face, the little hands, the tiny feet. Then I took an unlit silver lamp and poured the scented myrtle oil over the cradle, I took one of the glowing alabaster lamps, and set light to the oil, and when Kat-Senet awoke, shrieking, and other women, shrieking, ran in, it was too late, the fire that makes all clean had reached his body, and he was burning; they could not have him, soon he would be ashes, as his father had become in the funeral pyres of Byblos.

Chapter Twenty
Staphylos

My God, how soon the news flew around Amarna! The Queen brought to bed of a child, a most perfect child, but dead, dead at birth, the Queen, mad with grief, had burned the body. She had lost her reason. She was dying. She might be dead already.

The grief and panic was indescribable. Panic? Yes, for now the whispers were louder than ever. There was a curse on Pharaoh. His Queen had at last conceived a son, and the child was dead, never drawing a single breath. It was two or three days later that I heard them whispering something more. "She lost the child because she heard the news from Syria — so Amen exacts vengeance."

"She always suffers, the innocent one."

"And Egypt."

"The river has not flooded yet."

A great crowd of sullen men and weeping women gathered outside the Palace. I knew because I had hurried there the moment I heard that Byblos had fallen, was trying desperately to obtain what additional information I could. Akhnaten was not there; the crowd's rage increased. Mahu, neither the most optimistic nor the most efficient of men, said "There will be a massacre."

No one, I noticed, thought of consulting Pharaoh.

"We must tell Her Majesty," continued Mahu. "We must prepare her — she may have to be moved."

"Tell her by all means," said Horemheb, striding up. "But move her? They may tear us limb from limb, but they won't touch her."

He stared at Mahu in angry astonishment. Mahu, cringing slightly, nevertheless muttered pessimistically, "When a crowd goes mad — "

"Let the Queen know," said Horemheb, "I'll stake my life she won't agree to be moved."

It was just as well that no one took him at his word, for Nefertiti asked to be moved – but in a direction no one had dreamed of. I don't know if she had asked herself, "What would *he* do?" as if consulting an oracle, but, whatever prompted her, she had herself carried out of the palace on a litter. She looked broken, beaten down. The great eyes seemed the only living thing about her. She lay propped up on pillows, her dark hair spread over them. Her arms were extended over the coverlet. She looked dreadfully like a victim for sacrifice – a willing victim. At first there was absolute silence. Then the people began weeping, tearing their clothes, throwing dust over their heads. At first it seemed as if she did not possess the strength to speak to them, far less raise her head. All that she could manage was to lift her hands a little, to hold out to them for a moment.

The litter bearers began to turn. I thought her appearance might have done some slight good in that people knew that she was alive and sane, but the look of her – that utterly shattered, desolate look of her! – could give no comfort, only foreboding. Already the horrified silence had fallen on the crowd again, to be broken abruptly by the feeble wailing of a very young child. Sudden colour flooded Nefertiti's face. She told the bearers to set down the litter, asked weakly but in extreme agitation, to have the mother brought to her. The crowd pushed forward a shamed, wretched figure, a child, half-starved herself, holding a poor wizened little thing to a breast that seemed all skin, no flesh. She fell on her knees, apologetic, weeping. She was sorry the child had cried, but he was hungry, starving. She had no milk in her breasts.

"You are starving yourself," said Nefertiti gently. "How old are you?"

The girl said she thought she was nearly thirteen.

I caught the whisper, "Too young. I was that age when I had my first child. I had no milk for it, and I was not starving. But wait." She turned to one of her attendants. "Help me up. And tell all the men who are here that they must leave."

I had been one of those accompanying her, had stood close enough to her to catch all she said so weakly. Reluctantly now I went away – but, by God, once I was back in the Palace, I was seeking out a good vantage-point from which I might see the extraordinary scene developing outside. Nefertiti, still flushed, but smiling a little now, held the tiny dark figure in her arms, and fed it. When he had emptied one breast, the child fell asleep. Nefertiti handed him back tenderly to his mother. There was a wild cry, "Majesty! Feed my little one too!" Another child-mother, starving. Another tiny figure clasping a greedy mouth to the other breast.

"You must come back with me to the Palace," said Nefertiti gently. "I have enough milk to feed your two babies, I think. And I will do my best to see that the reserve grain stores issue corn so that no one need starve before the next harvest." After a moment, she added, "I think the river will flood again this year."

For what it is worth, the river did. The most teeming flood within living memory. God knows that flooding, so overdue, was more or less inevitable, but popular opinion attributed it, sentimentally, solely to the fact that the sorrowing Queen, Hathor incarnate, had acted as foster-mother to two starving children of the poor.

The sorrowing Queen. Doubly sorrowing. And in one respect at least, popular opinion was uncannily accurate. I knew about this because I was particularly involved. I had finished the bust of painted limestone, the woman dreaming of her lover, awaiting him. I had almost finished the head of quartzite — the face, still dreaming, lifted to the lover, but I had not the heart to complete it. Then about a fortnight after the news had come from Byblos, I was summoned to the Palace again. She did not like me any more now than she had liked me before, but I think she wanted to see someone who had known him — and I was now the only person falling into that category. For Sophronicos, meekest of poets and singers, seemed afflicted by the gods. He was going off to ruined Byblos, to find out exactly what happened to Acamas, walking into what had become reduced to nothing more than a den of cut-throats, expert in the most atrocious and protracted methods of despatching you from this world, for no better reason, he confessed, than to "set her mind at rest."

"Set her mind *at rest*?" I said, amid much blasphemy. "You've heard rumours of what they did to the garrison. How would getting confirmation of the details set her mind at rest?"

"But can't you understand? That she feels she must know what happened to him?" I did not understand. Whatever obscene atrocities had been inflicted on that splendid body, living or not, I did not want to know. He was dead. I should never see him again. This was as much knowledge as I could live with. But Sophronicos, god-afflicted, woman-afflicted, set off on his crazy quest. Leaving Nefertiti to summon me to the Palace.

Not that she spoke directly of him to me, except very rarely. But at least I, when I saw her fall into sad reverie, did not try to rouse her, as her attendants did. In fact, after the first day,

I would not have roused her for all the gold of Nubia. For – the mask being gone for good now – here was the face of unappeasable grief, silent mourning. The sorrowful, brooding face, the drooping shoulders – my third study of the living, feeling woman that was a dead man's achievement.

It was done for my eyes alone. But my Egyptian servants talked. I had not been angry with them when I found they had stolen into my studio to put bunches of lilies and lotus-flowers before the completed statue, but when that same studio began to suffer constant invasions from some of the most unlikely visitors ever to infest an artist's workshop, I lost my temper. Yet, despite my fury, I could not help being interested in one word which was repeated again and again. Not Hathor now. All that they knew of Nefertiti the Queen was that she mourned a dead child. But looking at the statue of Nefertiti they murmured, "Isis". And Isis was Isis of the Sorrows for she mourned, not a child, but a lover and husband.

Well, I paid dearly enough for my third triumph. Indeed, it proved my undoing. God knows Pharaoh was keen enough on proclaiming – fairly stridently – his devotion to The Truth. God knows he will no doubt enjoy distinction among monarchs because he insisted upon realism in his own portraits. He couldn't quarrel with the realism of the last statue I did of his wife. But he didn't like the stories of the great throngs of ordinary people coming to my house, putting flowers before the grieving Isis mourning Osiris. Or did someone else dislike the reports even more than he did – and not on grounds of religious fanaticism?

I was summoned, harangued, reviled, threatened. My anger and fear did not blind me to the fact that the man looked dreadful, almost corpse-like. I was additionally angry because he scarcely seemed to hear my reasoned objection that I had portrayed the Queen mourning a child, and bereaved mother had never been one of the attributes of the false goddess. In fact, I think his looks scared me more than his words. I decided it was time to leave Egypt. I had done not too badly during my comparatively brief stay – and now I recalled the words of warning and advice given me as I had journeyed up-river from the Delta. Make as much money as soon as possible; then get out in double-quick time.

There had always been the whiff of corruption beneath the tinkling, perfumed world of Amarna. Now there was something else. Worse than decay. Decay, after all, is a natural process. I didn't know what it was – degeneration, madness, or merely the threat of darkness beneath the seemingly unending brightness. But it scared me. I was getting out.

When I told her, she looked at me in a way that reminded me

unpleasantly of the way she had looked at me all of eighteen years before when I had told her I was bringing her to Egypt. For a moment, indeed, I thought she might even weep, beg me to stay — for, as she had wept and clung to me as a child because I was the only remaining contact with a lost loved condition, so, I suppose, I was now. But all that she said, after a moment's silence was, "You don't like me, I know, yet because you knew him, your presence helps me." But then she looked searchingly at me, and gave a sigh. "But you have never listened to any appeal from me. Very well, go."

There was another reason which had been nagging me to leave for weeks now. For, after the period of deepest dejection and grief, she had more than regained her amazing beauty. She had been fully roused to sensuous pleasure, and myrrh, I thought sardonically, never gives off its fragrance until it has been warmed. I watched with incredulity — and, I confess it, ludicrous jealousy. I harboured dark thoughts of a new lover in the Palace, an ardent, adoring young officer — even a regiment of ardent, adoring young officers. But then, from brief, infrequent remarks she dropped, more as if speaking to herself than to me, I realised that she dreamed constantly of Acamas, and bloomed brilliantly on these nocturnal fantasies.

Within a month of my leaving Amarna, the statue of mourning Nefertiti-Isis was smashed by order of the Pharaoh — on religious grounds. For the same reason, of course, countless other statues of false deities had been destroyed. Within a year of my leaving Amarna, the two busts I had done of her were also marked down for destruction — for reasons largely unconcerned with religion.*

When the news reached me, I writhed in impotent anger. My masterpieces! If I lived until I were a hundred, with clear eyesight, a strong and steady hand, I should never again achieve anything like them. But then, years later, with myself hundreds of miles from Egypt, I received a message — from Tuthmosis, old, ill — for all I knew he was dead before his messenger reached me. He had never liked Nefertiti because a good likeness of her had always escaped him; myself he detested because the likeness hadn't evaded *me*. But at least he was an artist, and, however grudgingly, had to acknowledge good work when he saw it. So when the order for destruction was made, he hurried

* But, of course, although the true cause was immediate malice on the part of Tiy, I have no doubt she intended to give another impression. I did not for a moment suppose that *she* ever believed that the people of Egypt had abandoned their old beliefs, and accordings to those beliefs statues are dwellings for the soul. So no future life for Nefertiti!

to my derelict studio, seized those best specimens of my work, left in their place stuff he himself had toiled over, frustratedly, in the past. The agents of destruction were brutish oafs with a civil service mentality. In other words, they were blind to what was good in art — but they could count. Two likenesses of the Queen that was — and up with the sledge-hammers. And concealed amid what remains of Tuthmosis' workshop, my masterpieces presumably rest until this day.

Chapter Twenty-One
Nefertiti

After I had destroyed the body of our child, I fell into a deep sleep. I don't know whether this was natural, or drugged. When, eventually, I awoke, I looked about me wildly, pleadingly asking my attendants where he was (that, at least, it appears I remembered, I had given birth to a son.) I knew I was weak, I thought that perhaps I had had a difficult childbirth, but I could feed him, the milk was here in my breasts, *I could feed him*, for the first time I could suckle a child!

Eventually recollection came back to me. My little son, who had never opened his eyes, or drawn breath, was ashes — and the milk that should have fed him was still in me. There are obvious ways of relieving the pain in the breasts of a mother who has lost her new-born child. I chose the most obvious way of all — and the most natural. Akhnaten was angry, but the people knew of my action before he did, so he could not stop it. I fed the children of two starving child-mothers for months.

Sophronicos left Amarna to go to Byblos. I did not ask him to go, but he correctly interpreted my thoughts.

And Staphylos left Egypt. I did not know then that a hurried departure by this man, always obsessed by his own safety and prosperity, was for me as accurate a presage of a forthcoming storm as the sudden silence of birds beneath a darkening Cretan sky. About a month after Staphylos had left Amarna, Sophronicos, against all hope, returned. He said he had done nothing extraordinary — poets, minstrels, were rarely attacked, often welcomed — and he had remembered how I had read to him part of Acamas' letter in which he had told me that barbaric mercenaries — Dorians from the extreme north of Achaea — had joined the besiegers. They were still there, and welcomed Sophronicos boisterously — their leader wanted a poem made of his exploits at Byblos.

The information Sophronicos and I sought came late at night. The leader of the barbarians had drunk a great deal, and grew maudlin. Sophronicos said he and his tribe frequently did on the subject of warfare. Battles were exquisite things — and what could be more beautiful than to die in one of them! A gashed corpse to them spelled perfection. And, after much childish generalisation, suddenly the slurred words achieved significance.

". . .You mightn't know it, poet, but you can take one look at a man on a battlefield, and never forget him. . .I hadn't forgotten him. . .Eyes the colour of the first sunlight on a stormy sea — and he could fight!. . .half-lying, half-sitting across the gateway of the palace, sword hidden under him. They'd got their hands on the old king. . .been talking for days about what they'd do with him when they got him. This one wasn't quite dead, either. I said he belonged to me — blood-feud between our tribes. They laughed, made suggestions, dragged the old king off. I went up to *him*, then. He was half-sitting, half-lying there — did I tell you that? Blood all over his face, but he looked up at me and there were those eyes — bright through the mask. And — fill my cup again, poet — he seemed to know me too. He smiled and said, in Achaean, 'Straight through to the heart, friend'. And so it was done. And then — well, we're not barbarians. We don't mutilate dead bodies, except in the heat of the moment, perhaps. So I dragged him inside the great door of the palace, and got a torch and set fire to the place, and gave him to the flames."

Sophronicos thought he had fallen asleep, and rose as quietly as he could, having learned more than he had dared expect. But barbarians have ears like cats; the movement, slight as it was, brought the yellow-haired head jerking up. "Before you go — something you might be able to tell me. I never heard of an Achaean warrior worshipping any goddess except Athene. But this one — when I bent over him and unbuckled his breastplate, to make sure of a quick job, looked over my shoulder, and *spoke to the Dawn Goddess*. 'Time to forget me, Eos,' he said, as I took my sword in my hand. Although he was looking westward into the setting sun as he died."

I sat in the garden, and wrote down my thoughts to Acamas. A prayer of parting, or a prayer of greeting?

"*I inhale the sweet breeze that comes from your mouth, I know your body afresh each day, my prayer is to hear your voice, like the breath of the north wind. . .let me feel your hands which hold my soul. . .call my name again, again, forever, I shall always respond to it, beloved. . .you are with me to all eternity.*"

A prayer of greeting, or a prayer of parting? Both, I thought.

A last greeting to him. Parting to the Nefertiti I had been — briefly — because of him. No, the Nefertiti who might have been. She had died more slowly than he, but was quite dead now. The dream was over. Only the old Nefertiti existed still, imprisoned here in Egypt for the rest of her life, imprisoned by time and place and circumstance. Whether she would be influenced by the — episode, I suppose I should call it, I did not know. It had been an isolated incident. The child was dead. No one save myself had been affected by what had preceded his conception.

"*Time to forget me. . .*" He was right, I must do my best.

Meritaten was standing before me. I did not know whether to be surprised or not — for months now half the time she seemed to avoid me, the rest of the time she stood staring at me, saying nothing. She had, I think, found my pregnancy half-distasteful, half-fascinating. While Nefer and Ankhesenpaaten had been angry when I, the Queen, had suckled the starving babies of starving mothers, Meritaten had expressed disgust of another sort, physical disgust. Yet she was not disgusted by other aspects of woman-hood. She was angry because her moon-courses had not started. Once they had, by tradition she was marriageable, so she and Smenkhare might — How she yearned for the physical consummation of marriage! Her passion — that unchildlike passion beginning when in years, and body, she was still a child — had increased almost obsessively over the past months. On the few occasions that Smenkhare came to the Palace she stared at him yearningly, devouringly. Her manner left me profoundly uneasy. It was not the manner of a young girl, gazing at her betrothed; it was more the look a woman gives her lover, a woman who had felt his flesh inside her own. Recollection, awareness, *knowledge*.

She had come to speak to me now because of the way he obsessed her. "From the moment I'm married to Smenkhare," she said, in the hoarse voice that always sounded as if she had wept endlessly, "only *he* is to call me Mayati. No one else."

Only he, who of all her relatives felt least tenderness for her, was to call her by her pet name.

"If it will make you happy," I said.

"What have you been doing? Have you been alone here all the time?" She sounded almost accusing.

"You don't mind being alone, darling."

She scowled, but when I rose to go back to my apartments, she accompanied me, although she said nothing. Even when I went to my bedroom, she came with me, lingered, watching me, almost as if she were Nofret. She began to play with the bottles on my dressing table. "Can I come here one day and use your cosmetics and perfumes?"

"Darling, you can have them all now, take them away with you — you know I use hardly any of them."

She scowled again. "No. If I took them away, the others would know what I was doing, Ankhesenpaaten would make fun of me. I want to come, alone, when you're not here, and try out things."

I recalled how in the last months she had suddenly become excessively modest before me, never letting me see her naked. Well, I had been like that once! "You can come any time you like," I said. She nodded in her stiff, ungracious way, and left me. I realised with a start that I still held the writing palette and papyrus I had been using when she had approached me — I must find a safe place for the papyrus — although I did not think I could ever bring myself to read it again. But I did — three or four months later. At least, I tried to, one night, when I awoke weeping silently, and took the little inlaid casket where I thought I had hidden the papyrus. But it was not there. I had been so preoccupied with my anxieties for Meritaten, I thought, that I had put it in a place other than the one I intended. In a day or two, when I was alone again, I would make a real search for it, But two days afterwards I had left the Great Palace, it seemed for ever.

Chapter Twenty-Two
Nefertiti

Akhnaten had sought me out only once since the child's birth — if one can speak of the visit of formal commiseration paid me when I was still so stupefied with grief and exhaustion that I was only dimly aware of an embarrassed voice, an awkward kiss on the forehead. I said, "It is gone," and turned my head away. (They thought I spoke of the child, but the child to me was always 'him') Once or twice, when I had recovered, I had tried to speak to him, but I shall write of this later.

But the second of the two men staring at me when I cried, "You have killed my child!" pestered me with requests to be received. He had returned to the frontier when I was out of danger, but still unfit to give audiences, but now he was back in Amarna, plaguing Akhnaten with demands that some Northern troops should be stationed in the capital and asking me to receive him. Every day the request was made. And refused. At first, although I was no longer distraught, I was still sunk in misery, irrational dreads, suspicions. And Horemheb I suspected most and worst; Kat-Senet, watching me narrowly, told me that as I had tossed in fever, I had repeatedly cried out to him. I knew he hated Akhnaten, was convinced his rule was disastrous, *he* must know what the people believed since I had never given birth to a son. And then I had become pregnant again. If the child were a boy. . .He must have known I was drowsing there in the Pavilion, that was why *he*, the most impassive of men, had shown such angry emotion in describing what happened at Byblos, because he hoped to make me miscarry. . .And even when this dark thought did not continually recur, I dared not see him, for I did not know what emotions would be revived by the mere sight of him. Yet he persisted in his request, although I did not think for a moment that he really wanted to see me. I could only suppose that his arrogance was piqued by my steady refusals.

Why could he not leave me to the only thing approaching a narcotic to grief, guiding the two hungry baby mouths to the fullness of my breasts, even sometimes smiling a little when the dark little hands clutched and clung and kneaded?

But Horemheb must have had more sympathisers than I had ever suspected, for he was kept well enough informed of my movements. Thus when one day I decided for the first time for many months to go to Maru-Aten, and walk beside the lake, he was there, waiting for me in the little glade sloping down to the water's edge that was my favourite spot. I had left my attendants far behind, wanting no company. Now there was no one who could keep him from speaking to me. With tears of helplessness in my eyes, I said, "You know I have no wish to see you."

"Because you think I killed your child?"

So he had not forgotten. "I have blamed you," I said.

"For accidental or deliberate murder? Women think deviously. But consider. Deliberate murder of an unborn child carries danger for the mother. Would I risk losing possibly my only ally here at Amarna — however reluctant an ally?"

"I have thought sometimes that you would have been glad to see the child born dead," I said with an effort.

"You would have been nearer the truth if you had said that I regretted the fact that you were pregnant at all. But you wanted the child, didn't you?"

"More than I have ever wanted anything in the world."

"Well, then, I've hurt you dreadfully. But without meaning to do so."

I considered. He was a clever and formidably efficient man. If he wanted me to miscarry, he would surely have acted before I had almost carried the child to full term. And, I thought suddenly, he could not have known what Byblos meant to me.

He said in a sudden anger, "Who was more responsible? The man who brought news of atrocity, or the man responsible for that atrocity because he sent no help?"

I said with an effort, "You should not say these things." After a moment I continued, "I think the real reason I refused to see you was that seeing you would remind me of what happened. Merely seeing you. If you had been there — quite silent, but *there* — it would still have been hard for me."

"You must forget it."

"Yes, I see that. For my own sake."

"It will grow less difficult."

I nodded. I did not believe him, but would not argue. I was still nervous when talking to him, so as usual I fell back on sheer formality. He would be leaving Amarna soon, I supposed. I said I was sorry that I had never really congratulated him on his appointment as Commander-in-Chief. But this was the worst opening I could have chosen. His face seemed to settle in even stiffer lines.

''Appointment to this command!'' he said between his teeth. ''The only tactic you need know is how to carry out a retreat!'' But after a moment he controlled himself with an effort. ''But you meant no irony,'' he said, and then went on to give a dryly factual account of the way in which the revenues of my estates were being administered for the relief of distress. I thanked him in a low voice, hoping that the uncomfortable conversation would now come to an end. But it did not. The Commander-in-Chief, it seemed, did not accept dismissal, he would only dismiss himself. ''Yes,'' he said, when I said, still nervously, that no doubt he had many preparations to make before returning to the frontier, ''I shall be going back soon.'' I turned away; he obdurately fell into step beside me. ''When I first went to Syria,'' he continued violently, ''the older officers would suddenly shoot questions at me — to keep me on the alert. Suppose — just suppose — you wanted to hold up the enemy on a retreat, which positions would you choose? All purely theoretical, an exercise, a war-game. But, by God, it's not a game now! Every time I go back, I have to look about me marking out places for use in a year — a month — when we've fallen back again.''

I did not know what to say. A professional soldier was a creature completely alien to me. Father had sincerely shared one of Akhnaten's convictions — both had great contempt for soldiers, walking embodiments of stupidity.

'' — you can't make sense of your orders, and you know it's not because of your own stupidity. There never was any sense in them.''

My step faltered. It was almost as if my unwelcome companion were reading my thoughts.

'' — the only suggestion I get is that I should build walls. *Walls*? It's *men* I want!''

Where were my attendants? How much longer must I be left exposed to this. . .I opened my mouth to say, ''This is no way to talk to a queen!'' Instead I heard myself saying, ''That is no way to talk to a minister.''

''No?'' He considered. ''Perhaps. My trade doesn't help. First you learn to obey. Then you learn to command. What they never teach you is how to cajole like a woman..''

Again I tried to end the conversation, repeating ineptly

that with so many preparations. . .

"Before I can get away from here, back to reality, dust, heat, thirst, defeat, *death*!" He should not have said that. It recalled with searing pain another voice.

I must myself go, in any case; my breasts were heavy, aching, it was time I fed my foster-chldren. Soon they would be able to do without me. Whether I could do without them was another matter. Suckling them was the sole sensual pleasure left to me. Until one has given suck to a child, the physical joy of it is unimaginable, the strong, hard tugging at the nipples that leaves the whole body shuddering with delight. Why must this hostile, angry man keep me from that last pleasure, why must he stand there stubbornly in the sunlight, face hard as bronze, cruel, no, *implacable* as bronze. . .yet the skin tightly stretched as it was over jutting bone, coiled muscle, covered flesh, vulnerability. A man could be strong, even splendidly strong, like this one, filled with violent life as he sped northwards in his chariot — and yet no more his own master than the stupid sacrificial beast plodding to its own slaughter.

Oh, why would he not go? My breasts were so heavy, so aching! Almost I moaned with pain. If only I could put my hands up to cup them, ease them, but this could be done only if I were alone. . .How agonisingly I was aware of their aching urgency. . .

"Please leave me now," I said in a whisper, and after subjecting me to a brief, hard stare, he abruptly saluted, apologised with no contrition in his voice for imposing on my patience, and strode away. Then at last I could put up my hands to ease my breasts a little — only to drop them with a sudden cry of shame. The front of my dress was wet; the milk had come leaking out and he must have seen the widening stain. I found I was backing away, as if he were still there, staring at me with angry contempt. "I will never see him again," I whispered. "Oh, Goddess, spare me the misery and shame of being seen by him again."

Although I did not know why I should feel such wretchedness and humiliation. All Egypt knew I had only months before borne a child. *Who should know better than he that I had borne that child*?

But I lost my foster-children before ever the Commander-in-Chief went back to the frontier. The Nile had flooded; the people who had crowded into Amarna from the dying villages wanted to return to prepare for the first good harvest for years. Now there was no distraction from my thoughts: thoughts of dust, heat, thirst, defeat, death.

If I had felt less constraint, self-consciousness in Horemheb's company, I might have told him that, since my recovery, more than once I had gone to Akhnaten and begged him to send help to the garrisons still holding out in Syria. I was suffering my defeats too, but defeat is the most private of things, and I could no more share such intimacy of thought with this gigantic man with the impassive face, than I could have exposed myself in physical nakedness.

Defeat was inflicted on me in an odd fashion. "No," Akhnaten replied invariably – but not strongly, not in anger, always shrilly with a kind of imploring hysteria. Then he would say, several times, "You must not to try to influence me in matters of state." And, sometimes, with that shrill note of entreaty which bewildered me, "Please don't try to influence me."

"I'm not succeeding very well, am I?" I asked wryly.

"You shouldn't try," he said, in a strange, almost fearful anger. "If it were known – "

"Well, who but you could tell anyone?" I asked in a puzzled voice.

He gave me a sideways, startled look, oddly childlike, then said, almost placatingly. "Your only interest used to be the children. Why can't you be like that now?"

"But when I was like that, when we first married, you were angry because I wasn't interested enough in religion. Don't you remember, you liked people to believe that I took a far more active part than I really – "

He gave me an angry, miserable, defiant look, and left me. Not so much a Pharaoh, I thought with some incredulity, as a child unhappily, apprehensively swaggering in the belief that some misdemeanour would soon come to light.

I was uneasy, but no more. I thought of petty misdemeanours. So my ancestors in Crete might have been aware of a darkening of the sky to the north, a distant roar – never guessing all the while that total catastrophe was at hand.

I sat in the garden, on the upper terrace. Below me came Akhnaten and Tiy, the Foreign Minister and the Chief Scribe in attendance. But not Father – surprising, this, for he had been back in Amarna for several days now. Was he losing favour?

Against the willows and tamarisks, Tiy blazed with gaudy splendour. On her arms and breasts silver jewellery, gaudily ornamented, glittered against her dark skin, and on her head the double plumes of empire. In my plain white dress, unadorned, my hair put up under a simple cap, I must have looked, in contrast, like a not particularly valued slave. I shrank back on my seat, fortunately concealed by a flowering acacia. But not before I had seen Akhnaten – only too clearly. His face was the colour of clay and even from this distance, I could see a sudden twitching of the right cheek, from eye down to mouth.

The four of them went into the pavilion. Were they, then, to have one of those mockeries of council meeting in which the Foreign Minister told lies, and the Chief Scribe intoned deferential platitudes?

There was a soldier's tread on the path beneath me. A tall, powerfully-built figure, bitter eyes in an unsmiling face. I had forgotten that this was the day that Horemheb went back to the north. Now, presumably, he was taking his formal leave of Akhnaten.

It was the thought of Acamas that brought me out of hiding, sent me along the path after Horemheb. True, he was not returning to a doomed city, but he was another man going north in angry helplessness. I felt nothing approaching liking for him, but it was wrong that his last memory of the court should be stares of bland incomprehension as he stated his case for the last time. In the pavilion where my darling had poured out his own bitterness, the pavilion where I had learned of his death.

"*Time to forget me, Eos.*"

Yes, I must forget him — after today. Today, remembering him for the last time, I would disobey the warning given me by May — even the odd warning given me by Akhnaten. "*If it were known* __ "

By the time I entered the pavilion, Tutu was telling a stony-faced Horemheb that he was, as usual, overstating his case, while Akhnaten, as usual, was quoting letters of explanation, reassurance, sent by Aziru, who was so interested in the will of Aten, who never failed to end his letters stressing this, asking for fresh instruction. . .It was the mention of Aziru, who had killed Acamas and Ribaddi and massacred the population of Byblos, that brought me, not only to break in upon them, but to break into their conversation.

"You talk of a universal god," I said to Akhnaten, "yet your interest doesn't really extend even the length of the Nile Valley. Only Amarna counts for you."

"Be silent!" Tiy's furious voice; Tiy's eyes, shallow, implacable.

But I caught Akhnaten's hands and stared up at him in desperate appeal. "And there's never been greater need for thought of things outside Amarna. Amarna is a room where there are no windows, only mirrors. You can't see the world outside, you can see only yourself. In *everything* you see only yourself."

"Be silent, I say!" I thought Tiy would strike me.

"There's a curse on Amarna," I whispered to Akhnaten. "You made the desert bloom here — but Byblos is a blackened wilderness.'

"You will be sorry for this," said Tiy. "You will be so sorry for this that every breath you may be permitted to take in future will be a moan of regret that you spoke as you have done."

But I was looking only at Akhnaten, who was not looking at me. It would have been easier if his eyes had consciously avoided mine, but he simply did not seem to see me. I went on looking up at him for some moments longer – and now I was deaf to Tiy's furious abuse. But he remained equally blind to me, so, head down, shoulders sagging, and with a slow step I turned and came away, past the shut-in courtier faces, down the steps, out of the pavilion. Tears of despair blinded me. At the third step I missed my footing, and would have fallen but for a hand catching my elbow. It was Horemheb. I looked up at him despairingly. "I've done more harm than good," I whispered.

"You tried," he said. "I don't forget such things. *And remember this – I've succeeded in one thing at least. There are a few Northern troops in Amarna now*!" But when I looked up at him in bewilderment, he only said tersely, "Raise your head, Majesty! Weep if you must – *but walk like a Queen*!" Then he saluted, and went back into the pavilion.

I expected a summons from Akhnaten or Tiy all the rest of the day. But nothing happened then, or the next day, or the day that followed. And then, when it happened, I was not summoned —they came to me. It was mid-afternoon. Still I thought only in terms of a storm, not catastrophe. But when they came in together, the very sight of him – I would not look at her – told me that something irrevocable had happened. But I had no idea what it was. I was frightened, but still had no idea that on this very afternoon the life to which I had become accustomed was to end completely. His eyes were staring, feverish. He had looked like this when he had announced his sudden decision to leave Thebes to found a new capital. But this time *he* said nothing. All the talking was done by her. He was content to gaze at her not so much with devotion as docility; not so much as the bidden, obedient child with his mother, it was as a domesticated animal staring at its owner, taut, coming to life only at the possessor's approach. Yes, he was possessed, body and soul. His eyes devoured her with a dazzled, unwinking stare.

She said for him that he repudiated me. By my attempts to interfere in affairs of state, above all, my open setting myself up in opposition three days before, I had fully earned the disgrace that was to be mine. And suddenly, because of the unwavering way in which he stared at her, I felt a horror of the body, a horror of the spirit. *This* was the look of – I think I managed to keep my face unamazed, almost unmoved, but when I spoke, it was in a high voice I scarcely recognised. "You are really saying that because I've tried to challenge *your* political power, I must go, there's no room for the two of us. But that's only the pretext." Almost retching with horror, I whispered, "Now I know why his father said that day to you that *his* own pleasures were natural ones, unlike yours — " I turned to Akhnaten. "And I wondered why, after she came to live in Amarna, you would never be a man with me!" I forced my lips to form the word. "Incest. Starting all those years ago, when your father sent you to Syria. But it didn't cure you."

At last he looked at me. "Tell her!" said Tiy, Sphinx tearing her prey to shreds. "Tell her!"

"You went to Syria," I repeated, "but it didn't cure you."

He replied in a dreadful mixture of boast, confession and pedantry. Boast and confession were vague; I have forgotten what details there were — probably because I wanted to forget them. But the pedantry — Oh, that sticks in my memory now as much as it stuck in my gullet then. He had gone not to Syria, but further east, to the Iranian plateau, where union between son and mother was commended. This was the most complete of unions, the holiest of unions — their priests, the *magi* were usually born of such unions.

"Like — Tutankhaten," I said, in dawning realisation.

"And Smenkhare!" said Tiy, jeering.

I whispered, "And I thought that I might be blamed for the famine, the barrenness — but it's no fault of mine — *it's your sin* — "

"Sin? Have you forgotten who I am? There can be no moral restrictions on *my* actions." He spoke like an offended child.

"That's what she's told you. That you can do what other men dare only dream of, think secretly of in sick fancy. Can't you see that's what it is — *sickness*, and she's taken advantage of it because her ambition, her greed for power, can batten on it."

"*You will pay for this*," said Tiy.

I ignored her. "Don't you remember how you told me we must leave Thebes because of the spiritual evil there? But *this* was the spiritual evil — and you brought it with you to Amarna.

As he stared at me, he began to tremble uncontrollably. "You know you don't really glory in it," I whispered. "Remember the name you took when you began to reign — 'Who lives in truth'. And you *know* I am telling you the truth. Sick imagination," I said in a low voice. "Not triumphant sin." I wondered how much longer I could keep my apparent calm. Yet as I stared imploringly up at him, I saw the false exaltation had left his face; head drooped as shoulders drooped. Suddenly his whole body shook convulsively.

"I warned you," he faltered. "And I — kept silent about what you said to me in private. But after you stood there beside Horemheb and said those things — when she asked me, afterwards, if you'd ever talked to me before like that, I couldn't keep it from her — " His eyes were suddenly those of a bewildered, despairing, desolate child. And he looked as brittle as old papyrus, as if he would crumble into pallid dust if I clasped his hand — to say, "Let us start again"? *As I must.* But could we start again when I should remember. . .every time he. . .The bile rose in my throat.

I hesitated, and was lost. She had grasped the hand I had not taken, was muttering fiercely to him, a mixture of threats, cajolery, promises. There was an air of assured grossness about the way in which, with the other hand, she suddenly, openly caressed him, lower, lower, more heavily, until *before me*, she. . .I groped behind me, felt for my chair, sat in it, heard him repeating, docilely, that he repudiated me.

"Tell her, too, that her children will be taken from her," said Tiy, smiling, stroking still.

I had forgotten the children. I lost all pretence of calmness then. I cannot remember precisely what I said, but I know I pleaded, I wept, I fawned on him, knelt to him. I think I would have crawled to him but for the fact that she led him away in triumph, leaving me to the silence and brightness and emptiness of the room that had become a torture-chamber.

Terror, succeeding horror, had left me a little insane, I think. There can be no other explanation for the fact that, when I could control my hands, I sent a brief appeal to *Father* to come to me. I can only think I acted as I did because, when I lay face downwards on the ground after they had gone I kept repeating to myself stupidly, "The children. The children" — and so, possibly, became childish myself. Or at least childish enough to remember an episode of my own near-babyhood; Ariaea, making one of her rare references to my grandfather, Ariaea, angry with my mother, because she had had such blind love and trust for her father. "*Father will come*, she'd say when she was frightened — and she was always frightened! — *and then everything will be all right.*"

But my own father, predictably, did not come. I was sure the letter had been delivered. Any order I gave was still obeyed. No one about me yet suspected exactly what had happened. They had heard angry voices — this made their attitude towards me cool, but it remained correct, for at this point no one (with the exception of Father?) dreamed of anything as extreme as repudiation.

Having written the letter, I knew what I had to do. I must go to the children — yet I could not go until I was composed. I sat with my head in my hands, trying to face the future. Once he had sent me away, he would not bother to hide his relations with her. But my thoughts also harked back to the past. "You are so calm, cold. Other women are excited." Yes, she would be excited. Power always excited her.

Why had he wept in the night, talked in his sleep. Why had he always seemed to be thinking of someone else. Thinking of doing *that* to *her*. I managed to get into my bedroom before I vomited.

Kat-Senet came to me as I lay, hands and forehead cold and clammy, unable to speak. "What is it?" she said, fussily, peering at me. "What is it, my little Beautiful One?"

I said, in a whisper, "They are plucking out my heart. They are taking my children away from me."

But they did not take the children away that day. When I had achieved some kind of composure, I went to the children's wing, and there nothing had changed. Meritaten scowled over a piece of embroidery, Ankhesenpaaten had the harpers playing so that she could dance, Nefer sat watching her sisters with her usual hostility, and Nofret — Nofret, as usual sat with her eyes fixed on the door, waiting for me to come. I thought, 'They can't take *her* away. They know she's delicate, almost as delicate as Setepenre. They know she — depends on me. *She* at least, they'll never take from me.'

I could not hide my pallor, my sadness, but the two elder girls did not notice it. Nefer did, and sat watching me with characteristic detached curiosity. And Nofret was aware of it, as a loving little dog is aware of the unspoken misery of an owner. And like a loving little dog, she crept to me, mutely pressed herself close to me, every part of her small body trying to comfort me.

But nothing happened that day.

The night that followed was not entirely sleepless for me, but if at last I slept briefly, exhausted by silent weeping, it was to moan and struggle in the grip of the old nightmare, the pursuing demon, but worse than ever before, because now my attempt to escape to the sunlight and the heavily beating wings, "sweet as the wind from the north," I said to myself, was prevented by small, cold, clinging hands, and my breasts were heavy — so aching and heavy they impeded my flight. Weeping, I besought the little things that clutched at me to ease me by letting me suckle them; I knelt and cupped the great swollen globes, offering them, but the tiny skeletal shapes rejected them at the same time as they grasped at me. "Oh, take them! Take them!" I moaned, but instead they tore at my womb. "For pity's sake, ease me!

ease me! Ease me!'' I sobbed. ''Tug at my nipples! Don't deny me this last physical pleasure.''

''Stroke them! Draw them out!'' said Father, seizing me from behind, and setting briskly to work with elegant, cruel fingers.

''Your father,'' said long-dead Naya, cackling, ''has no complaints now! He can't keep his hands off them, can he?'' Great jets of milk spurted from my breasts under Father's skilful fingers, but still they ached. ''Apis-bull!'' I moaned, ''Help me! Ease me!''

''You whore!'' muttered Father, in time to his rhythmic pulling at my nipples, now directing the milk, which he had first jetted as high as the low roof of the passage, down in great spurting bursts to the ground so that I slipped in it, for it was as sticky as blood, woman's blood.

''Acamas!'' I cried in my soul. ''Help me!''

''Time to forget me,'' came a voice that must have been his, although I could no more recognise it than I could remember how he had looked. Now moaning again to Apis-bull for help, I tried to crawl upwards to the light, but Father seized me by the shoulders and threw me down. ''No, Apis-bull mounts *this* heifer of my breeding!''

''You will be sorry for this,'' cackled the pursuing demon Sphinx about to rend and tear. ''You will be so sorry for this that every breath will be a moan of regret — ''

And I was moaning when I awoke, shuddering, to find my own hands were pressed against breasts that were heavy, swollen, while my womb ached, ached. I staggered to my feet, fell on my knees. ''Mother-Goddess, help me!'' — lay prostrate, imploring help, shortly after dawn received that help, it appeared in the form of feverish self-reassurance. If they had truly intended to take the children from me, they would have done so immediately. ''And'', I said to myself, ''they are only the children of a concubine now. *She* will be the Great Wife. So Smenkhare and Tutankaten are the heirs.''

My crassness was monumental. I should have known Tiy better. My daughters might be no more than harem-children now, but they were mine, loved by me — so they would be taken from me. But to strike a second time while I was still stunned by the shock of the first blow? Never. Wait until I had recovered a little, even to dare to hope — and *then* strike. Let one day pass, two, until the trapped animal thought, as I thought, ''If they had really meant to do it, they would have done it by this time — '' And then strike.

It was late afternoon. I was playing with Nofret in the last rays of the setting sun stretching across the floor. Suddenly we heard the sound of many feet approaching. Men's footfalls. I straightened up, my heart-beats suffocating me.

Nofret, always timid in any case, and now sensing my terror, clung to me. Before I could say a word to her, they were in the room, a dozen eunuchs, Pentu, the court physician — and Father leading them.

And now my crass stupidity reached its supreme height — or depth. (*Father* has come; everything will be right.) Gently I detached the small, clinging fingers. "It's all right, my darling," I whispered. "Your grandfather has come." And I ran across to him, flinging my arms about him, kissing him spontaneously for the first time in my life. "I knew you would come!" I whispered, taking his hand, and carrying it gratefully to my breast.

He detached himself roughly from me. The expression on his face was sheer fury that this failure of a daughter should try to involve him in her ruin. "I've come to take them away," he said.

When I could think clearly again, I said to myself. "I must seem to be calm. I mustn't distress my darlings by tears or outcries." And I think I could have managed it if it had not been for Nofret. Meritaten went from me with complete indifference, surrounded by smiling eunuchs. Ankesenpaaten following with a look of anticipation on her face. "Now perhaps we shan't be treated so much like children," she said. Neither looked back. Nefer did so when she came to the door, but the expression in the eyes that had never been childlike said only, "I know how brittle that composure of yours is — how soon will it break?" But Nofret was different. She clung to me, screaming that if she had done something wrong, she was sorry, she would never do it again, for she would die if she were taken away from me. And then my brittle composure did indeed break.

Kneeling, partly as suppliant, partly the better to shield Nofret, clasped in my arms, I wept, besought Pentu, "I know you are a father, with children of your own. Surely you, a doctor, are not a cruel man, you would not willingly be party to the torture of a child. . .I know this was intended as my punishment, but, can't you see, it hurts *her* more?" I besought pentu, for with whom else could I plead? Not the two grinning eunuchs who remained, least of all my own father. But it was he who came from behind me and — ignoble victory! — enabled the others to take Nofret from the fragile barricade of my arms. He came up behind me — never the open approach from him! — dragged me to my feet, squeezed my breasts so savagely that I screamed like an animal through sheer physical pain, and slackened my clasp on Nofret. "Take the brat," he said hoarsely to Pentu, "and I'll deal with *her*'' and went on squeezing my breasts so cruelly that, although prepared now, I no longer screamed, I groaned despite myself, instinctively began to bring my own hands up to tear him away — and so Pentu could drag Nofret from me. She could no longer scream, but she kept calling ''Mother! Mother!'' in her hoarse little voice as Pentu and the two eunuchs of the bed-chamber prised each of her fingers one by one from the folds of my dress, and her grandfather wrenched at my nipples now, and I moaned, and threshed against him and found suddenly that terrified hatred can produce a dreadful travesty of sexual passion — Father, orris-scented as in my childhood, held me in that hideous parody of a lover's embrace, of Acamas' embrace, and I groaned and my body arched, shaken by a great tremor, and for a moment I lay against him as if unconscious.

''It is not true,'' I told myself heartbeats later, eyes still closed. ''This is part of the dream still, you dreamed last night he did this to you — '' But the dream had not taken place in daylight, and Nofret — Nofret! ''Mother! Mother — '' the hoarse little voice called to me, I opened my eyes dazedly, and there she was, my delicate Nofret, my darling, the little struggling thing, fighting every inch of the way while I, her mother, who should have fought for her, had let her go because a hand wrenched at my breasts, had fainted after one spasm of physical pain. . . ''Mother! Mother!'' — Nofret clinging to every article of furniture on the path to the door, Pentu prising each thin finger loose, one by one, myself trying, too, sobbing with desperate hatred, to prise loose other stronger fingers, unsuccessfully, *how* they wrenched at me, Nofret clinging to the door itself, my hands tearing, ineffectually at Father's, and then, as Pentu and the eunuchs dragged her through the door, out of my sight, another great shuddering spasm, another uncontrollable arching of the body, and my head fell back on Father's shoulder.

His eyes, never more brilliant, glared down into mine. My womb seemed suddenly to melt in silent weeping. I spat up in his face. ''May whatever gods there are, damn you,'' I whispered. But then I forgot him. Whatever physical pain he inflicted on me — physical pain, the violence of it would indicate, he had contemplated lovingly for many years — it was irrelevant beside what was happening to Nofret, I must strain my ears to catch the broken little voice echoing back along the corridor, more and more faintly, ''Mother — Mother — Mother — ''

I had stopped struggling. Now that I could not see Nofret, I concentrated all my thoughts on that emotion so much easier to attain than love. Hatred of the men who had dragged her from me, but above all, hatred of Father. ''Beast, monster, I am willing you to die in misery, I can't hope you'll ever know misery like mine, because you'll never love anyone but yourself, but may you die in what wretchedness is possible for you — *because of me*.''

But I became conscious of Father as a person only when no broken childish voice was audible from the corridor. Possibly because I was no longer struggling, his hands were less-violent. His fingers still plucked at the nipples that jutted erect; the palms pressed close, cupping, almost caressing the breasts that thrust outward against them. How hatred can stimulate! I thought, noticing without much interest that at some point, after they had dragged Nofret through the door, he must have drawn down the material that had sheathed the flesh. But I was glad he had bared my breasts, so that his hand now stroked my naked flesh, for only in that intimacy of touch could I be reminded of — *Ah*, I gave a sudden shuddering sigh — the ineradicable scar inflicted on it years before by that other female animal he had robbed —

''There was a time,'' I said to him, indifferently, leaning back against him, looking up at him, ''when you were angry because I had no paps. Why are you still squeezing them now that the need for it has gone? Is it because they're now as big as your Mother's were? Do you suffer from the family failing, Father? Was it strong in you too? Did *you* lust after your mother as *he* lusts after his?'' But I did not try to release myself, I let him go on stroking, plucking — I was beside myself with shock, grief; shivering suddenly I began to moan. *I wanted to remain close to him, hating him*. For once he left me I should be alone with desolation. ''I want you,'' I began, went on with an effort, ''to stay with me. . .''

But Pentu and the eunuchs were calling him urgently from the corridor. ''Great Lord! Great Lord!''

''Don't go,'' I whispered, still shivering. ''*Don't leave me*''. I put my hands over his, imploring again, but he let me go; to report on the success of his mission, to disown me. I wondered how many letters he had already written in frantic, sweating haste, deploring my wicked folly, my eternally rebellious nature as once he had deplored my frigidity. Then, just before he reached the door, another thought struck me.

''Father!'' I said. Now that he no longer had his hands on me, all awareness seemed to have left me — grief held me in such a stupor I could think of no other way of addressing him. I don't know what he expected me to say to him, but he swung round quickly enough. But now that I had his attention, I did not bother to look at him. I concentrated on easing, cupping the breasts that he had tortured. Why was Father waiting so tensely? I had almost forgotten. Why had he taken a step towards me? What was he saying? I was shivering again, moaning softly. . .

"You will come back to my house," said Father in a low voice, "never to leave it." But then Pentu called again, urgently, from the corridor. "Great Lord!" and he halted, and I remembered what I had wanted to ask him.

I said, "You always knew about the relationship between your sister and *him*, didn't you? Did you think — like her — my marriage would never be consummated, is that why you're both so happy to take the living proof that once I *was* his wife? Why are you so happy — *you*?"

He only repeated, "You will come back to my house, and this time I'll never let you leave it again," and went out quickly. But I knew it was the truth; despite his boiling cauldron of ambition, he had hoped my marriage to a *Pharaoh* would remain unconsummated.

So here I was, childless, husbandless, fatherless. And crownless. But if I had never worn a crown, I might still have possessed children, a husband. There were no dreams that night. I lay staring into the darkness, wondering if Nofret, too, lay awake, her sad, dark eyes mournfully staring at the first of the walls which separated us, or if, like a terrified little animal, she had now accepted her fate.

But I did not go back to Father; next day I was told that I was to be moved to one of the smaller palaces, where I should have a greatly reduced household. I could have done without that household altogether; every member (save one) was of course chosen by Tiy, and therefore inimical to me. The exception was old Kat-Senet. I suppose they let me have her with me because she was old, and deaf — and of peasant stock and, therefore, they thought, inconsiderable. But it was her love that, I think, saved my reason in the days after they took my children from me.

Meanwhile Tiy was openly proclaimed as Akhnaten's Queen. In temples and public places my name was obliterated, my feature defaced. This took some considerable time; such was the drawback to parading an affection which did not really exist. And stone is a material retaining impressions longer than flesh does; the bruises Father had inflicted on my breasts had faded long before the last inscription was erased. But at last the operation was completed.

Officially I no longer existed.